"Afraid, Green Eyes?"

Jordan asked softly, the whisper somehow seeming loud in the heavy silence of the desert around them.

"No. I am not afraid of you, Jordan..." She wasn't afraid of him, not like he meant. She was more afraid of herself and her own reaction to him. Jolie tingled with excitement as Jordan's mouth moved to scorch a path from her lips to her temple, then her ear. Burying his face in her hair, he muttered love words, sex words that brought out a primitive instinct in Jolie.

Her hands moved boldly across his chest, her fingers sliding beneath his belt and buckle, undoing it with swift, deft movements that took away his breath. When her hands slipped inside his pants to caress him he gave a rough groan that was immediately lost in a fevered response. Impatient with the buttons of her shirt, Jordan jerked them sharply, and they popped off. Then he shoved aside the open edges of the shirt until it slipped from her shoulders and down her arms...

*

"Beautifully sensuous... based on two memorable characters whose love truly transcends time."

—*Romantic Times* on *Legacy of Shadows*

*

"Virginia Brown is a bright new star on the romantic horizon."

—*Affaire de Coeur*

Also by Virginia Brown

✳

Legacy of Shadows

Published by
WARNER BOOKS

Desert Dreams

Virginia Brown

WARNER BOOKS

A Warner Communications Company

WARNER BOOKS EDITION

Cover illustration by Sharon Spiak

Warner Books, Inc.
666 Fifth Avenue
New York, N.Y. 10103

 A Warner Communications Company

Printed in the United States of America

First Printing: August, 1988

10 9 8 7 6 5 4 3 2 1

Dedicated to my sister,
Deborah Gray Fite,
who has proved that,
in spite of life's obstacles,
a courageous heart always
picks you back up.

Part One

*

Prologue

April 3, 1880

Perched on the bank of a clear running stream in the Organ Mountains, a young girl stared into the waters without really seeing the smooth white rocks on the bottom. So much had happened in such a short time, and she was afraid. Of course, Papa had said they were safe here in these mountains where no one could find them, but she still remembered those long, frightening nights before they'd come here, before they'd joined the *Chihende* again.

Sunlight glinted in raven tresses that had a bluish tint, and she tossed back her loose hair. It was held out of her eyes with a strip of red material, and she wore a shapeless dress that fell to just below her knees. Apache boots covered her feet and calves, and as she rose in a graceful motion to balance on the bank she heard a shot. Startled, she made a quick movement, and the slick soles of her boots slipped on the grass, sending her plunging into the stream. Her heart pounded as she blinked water from her eyes. Poised for flight, she paused, turning to listen.

"Gáadu! Gáadu!"

It was Cháa, calling her by the secret name they used, the name of an animal. She was Gáadu, the cat, because of her eyes, and he was Cháa, the beaver, because of his prominent front teeth. If he was calling to her so loudly, things must be safe.

"*Yáá!* Cháa, over here!" Rising from behind the shelter of a rock, the girl waved both her arms.

"*Ayiie,*" Cháa said, coming to a halt in front of her, "look at you! You are *náyiist´u!*"

"Of course, I'm wet!" Gáadu replied indignantly. "I'm standing in water! Help me out." She lifted a hand, and the boy reached down to tug. "What did I hear?" the girl asked, sitting on the bank and wringing water from her buckskin dress. "It sounded like a shot."

"It was only a bobcat. Too bad it wasn't a *bélu.* . . ."

Gáadu slanted him a sour glance. "Are you forgetting that *I* am half-white, Cháa? Only my mother is one of the Apache. And anyway, no white would venture this close to our camp. They would be afraid of Victorio. Sometimes I'm afraid of him myself."

Cháa gazed down into Gáadu's eyes, huge green eyes that resembled those of a cat, slanted and glittering with mischief. He scowled, not liking to be reminded that this girl of his childhood was not completely Apache. "*Guzéé gútsa',*" he muttered

"I don't have a big mouth," she retorted, "I'm just stating fact." Pushing to her feet, Gáadu met his hot gaze with a slight smile. "Besides, you wouldn't like me if I was any different, now would you?"

"No," the boy admitted, tossing a rock into the stream.

"Why do you go away every year with *niztaá*?" His thin brown arms were already rippling with muscle, though he was not much more than ten summers. This would be their last year as friends, for he would soon be too old to play with girls, especially a girl like Gáadu. "Why do you go?" he persisted.

"I have to." Gáadu smoothed the wrinkles from her buckskin dress with one hand, a frown knitting her brows as she concentrated fiercely, muttering beneath her breath that her *'eutsa* was ruined this time, and her mother would fuss. "Shitaá must hunt the furs," she said aloud, "and I like to go with Papa when he hunts. I look for many things along the way, Cháa. I don't want to stay with the Apache forever." She looked up, staring across the broad, flat plains below toward a distant horizon. "I dream of going many places one day, maybe riding on a *bésh nangu'í* to a faraway village."

Cháa stiffened. "The big metal monster would swallow you up," he warned. "It has clouds of steam coming from between its wheels, and it can only run on that metal path . . ."

"*Chée!*" Gáadu commanded sharply. "I don't wish to hear any more! I *will* go away one day, I *will!*" Turning, she ran away from the stream and Cháa, leaping like a startled doe over bushes and fallen logs until she arrived back at the village out of breath.

Her father was back from a day of hunting, and she ran straight to him. "Papa! We will leave one day, won't we? I want to travel far away, out of the mountains. Let me go with you when you go, *s'il vous plâit.*"

"Patience, *chérie*," her father answered, smiling down at his breathless daughter. He smoothed back the ebony strands of hair from her forehead, gazing into her clear green eyes.

"Someday you will leave, *oui*. But not until it is time. You are safer here than anywhere else right now."

"But, Papa . . ."

"*Non!* Do not argue. It is dangerous on the flat lands with all the fighting. I will not risk your life. But one day, you shall get your wish." Giving her an affectionate pat on the head, Henri La Fleur ducked and entered the tipi where Gáadu's mother waited for him.

Gáadu remained outside when the flap closed behind her father, knowing better than to intrude on their privacy. Her lower lip was thrust out rebelliously, and she scuffed her still wet moccasins through the dust and dry grass. A hot breeze blew across the land, and she lifted her head, looking toward the east. Somewhere out there was a world she had never seen before. It waited for her.

It was night finally, and the fighting had ceased. Somewhere in the distance a coyote howled, its quivering wail rising above jagged rock peaks and dry arroyos, hanging in the air like a cloud. Fickle light from a jagged half-moon sprayed over the lava beds and the men sprawled in postures of death. They wore blue uniforms, bloodied now, their carbines and sabers gone with the Apache who had ambushed them. An entire command—fifty-three men—dead. Only one man had survived, and he lay gravely wounded.

Captain Jordan Sinclair stirred slightly, blue eyes opening and his throat constricting. Cautiously lifting his bloody head, he peered through the night shadows at the stiff bodies of his command. Fred Grimes, his very young bugler, lay with gaping mouth and open eyes; and there was Dave Stewart only a few yards away, a good cavalryman and friend, dead now. He'd known all of them by first name, had ridden with them, drunk with them, and fought with them. He should have died with them, Jordan thought bitterly.

His head lowered back to the rough surface of the lava bed. The rock was still warm from the heat of the sun, pressing against his cheek, cutting into his forehead. The instinct for survival urged him to action, and Jordan once more lifted his head, squinting into the shadows.

Moonlight lay eerily over humps of rock, wavering like ghostly shadows, creeping into crevices. To the east lay a towering black wall, dark against the paler sky, silent and forbidding. Stifling a groan, Jordan moved forward on his belly, crawling through the rocks to lower his aching body into a hollow winnowed out by time.

There was a wall of lava about fifty feet high, great ebony blocks of it, wrinkled in places like the sagging skin of a circus elephant, and in other places as slick as a mirror glass. Thorny clumps of brush, stiff and wiry, sprouted in unlikely spots, and prickly-pear cactus pushed its way through beds of rock. Sparse pines more like sticks than trees dotted the ground, jutting defiantly skyward, throwing skinny shadows across the barren landscape.

Wetting his dry mouth with the tip of his tongue, Jordan tried to recall a small cave he'd stumbled across once, a long time ago. It wasn't large, but it had an underground spring that trickled through it, and right now he needed that water badly.

Levering his body up with the help of a gritty boulder, Jordan swayed on his feet at last. He moved forward slowly, with a dull, throbbing ache in one shoulder and his head pounding from an Apache bullet crease. Blood matted his thick, dark hair. Feeling his way along, he searched for the cave, skinning knuckles and knees on the abrasive surfaces of the rock. Finding it at last, he wheeled into the opening like a drunken sailor at a waterfront tavern.

Water. It was cool and sweet, trickling over the rocks with the prettiest sound Jordan could ever remember hearing. It was the sound of life, and lurching forward, he threw himself to the ground to dip his head into the spring and drink greedily. Sated and dripping, he finally lay back on the cold rock, gazing at the dark ceiling of the cave.

He wiped a hand across his eyes, but it couldn't remove the memory of the bodies sprawled on the lava beds, those treacherous stretches of dangerous rock that had been their undoing. God, he'd tried to halt their flight, but the panicked men wouldn't listen. Any man who'd been in this country for any length of time knew that the lava beds would tear up the hoofs and legs of a horse, and the wily Apache had driven them there just as wolves would drive a deer. It had been pitiful, a turkey shoot, with stranded men flailing on the rock and the Apache picking them off one by one with their stolen rifles.

Turning over on his belly, Jordan frowned. He couldn't figure out why they'd not taken scalps from their victims, but the band had seemed to be in a big hurry. The Apache under Victorio and Nana had been on the warpath since 1879, killing, looting, and burning out settlers and miners with concentrated savagery. So far, the Army had not been able to do more than engage in a kind of guerrilla warfare with the Apache. Victorio preferred to hit and run; he would take a small band of warriors and attack where he could, then just disappear over a rocky crest. How did they do it? The Apache seemed to melt into rock and tree and stream, disappearing without a trace.

Shifting position, Jordan stifled a groan. He would have

to walk back to Fort Wingate unless he was lucky enough to run across a friendly patrol of soldiers or white settlers. And that hardly seemed likely in the Malpais lava beds. Considering his options, he decided to head for Acoma. It was the closest town, and lay northeast. Best to leave now, while it was still dark and the shadows might hide him from enemy eyes.

"Halt! Who goes there?"

Challenged by a posted sentry who was very young and quite nervous, Jordan paused. Standing in a jumble of rocks below, he couldn't see the man above and squinted against the sunlight with both hands above his head. "Captain Jordan Sinclair, Seventh Cavalry," he answered wearily, "and don't keep me standing too long or I just might not . . ."

It was the last he remembered saying for a while. When he woke, it was night and he was lying on Army blankets. Blinking, he stared up at the face above him. White teeth flashed brightly against ebony skin. " 'Bout time you woke up," the friendly face said. "Thought you'd done gone home fer shore!"

Jordan managed a weak grin. "Not yet," he replied in a hoarse whisper. "Who're you?"

"Corporal Rufus Washington, Cap'n, Ninth Cavalry. An' you be . . . ?"

"Captain Jordan Sinclair, all that's left of the Seventh Cavalry," was the slow answer. "Ambushed yesterday at the Malpais . . ."

" 'Paches?"

"Victorio."

The black corporal shook his head and whistled long and low. "Whoooeee! Victorio! Tha's who we goin' ta find

–9–

now, Cap'n. We been trailin' him from th' Sacred Mountain fer th' last day or two."

Jordan frowned, his laboring brain recognizing that something was the matter with that statement, but uncertain what it could be. He closed his eyes, his head throbbing with a pounding rhythm like Apache war drums.

"Corporal!" a voice cut in coldly. "Let the man rest for now."

"Yassuh, Lieutenant Weatherby, yassuh!" Backing away, Washington disappeared into the shadows and was replaced with another man. Hunkering down on his heels, the lieutenant opened his mouth to ask questions, then realized it was useless. The tall cavalry officer had drifted back into unconsciousness.

"Dammit," Amos Weatherby muttered, shoving his hat to the back of his head, "I need to know if that was really Victorio." He stared down at Sinclair for a long moment, his broad ebony face creased in a frown as he thought furiously. Victorio was supposed to be just a little bit ahead of the Ninth, yet this man claimed to have been ambushed by the Apache chief yesterday. No one, not even Victorio, could be in two places at once. If true, this was news that General Hatch should know.

"But, sir," Weatherby protested, "what if he isn't just delirious? That would mean that Victorio is not leading the Apache we're following. . . ."

Captain Carroll gave an exasperated snort. "I have my orders, Lieutenant, so it doesn't matter if we're following women and children! General Hatch said follow—so we follow them. Now get back to your post."

"But, sir, he'll get away. . . ."

"That's an order, Lieutenant!"

Stiffening, Weatherby snapped a salute and pivoted, marching back to his men. Army regulations didn't allow for deviation, even at the cost of an entire command, it would seem.

"So what now, Lieutenant?" Washington asked.

"We follow the Apache even if they're women and children," Amos answered firmly, his voice carrying the ring of authority.

And as it turned out, the Ninth *was* following women and children. About fifty of them, with only a dozen warriors led by Nana, Victorio's son-in-law.

The black cavalry troop commanded by Carroll camped on the evening of April 5 at the Malpais Spring. It was beautiful flowing water, clear and cool and inviting, and most of the command luxuriated in the welcome supply. But before morning, nearly all of the horses and half of the men were extremely ill.

"Gypsum," Sinclair muttered, glad he had sipped from his own canteen and not taken any spring water. "Has an effect like Epsom salts on a man."

Corporal Washington, deathly ill and ash gray beneath his dark skin, moaned pitifully. "Lawd, Lieutenant, I'm lak ta die. . . ."

"You won't die. You'll just feel like it," Sinclair said, shifting on his blankets to peer at Washington. He'd been carried along on a litter rigged up something like a travois, until the troop had ridden into the hills. Then, in order to keep up, he'd been forced to ride a horse. Now Carroll had given the order to break camp. They were moving into the mountains where Carroll expected to find a fresh-water spring he'd discovered the year before while a scout against these same Indians.

Unfortunately, when they reached the locality, there wasn't

a drop of water to be found. The Ninth moved southward to reach a canyon where there was certain to be plenty of water.

It was about six o'clock when, totally exhausted, the troop entered Memtrillo Canyon. Their bad luck held out. In this very cañon waited the Apache.

There was only one entrance to the Hembrillo Basin from the east, from Alkali Flats above White Sands—the three-mile-long Hembrillo Canyon. The troops passed through overhanging cliffs, climbing steeply from the White Sands Flats, up to the floor of Hembrillo, fifty-one hundred feet above sea level. The entrance was close and tight, and between it and a narrow gap only a short distance back was a spring. Beyond the water, the walls loomed so close together that only one horse at a time could pass through—a deathtrap for men coming in from the basin. At the crest, once clear of the defile and just before entering the basin floor, stood a clump of trees. It was here that the black cavalry troop was forced to build their fortress.

"Pretty valley," Amos Weatherby observed, standing up to see better. He had climbed a steep bluff to gaze down. As a mist cleared, he saw a valley surrounded by jagged peaks and cut with three deep canyons converging in the center. Standing slightly behind him, one of the scouts casually mentioned the fact that it had once been the location of Victorio's camp, and Weatherby slowly turned to stare at the man.

"Victorio's camp?" he echoed.

"Yep." The scout squinted at the valley. "We must have scared him off."

Sliding back down the bluff, half on his stomach and half running, Weatherby relayed this information to his captain, but it was too late. Bursts of fire from the encircling rocks indicated that the Apache were well aware of their arrival.

While Hatch's remaining troops attempted to close the circle, the Apache moved into Hembrillo Basin, stationing warriors at ledges guarding the narrow canyon entrances. It was early the next morning before the main attack, with the Apache taking the offensive and surrounding the command, shooting at the soldiers randomly from every direction and blocking them from the water supply.

But the darkness of night had provided the cavalry unit with enough time and secrecy to erect their rough stone fortress against the Apache, stacking the largest stones they could find to form a makeshift wall. They fended off the worst of the attack until Cruse's unit arrived to form a relief column. Cruse, part of Hatch's command, drove back the Apache so that the black unit could obtain water, though at a risk. The rocks sprouted with rifle barrels from peaks and bluffs overlooking the spring.

For Amos Weatherby, daylight had brought more than the Apache. He found himself gazing up at a rock mural on the face of the cliff behind them. It was awesome, an ancient painting by Indians from another age, another time, and Amos was impressed.

"Looka here," he muttered, elbowing the man next to him. "Look at that painting. . . ."

"Are you crazy? We got 'Paches screamin' an' yellin', an' wantin' ta take our scalps—" The man clutched at his close-cropped hair, eyes rolling with fear. "Man, I ain' got no guarantee they don' lak my hair jus' as well as they lak th' hair of a white man! Ain' got no time ta look at no damn paintin', fool!" Then, realizing that he was speaking to a superior officer, the corporal added, "I mean—Lieutenant."

A wry grimace twisted Amos's mouth. It wasn't that he wasn't afriad to die, for if the truth was known, he was just as scared as the next man, but he figured it wouldn't do him any good to waste his bullets against rocks instead of Apaches he could see. And while he was waiting for a decent target—which wasn't likely to show itself for a while—why not stare at something prettier than the buzzards already circling in the sky overhead? This mural was prettier than anything he could ever recall seeing since arriving in this barren, desolate country. God knows, even Mississippi was better than New Mexico.

Heat shimmers rose from the ground, and the air was thick with tension and the muffled sound of the cavalry unit as they peered anxiously over the stone wall looking for Apache. There was the scuff of boots against dirt, the occasional metallic clink of scabbard or gun against rock, and somewhere in the jumble of stone a man swore softly with a verse more like a prayer. Brief, sporadic shooting kept up during the long day, with Apache shooting at the black cavalry and the cavalry shooting back at the Apache. It was a waiting game, a ploy at which the Apache were highly skilled.

Amos chewed thoughtfully on the end of a matchstick, letting his eyes drift some forty feet across the rock painting. It was almost ten feet high, and it appeared to be two entirely different paintings on the one single ledge. Faded paint underlying the newer mural depicted two stick figures wearing skirts and pointing at smaller stick figures. It was decorated with suns, moons, snakes, and geometrical designs. Squinting, Amos could barely make out the shape of a mountain that seemed to be exploding—a volcano? The newer, more vivid mural did not obliterate the ancient one and reminded him of Apache art he had seen in abandoned villages. It had many colors—red, blue, yellow, black, white—and clearly showed a huge figure of an Indian warrior leading smaller warriors in an attack on a wagon train. Oddly enough, between the warriors and the wagon train appeared a ghostlike apparition, taller even than the giant Indian warrior, like a being surrounded in an aura of light. It was, Amos reflected, a surprisingly beautiful primitive painting.

"Still lookin' at that paintin'?" Corporal Washington grunted, sparing the mural a brief glance. "I think ya need ta be lookin' at th' real thing instead of dumb pitchers of Injuns. . . ."

"Show me an Apache to shoot, Corporal," Amos returned calmly, "and I'll shoot him. If you like wasting ammunition on rocks and clouds, go ahead. I don't."

"Hmmph! What'cha think yer gonna see in that stupid paintin'—a damn map outa here? Fergit it!"

Turning back to look at the mural, Amos frowned. Come to think of it, it did look a bit like some kind of map. He leaned forward, hunching his shoulders to stare at it more closely. If the bright light in the center was, say, the mountain, then maybe these other little cuts were paths out of the Basin. Or maybe not.

Intense rifle fire ended Amos's idle speculation for several hours as the cavalry fiercely defended their position. More of Hatch's troops arrived, and Cruse readied a final charge up the canyon and into Apache lines. Word was passed down the line—"Advance is to be continued on the run. Fire at will until reaching the hostile line. No halts for any purpose."

This final charge was a dud. There were no Apaches left in Hembrillo Basin. Colonel Hatch's force arrived about noon, but reported no sign of hostiles.

Lieutenant Weatherby was one of three men chosen for a reconnaissance a few days later. Scouting the region, the three men discovered telltale tracks that proved Colonel

Hatch had narrowly missed the Apache. Had he taken the path he'd intended to travel in the first place, he would have apprehended Nana, his warriors, and the women and children. It was evident that Nana and his group had hidden against an arroyo wall while the troops passed above them.

Stepping a short distance away, Amos followed another, fainter path. It lead up the peak, a winding, twisting path through rock and dry grasses, buffalo gourds, and rabbit bush. Slapping at a stinging insect on the side of his neck, Amos walked slowly, leading his horse. He finally paused for a rest, leaning against a ledge of rock and staring out over the basin spread below the peak. About a mile away, across the flat white plains, stood a sister peak, the dark cone jutting into the air. Mopping forehead and neck with his regulation scarf, Amos squinted into the distance.

The sky was cloudless and blue, burning down with a fierce intensity that made the ground shimmer. It was quiet all around him, only the soft jangle of the metal curb bit on his horse making any sound.

"Damn," he said, just for the sake of hearing a voice pierce the silence pressing down. His bay pricked its ears and went on munching disinterestedly at a bunch of dry grass. Amos laughed then, a deep rich laugh that welled up from his belly and into his chest before bursting into the steamy air. Snorting, the bay jerked his head, then reared in terror as a black object skimmed from under the ledge Amos was sitting on, almost bumping into the horse.

"Hey! Whoa!" Amos yanked on his reins, a big hand swooping out to smack the fluttering black creature out of the air. It was a bat, squeaking and flopping about on the rocks. "Well, I'll be damned," he breathed, and turned back to peer under the stone ledge. "What have we got here?"

Amos hunkered down on his heels and discovered that the space under the ledge was just big enough to allow a man to squeeze through. He debated a moment, then shrugged. Why not?

Jordan Sinclair stretched his aching muscles and winced as the cavalry doctor removed the bandage around his head.

"Hmmm," Perkins murmured. "Looks to be healing just fine, Captain. I don't know how, what with all the bumping and banging you've gotten in the past few days."

"It was better than lying in the rocks and waiting to be found," Jordan observed. "Besides, I heal better when I have a rifle in my hands."

"No doubt." Perkins snipped the last of the bandage away. "You were lucky to stumble across the Ninth instead of Victorio and his bunch."

"Yeah. I seem to be a very lucky man." Jordan winced again, not at the less-than-gentle touch of the Army doctor, but at the memory of his command sprawled upon the unyielding surface of the lava beds. It would take a long time for the memory to fade.

"Guess you'll be going back to the fort and getting another regiment," Perkins commented. "The Ninth is headed for a well-deserved week's furlough."

"Yeah. Guess I will. Or maybe I'll take that desk job I was offered not long ago. . . ."

Perkins laughed. "You don't seem like a man suited to a desk job, Captain!"

Sinclair's hard blue eyes met those of the doctor, and his grim expression gave Perkins pause. "No," Jordan agreed softly, "maybe I'm not suited to a desk job, but I'm not suited to chasing shadows, either."

Puzzled, the doctor dabbed alcohol on Sinclair's almost

healed wound and asked, "What do you mean—chasing shadows?"

"That's all the Army has been doing lately. They won't listen to their scouts, they won't keep their treaties with the Apache—what the hell do they expect? A goddamn miracle? I can't chase two hundred savages with fifty men and expect to walk out of it, and that's what they sent me to do...." Jordan halted abruptly, a muscle twitching in his lean jaw. "I'm not even sure I'm fighting on the right side," he muttered.

Perkins drew back, the eyes behind his glasses narrowing at his patient. "Now see here, Captain, your attitude is not one becoming an officer. We were sent to subdue the hostiles, and *that* is your job!"

"Is it? Pardon me," Jordan drawled, "but I had the impression I was here to steal back the dust we gave the Apache in place of mountains and green fields. No wonder Victorio and Nana are on the warpath. Have you seen the San Carlos reservation, where they put these Indians? Have you? No, I thought not. Instead of their ancestral range at Ojo Caliente, where they had land, water, and decent surroundings, the Army saw fit to transfer those Apache to San Carlos in Arizona. It's a death hole of disease and starvation, Doctor, presided over by corrupt agents. What did the Army expect? I wouldn't stand for it either."

"I must say, Captain," Perkins snapped, throwing his surgical instruments back into his black bag, "that you have a very peculiar outlook on this entire situation. What do those heathens mean to you?"

Shrugging, Jordan said, "Nothing. I just would like to know that I lost fifty-three men for a good reason instead of a bad one. That's all, Doc. That's all."

Chapter
1

June 8, 1883—Organ Mountains, New Mexico

Jordan Sinclair rode down through the Río Grande Valley, crossing the Jornada, that dry, flat tabletop that was barren except for prickly pear, cactus, and mesquite, then passed into the Organ Mountains. The Organs—twenty miles in length and at times shaped like a castle in a fairytale. An active imagination could easily recognize turrets and towers among the jagged peaks. In the past years, he'd ridden across the Organs a dozen times at least and still couldn't find all the hidden valleys and crevices tucked into the rocky folds of the mountain range. Those mysterious mountains held so many caves and tunnels and ravines that an entire army could be lost in them and never found again.

The Organ Mountains loomed dark against a red sunset, wreathed in gauzy veils of lavender shadows, paling to an eerie gleam like white sands at moonrise. Thorny yucca plants dotted the ground along with other desert vegetation such as the prickly pear with its lush yellow blossom, the desert willow festooned with pendants of pink and lilac, small pincushions of cactus bedecked in mauve petals that would put roses to shame, and the ocotillo cloaking its vicious barbs with tiny leaves until the long, snaking arms resembled fingers of green fur tipped with bright scarlet nails.

It was into this chaotic color that Jordan Sinclair rode early that June morning, his sleek-muscled gray gelding picking its way carefully among rocks and brush. It was still cool, the fresh air biting at his ears and nose, and Jordan was glad for the double layer of shirts he wore. The town of Franklin wasn't too far ahead, just beyond the Texas–New Mexico border and the far mountain ridges. He scratched at his beard-stubbled jaw, thinking of the future. He was out of the Army now, and headed for Mexico. Maybe down there he would find that elusive thing called peace of mind. Maybe. Right now he'd settle for a good bed and a hot bath.

Laying the reins over his mount's neck, Jordan steered the animal around a sharp outcropping of rock. He was concentrating on the ground, frowning down at the faint tracks pressed onto the hard shale by unshod ponies, when he became aware that someone was watching him. Jordan reined in his horse and looked up.

On the lip of a crest overhanging the path stood several mounted Apache, clad in leggings, breechcloths, and warpaint. They were gazing down at him with that same stony regard they gave any white man who was either brave or foolish enough to ride into their country.

Swallowing, Jordan considered several options: he could ride hell-for-leather and invite certain chase and death, or he could wait and try to parley. If talking didn't help, there was always his gun. He could still go down fighting. So Jordan waited, his calm countenance revealing none of his inner turmoil, and his hand only inches from his gun.

Four painted braves drew abreast within a few short moments, and one of them gestured with his rifle and said in excellent English, "You ride alone, white man."

Jordan nodded shortly. "Yes."

The Apache waited a moment, then said, "You will ride with us."

Left with little choice in the matter, Jordan soon found himself riding deep into the mountains, escorted by the Apache. It was well past noon when they dipped into a green valley by a clear, running stream, and he muttered a soft curse under his breath. This was obviously not going to be a social visit on his part; the village was teeming with painted, armed braves, and it didn't take a genius to realize that he had stumbled across Geronimo's camp. If nothing else, the circumvented route chosen by his escort would have alerted him—they had doubled back on their trail several times to confuse him, and had even blindfolded him at one point. Yeah, this was Geronimo's camp, all right, and he was as good as dead.

Watching him carefully, the Apache who had spoken to him in English said, "*Shái'ánde*," and then, at Jordan's blank stare, translated, "Geronimo's band," thus confirming his suspicion.

"Great," Jordan muttered. "I've always wanted to meet him."

The Apache gave a brief snort of laughter and dug moccasined heels into his pony's ribs. "Then you shall, white man!" Leaning forward with a swift, agile movement, he grabbed the gray's reins and jerked Jordan along beside him, trotting through the village and shouting in his own tongue to those watching.

Obviously being exhibited as a prize, Jordan resisted the urge to stare back at the men, women, and children crowding around him. He stared straight ahead, his back stiff and his head held high, wishing he still had his gun. It had, of course, been taken from him long before. His throat was dry and constricted, and his jaws were clenched tightly together as he was paraded through the milling throng. Jordan could sense the hate and animosity surrounding him and steeled himself against the oddly prickling expectation of a knife or bullet in the back.

Then, by chance, he happened to catch the gaze of a young girl standing off by herself, perched upon a hummock of dirt and rock, looking at Jordan with pity and interest in her expressive eyes. He couldn't tell the color of her eyes from the distance, but he was aware of the unspoken message of sympathy she was sending him and wondered at it. His head turned in her direction, and he looked at her with a bold stare, catching a glimpse of long dark hair and a bewitching smile before his captor yanked hard on his horse's reins.

Now what? Jordan thought when his horse was jerked to a halt in front of a large, brush-covered structure. The "what" turned out to be Geronimo himself, a short, powerful-looking man with a fierce expression. Wisely, Jordan decided silence was his best alternative.

It wasn't long before he found himself sitting cross-legged in a crescent of men, wondering why he hadn't been killed or actively "questioned" by the Apache. This time, it seemed, Geronimo intended to be more subtle than his actions in the past had proved him.

"Tell me about the white soldiers," the chief asked him in a civil tone that left Jordan sweating under his double layer of clothing. "You were one of them, yes?"

"Yes," Jordan admitted, glancing at the men gazing at him with distinctly unfriendly expressions. "But now I am no longer one of the soldiers. I ride alone."

Geronimo nodded, his small eyes narrowing at Jordan. "So we observed," he said with a smirk. "Were you not afraid to be riding through my land?"

Jordan's brows rose. "*Your* land? I thought the land belonged to no man—not even the Apache." He made a sweeping gesture with his hands, adding, "It belongs to the sky, and the wind, and the sun. . . ."

Staring at him with a thoughtful gaze, Geromino nodded slowly. "Perhaps you have a point, white man. But you seem to be the only white man who thinks this. Why were you sent here?"

"I told you," Jordan explained patiently. "I was just riding through. I am going to Mexico for a while."

"Ahhh, Mexico! I go there frequently myself!" Geronimo laughed hugely, enjoying his oblique reference to the fact that he and his braves continually raided in Mexico, killing and looting the hapless Mexicans with savage abandon. Then he leaned forward, his dark eyes glittering slits in his sun-bronzed face, staring at Jordan as if he was trying to read his mind. "You go back to the pony soldiers and tell them that Geronimo is not an old woman! Geronimo will not back down as some have done, and I will kill every white face I can find until no more come to steal our lands, our food, our lives. . . ." He paused, and some of his intensity transferred to Jordan.

"I will tell them what you say," Jordan answered, "but they will still come. There are too many for you to stop, too many even for a great chief like yourself to turn back. The white man will come like storm clouds, to roll over this land and everything in its path." His eyes met those of Geronimo, and there was a quick flash of defeat in the chief's gaze before he masked it.

"No!" Geronimo said forcefully. "We will fight! Tell them this, '*indaa*'. Tell them what I—Geronimo, the greatest chief of the Apache—have to say!" He rose in an abrupt motion, indicating the interview was over.

A sense of relief filled Jordan as he realized that the chief meant for him to go on his way unharmed, and while he questioned the motives, he didn't pause to question his release. He was led outside again, blinking at the sudden change from the dim, smoky interior of the thatched hut to the blazing sunshine blanketing the village.

While he was standing and trying to adjust to the light, he heard a soft giggle and half-turned. It was a feminine laugh, not the voice of his captor, and he turned blindly in that direction. Jordan caught a glimpse of dark hair as two girls stepped quickly behind a cone-shaped tipi with strange markings painted on it, but he was aware of them watching him. He looked away, then glanced back, and caught them peeping at him again. One of the girls wore a necklace that dangled against her almost flat chest, glittering as the sun struck it. It was huge, a medallion of silver, Jordan guessed, flinching as the glitter from it almost blinded him. His gaze shifted to the other girl, who was staring at him boldly, and he was struck by her beauty before she ducked back behind the tipi.

The Apache growled something at him Jordan didn't understand, but his meaning was clear enough and he followed him. He could feel the girls' eyes on him as he moved across the bare, dusty ground behind the warrior who had brought him to the village, but he shrugged away the uneasy feeling.

"Do not cast your eyes in that direction, white man," his

captor warned, jerking Jordan's head around. "That is the unmarried maidens' tipi, and Victorio's granddaughter wears *his* amulet for protection. If you value your scalp, get on your horse and leave." The brave leaned forward, his eyes cold and cruel. "You are lucky to leave alive—if I were chief, you would be killed very slowly. . . ."

Watching with Gusts'ile from the safety of the shadows stretching behind the unmarried maidens' tipi, Gáadu whirled when she heard a spiteful voice say, "Don't look upon '*indee*' with longing eyes, Gáadu!"

"And why not?" she asked her childhood friend indignantly. "What harm does it do to look upon a well-favored man?"

Cháa's fierce gaze moved from Gusts'ile to Gáadu, and then back. "It is not done," he stated in a flat tone. He was gazing at Gáadu with that strange intensity that was so disturbing lately, and she moved away several paces.

"I may look upon whom I please," she informed him. "I am not bound to you or any other man. . . ."

Cháa grabbed her by one wrist. "*Dah*! 'Aal! You will be bound to me soon enough!"

Gusts'ile, who stood silently fingering the silver amulet around her neck, was more easily frightened than her friend. She gasped and ran away, leaving them alone.

Yanking her arm from Cháa's grasp, Gáadu shook her thick mane of hair from her eyes and glared at him defiantly. "No, I am not one of the people. Not like you are, or like timid Gusts'ile. . . ."

Cháa stepped closer, his eyes hot. "But I want you for my wife."

Shaking her head, Gáadu moved away. "*Dah*," she said sadly. "I can never marry you. I will marry only for love, Cháa. Or I will be like Lozen and never marry."

Turning, she gazed after the tall man riding away from

their village. She had seen him in her dreams and in her heart. He was so handsome, with strangely colored eyes and hair that gleamed with red lights in the sun. His body was hard and firm like the Apache, but different somehow, with long, taut leg muscles well defined in the snug-fitting pants he wore. How could she look upon another with favor when this man had caught her imagination?

Chapter
2

The tinkling notes of an out-of-tune piano trickled into the hot air outside the saloon, only adding more noise to a street already filled with sounds. Listening to the clamor, Jordan Sinclair leaned against an unpainted wooden post holding up the sagging roof of Morton's General Store and patiently built a cigarette. He sprinkled tobacco, then twisted the ends of the brown cigarette paper with quick, expert motions. A match flared and Jordan inhaled sharply, letting a thin curl of smoke drift into the air.

The day had been hot—107 degrees in the unprotected sun. It'd been hot enough to fry an egg on the wooden sidewalk unless one was standing in the shade. In the shade, it was almost pleasant with the dry breeze blowing up dust. He'd ridden hard after leaving the Organs, but now he was here, and he was thirsty.

Tossing down his cigarette butt, Sinclair ground it into the dust with the heel of his boot and stepped into the saloon. He was greeted with a raucous burst of laughter and smoke that struck him almost physically as he strode across the sawdust floor to the bar. It was a short bar, with rows of glasses placed on shelves behind it and the inevitable painting of a nude reclining on cushions of clouds between the long mirrors. There was a short wooden plaque with the bartender's name, Pete, burned into it.

"What's your pleasure?" asked the moon-faced bartender.

"Rye." A shot of whiskey was poured into a short, round glass and slid across the bar toward Jordan. It went down fast, and Jordan plunked his glass back to the somewhat grubby surface of the bar.

The bartender's brows rose in twin crescents at the man, but he silently poured another shot, swiping aimlessly at the bar top with a less than clean rag. The second glass went the way of the first, but it seemed to satisfy Jordan finally.

Leaning one elbow against the edge of the bar, Jordan let his gaze drift curiously around the room, peering through the haze of smoke. It was crowded, with tables placed randomly across the wide floor. Only two more men stood at the bar; the rest were seated around the small tables. Poker games were in quiet progress, but most of the men just seemed to want to kick back in their chairs and talk and drink.

There were no familiar faces in the room, and shrugging, Jordan returned to his empty glass. He held it up, and it was refilled.

"You new in town?" Pete, the bartender, eyed him from the corner of one eye, obviously trying to guess his reason for being in Franklin.

Jordan didn't care for the way the man's eyes wouldn't meet his, and didn't feel one bit obligated to answer any questions. He looked up at the bartender. "Do you care?"

"Naw, I don't. But others might."

Now Sinclair's brows rose, and Pete began to wish he'd kept his comments to himself. There was no congeniality in those cold blue eyes that were boring a hole through him, and no humor in the thinly chiseled lips that were compressed in a straight, tight line.

"Curiosity got the cat killed," was the soft answer, and the bartender nodded shortly.

"Yeah. So I heard." Pete shifted from one foot to the other and began to edge away, but Jordan reached out to capture the bottle of rye with one large hand.

"I'll keep this a while. You can move on."

Wordlessly, the bartender moved on down the bar away from Sinclair, but his glance kept returning. Strangers in Franklin were common, as the little town perched on the border between Texas and Mexico, but there was something about this tall, lean stranger that nagged him. He was still thinking about it when trouble walked in the door.

It had been eighteen long years since the end of the Civil War, but there were still men around who bore a grudge toward different colors of uniform and different shades of skin. One of these was Pete McCall.

"Hey!" he shouted. "You can't come in here!"

The music stopped and voices died, and all heads turned toward the double swinging doors.

"Sez who?" Trouble walked slowly across the sawdust floor, two pistols on his hips and a shotgun in his hand. He set the double-barreled weapon on the bar and met the bartender's hot-eyed stare with one of his own.

"*I* sez!" Pete blustered. "We don't serve niggers or Injuns in here."

There was complete quiet for several moments as the big black man just stood there, looking at Pete McCall with contempt. When he spoke, it was in the same quiet tone he'd used before.

"Well, I ain't no Injun, but I've done my share of

fighting 'em. I think that qualifies me for a drink any damn where I please. And if that don't qualify me," he said as he lifted his shotgun, "this will."

"You aimin' to shoot up the whole saloon?" another man asked, pushing back his chair to stand up.

Trouble half-turned. "If I have to."

"Alone?" the man sneered.

Again, softly, "If I have to."

Jordan, standing still and quiet at his end of the bar, stared at the Negro with narrowed eyes. It'd been a long time, three years in fact, but he still had good memories of the Ninth Cavalry who had saved him that day back near the Malpais. And anyway, injustice of any kind just made him plain, damn mad. He stepped forward.

"He's not quite alone."

"Stay out of this," the Negro snapped, keeping his eyes on both Pete and the blustering man who had challenged him. "It's not your fight."

"I can make it mine if I want to. It's a free country, ain't it?"

There was a short pause, then the black man said, "Yeah, I reckon you can at that."

They stood there, both of them with hands hanging loosely by their sides, the Negro's shotgun within easy reach and their pistols ready. Boots scraped through the sawdust as other men stood, eyeing the waiting pair with wary gazes. The saloon men formed a rough half-circle in front of them, obviously reluctant to be in the shotgun's path but determined not to let these two men bluff them.

Though Pete had started the argument, he had a strange reluctance to see his saloon shot to pieces. Relenting, he said, "Dammit, have your drink, then! I don't want my place shot up, and that's what it looks like it'll be."

"Right," Trouble answered quietly.

The crescent of men slowly sat back down and resumed card games and drinking as Pete flashed the huge Negro a sour glance and said, "What's your pleasure?"

Jordan grinned, and, relaxing slightly, flipped a few coins to the bar. "Enjoy your drink," was all he said to the black man before turning to go.

"Wait a minute." The Negro plunked down enough money on the bar for an entire bottle of rye and hoisted it in a beefy hand. "Come have a drink with me."

"Thanks, but I need to be moving on. . . ."

"Too good to drink with a man of color?" came the mocking taunt, delivered with a grin. "Come on, Captain Sinclair, it won't hurt a bit."

Jordan paused, looking closely at the Negro. "How did you know my name?"

"I know lots of things, Captain. Like how you got that scar across your forehead, for instance, and how you were the only survivor of your command."

"The Ninth. You were with the Ninth," Jordan said, and the Negro nodded. "What's your name?"

"Amos Weatherby. It was Lieutenant Amos Weatherby when I was still in the Army."

Jordan held out his hand. "Plain Jordan Sinclair now, not Captain. And I *am* still thirsty, Weatherby."

They chose a table in the corner, sitting with their backs against the wall in case of trouble, and put their boots on the table and began to drink.

"You know," Jordan said a few hours later, pushing back his hat to peer at Amos, who had a tendency to waver suspiciously, "it wasn't that I grew to hate the Army, but I just couldn't understand it at times. Hell, we had enough men to rout the hostiles and win, but we had to wait for orders. And when orders came . . ."

"It was too late to do anything but clean up after the massacre," Amos finished. Shrugging, he downed another glass of rye. "Don' matter none now, I guess. The Apache are about finished. Victorio's dead, and Nana's almost shot his last."

"They've still got another year or two, maybe three, before it's over," Jordan predicted, staring through bleary eyes at Weatherby. He waggled his empty glass in Amos's direction. "Then they'll be cooped up like chickens in a pen, with all th' fight out of 'em."

Amos leaned forward and snared the bottle of rye. There was only a small amount left, and he tilted up the bottle and finished it off before saying, "You 'member that fight at Hembrillo Basin, Cap'n?"

Jordan squinted thoughtfully. "Yeah, of course I do. It was a waste of ammunition and time."

"Yeah, for most ever'body it was. Not me, though. I found sumthin' worth going back to that peak for, Cap'n." His chair legs thumped down as he leaned forward, one hand fumbling in the pocket of his faded cavalry pants as his voice lowered. Both of Amos's eyes wandered drunkenly for a moment until he was able to focus on Sinclair. "That's th' reason I got outa th' Army, Cap'n, and that's th' reason I come back to this territory. I got plans—*big* plans!"

Jordan had heard plenty of this kind of talk lately, usually from tattered old miners with a glazed look in their eyes, a scrawny mule, and a small grubstake. But somehow he knew that Amos was different. For one thing, Amos Weatherby wasn't the usual, run-of-the-mill miner; he was an intelligent man with a purpose and twelve years of army duty behind him. And for another thing, he was holding in the pink palm of his hand a dull gleaming chunk of gold. That was enough to sober up Jordan.

"That chunk is big enough to choke a mule, Amos," he commented casually. "Had it assayed?"

"Don't have to. Besides, you think I want anybody knowing I might have an idea where to get more? Shit! I'd be strung up quicker than a hawg on butchering day! No, Cap'n, this is our little secret."

"How do you know you can trust me?"

Amos sat back with a smile on his face, sliding the gold nugget back into his pocket. "I've learned a few things the hard way in my life, Cap'n, and one of 'em is who I can trust and who I can't. I've seen your face, and I've heard your talk, and I know you. You'll do."

Amused now, Jordan sat back in his chair, blunt fingertips thumping against the table top as he regarded Amos with benevolence. "I'll do what, Amos?"

Amos grinned. "You'll do as my partner, Cap'n."

"Whoa! I'm not into gold mining. Too much hard work, long hours, and risk for me."

"Hell, man! I don't want to do no gold mining neither! I'm talking about treasure, Sinclair, money and rifles and gold bars and silver a man can dig out of rock with a spoon. . . ."

"You're crazy."

"Am I?" Amos reached into his pocket again. "Look at this *nugget*, Sinclair, look real close. What do you see?"

Taking it, Jordan inspected the chunk of gold closely. It wasn't raw gold like he'd thought, but part of a gold bar. He quirked a glance at Amos. "Where'd you find it?"

Amos was silent for a moment, then shrugged and said,

"Damned if I know, Cap'n. I've been back over every inch of that peak and I can't find the cave. I've spent the last two months up there, tracing and retracing my steps, until I've gone plumb damn crazy looking for it. I need help, somebody who can stand back and look at the area with a new eye."

"How did you find the cave the first time, and when?"

"I was scoutin' around after that fight, right after we realized that Hatch's command had backed us up, but the 'Pache had slid over the west saddle of the basin during the night. Well, I was on reconnaissance a few days later, looking for a sign, and I just kind of stumbled into it. You've got to slide under this rock ledge, see, and then you drop down into this tunnel that leads into the cave. I found Wells Fargo boxes, letters, silver cups and plates and dinnerware—hell, I even found an old Spanish scabbard and sword down there! Looks like the Apache been using it as a storage area for all their raided loot." Amos sighed, scratching his head for a moment as he pondered, then obviously decided something.

Hunching his broad shoulders, he leaned forward and met Sinclair's eyes. "There's more," he said. "Cap'n, let me tell you what else I found down there . . . gold bullion stacked like cordwood, thousands of 'em! They're just sitting there waiting on us to come back for 'em, Cap'n!"

"So why did it take you so long? That was back in '80, wasn't it?"

"Hell, you know the Army, Cap'n, and how slow they work. I got transferred to a post in Kansas, and then from there to Texas, and it took me this long to do my time and get out." Amos gave a shake of his head, his expression forlorn. "And now I'm here and can't even find the cave."

"So how do you think I can help?"

"Well, you know the area pretty good, right? And you've got experience with fighting 'Pache, right? And you give the impression of being a man who can keep a secret. That's about all the qualifications I need.''

Jordan remained silent for several moments. The saloon had just about cleared out, and only a few scattered tables had anyone at all sitting at them. Pete was still at the bar, occasionally glowering at Jordan and Amos but other than that leaving them alone. Even the piano player was gone. Finally, looking up at Amos, Jordan said, "Give me some time to think it over, Weatherby. It sounds good, but there's a lot at risk."

"Like what?"

"Apache, for one thing. Nana's still loose, remember? And it seems to me that most men who go looking for gold end up losing their gold and their lives in the process. Gold will make a man do a lot of things, Amos."

"Gold makes *greedy* men do a lot of things, Cap'n. I don't want to be greedy. I just want enough to buy me a little farm somewhere and settle down and raise pigs and pickaninnies."

Jordan grinned. "Now, that sounds reasonable, Amos. I can't see a problem with that at all."

Chapter
3

Noon bore down on the south Texas town like a freight train, hot and steaming. Jordan had been up since right after sunrise, and had already eaten a hearty breakfast of steak and eggs when he saw Amos. The big Negro was strolling up the dust-thick street with long, easy strides.

"Amos." Sinclair tugged on the brim of his battered gray hat in greeting. He was sitting in the shade of an awning, watching the busy street as old men do.

"Good morning to you, Jordan." Amos stopped, grinning that wide grin that reminded Sinclair of a row of gleaming pearls. "You look rested, and as well fed as a coon dog during hunting season."

"You mean it shows?"

"It shows, Jordan."

"Well, you might be right about that. You know, I've been thinking. I had a little idea come to me sometime during the night that might help out with this hunt."

"You mean you're in?"

"You taking back the offer?"

"Hell, no! The offer stands!" Amos's grin widened even farther and he stuck out his hand. "Shake on it? We split whatever we find fifty-fifty."

"Okay." Rocking his chair forward, Jordan rose and took his hand. "Now listen to this idea, Amos." He slung one arm around Weatherby's broad shoulders and walked him down the wooden sidewalk several feet until they stood in a deserted alley.

Lowering his voice, Jordan began, "We need to find this Apache hideout, right? And the Apache, they aren't going to be too thrilled about us looking for it, right? So I thought we might just carry along a little extra insurance against any, shall we say, unpleasant surprises. I came to Franklin down through the Organ Mountains, and I happened to . . . visit . . . a remote little village stuck back in one of the canyons." He grinned at Amos. "Remember me telling you yesterday about meeting Geronimo? Well, this village, my friend, is filled with Victorio's relatives."

"How do you know that?"

Jordan's brow lifted. "I was informed of it by one of the residents, and warned away—as if I needed any warning to stay away from that village!"

"How do you know he was telling the truth? He could have been lying, and anyway, what the hell difference does this make to our plans?"

"Be patient, Amos, be patient. I know it was the truth, and I know that Victorio's granddaughter is staying in this little village because I saw her, too. And it makes a hell of a lot of difference if you think of the girl as life insurance, Amos, *life insurance*. She could be our guarantee that no harm comes to us from the Apache while we're up there poking around Victorio's hideout. And she could also tell us where it is, I'm willing to bet."

Amos shook his head. "I don't know, Cap'n. Sounds pretty risky to me."

"More risky than going up there without any insurance? Our lives wouldn't be worth a nickel, Weatherby. You can count on that."

Amos pursed his thick lips, rocking back and forth on his heels for a moment. "Wouldn't hurt the girl, would we?"

"Of course not. Do I look like a child murderer?"

"Yeah, you do, but appearances can be deceiving."

"You don't look so reputable yourself, old man."

"My momma thinks so, Sinclair!"

Grinning, Jordan agreed, "Okay, so I look pretty bad. With a bath and a shave, I'll look a sight better, but you haven't got a prayer."

"Don' worry about it—I ain't religious." Tilting his cavalry cap over his eyes, Amos said, "So when do we start this little adventure, Cap'n?"

"Morning suit you?"

"Suits me just fine, Cap'n, just fine."

But morning brought delay instead of departure. This delay was in the form of a lean young man of sixteen years, blond and brash and looking for his uncle.

Jordan wouldn't even have known his nephew was in town if Griffin didn't have such a trigger-temper and mouth to match. It was barely past nine o'clock when Jordan's attention was snared by a commotion in the street. He was leaving the General Store with saddlebags full of supplies, stepping down from the rough wooden porch to the hitching post and his horse, when he spied two men facing each other in the street. It had not yet progressed to an actual duel between them, but it was quickly headed that way. Pausing, Jordan stared at the kid with a gleam of recognition.

"You think you're so tough, kid?" a beefy man in a dark, dusty suit growled at the youth. "Let's just see if you're as bad as you think you are...."

"Come on," the kid replied coolly. "Anytime you're ready, old man." He stood with hands loose at his sides, his pistol tied down low on one lean thigh, bright blue eyes narrowed and intent. "Come on, Cooke," he urged softly.

His antagonist hesitated, squinting at the brash youth who was so cocksure, then blustered, "Who d'ya think you are—Billy the Kid? Hell, boy, he's dead and gone, like you're gonna be...."

"Leave your gun where it is, mister," Jordan warned when the man's hand dropped slightly, "or you're going to be the one who's lying in the street."

"What th' ... who in th' hell do you think you are, gettin' in a fight that don't concern you?" Cooke half-turned to glare at Jordan, saw his drawn weapon, and held his hands well away from his sides.

Jordan reached out to pluck Cooke's pistol from his holster, keeping his .45 trained on a spot between the man's neck and navel.

"I don't have to think," Sinclair responded lightly, "I know who I am. I'm this boy's uncle..."

"Uncle Jordan?" the youth under discussion cut in. "I been looking for you!"

"...and I don't care to see him sporting any bullet holes," Jordan finished. Cooke's pistol dropped to the dust, and Jordan kicked it several feet away. "Why don't you go on and mind your own business, and forget this even happened," he advised.

"I don't mind," Cooke said, "but tell this hot-headed little banty rooster that he can't go around accusing a man of cheatin' at cards without gettin' into trouble—killing trouble."

"I'll tell him. Go get yourself a drink, mister."

"You should have left me alone, Uncle Jordan," the boy said as Cooke walked away. Thumbs hooked into his belt, he shook his fair head. "I could've taken him easy."

Jordan's response was a wicked backhand to the jaw, sending Griffin Armstrong sprawling into the dust of the street. "You young idiot! What in the hell do you think you're doing? That man could have killed you and left you in the middle of the street for the buzzards to pick!"

Griffin rolled to his knees, staring up at his uncle with a fair measure of reproach. "I'm telling you that I could have taken him. I've been practicin', Uncle Jordan."

"Does your mother know you're here? And why in the hell *are* you here?"

Griffin grinned. "Why don't we talk about this over a beer?" He massaged his bruised jaw and gazed hopefully at Jordan.

"I can have a beer," Jordan said through clenched teeth, reaching down to haul his nephew up by his shirt collar. "You drink sarsaparilla."

"Shit . . ."

"And soap in your mouth if you don't watch it."

Propelling the youth ahead of him, Jordan stopped first to sling his saddlebags over one shoulder, then headed for the nearest café. After ordering eggs and coffee for both of them, he crossed his arms and leaned on the table, piercing Griffin with a hard look.

"Now tell me what you're doing here."

Griffin's grin was disarming, but it wasn't having the desired effect on his uncle, so he shrugged. "Okay, I came looking for you, Uncle Jordan. I got tired of the same old thing every day, with Mama nagging at me and Pa just going on and on about the ranch . . . it was driving me crazy. I don't want to spend the rest of my life in a one-horse town in northwest Texas doing nothing. After listening to you talk about your adventures on your last visit right before Christmas, I decided that *I* want adventure. I want to see more than sagebrush, cactus, and the back end of a cow.''

"So you came here?" Jordan's mouth twisted in a mocking grin that made Griffin flush. "Good choice, nephew."

"I came here for a reason," the boy defended himself. "I came to find you. Mama had just gotten that letter you wrote about getting out of the Army and heading to Mexico for a while, and I thought that if I could find you, you'd take me with you."

"Did you? I sent that letter three weeks ago. How'd you know where to look for me?"

"Easy." Griffin grinned again and took a quick gulp of scalding coffee. "I read in the letter where you were leaving the fort sometime around the last of May, and Franklin is between Fort Wingate and Mexico, ain't it? Well it stands to reason a man would stop here for a day or two before heading south again. After all, Franklin is the main border town between Texas and Mexico."

"How'd you get here?" Jordan asked mildly, impressed in spite of himself by the youth's deductive reasoning. "And how long have you been in town?"

"I took the money I've been saving and bought a ticket on the Overland mail stage. It goes all the way from Pecos to here with no problem, but it's one hell—heck—of a hot, dusty ride. I've been waiting two days. When did you get in town?"

Leaning back in his chair, Jordan draped one arm over the chairback as he gazed at his nephew, debating on a solution. He was on his way out of town, heading into the unknown, and he sure didn't want to subject his only sister's boy to that kind of danger. But what guarantee did he have that if he put impetuous Griffin on the Overland mail stage back to his mother, he'd get home? If he escorted the boy home, he'd lose precious time, and if he didn't—Griffin might end up in a shallow grave outside some small town.

"What were you going to do if you didn't find me?" Jordan asked instead of answering the boy's question. "Go back home?"

"Hell, no! Excuse me—no, I wasn't. I was going to head for California," he said recklessly, hazarding an answer that just might persuade his uncle to relent in the face of his determination and take him along. "Figured maybe I'd pan for gold or something."

"How old are you now, Griffin?"

"Seventeen—well, sixteen, but I'll be seventeen next March."

"And this is June? Great. How do you think your mother would feel if you went and got yourself killed panning for California gold? You're her firstborn son, and she always took a lot of pride in you, Griffin. Do you think you're being fair to her?"

Griffin stared down at his coffee mug, mouth set in a tight line that reminded Jordan of Griffin's mother, Jasmine. A faint smile slanted Jordan's mouth. Hell, it must be a family trait, this restless urge to see what there was to see, because he could remember his own youthful urges.

Glancing up, Griffin caught that faint gleam of sympathy and understanding in his uncle's eyes and decided to strike while the iron was hot.

"I'm being fair to *me* right now, Uncle Jordan, and don't say you don't understand. Mama understands more than you think she does, you know. She always had that wild hair when she was a girl, and sometimes when she's sitting out on the front porch at the end of the day, I listen to her talk about the times before she met Pa, how she took care of you when she wanted to be roaming. . . ."

Jordan's mind flew back over twenty years to when he'd been only six years old and had no one to look to but his older sister. She'd been only a girl, just sixteen, and saddled with a younger brother to care for. Times had been hard, especially after their mother's death, and they'd had to scratch just to survive on the meager amount of money brought home by their father. But somehow, Jasmine had made their shabby house a home, filling it with love and laughter, and he'd never forgotten. He'd lived with her and Fletcher after they married. Pa had died and he had no place else to go, and Fletcher Armstrong was a good man. Fletcher made sure that young Jordan had schooling; maybe he could repay that debt by seeing to Fletcher's and Jassy's son, give him a different kind of education that would help him become a man.

"Tell you what, Griffin, I've got a proposal to put to you." Jordan smiled at Griffin's eager expression, the widening of blue eyes so much like Jassy's. "I'll take you with me, but you've got to promise that at the end of the summer you'll go back home to your folks and discuss your schooling. Ah-ah," he said when Griffin's mouth pursed in automatic protest. "If you don't agree, I'll put you on the first stage back right now, even if I have to tie you into a burlap sack."

Griffin sat back in his chair, his youthful mouth curved in a frown. "All right," he finally said, too elated at the prospect of finally spending time with the uncle he idolized to think about future restrictions, "but this better be one hell of a summer, Uncle Jordan."

Grinning, Jordan said, "Since we're going to be riding the trail together, just call me Jordan. And by the way," he added, spying Amos's dark shadow just outside the café, "I'm about to introduce you to Amos Weatherby, a friend and business partner. Finish your eggs and meet me outside."

Tossing down coins for their meal, Jordan rose from the table and strode out of the café, finding Amos waiting on the porch.

"Where the hell you been, Cap'n? I found your horse tied in front of the store, but no sign of you. Thought you'd done gone and changed your mind."

"No, but there have been some . . . ahh . . . alterations to our plans, Amos."

Amos gave him a hard look. "Alterations?"

"Alterations." Jordan leaned against the porch post and pushed back his hat. "I stumbled across a small problem a little while ago. I can't turn my back on it, so—I'm going to have to take it with us or back out."

Amos never had been quick to jump to conclusions or decisions, so he waited a moment before he spoke. Pushing back his cavalry cap, he took the makings for a cigarette out of his blue denim shirt pocket, shoving aside his suspender strap to reach the tobacco pouch. He filled and rolled two cigarettes with deliberate movements and offered one to Jordan, who took it.

"What kind of problem are we talking about, Cap'n?" he asked, lighting Jordan's cigarette. " 'Cause I might get second thoughts about this."

Jordan took a deep drag from his cigarette and blew the smoke into the air. "Fair enough. It's my nephew. He's here in Franklin, and I can't just leave him or put him on the train back home. I said he could travel with me for the summer if he promised to go home in the fall. I made the deal and I can't go back on it. Either Griffin goes with us, or I have to back out of our business deal. Sorry, Amos, but he's my sister's boy and I owe her."

"Hey, I understand, Cap'n, I do. No problem there, it's just that I don't know if I want to ride with some green kid, especially on something like this. You understand?"

"Yeah, sure I do. I don't blame you. Here he comes now, and I'd like you to meet him."

Griffin strolled out of the café, adjusting the gunbelt he wore around his skinny hips, flashing a bright grin at his uncle. His gaze went from Jordan to Amos, and he stuck out a hand. "Hello, Mr. Weatherby. Jordan tells me you're a friend and business partner. Nice to meet you."

Pumping his hand, Amos nodded. "Nice to meet you, too, Mister . . . ?"

"Sorry, Amos. Amos Weatherby, meet my nephew, Griffin Armstrong," Jordan put in. "He's a little cocky, but pretty well-mannered."

Amos's gaze went from Griffin's open, honest face to the gunbelt he wore slung around his hips. It seemed incongruous for such a lethal weapon to be worn by such a youthful lad, and he laughed and said so.

Griffin bristled immediately. "Hey, I can use this old pistol, don't you worry about it! I spent seven hours a day practicing behind our barn, and I can shoot the eye out of a hawk. . . ."

"Well," Amos said, amusement curling his mouth, "I ain't got much use for hawk eyes, but let's see what else you can do, boy." He met Jordan's curious gaze and muttered, "I just hate to lose a good partner, that's all. And who knows—maybe we can use him."

Jordan grinned and said, "Come on, Griffin. There's a stretch of ground just outside of town where nobody'll get hurt."

Puffed up with injured pride, Griffin followed Amos and Jordan down the street until they were just outside of the Franklin town limits. An ancient church stood not far away, and he considered ringing its bells with bullets for a moment before deciding that would not impress his uncle. Instead, the boy turned to Amos and asked, "You got a nickel?"

"Yeah."

"Throw it up as high as you can."

While Griffin backed away about four feet, half-crouched and waiting, Amos dug into his pocket, a wide grin on his dark face. "This is going to be good," he muttered. Sunlight glittered on Amos's brawny arms, dusky muscles glowing with perspiration as they flexed. Leaning back, Amos put his weight into the toss, and the nickel flew into the air as if shot from a cannon. It arced high, spinning in the sunlight so that Jordan could hardly see it, but it was soon apparent that Griffin could.

Moving with a smooth, easy motion, Griffin drew and fired. "You check the nickel," he said, rising from his crouch, "so that you won't think there's some trick to it."

Amos scuffed through the dirt to find the nickel. It was plugged through the center and still warm from the bullet. His gaze moved slowly to the boy who stood with studied poise.

"You're good, Griffin Armstrong, damn good." Amos looked down at the plugged coin in his palm. "Damn good."

When Amos's gaze moved to Jordan, he shrugged. "It's up to you, Weatherby. It's your decision now."

Puzzled, Griffin looked from his uncle to Amos and back again. "What are you talking about?" he asked.

Amos grinned, and he and Jordan both said at the same time, "Gold."

Chapter
4

It was dark, the night wind whipping through the pines outside the cave with a sighing sound, making Griffin's skin prickle.

"I thought you said we were going to hunt for gold," he muttered. "You never said nothing about sneaking into an entire village of Apaches!"

"Oh," Jordan said innocently, "did I leave that out? How remiss of me. Now listen, Griffin, this is important in case there's trouble. There's one tipi on the very edge of the village, and it is the one where Victorio's granddaughter sleeps. It has markings on it like this...." He drew some figures in the dirt, and Griffin squinted in the firelight to see them. "That's my objective. You hang back with Amos and cover me if I need you. Look for the tipi with those markings, and you'll know you've got the right one. All the men of any age are going to be gone on this hunt they're organizing—it's the season—so I shouldn't have any problem at all. Now something else that's important—are you listening?"

"Yeah, I'm listening," Griffin said, but his thoughts were on the night ahead of him. He glanced down at his breech-

cloth and Apache boots and made a face. The root dye
Jordan and Amos had put on his hair itched, and the
nutberry juice they'd rubbed into his skin stank. He was
miserable, plain miserable. This wasn't his idea of high
adventure at all. Where was the glory in dressing up like an
Apache boy and sitting back while someone else had all the
fun? There would be a lot more glory in riding into the
Apache village yelling and shooting his gun.

"Griffin!"

"Wha . . . what?"

"Did you hear what I said? Make certain you cover me or
I'm liable to get my hair shaved from eyebrows to chin!"

"Yeah, yeah, I know." Standing, Griffin stretched his
cramped muscles and shivered again. "This cave is cold.
How do Apaches stand going around without a shirt?"

"They don't. They wear shirts if they want."

"Great. *Now* you tell me."

Jordan grinned. "If you weren't in such a hurry to go
ahead and play dress-up, you wouldn't be so cold. Me and
Amos are waiting 'til right before we go, and the hour before
daybreak is usually the coolest time of the night."

"Right," Griffin said, following their example and stretching
out on his blanket in front of the fire. "I still don't see why
you won't let me sneak into the village, though. I could do
it better than you because I'm more the size of an Apache
and won't stick out like a giant sore thumb like you will."

"I told you," Jordan said in the tone of a man who has
repeated himself on the same subject several times. "Your
mother would never forgive me for letting a green kid . . ."

"Green kid!" Griffin exploded wrathfully.

". . . get himself hurt, and I'd probably never hear the
end of it," Jordan continued imperturbably. "Besides, Griff,
you wouldn't want me to feel bad if you got hurt, would you?"

"I don't know when everybody's gonna realize that I'm not just a little kid anymore," Griffin grumbled in answer. He flopped over on his side with his back to Amos and Jordan and drew a long, deep sigh.

Amos and Jordan exchanged amused glances and settled down to get a few hours' sleep before executing their plan. It was always wise to be razor-sharp.

The moon finally slid behind a peak, and Griffin knew it was time. These dark hours before dawn would be the best chance to sneak in undetected, according to Jordan, and he rose to his feet as silently as a cat, recalling every detail he could about what they'd said earlier.

"Remember what I said," Amos had said, "about walkin' on the balls of your feet, quiet like a cat. . . ."

"And look for these markings on the tipi for unmarried maidens," Jordan had said while scribbling his stick drawings in the dirt of the cave floor.

Griffin patted the leather strap holding his gun around his waist and flicked a last glance at the sleeping figure on the ground. They would be so surprised when he returned with the girl, and then they'd know that he wasn't just a silly little kid playing at being grown-up.

When Griffin slipped softly out of the cave on the balls of his feet, Amos opened one eye and watched, a half-smile slanting his mouth. Maybe the kid could do it and maybe he couldn't, but they'd never know unless he tried. Hell, Jordan was being a little too protective anyway. And there wasn't much danger in sneaking into an unarmed, unmanned camp and stealing a skinny little Apache girl. Besides, he'd wake Jordan up as soon as Griffin had had his chance to get to the camp, so the boy would have a back-up. This was the youth's rite of manhood, and he deserved a chance.

* * *

It was a lot easier to act brave than it was not to be scared, Griffin reflected an hour later as he squatted in thick bear bushes outside the Apache camp. He'd had plenty of trouble sneaking this close, even though most of the men and boys old enough to fight were gone on a raid.

Probably off scalping white settlers, Griffin decided gloomily, staring back at a skinny camp mongrel. The dog sat back on his haunches, trying to decide if Griffin was worthy of a fuss. The camp dogs were one reason it had taken him longer than necessary. Nocturnal prowlers through the refuse of the camp, the dogs were natural guards, barking at any unusual movements. So far, it had taken Griffin a half hour just to creep ten yards. Now he was within arm's reach of the tipi Jordan had described, and this stupid mutt was gazing at him with a toothy grin.

"Shoo!" Griffin hissed finally, "go away!" Maybe the dog didn't understand English, and he didn't know Apache. Griffin compromised with Spanish. "Vamos!" When that didn't work, he lost patience and lifted a nearby stick. That worked. The mutt, obviously accustomed to having sticks flung at him, yelped once and fled. Griffin froze.

Time ticked slowly past, measured by the frantic beating of his heart, and no one came out to see why the dog had yelped. Maybe that was common, too.

Creeping forward at last, Griffin reached the perimeter of the cone-shaped, buffalo-hide tipi. The bottom edges had been lifted for ventilation, an unexpected bonus, and he slid forward on his belly to peer inside. Another bonus. Only one girl lay on her mats, and she was sound alseep.

Griffin smiled to himself and slithered forward like a rattlesnake. There she was, his target, Victorio's granddaughter, their insurance. She was larger than he'd thought an Apache girl would be; not fat or chunky, but slender and long-legged.

Rising to his knees, Griffin quietly drew the burlap bag from his waistband, then frowned. Jordan had said something about some kind of proof that this was the right girl, but what? Damn, he should have listened better! But how could this be the wrong girl? he argued with himself. She was the only girl in the tipi. And besides, time was running out. It would be light soon, and this stupid disguise he wore wouldn't fool any Apache. It hadn't even fooled the camp dogs.

Leaning forward, Griffin hastily stuffed a rag into the girl's mouth, waking her so that she began to struggle wildly, arms and long legs flailing like an overturned beetle.

"Keep still," he muttered, then realized the girl probably couldn't understand English. He quickly tied the gag in a knot, then tugged the burlap bag over her head, pinning her arms at her sides. Now it was going to be touchy, pulling the girl out of the tipi and across the open area until he reached the stream. Downstream a short way waited his horse, and from that point on it should be a cinch. He began to drag his captive out of the tipi and across the bunchgrass, keeping a nervous eye out for any suspicious movements.

Griffin hadn't counted on the girl being so strong. And he hadn't counted on her being able to loosen her gag, either. It was bad enough when she kicked him in the shins, and even worse when she began yelling at him in some weird language, but when the girl managed to land a swift kick in Griffin's crotch, his patience snapped. As soon as he was able to breathe again, he clipped her on the jaw. Results were immediate and infinitely satisfying. The girl went silent and limp.

The rest of the short trip to his mount was relatively

uneventful. His captive did not regain consciousness until just outside of their cave hideout four miles away, but she regained clarity with a vengeance.

Crouched at the entrance of the cave, just awake and discussing what to do, Amos and Jordan exchanged alarmed glances.

"What in the hell is that?" they chorused, and started out of the cave at a run, pistols drawn.

"It's Griffin," Jordan said at last, pausing. Relief was evident in his voice. "And he's either got the girl or a wildcat."

"Wildcat's my guess," Amos said. "Listen to that squalling! Sounds like a whole cat fight."

Jordan peered into the darkness. He could hear Griffin cussing a blue streak, and smiled. "Well, against my better judgment, he's made it this far. Think we should help, Amos?"

Amos contemplated the question a moment, then chuckled. "Naw. The boy's got to grow up sometime, right?"

"Right."

Both men turned and walked back into the cave and crouched beside the campfire to wait on Griffin.

It was a wild-eyed and ragged Griffin who stormed into the cave on his horse, unceremoniously dumping the girl on the rocky floor. "Thanks a lot for your help!" he snarled, leaping down from his mount. "This bitch almost killed me!"

Amos looked down at the rocky ground, suddenly intent on the progress of a bug. Jordan found himself equally absorbed in the flight of a night moth.

"All right, you guys, this isn't a damn bit funny!" Griffin angled closer, one foot atop the squirming burlap bag at his feet, his eyes narrowed with anger. A strange, muffled sound was coming from the bag, interspersed with oddly familiar words.

"It sounds like she's speaking Spanish," Amos said.

"And Apache," Jordan added, "mixed with French." They looked at each other, then said together, "French?"

Jordan glared at Griffin, who was scratched as if he'd been run through thorn bushes. "Since you decided to be the hero," he ground out from between clenched teeth, "you better have gotten the right girl, Griffin Armstrong! Our lives won't be worth that nickel you plugged for Amos if you didn't."

Reaching out, Jordan untied the leather strips binding the bag over the girl's head and torso. When he tugged it away, the girl rolled onto the ground, her buckskin dress twisted up around slender thighs. She sat up immediately, fury contorting a very pretty face, a torrent of words rushing from her mouth.

"What's she mean, 'moan do' and 'sack ray blue'?" Amos asked. "Sounds like no Apache I've ever heard. What's a'ko shun'?"

"That," Jordan replied tightly, "is French for pig, Amos." He edged closer to the girl, who stared at him with narrowed eyes, finally growing quiet. "Goddammit, Griffin!" he exploded, his lean body straightening in a lithe motion, "You didn't even get the right girl!"

Griffin, busily examining his wounds, gave Jordan a sour glance. "Had to get the right girl," he muttered. "She was the *only* girl."

"Didn't you listen when I described what she'd be wearing—that Victorio's granddaughter would be wearing a special amulet around her neck? Sweet Jesus, this girl's not even Apache!"

"Well, how was I to know any different?" Griffin defended

himself. "She was in the right tipi, she looks like an Apache, and she was the only girl in there!"

Jordan's reaction was swift and unexpected. He reached out with both hands and pulled the girl up, turning her around so that her back was pressed against his chest, one hand tilting up her chin. "Look, Griffin," he said, holding her head still, "Apaches don't have green eyes."

Blinking in surprise, Griffin leaned close, staring into the girl's face. Huge green eyes like emeralds stared back at him. "Well, I'll be damned," he breathed.

"I don't doubt it," Amos observed tersely, dropping to a seat on a flat rock. "Now what do we do, Cap'n? Your great idea didn't turn out to be so great after all."

"*My* idea was fine. Your idea to let Griffin play hero didn't work out too good, though!" Jordan released the girl, letting go of her arms. He expected her to attempt flight, or at the very least to withdraw as far as she could, but she did neither. She turned slowly, staring up into his face with a strange half-smile curving her lips. Nonplussed, Jordan stared back for a moment. "You can sit down," he said brusquely, signing with his hands when she tilted her head to one side and toyed with a long strand of her dark hair.

"Thank you," she said finally, her English letter-perfect. All three men stared at her, and, smiling to herself now, she turned and chose a rock close to the fire. She gazed at them for a moment, then asked, "Do you have anything to eat? I'm starved."

Chapter
<u>5</u>

Amos and Jordan exchanged stunned glances, then looked back at the slender girl before them. She sat like a pert pixie, watching them curiously, her gaze lingering upon Amos for several moments.

"You're black," she stated, pointing a grubby finger in his direction. *"T'eeshínde."*

Amos's mouth worked silently for a moment, then he said, "No kidding! Hell, she's got me, Jordan. It's all up to you now."

"What do you mean—all up to me?" Jordan's eyes narrowed.

"She knows I'm black. *You* talk to her."

"And what does that have to do with anything?" Jordan demanded, but Amos was already walking to the other side of the fire and sitting down on the rocky cave floor.

"Nothing, but I'm damned if I'm going to try and talk to her. It was *your* idea to get the girl—you talk to her."

"Don't look at *me*!" Griffin sputtered when Jordan's gaze swung in his direction. "I went and got her, and now I'm like to bleed to death. It's your turn to do something besides think up lousy plans."

Watching with eyes so wide they were almost ludicrous, the girl smiled suddenly. Jordan stared at her suspiciously, and her smile grew wider.

"I'll get you something to eat," he muttered shortly. Kneeling by the fire, he hooked a chunk of almost burned venison from the coals, tossing the hot meat from hand to hand as he fumbled for a tin plate. Jordan held out the plate, his eyes meeting hers for an instant, and he scowled. Maybe she was Apache. She certainly looked like one, with her buckskin dress, bare legs and feet, and long black hair. But—what about the green eyes?

The girl took the plate then, murmured something in Apache, and began eating noisily. She had certainly neglected to learn table manners, Jordan decided as strong white teeth tore into the steaming chunk of venison and she began to chew.

"Now let me get this straight," Jordan said as the girl stared up at him with a wide smile, "you weren't captured by the Apache, right?"

"Right." Small fingers tore a huge strip of meat from the chunk they had given her and stuffed it into her mouth. Both cheeks bulged, and fat dripped down her round chin as she chewed on the venison.

"Disgusting," Griffin said with a grimace, and the girl's head whipped around, eyes narrowing. Her glance moved from Griffin to Amos, and when he looked away with a pained expression, she swallowed the meat. The boy called Griffin handed her a scrap of cloth and indicated that she should wipe her chin, which she did slowly and thoughtfully.

"So," Jordan persisted, "if you weren't captured, then you were in that camp and in that tipi willingly. Why?"

"Why not?" Another strip of meat was torn from the half

burned chunk of deer meat. This time she bit off a small amount and chewed it with her mouth closed. She had no intention of telling him that she had been in that tipi for the simple reason that it was her time, and the unmarried maidens were set aside at that time of the month.

Taking a deep breath, Jordan tried again. "Look, I heard you speak French. Most Apache don't speak French. Your English is perfect, and I heard you use Spanish as well." He reached out to lift a strand of her dark, heavy hair, letting it slide through his fingers like silk. "You hair is black, but it's not as coarse as an Apache's; your skin is dark but doesn't have the same cast an an Apache's; you have high cheekbones, but your nose is straight and thin—who are you?"

Wiping greasy fingers on her outgrown buckskin dress, the girl drew her sleeve across her mouth and said, "Sometimes I am called Gáadu." She smiled and pointed to her eyes. "It is because they are green like a cat's."

"And that is your name?"

"*'Izhi' shiyéé*," she said, and at his blank look translated, "names are personal possessions and not to be given to one who is not a friend."

"So, consider me a friend. Do I call you Gáadu?"

Beaming at this suggestion that she be his friend, she said, "If it pleases you. I also have another name."

When she stared at him expectantly, Jordan lost some of his patience. "Well, what is it, dammit!"

Gáadu stared at him for a moment. "Jolie La Fleur."

"Aha! I knew it. She's French. . . ."

"Shimá—my mother—was one of the people—*Chihende*," she interrupted Jordan. "She's dead."

Jordan didn't know what to say for a moment, and he didn't like the way the girl kept staring at him. It reminded him of a time not long ago when another girl had stared at him like that. It was unnerving.

"So, that explains why you were in the tipi for unmarried girls." Jordan threw Griffin a withering glance that plainly said *I told you so*. "Now, boys, what do we do with our little captive?" He turned to face Griffin and Amos. "She's of no use as a hostage like I'd hoped. Her mother's dead and her father's French. She's more of a liability than an asset, and we can't afford any more mistakes. Any suggestions?"

There was silence for a moment as the men contemplated their options, and the girl digested this turn of events. She'd recognized him at once as the man brought to Geronimo's camp, of course, and was pleased that he had obviously seen and wanted her also. She didn't understand all the words he used, but it was obvious he might have changed his mind about taking her along with him. It didn't sound good.

Crossing her legs, Jolie La Fleur propped her bruised chin in a cupped palm, rested her elbow on her knee, and gazed at Jordan. She remembered him quite well, and he hadn't changed at all. He was so handsome, and when he had held her against him, she had wanted to melt. Lozen, Victorio's granddaughter, who had been named after his sister, had told her she would one day feel this way, but somehow Jolie had always thought it would be for a man in the tribe. This man was a *bélu*, a white man and her natural enemy. But her father was white, French, and that was the same thing. Hadn't her mother married a white man? And besides—he had remembered her and come after her. She'd heard him admit it. Jolie smiled.

Glancing toward the girl, Jordan saw her smile and paused in midsentence, his brain ceasing to function. There was just something about the way she looked at him.

"Stop that!" he told her crossly.

"Stop what?" Her expression was innocent.

"Stop looking at me." Jordan was well aware of Amos's, and Griffin's interested gazes, and he scowled.

"Why?" the girl asked, scooting closer to Jordan. He edged away.

"Because I said so, and because you're looking at me like you were planning on adding my scalp to your lodgepole, that's why."

Jolie laughed. "Women don't take scalps. Except on special occasions."

"Great. Look, can you just stare somewhere else?"

But Jolie couldn't. She tried, but her thoughts were full of this man called Jordan and she couldn't keep her gaze from drifting back to him. He was tall, much taller than any Apache, and he was so handsome. His hair was not as dark as hers, and when the firelight hit it, the dark brown strands glowed red. And his face—it was lean and hard, but very attractive. He had high cheekbones like an Apache, and his nose was straight and thin, not broad. But it was his lips that really attracted her attention. They were neither too thin nor too full, and she suddenly wondered how he would taste if she kissed him.

"She's looking at you again," Griffin pointed out, and Jordan glared at his nephew.

"Go wash that brown stuff off your face," was all he said, "and let's get some sleep. We'll decide what to do in a couple of hours."

Amos rose, stretched, and stared at their prisoner with a thoughtful expression. "Shouldn't we tie her up or something? She might go bring back some of her relatives."

"Sure. Tie her up," Jordan agreed, turning his back on the girl. "And tie her tight."

Shrugging, Amos bent and scooped up the leather strips

used earlier and advanced on the girl. She obediently held out her hands as he hunkered down on his heels in front of her.

"Now, there ain't no need to be afraid, little gal. We don't intend to murder you...."

"The hell we don't!" Griffin put in irritably. "Look what she did to me!" He held out arms that had been badly scratched. Even one cheek bore a long mark from her fingernails. His shins were bruised, and his crotch still ached, and he glared at the captive girl with a mixture of dislike and admiration. Jolie stared back. Green eyes rested on Griffin for a long moment until he flushed and looked away. "Here," he muttered to Amos, "give her my blanket."

"There's no need for that," Jordan put in. "We brought an extra, remember? Now let's get an hour's sleep before we have to start moving. This cave won't keep us hidden long, and I've a feeling that there might be a scouting party headed our way soon."

"No, there won't," Jolie said unexpectedly. "All the men are gone for a time. No one will look for me. You are safe for now."

Amos, Jordan, and Griffin exchanged glances again. It was Amos who decided to ask, "Why are you telling us this? Do you think we're fool enough to believe you? Why, girl, we're liable to step outside that cave and meet forty rifles business-end first if we're dumb enough to believe what you tell us!"

Jolie shrugged. "Suit yourself. You will see that I tell the truth." Meeting Amos's gaze with a direct, steady stare, she asked, "May I have my blanket now?"

The blanket was tossed to her, and she said politely, " '*Ixéhe*," then smoothed it out as best she could with tied hands, lay down, and closed her eyes.

"I don't like this," Amos muttered under his breath to Jordan. His face was creased in a frown. "Nope, I don't like this at all. She acts damn funny."

Griffin snorted and scooted close to the dying fire. "And we act normal? This whole idea is crazy if you ask me. I don't think this girl is going to be one bit of protection against anything, Jordan. Even if she is Victorio's granddaughter. . . ."

Lying on her side with her back to the fire and the men, Jolie smiled. She didn't know what they wanted, except safe passage, but she knew what she wanted. She had seen her own Gray Ghost.

It had been Lozen, Victorio's sister, who had first seen the Gray Ghost. Though a legendary beauty, Lozen had chosen never to marry because no man could measure up to the Gray Ghost. The warriors called him Gray Ghost because he was very powerful, a man of great stature, and always rode alone. No man could ever approach him. After three warriors warned the Gray Ghost of chasing cavalry and pointed out a hiding place, he had visited in their village for a time, and that is where Lozen had fallen in love with him. Gray Ghost had stayed until a wagon moved through the land, carrying a beautiful woman. He knew her and followed it west, away from the Apache. Lozen had been too young then for marriage but had never looked upon another man with interest after the Gray Ghost. Instead, she had carved a place in legend as a warrior, fighting beside her brother Victorio, and was respected above all living women.

Jolie had always thought it a beautiful story and knew it to be true. Now she had found her own Gray Ghost, a man no other man could hope to match. In all her nineteen winters, she had not seen a man who sparked her desire to sleep in his tipi, but this one did. Jolie was still smiling when she fell asleep.

She fell asleep only to be wakened in what seemed like minutes. She muttered a faint protest that was ignored as Amos tugged her from sleep, his big hands finally reaching down to lift her from her blanket and stand her on her feet.

"You got to get up, gal, because we're moving on," he said. After a brief hesitation, he untied her wrists and tossed away the leather thongs.

Jolie yawned and stretched, her slender body straining against the material of the buckskin dress. It wasn't even her dress, but borrowed, and it was too small in all the wrong places. In the clearer light of day filtering in through the cave entrance, even Amos noticed the press of young breasts against the material and how the hem rose well above her knees. He cleared his throat and glanced at Jordan, who was staring at Jolie with a bemused expression.

"We got to decide something, Cap'n," he said, and Jordan nodded agreement.

"Yeah. We do." Jordan regarded the girl with a sober expression on his face. She was trouble. He could sense it.

Blinking sleep from her eyes, with her sable hair rumpled and tumbling over a bare shoulder where the dress had slipped, Jolie La Fleur looked no more than fifteen. Until you looked in her eyes. Then she seemed ten years older, with that special awareness women have when they look at a man they find attractive. Oh, Jordan knew that look all right, had had it turned on him before by quite a few women, but for some reason, this one spelled danger with capital letters. And it wasn't just that they'd captured her from an Apache village, either, though that was trouble enough. Jordan had a sixth sense about these things, and he knew Jolie La Fleur had set her sights on him. Well, so had others, and he was still unattached.

"Get her on a horse," he said abruptly. "We'll put her usefulness to a test."

Griffin and Amos looked at each other, then at Jordan. "Uh, how do you mean to do that, Cap'n?"

Jordan smiled, but there was no humor in the slant of his mouth. "We'll let her ride out as bait and see what happens."

Amos shifted uneasily from one foot to the other and scratched his head beneath the cavalry cap, then pulled it down to shade his eyes. Broad nostrils were flared with distaste, and his wide mouth tightened to a thin line. "I don't think I care for that idea too much."

Jordan glanced at him and gave a short bark of laughter. "Hell, Amos, I didn't mean *that* kind of bait! I'm not in too big a hurry to risk *my* life. We'll put her on a horse, let her ride with us, and see what happens."

The Organ Mountains lay forty-three miles south of Hembrillo. Irregular, columnar peaks that resembled organ pipes had earned them their name, and some still called them Los Organas, or Pipe Organs. The little caravan of four rode out of the Organs and onto the fringe of the Jornada.

This trackless waste of what was once an old Spanish route between Mexico City and Santa Fe stretched forty-five miles wide by ninety miles long, with rugged mountains ringing each side, a lava bed on the north, and the Río Grande River snaking across its southern boundary.

"Where in hell are we?" Griffin asked, looking around uneasily at the barren landscape.

"I'd say hell was as a good term for this place as any," Jordan answered. "But the Spanish called it La Jornada del Muerto—the Dead Man's Route."

"Great," Griffin muttered. "That fact sure makes me feel better."

Iron-shod hooves clattered on the sun-baked red sand as they rode at a walk across the flat land. It was late afternoon, yet the sun still beat down on them with a vengeance.

"Stay out of the arroyos," Amos warned. "A summer storm in the mountains can fill up one of those gorges quicker than a man can blink an eye. You'd drown before you knew what hit you."

Griffin eyed the lateral ravines across the Jornada warily. "Do you mean to tell me a man can drown in this desert?"

"Can and have," Jordan commented. "There's never any warning, just a five-foot wall of water."

"Well, damn!"

Jolie had remained silent during most of the day, her thoughts straying. Now she looked at Jordan. He sat his horse, a big gray, easily, his broad-brimmed hat tilted forward to shade his eyes and face. Her heart gave an irregular thump when he half-turned to glance at her, saw her looking at him, and jerked away with a dark scowl. She nudged her piebald mount a little faster, catching up with him.

"Hello . . ." He said nothing, didn't even glance at her, and Jolie tried again. "I said 'Hello.' "

"I heard you."

She thought for a moment. Perhaps she should have used his name. The '*indaa*' seemed to prefer using personal names freely, while the Apache refrained from doing so. Since she was with these white men, she should adapt herself to their habits, so she smiled pleasantly and tried again.

"Where are we going, Jor-dan?" She pronounced his

name with a French *J*, Zhor-dahn, and he flicked her another scowl.

"We are going to get rid of you as fast as we can, that's where we're going," he muttered.

Jolie dimpled, and Jordan tried not to notice how pretty she was when she smiled. It must be the combination of French and Apache blood that made her so enchanting, with her dusky skin and jet hair, those huge green eyes and thick fringe of lashes, the full, sensual lips that quirked invitingly whenever she looked at him. And her damn long legs were a definite distraction, especially as she insisted upon riding astride, those golden limbs dangling sinuously on each side of her horse. Oh no, he knew her kind and knew to keep away.

"But you don't want to 'get rid' of me, Jor-dan," she said. "And I want to stay with you."

Jordan could hear Griffin's muffled snort of laughter and Amos's amused cough, and his patience snapped. Jerking on his reins, he wheeled his gray to a halt and blocked Jolie's horse. One brawny arm rested on his saddle horn as he learned forward to meet Jolie's surprised gaze.

"Now listen to me and listen good," he growled, "or you'll wish you had! I've no intention of pretending to be nice to you when I don't want to be. I don't like your kind, Jolie La Fleur, or Gáadu, or whatever you choose to call yourself. You're half Apache, and I've got no use for Apache. I lost fifty-three men, men I'd lived with for a year, because of Apache, and I *don't* want to be friends! Got that?"

Jolie stared at him for a long moment, until her horse sensed the tension and began to prance nervously. She easily soothed the restless piebald with a careless nudge of bare heels in his ribs, her long, tan legs flexing in the high sun.

"*Oui*," she said at last in the hot, oppressive silence, "I've 'got that,' Jor-dan. You're fortunate that you only lost fifty-three men to Apache." She gave a toss of her head, blue-black hair rippling back over her shoulders. "I lost my mother, grandparents, and a brother to bluecoats. My brother was only two years old, and my mother was pregnant. Yes, you are fortunate you only lost fifty-three men to Apache."

There was nothing Jordan could think of to say that wouldn't sound trite or foolish. He just gazed back at Jolie, whose green eyes glittered suspiciously though she obviously had no wish to show weakness with tears. Half-ashamed, Jordan wished he hadn't been quite so hasty with his temper. Where was his normal objectivity—his compassion and sense of justice? He felt like a dog, but pride wouldn't allow him to offer an apology.

Amos cleared his throat again. "What say we ride on now, Cap'n. I'd like to find a good place to camp for the night."

Griffin walked his horse forward and grasped the pie-bald's rope hackamore. "Come on, Jolie," he said, not looking at his uncle as he led the girl's horse forward. "I'll teach you a little song I heard not long ago."

Jordan remained still as Griffin and Jolie stepped around him. He could feel Amos looking at him but didn't want to look back. He knew what he'd see in the big man's eyes, and he knew he deserved it.

"Cap'n, I know you're still mourning those men you lost, but you can't feel guilty forever."

Jordan's eyes shot to Amos and narrowed. "Say exactly what you mean, Weatherby."

Shrugging, Amos mopped his forehead with his yellow scarf, coolly returning Jordan's stare. "*You* were responsible for those men, not that girl. It wasn't your fault they got killed, but it wasn't hers either. Quit trying to blame anybody. It was war, Cap'n, plain and simple, and their luck ran out. Our luck could run out, too. We're looking for gold that ain't ours in a land that ain't ours. We don't have the time to fight old battles.''

Jordan nodded. "Guess you're right. It's only a matter of time and luck before the Apache find us, so we need to do what we've got to do and get back out of their territory." He paused, glancing toward Jolie and Griffin. The boy was teaching her a bawdy song he'd obviously picked up in some saloon, and she was mimicking him perfectly. "I just don't know about the girl, Amos."

"I think she could be useful as long as she likes us," Amos said carefully, and Jordan grinned.

"In other words—don't antagonize her, huh?"

Amos nodded. "Something like that. Look at it this way, if she likes us—and she definitely likes you—we might can use her as a guide, and maybe even as go-between with any Apache we run across. If she don't like us—and after this I wouldn't blame her—then she could just as easily find a way to signal her Apache kin. Think about it . . . *Zhor-dahn!*"

Gathering his reins in one hand, Jordan wheeled the gray to follow Jolie and Griffin, and Amos fell in with him. "All right," Jordan said. "But I have my pride, Amos. The girl stays, but she stays away from me."

"Sounds fair," Amos said, slicing an amused glance toward Jordan. Sometimes a man didn't even know what he wanted until he got it. This trip should be even more interesting now.

Chapter
<u>6</u>

Night comes swiftly in the desert. It descends like a hunting hawk, like dark shadows of great wings sweeping from mountain ridges to the hard, flat plains in a silent rush. The day creatures hide in burrows or beneath rocks while night predators are on the prowl.

It was almost dark when Amos chose their campsite. It was a simple matter of choosing the best of the worst, and he briefly considered pushing on through the night shadows instead of stopping. Perhaps they would have if the horses weren't so tired and their water supply so low. Poor visibility was also an important factor, as they could easily misjudge in the dark and plunge into an arroyo or hole without warning.

The decision made, they camped on a flat stretch of barren ground that night, far from trees and water and safety. It was an uneasy night for all of them. They didn't dare light a fire, so they ate dried beef, or jerky, and took sparing swallows from their water pouches. Even the horses were nervous, shifting across the rocks and nickering softly at times. Jordan tied them to a single length of rope stretched between two large rocks, forming a rough remuda not far from where they would spread their blankets. The horses would warn them of approaching danger.

Pausing for a moment, Jordan stretched, catlike, loosening his cramped muscles as he glanced in the direction of Jolie and his nephew. Blue eyes narrowed to slits, and he stiffened. She was helping Griffin unload a pack, bending over from the waist, her slim legs stiff and straight. The form-fitting buckskin dress was snug across her firm posterior, outlining the utterly female shape that would have been intriguing if he didn't know that she was so young. Her long, silky hair fell forward as she bent, held out of her eyes with a knotted cloth wound around her head and almost brushing the ground on each side of the pack. Jordan's mouth tightened as his gaze returned to that expanse of tan, bare leg. It wasn't right that a girl should show so much leg, but he was damned if he was going to admit that he'd even noticed she was female, much less attractive enough to catch his eye.

Jolie was laughing at something Griffin had said as she straightened, flinging back her mane of hair with a careless toss of her head. Young arms flexed backward as she stretched with a lithe, feline movement, straining the thin material of her dress across her small breasts.

Grinding his teeth, Jordan picked up his bedroll and chose a spot several feet beyond the others. He had no intention of sleeping anywhere near that Apache vixen.

Although Amos and Griffin noticed Jordan's tight-lipped silence, they didn't mention it. After an exchange of glances, they went about their few tasks with the same cheerful attitude. It was Jolie who noticed Jordan's deliberate silence and started toward him, but Griffin caught her arm.

"No, Jolie," he advised. "I wouldn't do that. Just roll out your blankets and let's get some sleep."

Puzzled, she glanced toward Jordan, then back to Griffin. "I was only going to talk to him for a moment. . . ."

"Like I said, I don't think you should. Come on, and I'll teach you another song." He held up a small, shiny rectangle and grinned. "I brought my mouth organ with me, and I play it pretty good."

Diverted, Jolie agreed. Perhaps she should not forgive Jordan so quickly anyway. He had behaved badly, saying angry words to her that had nothing to do with anything she had done. But still, as Griffin played softly and Amos sang a low, sweet song about chariots flying over Jordan, she let her attention wander in his direction again and again. Why did she feel so young when she was near Jordan? It wasn't her age, because she was certainly old enough to be married; it was the way he made her feel, as if she was silly and childish instead of a mature female. Her mother's people learned to laugh at an early age, seeing amusement in the most trivial things, because the reality of life could be harsh. The white man seemed to think it frivolous to behave with humor at times. At least Amos and Griffin were not as dour as Jordan, she reflected, her attention returning to the soft music they were playing.

"That's a nice song, Amos," she said when he had finished. "But why did you write it about Jor-dan?"

Amos gave her a blank stare for an instant, then grinned, his teeth shining brightly in the dark. "You're a funny thing, Miss Jolie," he said. "I didn't write that song, and it ain't about Jordan. The song's talkin' about a river named Jordan, not a man."

"Oh. Well, it's still a nice song."

"Thank you."

"And you play your . . . mouth organ . . . well, Griffin."

"Thank you," the boy said solemnly. His watchful eyes

had seen Jordan's shoulders shaking with silent amusement, and he was having a hard time himself trying to keep from laughing at Jolie. She sure was a funny one.

Spreading blankets on the hard ground, they all lay down for the night and stared up at the starry skies, listening to the night sounds of puma, coyote, and hawk. The desert came alive at night with a wide variety of predators—animal and human.

Edgy because of the unfamiliar noises, Griffin's head often swiveled as if expecting trouble, and finally Amos's soft voice drifted across the semicircle of blanketed mounds to ask, "What you looking for, Rooster?"

A faint smiled curved Griffin's mouth, and his blue eyes lightened a bit as he turned his fair head in Amos's direction. "I'm looking for Apache, I guess. This place seems like the perfect spot to be ambushed."

Jordan spoke up from his mound of blanket and curls of fragrant tobacco smoke. "Not even the Apache like hiding in the arroyos, and we can see a pretty far distance from this spot. We're fairly safe."

It was quiet a moment, then Griffin said, "Thanks anyway, Jordan, but I heard you tell Amos earlier that the Jornada was the worst possible place for anyone who isn't mountain lion or Apache—which means that only Jolie is safe."

Jordan grunted, "Yeah, she's part Apache and part mountain cat, so she's pretty damned safe."

Jolie, already wrapped up in her blankets like a caterpillar in a cocoon, said nothing. She just listened. In spite of Jordan's harsh words earlier, she had decided to forgive him. After all, he had not yet learned how to accept the cruelty of everyday life as the Apache had. It was only normal that he should still grieve for his dead friends.

It occurred to her to wonder where these men were going, though she didn't really care as long as she could go with them. This was a true adventure, and she had finally met the man she wished as husband. A higher power must have sent him to their camp that day, for she had thought of little else since that first glimpse. And he must have thought of her, too, for hadn't he come back for her? A satisfied smile curved her mouth as Jolie snuggled deeper into her blankets.

Long lashes lifted as she shifted to gaze thoughtfully at Jordan Sinclair. Sudden doubts flew at her like bats in the night, and she wondered if she was making a mistake. Perhaps he was not the man she thought him to be . . . He was lying on his back looking up at the stars, his arms behind his head, a thin brown cigarette between his lips. Jolie watched, fascinated, as he inhaled deeply and blew smoke into the air. Her intuition had never been wrong before, and she suddenly knew it had not failed her now. Sinclair was the reason she was still with these adventurous *'Indaa,'* and she intended to remain with them. The handsome Jordan had not known what he was getting into when he'd ordered her capture, but he would soon.

Jolie's gaze drifted over Jordan's long body. He was lying atop his blankets, his booted feet crossed at the ankles as he stared at the sky. He was much taller than her father, whom she'd always thought very tall. But where Henri La Fleur was broad and fleshy, Jordan was lean and muscular. Both had wide shoulders; her father's were thick like a bull's, while Jordan's were trim with the sleek muscles of a mountain cat. Though not overly muscular, both men possessed a natural grace and ease of movement that Jolie admired.

Frowning suddenly, she wondered if Sinclair found her unattractive. She'd never thought much about it before, but now the thought that he found her ugly lurked at the fringes of her mind. Did he? She wasn't beautiful like the young maidens of her mother's tribe, true, but neither was she so ill-favored as to frighten away suitors. Several young men had approached her father with offers, but Jolie had turned them all down.

Twisting underneath her blankets, she writhed with uncertainty. Perhaps Jordan did find her ugly. After all, she wasn't as dark as the smooth-skinned, sturdy Apache girls, nor as fair as the '*indaa*' girls she had seen at the fur-trading post that her father frequented. Those girls had possessed pale skin the color of mare's milk, with cheeks blushing the shade of squawberries, and eyes like the summer sky, while she, Jolie, had stood near with her brown skin and thick black hair, feeling very awkward and plain compared to such fragility and fairness. Was that how Jordan saw her— skinny and dark, with hair hanging like night shadows down her back? Maybe she was.

Jolie blinked back the hot sting of tears. No woman of the people cried needlessly. Her small rounded chin with its hint of a cleft thrust out firmly, and her hands curled into determined fists. She would not give up. She would be like Lozen, faithful and steadfast, only she would not lose her Gray Ghost as Victorio's sister had done. She, Jolie La Fleur, daughter of Henri La Fleur and Nańdile, would pursue her quest until it was gained. Her decision made, she snuggled deeper into her blankets and closed her eyes again. Sleep came easily to those with a firm purpose.

At least, to most of those with a firm purpose. Jordan had a firm purpose in mind—gold; yet he was finding it difficult to fall asleep. It wasn't just the thought of the gold at the end of their journey or even the dangers they risked that kept him awake. Jolie would have been quite gratified to know that she was the cause for his sleepless night.

Taking the last drag from his cigarette, Jordan thumped it into the air, watching as the glowing stub sailed in a graceful arc like a shooting star. Damn, but he'd be glad when this was over. In light of the consequences, he now regretted his idea to capture Victorio's granddaughter. It hadn't worked out at all like he'd planned, and now they were stuck with this girl who seemed to have developed an irritating affection for him. Even his angry, hasty words had not deterred Jolie from gazing at him with tender reproach. He would have much preferred fires of hatred in those glowing eyes that reminded him of bits of green glass.

Females of any race were nothing but trouble, as he had learned to his dismay several years before. This untaught half-Apache girl would be even more trouble, with her soft eyes and blunt admiration. At least other women hid their motives better. Jolie had removed any pretense of coy surprise from the situation. Whoever had said that honesty was the best policy couldn't have been referring to the games men and women play, Jordan reflected with a wry smile. Honesty in this case was irritating.

Jordan stared up at the sky with an unblinking gaze. In the distance a coyote howled, and there was a short, muffled shriek as a hawk found its prey. New Mexico territory was still raw and primitive, and it still belonged to the desert predators such as coyotes, hawks, and the Apache. He'd had enough of it in the past few years. Death and danger had been his constant companions, and now he just wanted solitude and peace. If it wasn't for the lure of gold, he would be far away on the coast of Mexico where there were sleepy little fishing villages and cool breezes.

Jordan stretched lazily and yawned. When this adventure was all over, he would take his gold and go to Europe. He'd always wanted to visit those places he'd only read about in books. With the gold he would be able to realize that dream.

Tilting his gray felt hat over his eyes to blot out the stars, Jordan slid beneath his blankets and shut his eyes.

To her surprise, Jolie was the first one to wake. She blinked sleep from her eyes, long lashes slowly lifting as she focused on the gray, pearly light blanketing the ground. Dawn diffused the harsh angles and sharp lines of the rocks and mountains, softening them into shadowy blurs against a pale sky so that the desert seemed almost hospitable instead of alien. Breathing deeply, she inhaled the sharp tang of sage as well as the fresh smell of a new day.

Along the line of the remuda, fresh horse piles steamed in the early morning air, and Jolie turned her head in that direction. The piebald she had been riding turned his head slightly, ears pricked forward and nostrils flared.

Stealing a glance toward Jordan Sinclair, who lay with his saddle pillowing his head and his hat over his eyes, Jolie wondered what would happen if she pretended an escape attempt. Would he try to stop her?

Testing the boundaries, Jolie stuck one bare foot from beneath her blankets, then the other. Jordan made no move. Amos was snoring loudly, his rifle slanted across his wide chest, and Griffin was lying with arms flung out to both sides in careless slumber. Somehow, she sensed that Jordan was faking sleep. Why? To watch her, perhaps?

Still hesitating, Jolie pondered the situation. She did not intend to escape, but it might be interesting to observe Jordan's reaction if she did try. Then again, why go to all that trouble?

A smile curved her generous mouth as Jolie slid both feet back beneath the blankets. There would be no easy solution for Jordan Sinclair. He would have to deal with her boldly. She made a great deal of noise then, coughing, sneezing, and thrashing about in her blankets until she saw the glitter of blue eyes peering from beneath a gray hat brim.

"Makin' enough noise?" Jordan demanded testily. He flashed Jolie a sour glance as he kicked off his blankets and sat up.

She stared at him with an innocent expression. "Why? Do I bother you?"

"As a matter of fact—yes." This last was almost snarled at her as Jordan rose in a lithe movement, reaching for his gunbelt as he stood. There was a faint protest of leather and metal as he buckled on his twin Colts, and she lifted a delicately arched brow in mild surprise.

"Two guns, monsieur? Are we in danger?"

"In case you you haven't noticed, we're not exactly sitting on a front porch in our rocking chairs," Jordan responded shortly.

By now Amos and Griffin were awake, Amos propping himself on one elbow to gaze at his partner and the Apache girl with a resigned expression. "Don't know how long those two are gonna fuss," he muttered to no one in particular, "but I'm all for givin' the gal back to her kin."

Griffin nodded morosely. "Yeah, they sound like two bobcats, don't they?" He tugged on his boots and raked a hand through his blond hair. "If I didn't know better," Griffin observed with a perceptiveness far beyond his years, "I'd say Uncle Jordan kinda likes our little captive Apache, wouldn't you?"

Amos grinned, rolling from his bed of blankets to stretch. "Rooster, I think you just put a tail on the dog!"

Griffin gave him a blank stare. "Do what?"

"Put a tail on the dog—you know, recognized the truth."

"Oh. Between you and Jolie, I can't understand most of

what you're talking about!'' Griffin shook his head. ''I feel like I just got off the boat in some foreign country.''

''You did, Rooster, you did.'' Amos lifted his rifle, heaved his saddle to one broad shoulder and strode toward his horse. ''This is about as foreign as you can get and still be on the North American continent.''

Even Jolie began to wonder if she was in a foreign country when they finally rode from the Jornada into Hembrillo Basin. It was different than she remembered it, with a craggy rim encircling a rough desert floor that made it look somewhat like a dormant volcano. The basin floor held two peaks shaped like cones, roughly a mile apart. One of these, Amos commented, was Hembrillo peak.

Jolie could feel Jordan's gaze resting on her and knew what he was thinking.

''You're wondering how much I know about what you're looking for, aren't you?'' She met his gaze with a steady stare of her own. ''There could be only one reason you are here risking your lives, and I think I know what it is.''

Jordan edged his mount closer. ''Do you?'' he asked softly. ''What are we looking for?''

''The French padre's mine!'' Jolie stared at him with an expression of triumph that began to fade when he gazed at her blankly. *''Non? N'est-ce pas?''* she asked, translating when he still stared at her, ''isn't that so?''

''What French padre's mine?'' Jordan demanded.

Jolie's bewildered gaze moved from Amos—who had frozen to rapt attention—to Griffin's interested face, then back to Jordan. ''Why, Padre La Rue. Everyone has heard of it, how the old priest hid Spanish gold for his people, the Indians who mined it, and how the Spanish came for it and murdered the padre when he would not tell where it was hidden . . .''

"No," Jordan interrupted, "everyone has *not* heard of it. Me, for instance. Why don't we dismount and hear what you've got to say, green eyes?" Signalling to Griffin to grab the piebald's reins, Jordan swung down from his gray at the same time as he grasped Jolie around her slim waist.

Content just to be in Jordan's arms, Jolie put her arms around his neck and snuggled close, earning a wary glance from the man who held her and a concert of chuckles from Amos and Griffin. *"Oui,"* she murmured in Jordan's ear, nuzzling his neck with her nose, "I will tell you whatever you wish to hear, Jor-dan." She drew *Zhor-dahn* out even longer than usual, and he frowned.

Releasing his grip, Jordan dropped Jolie like a hot rock. She landed on hands and knees, barely managing to keep from sprawling on the ground, and glared up at him through tangled strands of jet hair.

"Gúuchi," she muttered, and Amos laughed.

"What'd she say to me, Amos?" Hands on hips, Jordan glanced from his partner to the girl.

A wide grin split Amos's face as he replied, "Sounds close to the Apache word for pig, is all I know."

"Great." Jordan reached down to haul Jolie to her feet by one hand. "Look," he said into stormy eyes, "you speak very good English, so I don't want to hear any more of this French or Apache stuff you talk. Stick with what I understand."

For reply, Jolie launched into a torrent of French, Apache, and Spanish, her angry tone leaving her listeners in no doubt as to the content of her diatribe.

Jordan's voice was soft and faintly menacing as he said, "Speak English when you're talking about this supposed mine, green eyes."

"It's not 'supposed.' It's real." Jolie defended herself sulkily. Sitting on the flat surface of a rock, she folded her arms around bent knees and faced the three men. "I know it's real," she said, "because I've seen it." Leaning forward, her voice dropped to a dramatic whisper, all the more dramatic because of the hot wind and burning sky that shimmered around them. "I've seen gold bars stacked like logs for the winter, as high as I can reach on my tiptoes, and they're heavy—almost too heavy to lift."

"How'd they get there?" Griffin demanded. "Did the French padre run a smelting operation, too?"

"*Oui*, but not like you think. Padre La Rue was a great man among the Indians; he protected and cared for them. In the *tsé deezha* where my village is . . ."

"The mine is in the Organ Mountains?" Amos interrupted in surprise.

Jolie bent a stern glance on the three men. "You must listen quietly so that I do not become confused. *Comprendez*?"

"We understand. Sorry," Griffin said quickly when Jordan leveled a narrow glare at the slim girl who was perched upon a rock with all the grace and authority of a learned instructor. Bare brown legs crossed at the ankles as Jolie slanted Jordan a defiant glance, her small chin thrusting out stubbornly as she waited for Jordan to agree.

His mouth tightened. Damn this cheeky girl with bold eyes and bolder ideas! She was enjoying herself entirely too much! "All right! Go on," he said tersely.

"*Bon*! Now, Padre La Rue once lived in north Mexico with a mission of peons and poor Spaniards. He had been sent by France to lead these people and took his position quite seriously. An old man befriended by the padre became ill, and on his deathbed he told the priest about an area where there was an abundance of gold. The old Spaniard had discovered this place during his former scouting days, and he described it as being two days north of *tsé táhúaya*. I think you call that place Franklin now," she added, and all three men jerked in surprise. "Anyway, it was in the range known as . . . Sierra Organos, near San Augustine Pass to the east, where there was a spring, which he called Spirit Spring, near which was Cuerza Vegas, cave of the meadows." Jolie paused in her memorized recital to take a deep breath, her mouth curving in a satisfied smile at her small audience's rapt attention. "A short distance from this spring, the old man told the padre, was a very high rock, or cliff, and near this would be found rich—how do you say— streams, or veins of gold in the rock.

"Soon after telling this legend to Padre La Rue, the old Spaniard died. The people, always hungry like the Apache, soon suffered a time of drought. Famine threatened. That is when the priest called his people together and told the story of the old Spaniard. He asked if they were willing to risk a search . . . en masse . . . to this place. To remain meant that many would die. To go gave them hope. The people decided to go. Only a few days after they reached the . . . Organs, one of the men found much gold in a nearby canyon.

"Padre La Rue then decided that the Spaniard had been right, and he established a permanent mission. For himself, he had a large room hacked into a high chalk cliff near Spirit Spring. The other homes were built of rock and mud mortar before all the people began to look for gold. After a long while they decided upon a vein of gold where no one could observe them, and made a tunnel. They worked this gold for many years, and Padre La Rue, who acted as a . . . a . . . treasurer . . . used only what was necessary to purchase supplies and tools from faraway settlements. He did not wish word about the gold to be heard."

"What happened to the rest?" Amos couldn't help asking, earning a severe glance from Jolie for his interruption.

"The rest," she answered, "was hidden in the false cave where he lived. They eventually built a high stone wall around their little mission. Years passed, with the gold bars being stacked higher and higher. If the world found out about their wealth, it would be disastrous to their colony, the Padre rightly feared. He became old and greatly revered by his people.

"Finally, after many years, Mexico City began to wonder about Padre La Rue. They sent an expedition to find him, which they did only after a year of searching in the Las Cruces region. When they demanded entrance at the colony gate, they were refused. The leader of the expedition, a man known as Maximo Milliano, then formally demanded that Padre La Rue give him—as a representative of the Church in Mexico—all the gold and reveal the location of the mine. The priest refused, saying that the mine and its contents belonged to his people, not the Church. Naturally, he was killed for his efforts . . ."

"Naturally," Jordan muttered. "So where does that leave us?"

"Jor-dan," Jolie scolded, "I cannot tell you if you keep interrupting! The mine entrance had been hidden, and the gold was removed to several hiding places in the mountains. Not the mountains where they were, but in other mountains northeast of what you call the Organs . . ."

"She's saying the San Andres!" Griffin pointed out excitedly. "That's where you saw the gold, Amos . . ."

"Can you take us there?" Amos cut in impatiently.

Jolie threw him a glance. "No. You can't get there from here."

"Can't get there from here . . ." Jordan echoed faintly, then added, "dammit! Do you think I'm some kind of an idiot? Don't answer that! Draw me a map, Jolie."

"No. I will not draw a map. But I will take you," she added when Jordan's mouth tightened fiercely. "I will take you to Padre La Rue's hidden mine on one condition."

"I don't make deals," Jordan began, but Amos nudged him with an elbow. Answering the plea in his partner's eyes, Jordan shrugged and asked shortly, "What is your condition, green eyes?"

Jolie smiled sweetly. Tilting her head to one side, she looked up at Jordan with the same expression one usually reserved for a fractious child. "I will take you to the mine if you will sit with me, Jordan," she said.

"Sit with you?" Jordan glanced from the dark-haired girl to Amos. "That doesn't sound so bad," he began, but Amos was shaking his close-cropped head.

"Jordan. She means . . . *sit* with her . . . you know, like a man lives with a woman. . . ."

Jordan's calm expression altered swiftly. "What?! Hell, no, I won't do that! This brazen little heifer—what would a kid like her even know about such things?"

Then he looked at Jolie and knew better.

Chapter
7

Jolie waited patiently for Jordan's furious outburst to wear itself out, her eyes huge and green as she surveyed him with an interested gaze. Propping her elbow on one drawn-up knee, she rested her chin in the cup formed by her palm and fingers and tried not to show any reaction to the argument raging between Jordan and the combined team of Amos and Griffin.

"I refuse to let some impudent, cheeky brat blackmail me into doing anything I don't want to do!" Jordan ground out furiously, his eyes blazing with hot lights.

"Jordan," Amos was saying, "be reasonable. What harm can it do if we just"—one outstretched hand waggled back and forth suggestively, palm down, fingers spread—"play along with her, let's say?"

"And if I don't *feel* like playing along with her?" Jordan asked in a dangerously quiet tone. "What then?"

"Why, we just quit and go home," Griffin put in. "All our time and effort, our plans—wasted. But if that's what you really want, Uncle Jordan, then that's what it'll have to be."

"All that gold," Amos groaned.

"*Tons* of it," Griffin added morosely.

"Up there somewhere in the mountains, waiting for someone to find it—someone like us." Amos shook his kinky head dolefully. "Sure was a nice dream while it lasted." He glanced at Griffin. "What was it you were going to do with your share, Rooster? Give some to your ma, wasn't you?"

"Huh? Oh, yeah. Poor Ma. She would have finally gotten something for all those hard years she's put in, but now—guess she won't get nothing. . . ."

"Shut up!" Jordan growled. "I know what you're both doing, and it doesn't matter what kind of guilt you try and heap on me, I won't do anything I don't want to do. Do you understand that? I refuse—absolutely refuse—to go along with this insane idea of some baby-faced Apache who has no notion in hell of what's going on!" Folding both arms across his chest, Jordan gave first his partner, then his nephew a baleful stare. "I won't do it," he said adamantly.

Smiling, Jolie snuggled closer to Jordan. It was dark in the basin, and the stars were already out. She could hear the strong, steady thump of Jordan's heart beneath her ear as she kept her dark head on his chest. It was a comforting sound, and she gave a contented sigh.

Jordan, however, was anything but contented. He had compromised his principles by relenting even this far, but he had no intentions of "sitting" with the girl in the way she obviously intended. He'd go along with this for a while, just until they found the gold, but he had his limits—which he had firmly stated in terms she was forced to understand.

Slanting Jolie a glance from beneath his thick lashes, Jordan scowled. Ebony strands of silky hair strayed across his shirtfront in soft tangles that left him with the fleeting desire to touch them. Her cheek was fitted to the hollow of his arm and shoulder, while her slender arm angled comfortably across his chest. He felt her smile against the thin chambray shirt he wore, and his mouth tightened into a harsh line. She was enjoying this close proximity, while it left him feeling as itchy as a dog with fleas. All he wanted between them was distance—plenty of distance.

"Jor-dan," she murmured softly, drawing out his name, "do you not like me even a little?" Slim fingers toyed with the buttons of his shirt, and he slapped her hand.

"Do you like playing these games, little girl? You're too damn young. Didn't your mother ever tell you not to play with fire?"

Puzzled, Jolie tilted her head to gaze up at his strong square jaw bristling with a week's growth of beard. "Play with fire?" she echoed. "What do you mean?"

Shoving her away, Jordan crossed his arms behind his head and gazed thoughtfully at the girl beside him. "I mean, if you keep pushing me, green eyes, you may not like the results. Look," he added, "why don't you back off some? I think I'd like you better if you didn't force yourself on me. . . ."

"You would?" Jolie sat up, wide eyes staring at him in the light of their campfire. The glittering orbs reflected the firelight in twin points like shining green gems. "Why didn't you say so earlier?"

"I shouldn't have to say anything. Ah, Jolie, just lie back down and go to sleep. Sunrise will be here before you know it, and we'e got a lot to do tomorrow." He patted the rumpled blanket invitingly. "Okay?"

"'*Axah*.'" Jolie lay back down, nestling close to him again, her hand curling beneath her chin like a child. There was a lot of truth in what he had said. Perhaps she shouldn't have made that bargain.

Never one to agonize long over a questionable situation, she sat up abruptly, regarding Jordan with an earnest gaze. "Would you like to forget our bargain?" she asked.

Exasperation altered to suspicion as he stared back at this irritating, intriguing chit of a girl he had been foolish enough to snatch from her people. Bluntly he replied, "No. You agreed to lead us to this . . . hidden treasure . . . if I would pay more attention to you, and that's what you're gonna do."

"I will still take you, Jor-dan; if you want me to."

It was too good to be true. "No," Jordan refused again, this time more kindly, though he still didn't trust her. "Just forget it. Lie back down and go to sleep. . . ."

"For the love of all that's holy!" Amos exploded, sitting up in his bed of blankets across the campfire. "Do you two intend to talk all night? It's damn hard for a body to get any rest with this jabber, jabber, jabber. . . ."

"Tell that to her, not me," Jordan cut in. "You're the one who insisted on this bargain, so you shut her up."

"Why don't you *all* shut up?" Griffin suggested from his pallet. "If she don't have anybody to talk to, she's bound to go to sleep sooner or later."

"Sounds good to me," Jordan muttered, turning on one side with his back presented to an indignant Jolie, "but I'm willin' to bet she'll talk to a damn rock if it suits her."

"*Sacré bleu!*" Jolie stormed, flinging back the hair from her eyes as she glared at the three men in turn.

"There she goes with that 'sack ray blue' shit again," Amos said disgustedly. His big head swung back and forth in grim resignation. "Should have kept the gag," he muttered.

Stung by their caustic comments, Jolie flopped over on her side, her back to Jordan's back, her lips pressed tightly together. She lay with eyes wide open, staring at the shadowed shapes of rock and piñon trees.

In spite of her irritation, things had turned out better than she'd hoped. Jordan had agreed to be nice to her and agreed to treat her with all the respect he would show an *'indee'* woman. The latter point had been Griffin's idea, not hers, for she wasn't quite certain how well she liked the idea of being treated as she had seen some white men treat their women. But, still, they seemed to think it a great compliment.

Patience was not Jolie's greatest virtue, but she was willing to wait if that was how she could win Jordan. Time would be a small price to pay. And anyway, what else did she have to do? Papa was off hunting, and she had been left behind in the village to while away the hours in boredom. Though her mother was Apache and she felt a strong kinship with them, she was more French like her father. It wasn't surprising, since they had lived most of her life in the mountains where Henri La Fleur hunted, distant from even the Apache. She felt comfortable with these men and considered this the exciting adventure she had always longed for.

Besides, it couldn't do any harm to lead these men to what they sought. After all, her people would not touch the yellow metal the *'indaa'* called gold. It was considered sacred, being the color of the sun, which is the symbol of Ussen. The sun was Ussen, creator of life; earth the mother, receptacle of life; and stars were the children. It was all very simple in the Apache way.

Jolie lay still, listening to the murmurs of sound in the basin. "Jor-dan?" she whispered after a few more minutes of silence, turning over to poke him with an inquiring finger. "Are you asleep?"

There was a muffled grunt, then a resigned, "I *was*. What do you want?"

"What will you do with your treasure after you have it?"

"Do we have to talk about this now?"

"Yes. I must know before . . . before I help you."

"I can't believe this," Jordan groaned. "We've got a deal, right?"

Slowly, "Right."

"So what difference does it make what I intend to do with my share? Why don't you wake up Amos or Griffin and ask them, instead of pestering me?"

"You're angry. . . ."

"No, dammit, just sleepy!" Jordan turned over and sat up to glare at Jolie. "Please," he cajoled, "can we talk about this tomorrow?"

After brief consideration, she gave a short nod of her head. "*Oui*, tomorrow will do. *Bonne nuit* . . ."

"I suppose that means good night," Jordan muttered, flopping back down and flinging his blanket over his head. "Too bad it wasn't goodbye."

In spite of Jordan's irritation and sharp comments, Jolie smiled. He was beginning to soften toward her. She could tell.

Chapter 8

Sitting cross-legged atop her pallet of mussed blankets, Jolie just watched as Amos skillfully flipped a thick strip of bacon in the black iron skillet. It began to fry with a tantalizing sound and smell that was so delicious it made her mouth water, and her eyes gleamed in anticipation.

"Is that for me?" she asked, and the big man grinned. He was crouching on his heels beside the breakfast fire, having volunteered to be the cook, but Jolie was the only one evincing any interest in his culinary efforts.

"If'n you want it, Miss Jolie, it's yours. The rest of these sourfaces don't seem to care." With a quick flick of his wrist, Amos turned the bacon. "'Most as thick as a pork chop, ain't it?" he observed, and she nodded.

"*Oui.*"

Amos frowned. "'We' what? Why you always talkin' that 'we' stuff, and saying 'sack ray blue' like you do?"

Shrugging, Jolie explained, "It's my father's tongue that I'm speaking, Amos. He was born across the big water and taught me to speak as he was taught."

Amos gave a grunt of understanding, but it was Griffin who asked, "But where'd you learn to speak English? And Spanish?"

Jolie smiled at the young man so close to her age. She liked Griffin in spite of the fact that he had been so rough with her the night of her capture. After all, she had done her best to scratch out his eyes, so they were even. And he had been kind to her since then, looking after her as if she were a sister.

"When I was very young," she told Griffin, "we lived in the mountains alone. There was a family near by, and they had a daughter who was my age. We played together often, and I taught her French and a little Apache, and she taught me English." A sad smile curved her mouth for a moment as Jolie recalled Sarah Berryman, and how bewildered and hurt both girls had been at the elder Berrymans' reaction when they discovered that their child's playmate had an Apache mother. Young Sarah had been forbidden even to speak to Jolie again, and their friendship had ended. But she told none of this to Griffin or Amos, for the memory was still too sharp.

"Then how'd you learn Spanish?" Griffin prompted. "I've lived in Texas all my life, and I still can't say more than a couple of words of Spanish."

"Victorio was really Mexican, not Apache, and he spoke the language well. Besides, all Apache know how to speak Spanish. . . ."

"Whoa," Jordan interrupted, "wait just a minute! Are you telling me that an Apache chief was really a Mexican?"

"No."

"I didn't think so!"

"I was telling Griffin," Jolie finished with quiet dignity. "But I will tell you if you wish."

"Now look, green eyes, that story is just a little bit too farfetched for even you to tell." Jordan gave a snort of disbelief and stalked over to the fire. Kneeling, he poured himself a cup of coffee from the bubbling, blackened pot on the hot stones, slicing Jolie an amused glance.

She quivered with indignation. "It is true! When he was just a boy living in Chihuahua, he was taken from Rancho del Carmen. He adopted the ways and gods of The People and made them his. Victorio was a great chief, possibly the greatest, and a fierce fighter . . ."

"I'm not disputing that," Jordan muttered. "I just find it difficult to believe that a Mexican boy could grow up to become a great Apache chief."

"Why not?" Amos put in. "Sounds logical to me. I mean, look around at some of the men in Washington. How many of them were born Americans? Even the city was named after a man born in England. Why couldn't Victorio have been Mexican? Or even French, for that matter?" Amos shook his head and handed Jolie a plate heaped with bacon and beans. "It's just crazy enough to be true."

Exonerated, Jolie flashed Jordan a triumphant smile and began eating her bacon. Small white teeth crunched happily as she balanced the tin plate on her drawn-up knees and regarded Jordan with a steady gaze.

He gazed back at her with a less than pleased expression on his handsome face. Thick brows were drawn into a knot over the bridge of his nose, and his blue eyes were narrowed and glittering. This pesky child was just a nuisance, a starry-eyed girl who had romanticized their search for gold into an adventure, and he was tempted to call the whole thing off in spite of his promise. How much longer could he endure this charade? And besides that, the girl needed something more to wear than the short buckskin dress that barely reached her knees. It was almost indecent, and while she was still just a young girl, she shouldn't be allowed to parade herself before a group of men like she was doing. It wasn't right.

Surging to his feet, Jordan said tersely, "Griffin, get that extra pair of trousers you brought with you and give them to Jolie. If they don't fit, tie them on her with a rope, but just cover her bare legs with something."

As the three startled gazes riveted on him, he set his empty coffee cup down on the ground. Pivoting, he strode swiftly from the camp and disappeared into a thick clump of mesquite.

"Well," Griffin finally said into the sudden, heavy silence, "guess I'll find my extra pair of britches."

"Is there something...*wrong*...with my legs?" Jolie wanted to know.

Both men reflected for a moment, then Amos said, "No, not a damn thing's the matter with them legs, little gal, not a damn thing."

A dimple flashed enchantingly in Jolie's right cheek as she smiled at Amos. "I didn't think so," she said, "but I just wanted to hear it."

Griffin dug silently into his leather saddlebags and pulled out a pair of denim trousers just like the ones he was already wearing. "Levi Strauss made these," he pointed out, indicating the double-sewn seams and rivets. "Ma paid a lot for 'em, but they're the best."

"Then I shall take great care of them since they were made by your friend, Mr. Strauss," Jolie promised. Griffin opened his mouth, then realized the futility of explaining and shut it again. After a brief hesitation, Jolie shrugged and said, "I cannot put them on with you watching."

Stepping gingerly into the trousers, Jolie felt deliciously wicked at dressing in a man's garment. Not even the French would do so, and certainly not an Apache woman. Loose blouses and full skirts were the rule with her mother's people, with very few exceptions. What would her father say if he saw her now?

Though Griffin was taller than she was, he was very lean. Jolie's hips swelled in womanly curves that defied the straight-legged trouser seams to burst. The denims were too long, so she rolled the cuffs up to her ankles. Satisfied at last, she held the hem of her dress in a knot at her waist.

"I am done," she said, and Amos and Griffin turned around. "What do you think?"

There was complete silence. The trousers clung to Jolie like a second skin, emphasizing her narrow waist and the curve of her hips, skimming suggestively over her legs.

"Let go of the dress," Amos suggested when he could find his voice, and Jolie complied, letting the hem drop back to just above her knees. "That's . . . better. It looks kinda like you've got leggings on, don't it, Griffin? Yeah, leggings."

Silence prevailed again, then Griffin said, "What she needs now is shoes. Her feet are bare, and that ain't good. Got any shoes, Amos?"

"That will fit *her*?" Amos asked incredulously. "This sun must've got to your head, boy. I ain't got no shoes that'll fit that little gal. Shoot, I ain't got any shoes that'd fit *you*, Rooster!"

"That's all right," Jolie said, "I don't need shoes."

"You've got to have shoes," Griffin insisted, "don't she, Jordan?" he asked, spying his uncle watching them. "Don't she need shoes?"

"What she needs is a swift kick in those nice new denims she's wearing, but I don't have the heart for it," Jordan muttered.

Griffin puffed out his cheeks and turned to Jolie with a sympathetic smile, but she was gazing fondly at Jordan.

"He is so thoughtful," she said, "yes?"

"Jolie, *no*," Griffin retorted with a sharp glance at Jordan, "He is not thoughtful! Didn't you understand what he just said—*comprendez*?"

She looked surprised. "But of course I understand. My English is excellent. He said he does not have the heart to hurt me. . . ."

"Good God!" Griffin exploded while Amos burst into loud laughter.

"If that don't beat all I ever heard!" Amos said between knee-slapping laughter. "Th' little gal hears just what she wants to hear, Griffin. Let her alone."

Sparing his uncle a cutting glance, Griffin stalked to his saddlebags and knelt beside them. Muttered comments obviously meant for Jordan's ears floated back over his shoulder.

"Either speak louder or shut up," Jordan finally growled in his nephew's direction. This was getting ridiculous. The girl was the cause of dissension between them and had to go, hostage or not. They certainly didn't need to be arguing among themselves when they were in the middle of Apache territory. And the bright-eyed little wretch sat staring at him as if she was completely innocent.

"You are angry," Jolie said simply, stepping close to where he stood.

"Yes. I am angry," he confirmed.

"What have I done?"

Fully aware of Amos's gaze and Griffin's arrested attention, Jordan shifted irritably.

"Hell," he finally said, "you haven't *done* anything but

be yourself, I guess. It's just that we don't need another burden on this ride."

"And I am a burden?"

"Look," Jordan said flatly, "I think it's time you went back to your people, Jolie, or Gáadu, or whatever you want to call yourself. I know I made a deal, and I'll keep my word, but why don't you just go on back. We'll give you that piebald. It's yours. And you can keep the denims."

Jolie's eyes flashed dangerously, but her voice was soft and sweet. "And a sack of meal, perhaps? What about a blanket or two, Jordan Sinclair—do you throw those in for good measure? A handful of beads, maybe?"

Jordan blinked at her show of spirit, though he refused to back down. "Yeah, if I had any beads I'd throw 'em in."

"Ah, how generous! Cháa was right," she observed with a trace of bitterness. "He claimed the *'indaa' dogoyáádá*, and I see he was right. He forgot to tell me, though, that *'indaa' dos' aa bagochíídaa*." Whirling, Jolie concluded this obviously disparaging observation with an angry toss of her head, long hair whipping over her shoulder with the sinuous movement of an enraged snake as she slowly turned her back on Jordan. She stood that way for a few moments, her shoulders straight and stiff, arms crossed over her chest.

"Whew!" Amos said when she'd stalked away. "Th' little gal has just given you the Apache snub, Jordan."

"I'm not at all sure I care about hearing what she said," Jordan began, but Amos was enjoying himself too much to be stopped.

"Called you stupid, first; then she said you were ill-tempered and too critical. I'm surprised she didn't add *'adiɫkp̣ą* to the list." When Jordan only glared at him, Amos offered the translation, "Means arrogant or condescending. Thought you might want to know in case she hits you with that one.''

''Thanks.''

''And the worst snub was turning her back on you. 'Pache consider that an insult in itself.''

''I said thanks for the information, Amos.'' This time Jordan's biting tone and narrowed eyes managed to hush the big man, but Amos was still smiling broadly.

''Do you suppose,'' Jordan suggested, ''that we could go on now? Since we're stuck with our little guide, let's use her.''

They broke camp in silence, with Griffin and Amos scooping up the skillet and tin plates and kicking dirt on the fire. Jordan retrieved the horses, and Jolie, still sulking, watched with a defiant expression.

She stood apart from them with her back to a rock, leaning against it and feeling very ill-used. This was supposed to be a fine adventure, and Jordan was supposed to feel about her the way she felt about him, but somehow it was not working out quite as she had hoped. He didn't like her at all; in fact, he thought of her as an uncivilized Apache. It wasn't unexpected, but it still rankled.

Jolie's chin lifted slightly. Amos had been right. She did consider Jordan arrogant and condescending, but it was only because he did not know any better. She would show him the right way, but it would have to be done skillfully. With that thought in mind, Jolie pushed away from the rock and advanced upon Jordan with a smile.

He flashed her a sour glance. ''Not big on holding grudges, are you?'' he grumbled. ''I should have known better than to expect a rest. Want a leg up?'' He cupped one hand in an offer to help her mount, but she shook her head.

''*Dah*. I am able to mount,'' she said, and suited action

to words with a graceful vault onto the pony's broad back, not deigning to use the dangling stirrup. She gazed down at him with that distant, disdainful stare he had seen so often on Apache, retreating into the safety of dignity.

Jordan put one hand on the piebald's withers, toying with coarse strands of the horse's mane as he looked up at Jolie. How did she do that? Just when he was thinking of her as an incorrigible brat, she behaved like an aloof woman. It was disconcerting. "Do you know the way to this padre's mine from here?" he asked, " 'Cause if you don't, I'm all for following our original plan."

" '*Au*—yes, I know where the mine is, but I'm not quite sure where we are. Let's ride higher so that I can see."

It sounded fair enough, and Jordan nodded. Mounting his own gray, he led the way up the rocky slope behind their camp, through prickly pear, tall, belly-brushing grasses, buffalo gourds, mesquite, piñon trees, and rabbit bush. No birds added their song to the area, and there were no furtive movements in the tall grasses that indicated the existance of small animals, a fact Jordan found peculiar.

"It is haunted," Jolie informed them with an expansive wave of one hand that included the entire Hembrillo Basin. "Evil spirits roam here."

Jordan's derisive snort registered his opinion of this explanation, but Amos's eyes rolled nervously at her remark. "Say it ain't so," he pleaded, nudging his horse beside hers. "Why are you tryin' to scare us?"

"I would have no reason to lie," she replied. "No animals will come to this place. There is no reason for them not to, as it has thick grass and bushes, even thicker near the fresh spring at the base. And," she added, lowering her voice, "at night there are strange lights that cannot be explained." She lifted a dark brow at Amos. "Did you hear any animal noises last night?'' she asked pointedly, and he had to shake his head. "Then I shall say no more."

"Jordan," Amos said with a strange tremor in his voice, "I don't know about this. . . ."

"Amos, you spent several days in this basin three years ago. Did any ghosts come to carry you off? No? I didn't think so. Did you *see* any ghosts? I didn't think you had. Jolie is just amusing herself at your expense . . ."

"No, it is true," she insisted. "All Apache know this."

"Another point in favor of not believing it," Jordan retorted.

They all rode silently for a moment, hooves clattering over dry scrubbed rocks, and metal bits and curb chains rattling with a muted sound. The sun beat down through fitful clouds, and sweat ran from man and horse alike.

It was so quiet that Jordan and Jolie heard the noise at the same time. They were riding in a small arroyo that cut through the rock, steep walls rising on each side, when a dreaded familiar noise rumbled faintly ahead.

"Flash flood!" Jordan yelled, spurring his lathered mount to greater effort. He clambered up the path in a shower of rock and sparks from the iron-shod hooves, and the others followed. Flecks of foam sprayed from the horses' mouths as they struggled valiantly against rock and time. The little caravan of terror took a sharp bend in the gorge and discovered a path to the left. Jordan took it flying, leaving skin and leather scrapings on the rock walls as he did, but barely managing to escape the huge wall of water that was bearing down on them. He hadn't had time to look back, and had counted on the others to follow, so it was with a sigh of relief that he saw them all safe and huddled in a drenched knot on the lip of the cut-off as the flood swept past.

One moment there was only dry, scrubbed rock—the next, a wall of water five feet high loomed above, roaring down the twisting, turning arroyo with enough force to crush anything in its path. Geysers of dirty foam showered the four trembling horses and their riders.

"It wouldn't be so bad," Griffin was heard to remark, "if'n it was *clean* water. This stinks!"

"Well, it ought to cool us off," was Jordan's calm reply. He glanced at Jolie, who sat her horse as coolly as if she had been any young girl out for a Sunday stroll on her favorite mount. He stifled the desire to ask if she was all right, saying instead, "Let's go."

It was Amos who discovered the rock map, though, not Jolie. They had just topped a crest in the canyon and were gazing down at the area below while Jolie searched out familiar landmarks, when Amos let out a wild whoop.

"This is it!" he said excitedly, "this is the place we held off the 'Pache! And this is th' map I was telling you about—let's look at it!"

They nudged their horses down the rocky slope as quickly as they dared, finally arriving at the spot where Amos had been three years before. Dismounting, Jordan and Griffin joined Amos to stare with great interest at the painted figures on the rocky ledge. The ruins of Amos's old barricade tumbled beneath their feet, piles of stones still standing in a makeshift wall in places.

Only Jolie remained on her horse, gazing at the men and the spot with thoughtful interest. She remembered this, yes. It had been some time ago, but she had come here with her father. That had been in the days of Victorio, before the great chief had met his end in Mexico. And Amos was quite right. The painted figures on the rock ledge were a map of sorts, but he was reading it all wrong. It was not polite to call someone a liar, but still she felt the urge to correct him.

Couching her words in the most careful Apache terms, Jolie suggested, "Perhaps the map has another meaning, one that is hidden."

Amos, having had a great deal of experience with Apache manners because of his time spent on the San Carlos reservation with them, knew what she was trying to say. "I ain't interpreting it right, am I?" he said, rising from his kneeling position close to the ledge. "What does it mean?"

The piebald shifted position, one back leg moving forward to rest lazily on the tip of the hoof, and Jolie assumed a casual pose also, crossing her right leg over the horse's withers and resting her elbow on her knee. "It could mean several things. But I am of the opinion that it means we should leave this place and go that way." She indicated the direction with a wave of her arm, and Amos nodded.

"Sounds reasonable," he agreed. Pulling off his cavalry cap, he wiped his sweating forehead with one sleeve, peering up at the merciless sun.

Jolie smiled down at him. "*Gostood' né?*"

"'*Au. Gostood*'," Amos answered.

"Hey!" Griffin interjected, "what are you two saying?"

Amos grinned. "We ain't planning no mutiny, Rooster, so don't worry about that. She just said that it was hot, wasn't it, and I said that yeah, it was. Don't get nervous."

"I ain't nervous, just nosy," Griffin retorted. "Seems to me you could speak English instead of Apache."

"But then you'd know what we were saying," Amos replied with a twinkle in his dark eyes.

Griffin couldn't help a grin. He spread his fingers to brush back the shaggy mop of hair sticking like pale sticks of hay from beneath the brim of his hat, then his boyish face crumpled with amusement as he broke into laughter. "I think you're both crazy," he said, then sliced a glance toward Jordan. "I'm not too sure about him either, so that leaves me as the only one here with any sense left."

"So what's a smart boy like you doing here with all us crazy folk?" Amos wanted to know.

"Oh, I'm just tagging along, remember? I'm not supposed to get in any trouble or make any waves. I'm just supposed to do what I'm told without thinking. Isn't that what Uncle Jordan said?"

"Something like that, yeah." Amos was amused, sliding his sweat-stained cap back over his forehead to shade his eyes. Hands on hips, he looked from Griffin to Jordan, who was still examining the mural. "What say we take our guide's advice, Sinclair? She says go that way."

"Fine with me. That's why she's here, isn't it?"

Jordan's clipped tones caused Jolie no alarm. He was finding it dificult to admit that she knew something he didn't, just like most men. Why was that? she wondered idly, nudging her piebald into a brisk walk up the slope. It was good for a woman to carry water and prepare food, or wash the clothes on a rock in the stream and tend babies, but it was not good for a woman to offer opinions on subjects men considered sacred. And the sanctity of the subject varied with each man.

Amos and Griffin, for instance, had not objected to her bare legs, while Jordan had insisted upon covering them. It had been the same with her parents. Customs her mother considered taboo were regarded with amusement by her father, and the same thing had happened with her mother. There had been times Jolie had wanted to throw up her arms in frustration when confronted with two entirely different lifestyles, but she had managed to take what she considered the best of both. She would do the same with these men.

It was obvious that Amos and Griffin thought her attention to Jordan rather flattering, but he considered it irritating. The inconsistencies of men never failed to amaze her.

Crumpled folds of rock and dirt clattered beneath her pony's hooves as she urged him up the steep slope ahead, then took a faint, almost inperceptible path winding through sparse tufts of belly-high grass.

"Are you sure you remember the way?" Griffin asked an hour later when they still hadn't found the spot she was looking for. "It's kinda spooky around here."

They had paused beneath the scant shade of the peak towering above them and dismounted, hoping the sun's position in the sky would allow them a respite from the heat.

Standing beside her horse, Jolie glanced around her and nodded. "I remember the way."

Frowning, Amos muttered, "This looks like the place where I found *my* gold, little gal, and I don't recollect no damn gold mine, just a hiding place."

Slanting him a curious glance, Jolie asked several quick questions in Apache, which he answered, then she gave a satisfied nod. "It is the same," she said.

"What?"

"We search for the same place," she explained. "You saw only gold and silver in bags, and a few gold bars. There are more rooms to the cave that hold much more."

"Well, I'll be damned!" Exchanging glances with Jordan, Amos sat down on a rock ledge. A pleased smile creased his ebony face and he glistened with sweat, his broad features shining with pleasure and excitement. "How 'bout that, boys?"

"Sounds good to me," Griffin said.

"I'll wait and see," was Jordan's more reserved reply. "I don't like counting nothing until I have it in my hands."

"That's fair enough, I guess." Griffin paused, then added, "But I'm still wondering what you're going to do with your share, Uncle Jordan."

"Let's get it first, then I'll start spending it." He lifted his hat and raked a hand through his dark hair, a smile pressing at the corners of his mouth. "I haven't ever seen two people more interested in how another man's gonna spend his money than you two," he said with a grin, and they all laughed. Jordan pulled the makings for a cigarette from his shirt pocket and relaxed against a rock.

"Hey, where's Jolie?" Amos asked when he'd almost finished the cigarette Jordan had given him. Two heads whipped around to look. "She was here a minute ago."

There was no sign of her. Her piebald was standing with drooping head, cropping lackadaisically at the stunted wisps of grass sprouting between rocks and clumps of dirt, but the young woman was nowhere in sight. Only sky and tumbled mounds of rock greeted them when they turned.

"Jolie!" Griffin yelled, his voice reverberating from the hills to bounce back at him. He took a few running steps up the slope and cupped his hands over his mouth. "Hey, Jolie!"

There was no answer. Black specks circled in the sky, wheeling in great, sweeping arcs, and in the distance they could hear the piercing cry of a hawk, but other than that there was no sound.

His cigarette forgotten, Jordan stepped to the edge of a chasm and peered over the side. He saw no movement at all. Half-sliding on the loose rocks, he scouted down a shallow gully, but there was no sign of the slim girl anywhere, so he climbed back to the creast. "Where could she be . . . ?" he muttered, turning toward Amos. The huge Negro was gone. Only the flattened blades of grass were evidence that he had stood there moments before. "Now, this is getting out of hand!" Jordan said harshly, looking around him. "Griffin, did you see anything?"

Griffin's bewildered, wide-eyed face was answer enough. Straight wisps of damp hair trembled in front of his eyes, and his gun hand rested on the butt of his pistol. Uneasy now, the pair instinctively moved closer together. There was nothing unusual on the surface, but the quiet, pressing heat was unnerving. No breeze whispered across the peak; no blade of grass rustled with the stealthy movement of an animal; no small rock or pebble rolled down from one of the slopes to indicate that there was another living creature on the side of Hembrillo Peak.

"What do we do now?" Griffin whispered as if surrounded by hostile forces. "Where'd they go?"

Jordan squinted at the huge slabs of rock and granite lying in heaps and covered with dirt and grass. "They've got to be close, or Amos never could have disappeared like that. He's too big. Hell, the earth didn't just open up and swallow him!"

Gulping, Griffin reminded, "Jolie *said* this place was haunted! We should've listened, Uncle Jordan."

"Don't be an idiot!" Jordan snapped. "There has to be a reasonable explanation for this. You go that way, circle the boulder, then double back. I'll do the same the other way. And keep your eyes and ears open!" he added unnecessarily.

Grimly now, Jordan pulled his .45 from its holster, cradling the handle in the sweating palm of his hand. Damn, but this was the craziest thing . . . where did two people suddenly vanish to? In the middle of the day, in the middle of a conversation? In spite of the heat, he felt a shiver ripple down his back and cursed softly.

His boots scrunched on the dry ground, and dislodged pebbles rolled down the slope, bouncing with a patter like rain on a tin roof. Sweat rolled down his collar, and his shirt stuck to the middle of his back in wet patches. Only the sweatband on his Stetson kept sweat from dripping into his eyes. Jordan wet dry lips with a nearly dry tongue and cursed again.

Nothing moved. There was only the sweep of bunchgrass and dirt on the rocky slope and the forbidding thrust of the peak towering above them. He coughed, a welcome sound in the oppressive silence, and retraced his steps back to the spot where he and Griffin had separated. Only the horses were there, lazily cropping grass as if they hadn't a care in the world, which, he supposed, they hadn't.

Jordan took a swig of water from his canteen and leaned against a rock to wait for Griffin. Time crawled slowly past, and the irritating buzz of insects on his sweaty skin was the only thing to occupy him. Shadows lengthened and the western sky began to glow with a purple haze that meant dark was not far behind. Tension tightened Jordan's gut into a knot. Where the hell was everybody?

Chapter
9

Jordan didn't know how long he'd sat there in the sun and then the shadows, but he slowly became aware of a faint tremble vibrating along the ground. His gray gelding threw up his head and snorted, and Jolie's piebald stamped nervously. Jordan tensed, resting his hand on the butt of one pistol.

A thin cry drifted up from the ground at his feet, and Jordan leaped up from the rocky ledge where he was perched. What the hell . . . ? Then it sounded again, impatient this time, and demanding.

"Jor-dan!"

He crouched, gun drawn, to peer under the ledge where the noise seemed to come from. Squinting into the shadows, Jordan began to grin. Griffin's animated face was peering mischievously at him from a large opening between the ledge and the ground.

"Lose a few people?" the youth asked.

"Damn right, and I'm not too sure I want to find any of

you again. It's been mighty peaceful since you've been gone."

"In that case . . ." Griffin began to slide back into the rock cleft, but Jordan's hand flashed out to grab him by the shirt collar.

"Oh no you don't! What the hell is going on?"

"Gold, Jordan." Griffin held up a dully gleaming brick with both hands, his tone almost reverent as he said, "More gold than I've ever seen in my life—not that *that* counts for a whole lot!"

"Down there?" Jordan hefted the gold bar and stared dubiously at the opening.

Griffin nodded. "Yeah, and it's going to be a real trick getting it out. These walls are steep. . . . Hey!" he protested, half-turning to someone below him. "Just a minute, will ya?"

"Amos and Jolie," Jordan correctly observed, and Griffin nodded.

"Yeah, I'm standing on Amos's shoulders. Guess he's getting tired. Give me a hand."

Obliging, Jordan hauled his young nephew out of the cave entrance. Then, tying a length of rope to his saddle horn, Jordan lowered one end to Amos and Jolie, then backed his horse. Jolie was the first one pulled up, grinning at him with an impish expression that made his eyes narrow.

"Whoa," Jordan muttered to the gray, halting the horse's retreat across the dust and grass. "Untie yourself and throw the rope back down to Amos," he ordered Jolie abruptly.

"Mad, Jordan?" she teased, shrugging out of the make-shift rope sling Amos had fashioned. "I didn't mean to leave you out. . . ."

"Just cut the talk and lower the rope!" Jordan snapped.

"It's almost dark, and I don't want to spend the night up here on the top of a damned mountain."

Shooting his uncle a glare, it was Griffin who lowered the rope, gently moving Jolie aside. Once more the gray was backed up, pulling the much heavier Amos from the cavern.

"I was beginnin' to wonder if I was gonna get outa there," Amos grumbled, wiping at the soot and grime covering his arms, face, and clothes. "It's pretty dark down in that cave. We need to make a few torches before we go back in the morning."

Recoiling his rope, Jordan felt rather than saw his partner's eyes on him. "Yeah," he muttered, "we can do that in the morning."

"What's the matter?" Amos asked then. "Don't you want to hear about the gold?"

Lifting his head, Jordan gazed at Amos for a moment, and a frown cut between his brows. "Sure, I want to hear about it, but something's wrong. I don't know what it is, I just know something's not right here."

"Yeah," Griffin put in, "and the something that's not right is that we have to work so hard to get the gold outa there. Wait'll you see that drop! Hell, I bet it's all of sixty feet straight down, and that black stuff at the bottom ain't none too great either! I don't know what it is, but . . ."

"What's the matter, Jordan?" Jolie asked softly, moving to stare up at him with a troubled expression. "What has happened?"

Shrugging, he replied, "Nothing. I was just wondering where in the hell you were, that's all."

She matched his shrug. "I stuck my head into the hole to see if it was as I remembered it, but I couldn't see. When I went a little farther, I began to slide and couldn't stop myself until I reached a ledge. Then Amos followed, and then Griffin. . . ." She held both arms out from her sides. "It took a little while to work our way back up the incline to you, that's all."

"So glad you could make it," he returned dryly, tying the rope back on his saddle. Jordan leaned one arm on the seat of his etched leather saddle and stuck his other hand in his back pocket, looking down at Jolie with a slight smile. She had streaks of black on her chin and nose, and her long eyelashes were dusted with some sort of dirt. "You look like a coal miner," he remarked, and she laughed.

"I thought you were only concerned with mining for gold or silver, Jor-dan, instead of this . . . coal."

"I'm not interested in mining at all, only the—say—*collection* of gold or silver."

"Or the spending of it?" Amos suggested.

Jordan grinned. "Yeah, that too."

"I'm all for that," Griffin put in fervently, reaching down to grab the reins trailing from his horse. He pulled the animal's head up, rubbing the soft muzzle absently as he added, "You know, it's gonna be hard carrying that stuff out of here without any mules. Those bars are heavy. We need to make some kind of ladder instead of using ropes."

"Good idea, Griffin. Why don't Jordan and I go down and cut a tree and haul it up here? We can use that for a ladder," Amos said.

"Sounds fine to me. How 'bout you, Jolie?" Griffin asked.

She nodded. "Yes, but now I think it is time to make camp for the night. We can worry about the ladder and the gold tomorrow."

"Yeah," Jordan muttered, "golden days are just around the corner for everybody."

"What's botherin' you?" Amos asked. "Instead of bein'

glad that we found the cave, and that it's got more gold than any of us has ever seen before, you're actin' like we just found a snake pit or somethin'!''

"Let's just say that things are going so good that it makes me kind of nervous, okay? I like it better when I can *see* what's making me nervous."

Jordan's mood shifted to his companions, and they all exchanged solemn glances.

"It is nothing," Jolie finally said, cutting through the thick tension with cheerful determination. "It is just that we are all so tired, that is all. After we eat and rest, you will all realize your good fortune."

But long after they had eaten and the fire had died to glowing embers, the men were still gazing at the stars with wide-open eyes. No one spoke. Even Jolie remained quiet, listening to the night sounds with her own thoughts spinning. What if Jordan was right? What if their search for gold was frowned upon by fate? But if that was so, why had she not sensed it also?

Stirring uneasily, Jolie turned on her side, resting her head in one palm. She gazed across the rocky ground to where Jordan lay, stretched out in his blankets and smoking another cigarette. The crimson tip glowed brightly, and she could make out the thin spirals of smoke drifting upward.

"Jordan?" she said softly and heard the creak of leather as his head shifted on the seat of the saddle he was using as a pillow.

"Yeah?"

"Perhaps you were right. Perhaps Ussen frowns upon our disturbing the sacred yellow metal. . . ."

Jordan snorted derisively. "Look, green eyes, I didn't mean any of that. Like you said, I was just tired and hungry."

She didn't believe him for a moment. "That is not true, Jordan. You meant what you were saying."

"I don't believe in jinxes, and I don't believe in curses. I believe in hard work and honest pay, and that was what was making me think about it. It's just been too easy, but maybe it's like that sometimes." His tone changed from hard to soft, and she could see the flicker of his cigarette in the moonlight. "Go to sleep, little girl, and don't worry about it."

"I'm not worried," she snapped back, miffed that he had called her a little girl. "And I don't want to go to sleep yet!"

"Why not?"

"Because I'm only tired, not sleepy." There was a short pause, then she asked, "Why do you always pretend you are angry with me, Jor-dan?"

"What makes you think I'm pretending?"

"Your eyes give you away. . . ."

"And why do you think you can tell anything by that?" Jordan's tone was irritated, and he gave his cigarette stub a quick thump, sending it spiralling through the dark like a tiny meteor. "Don't try to act so grown up, little girl."

Jolie drew in her breath sharply, the sound almost a hiss through her clenched teeth, but she managed to keep her voice light when she said, "And what makes you think I'm not already grown up, Jor-dan?"

"It doesn't take a genius to see that you're still a child, green eyes. I'm not trying to hurt your feelings, but grown women don't behave as you do."

"How do 'grown women' behave?" she asked tartly. "Do they act solemn all the time, never laugh, and never have a good time? That is not the way my mother's people live. Life is full of sadness and sorrow, so it is only right that one should laugh and joke when it is possible. If a sad face is what you expect of me, then I am glad that I am not what you call a grown woman, Jor-dan Sin-clair!''

Before Jordan could offer any comment, Jolie had sprang up from her blankets and fled into the night, disappearing over the nearest ridge. Half-rising on his elbows, Jordan gave an exasperated sigh. She was such a touchy little thing, but dammit, she *did* behave like a child instead of a woman! Women of his experience did not stare at him with adoring eyes like a half-grown puppy; nor did they tease him like she did. Women were either bold like the saloon girls, or extremely proper and looking for a husband. Jolie La Fleur was too young for this kind of game, and Jordan was growing weary of pampering her.

Morning struck the sides of Hembrillo Peak with blinding force, not creeping up on them as it sometimes did but spearing them with bright shafts of light.

''Sunrise shakes heaven and earth up here,'' Amos was heard to grumble as he shook sleep from his eyes. He squinted against the glare and ran a hand across his close-cropped head and grizzled jaw.

As if summoned by his words, there was an ominous rumble in the distance, and Jordan flung up his head to look for telltale thunderclouds. ''The sky is clear,'' he muttered in a puzzled tone, shading his eyes with one hand as he stared across the sweep of land to the horizon. ''What was that noise?''

''Perhaps the gods are angry,'' Jolie offered, but she was ignored. The three men were standing now and gazing around them, shifting uneasily.

''Flash flood?'' Griffin suggested, but it was pointed out

that they were not anywhere near an area prone to that hazard. "Then what could it be?" he demanded.

"Perhaps we should not search for the gold," Jolie said quietly. Her mother's basic training in the possible wrath of the gods came back to her now, and she ignored all the teachings of the rotund little priest at the mission. "If the gods are angered by our search . . ."

"Jolie, please," Griffin said patiently, "we are trying to figure out what this is! We don't need to hear any of that junk about curses right now."

Gathering shreds of her wounded pride around her like a cloak, Jolie crossed her arms over her chest and lifted her chin in the now familiar gesture of affront. "Just because you choose not to listen does not mean it cannnot be true," she began but was interrupted by another fierce rumble.

This time the earth shook beneath their feet, and the terrified horses began to scream shrilly. Jordan and Griffin sprang to the horses, while Amos scooped up saddles and blankets. Nonessential supplies were left scattered across the ground as rocks tumbled down the sloping sides of Hembrillo Peak, bouncing erratically.

"It's only a matter of time before the *big* rocks come down on our heads," Jordan snapped, jerking up the leather water skins and slinging them across his saddle horn. "Let's get out of here while we can!" he flung at Jolie, but she was not where she'd been a moment before.

Jolie was already ahead of him, having vaulted to the bare back of her piebald heedless of saddle or bridle. She used only the simple rope hackamore left around the animal's head for guidance and was moving at a fast pace down the slope. The horse needed little urging to run.

Now the ground trembled and shook in rolling waves, and the earth cracked open as rocks pelted down in deadly showers. Crevices zigzagged across the ground in erratic patterns as the four riders made their way over yawning gaps in the crust, leaping chasms sometimes four feet wide.

Once Jolie glanced back to see Jordan several yards behind her, his head down and his gray stretched out in a dead run, with its nostrils pink and flaring. He was bent over the animal's neck, urging it faster, yanking it to one side when a huge rock slid toward him in a shower of smaller rocks. Her heart was pumping so fast that she did not see how it remained in her chest, and her mouth was dry and aching from the harsh clenching of her teeth. Did she look as frightened as the others? she wondered for an instant, then turned her attention back to the splitting ground in front of her.

Shards of rock showered down suddenly in a cloud of dust, and the piebald dodged them without breaking stride, landing smoothly on the other side of the jagged mounds. The rumbling gradually lessened as they neared the bottom of the peak and slowed their horses. Jolie was in front by several yards, and she half-turned her horse to wait on the others.

In spite of the cool morning air, her buckskin dress was plastered to her body with perspiration, and her long dark hair was damp at the temples. She had lost the strip of material she used to hold back her hair, and wisps hung in her eyes. But the picture she presented to the men who followed her was one of cool composure as she waited with calm hands and a half-smile of triumph curving her mouth.

"Dammit!" Amos grumbled. "Just look at her! She looks like she ain't got a care in the world!"

Jordan slanted her a sour glance, but Griffin appeared to be too frightened to do more than gasp for breath. His horse was white with lather, its sides heaving and head hanging low.

"Griffin?" Jolie said, nudging her mount close to his. "Are you all right?"

He nodded silently, his pale blond hair sticking to his scalp and his hat gone. Blue eyes flicked toward her for a moment, and he attempted a smile.

"Fine," he muttered after a brief struggle, then pierced her with a quizzical glance and the question, "Ain't you afraid of dying, Jolie? Why ain't you as scared as the rest of us?"

"I was frightened," she answered slowly, "but one cannot outrun death if it is meant to be, Griffin. There are times one can choose the method of dying, but not the time." She shrugged her shoulders and smiled at the youth who was only a few months younger than she in years, but much less experienced in the harsh ways of life. He had not seen death as intimately as the Apache did. To the Apache, death was a daily shadow.

"Sounds a bit fatalistic to me," Jordan muttered. He slapped his hat against his thigh and wiped his dripping forehead with the back of one arm. "And now that we've all enjoyed our little romp down the mountainside, what say we go back and see what's left of our supplies—and the entrance to the cave?"

Apparently no one else had thought of that, for they all looked thunderstruck for a moment. The ride back up the heated slope was silent except for an occasional scratch of small rocks still sliding down the peak.

The spot where they had camped was now littered with loose rocks and raw scrapes in the earth's crust, and bare patches had been gouged out of the ground. They found a battered shovel, a blanket, their black iron skillet, and part of a pack, but the rest had been buried underneath the rocks or carried away.

"Well," Amos said at last, his voice heavy as he pushed at a large rock with his foot, "guess we lost the cave opening again. I sure don't see it. Does anyone else?"

"All I see is a damned pile of rocks," Griffin said gloomily. He perched on the sharp edge of a boulder. "I don't even see my hat."

"This it?" Jordan asked, bending to scoop up a shapeless triangle of felt. He punched a fist into it in an attempt to straighten it out, but it was clearly hopeless.

Griffin's face was a youthful picture of woe and disgust as he gazed at the remains of his hat. "So what do we do now?" he asked. "Stick around and try to dig out the entrance to that cave? It'd take weeks unless we go back to town and get some more supplies, and that's gonna take a few weeks, too."

"Not mentioning the fact that we spent all our money on the stuff sitting under those rocks," Amos added. "What can we buy with . . ." He dug into his pocket and came out with a few coins. "Six dollars and thirty-eight cents?"

"Not much," Jordan said briefly. "I don't have much more money than that. How much do you have, Griffin?"

"Money? None," the boy said promptly. "But I do have something that might help."

"Like what?" Jordan snapped irritably, but Jolie slid from her horse with the beginnings of a smile on her face.

She recognized the gleam of triumph in Griffin's eyes, and knew what his answer would be even before he began digging into the small leather pouch he had tied to his waist.

"Well, I didn't have much time to grab anything when the ground started dancing with those rocks," Griffin was saying, "and I sure didn't have time to grab my hat, but I did manage to take this along with me, seein' as how it was tied to my belt anyhow."

A solid length of dully gleaming metal slid from the bag into his hand, weighing heavily as he held it up. "While the rest of you were busy runnin'," he announced, "I was busy lugging this heavy gold bar around."

Chapter
<u>10</u>

Franklin, Texas, sweltered under the summer sun as Amos, Jordan, Griffin, and Jolie rode down the dusty main street. There was no breeze to cool them. Not even a tumbleweed blew down the street as the weary horses plodded through drifts of dust. Very few people were on the streets, but as they moved toward the other end of town, passing through a line of clapboard false-fronted buildings, they heard faint calls.

"Hey, honey!" a sultry voice purred from a window. "How 'bout cooling off in here with me? Selena can show you cowboys a real good time! Much better than that Indian squaw you've got with you . . ."

Jolie's head whipped around and she narrowed her eyes at the half-clad woman leaning on a windowsill. She was clothed in a frilly lace chemise that appeared tattered and dingy even from the street, and her blond hair was frowsy and hanging in messy tendrils around her painted face.

"*Puta*!" Jolie muttered, and even Griffin understood enough Spanish to know what she meant.

"Yeah, she is, but that's her business," he said with a grin. "Don't let her worry you none, Jolie."

"Me?" She tossed her head and gave the woman a disdainful glance. "I do not worry about such a one. In my mother's camp, she would have her nose slit. . . ."

Jolie broke off when another skimpily clad woman called out, this one calling Jordan by name as she rushed from the house to clasp him by one leg, walking beside his gray and smiling up at him with delight.

"Jordan! It's been a while, sweetie. Why don't you come on in and see me again? Don't you remember how good Hayley can make you feel, honey?" Her fingers inched further up his leg, to the amusement of Amos and Griffin and the chagrin of Jolie. "I been missing you," the girl was saying, pushing at the curling strands of brown hair in her eyes. The thin straps of her lacy chemise sagged from her shoulders, the drooping bodice exposing the tops of pale, round breasts to any stray gaze as she pushed close to the side of Jordan's horse. Bright red lips stretched in a provocative smile that was full and ripe with promise as she gazed up at Jordan, goading Jolie into reaction.

Nudging her piebald with a bare heel, Jolie stepped up the animal's pace just enough to catch up with Jordan so that when he reined his gray to a slower walk, the piebald was right behind the girl called Hayley. She never noticed. Her attention was riveted upon Jordan, her smile growing wetter and wider by the moment as she moistened her lips with the tip of her tongue.

Jolie bridled, eyes glittering with determination as she nudged her horse even closer. This time Hayley noticed. A shod hoof came down upon her heel, and the scantily clad girl shrieked loudly, whirling with wildly waving arms and frightening the horse. Jolie made no effort to control the piebald's terrified lunges but allowed it to half-rear, sending Hayley skittering back to the comparative safety of the sagging front porch, limping with every step.

"You did that on purpose!" Hayley shrilled, holding her foot and glaring at Jolie, who was gazing at her with satisfaction. "Oh—I get it!" Hayley spat, recognizing the expression on Jolie's face. "You're just jealous, you wretched Indian squaw! Do you think you can interest a man, wearing those ragged, stinking clothes that make you look like a sack of cornmeal?! You're too brown and ugly for any man to look at!" she snarled, still holding her foot.

"Enough, Hayley," Jordan said sternly, though his mouth was curved into an amused line. "I may look you up later tonight. Right now we've still got things to do." He touched the brim of his hat as he nudged the gray into a trot, wanting to get away from the scene before Jolie exploded. He'd already recognized dangerous glints in her green eyes that boded ill if they hung around much longer.

"Hey, Jolie," Griffin said, nudging his horse close and grinning at her, "try this. She'll understand it." He showed her a crude hand sign that Jolie immediately copied, gesturing toward the porch where Hayley stood glaring at them. It made Jolie feel much better to see the girl sputtering in fury, and Griffin enjoyed himself hugely. "You're a quick study," he said in approval as they rode toward the end of the street, and Jolie smiled.

"You shouldn't be showing her that kind of stuff," Amos admonished, but it was easy enough to see that he was being ignored by both Griffin and Jolie.

"It's going to backfire on him one day," Jordan observed acidly. "Then he'll wish he hadn't been quite so quick to teach his star pupil obscenities."

"Maybe," Griffin agreed. "And maybe not."

Jolie said nothing, letting Griffin defend her. It was easier than challenging Jordan, and besides, Griffin usually won the argument.

"Let's cool off in the saloon," Amos suggested when they finally stood in the shade of the huge livery stable where they were to leave their horses. "I could do with a good drink 'bout now."

"Yeah, but what do we do with her?" Jordan jerked his thumb in Jolie's direction. "I don't think we want to take her in a saloon."

"Why not?" Jolie demanded. She faced Jordan with an indignant expression on her face. "My papa used to take me with him when he would drink. . . ."

"I ain't your papa, green eyes," Jordan shot back. "And I don't want to take you with me." Dropping his saddle into the dust and straw of the stable floor, he leaned one arm against a wooden post between stalls and raked her with a considering glance for several long moments. Griffin paused in rubbing down his horse to watch him warily, knowing what he was thinking.

"Jordan," the youth began, but his uncle shook his head.

"No, Griffin. Not anymore. Look, we found the cave without getting killed, and we don't really need her anymore. We got up there once without running into any Apache, and it's a fair bet we can do it again. I say we cut her loose. Send her back to her camp, or whatever, but I don't want to ride with her anymore."

"Shouldn't we all take a vote on this?" Amos put in. "I think we agreed somewhere along the line to give everybody his say on a subject."

"Oh, come on! Do you really think we should take her with us?" Jordan asked derisively. "I'm all for putting her on a pony and sending her home whether she wants to go or not."

"You don't really want to send me home," Jolie said confidently. "You are just angry with me right now. I will stay with you, Jor-dan. I saw you when the men brought you into my mother's camp, and I know you saw me, too. Our eyes met, and you knew what you wanted, just as I know what I want. Why else would you have taken me from my camp?"

"What makes you think that? Hell, I've been trying to shake you ever since we took you from your camp!" He snorted. "You're a mistake, Jolie La Fleur! We didn't want you—we wanted Victorio's granddaughter!"

"A mistake?" Jolie asked, feeling as if the world was crumbling around her. And she had been foolish enough to think he had seen her and wanted her for himself! Her cheeks were flushed and her eyes even brighter than usual as she stared at Jordan.

He could read the shock of his words in Jolie's eyes and shook his head. "No, Jolie," he said more gently, "I did not mean to get you. We took you because we thought you were Victorio's granddaughter and we could use you for safe passage while we looked for the gold."

Her chin lifted as she returned his gaze, and there was no trace of emotion in her eyes when she said coolly, "You found more than you were looking for, Jor-dan. But since I *did* help you, I deserve a share of your gold."

"I thought you didn't believe in taking gold," he said mockingly, while bending to pick up his saddle. Jolie just watched as he flung the leather saddle over a rack to air it. She kept her face expressionless.

"That does not matter. Give me a share now, or take me with you," she retorted. "It's only fair!"

"No," Griffin objected, slanting his uncle an exasperated glance. "How would that be fair? We stand to get a lot more when we go back. If we spend our gold now, it might start people wondering where we got it—and I don't think we need any more partners! We need to buy more shovels and picks and even dynamite to get that cave open again! I say you should go with us, Jolie, and get your share later...."

"Anybody else you want to cut in on this gold we ain't even got yet?" Jordan snapped. "If we're going to give some to her, how about givin' a share to the horses, and then to the bartenders in town, and the saloon girls...."

"Why don't we have a drink and talk about it later, when we aren't so hot and thirsty?" Amos suggested mildly. "I've got very little patience for talking right now."

"Fine with me," Griffin said shortly. "How 'bout you, Jordan?"

He shrugged. "I think you're both soft in the head when it comes to this girl, is what I think. But a good stiff drink might help out." Pivoting, he strode from the stable with loose, easy strides, leaving Amos, Griffin, and Jolie standing silently in the dusky shadows.

"Well," Griffin said after a moment of heavy silence, "guess we'll just meet up with him at the saloon. What you gonna do, Jolie? Do you want to get a room, maybe, take a nap or something? We can meet you later if you want."

Her gaze shifted from the vacant air where Jordan had just been, focusing upon the blond youth staring at her with an anxious expression on his face. He meant well, and so did Amos, but there were some things a woman had to do for herself if she was to triumph. "I'm going to the saloon," she announced. "Which one is it?"

Lifting his hat, Griffin raked a hand through his blond hair and shifted his feet in the dust and spilled hay of the stable floor. "Jolie, are you sure you want to do that?"

Ebony hair glinted in the soft light streaming through the open doors from a hayloft overhead as she nodded. "'Au—

yes, Griffin, I am sure. Jor-dan Sin-clair does not know what he wants, but I do.''

Amos and Griffin exchanged startled glances that quickly grew into consternation when Jolie asked for a small portion of money.

''Just a small amount will do,'' she said quietly, and Griffin surrendered his cash without a word. ''Thank you, Griffin. First I go to buy some things, then I will join you. Where will you be?''

Amos gave her directions reluctantly and shook his head as Jolie strode from the stable with her long hair swinging and her hips swaying in an excellent imitation of the girl Hayley. ''I don't know what she's plannin', Rooster, and I ain't too sure I want to,'' he muttered, shaking his head. Both men stared after her.

Jolie's mouth was in a thin, tight line as she stalked from the stable. Perhaps the girl Hayley had been right. No man would want her when she looked like this, not when there were women who wore soft, frilly things and smelled of soap and water instead of dust and horse.

Reaching up, she tore off the strip of cloth she now wore to keep her hair from her eyes and threw it to the ground, not giving it a second glance as she walked on. Her bare feet made soft patters in the dust as she walked, and the Levis covering her long legs made swishing sounds. Yes, all she needed was a dress and Jordan would see her as a woman.

At that particular moment, Jordan was thinking of Jolie in anything but kind terms. She had once again managed to irritate him beyond belief. How did the girl get under his skin so quickly? And why did he let her? Questions like these could drive a man to drink, he reflected sourly and headed in the direction of the local barber. If he was going to sit in a public place, he needed to clean off the smell of trail dust, horse, and mule as well as get a shave and haircut.

A quarter of an hour later found him sitting in a wooden tub of soapy water that came up to his armpits. He had demanded and paid for a bath with water that had not been previously used, and he leaned back to luxuriate in it. It felt great not to have inches of dust and grime coating his skin. And the clean, new clothes hanging on a wall peg would feel a hell of a lot better than his worn-out blues. Of course, those cavalry pants had a lot of memories tucked into the folds, creases, and pockets, some of them so raw he'd rather not remember.

Leaning his head back against the rough rim, he closed his eyes and tried to shut out the memory of similarly blue-clad bodies sprawled across the glossy black rock of the Malpais. Most of those men had been just kids, boys not much older than Griffin, and Jordan had been responsible for them. He should have been able to stop them from dashing recklessly onto that deadly patch of mirror-smooth ground somehow, but the solution still eluded him even after three years of mulling it over and over again in his mind.

Jordan let a long, drawn-out sigh escape with a sibilant sound, stirring the mounds of soap bubbles on his knee. Dammit. He was still haunted, and somehow Jolie was mixed up in all his bad dreams. He'd see her face floating over him at night, those fine, exquisite features framed by a mass of heavy, black satin hair, and her mouth was always stretched into a smile. How could he forget that she was partly related to the people who had killed his friends?

But as Jordan opened his eyes and glumly contemplated a mound of rainbow bubbles perched upon one knee, he reflected on the fact that Jolie was only one small part of his problem. The biggest trouble lay within his own mind, his struggle with the nagging feelings of guilt. Maybe that was why he reacted so strongly to Jolie's overtures, her loyal devotion that sometimes reminded him of a favorite hound when he was a kid. Kick her away and she bounced back just as if she was yanked on a string. Trouble was, he felt lower than dirt for shouting at her, or rudely rejecting her, or even just speaking sharply to her. How could he be such a villain when every time he closed his eyes he saw his sister Jassy's reproving face?

Jassy, sweet Jassy, who had been saddled with the care of a boy years younger when she was still a child herself. But she had managed, had seen to it that he had schooling, manners, and discipline, and had talked their ailing father into letting his only son join the Army when he wasn't much older than Griffin was now. Jordan smiled at the memory. He'd been hell-bent and determined to go into the Army in spite of Jassy's entreaties and their father's firm refusal to allow him to, and his sister had at last relented in the face of such determination.

"It'll be best, I suppose," she had said with a sigh, "or you'll do something like running away. Just remember, Jordan, that you're a Sinclair. Sinclairs never do anything dishonorable or wicked."

He'd done his best to live up to Jassy's expectations. And last Christmas, when he'd gone to their home in Texas to visit with them, he'd tried to explain the reasons behind his decision to leave the Army.

"It isn't right, Jassy," he'd said sadly. "The reasons for being there are right, but some of the things I see and have to do go against my grain."

"Is the Army corrupt?" she'd asked, and he'd shaken his head.

"No, not the Army. Just some of the commanding officers. And some of the men who join are worse than criminals. I've seen them do things to Indian women and children that would turn your stomach."

"Well, how about the atrocities committed by the Indians?" Fletcher Armstrong, Jassy's husband and Griffin's father, had asked. "Is that right?"

"Of course not, but when did two wrongs ever make a right?" Jordan had countered. He thought of that now. Two wrongs did not make a right, and he was doing the same thing to Jolie now. . . .

Jolie was right in her prediction about Jordan's reaction. When she strolled into the Last Chance Saloon, he didn't even recognize her. He was sitting at a table in the back with Amos and Griffin, still working on their first bottle of rye, when the double doors swung open. For a moment he caught a brief glimpse of a feminine form in a pale green dress. Pushing back his hat, he turned to get a better look at the faintly familiar form, but she was gone.

Frowning, Jordan turned toward Amos and Griffin, opening his mouth to ask if he had really seen a woman, when a hand tapped him on the shoulder.

"Jor-dan?" a familiar voice asked. "Do you look for me?"

His brows drew into a knot as he recognized her voice and began, "No, I was *not* looking for you . . ." when he tilted back his head and saw her. It was Jolie, but it was not Jolie. Gone were the Apache headband, the buckskin dress, the Levis, the bare feet. In their place were a demure bonnet with tiny flowers and a net, a curve-hugging dress with a bustle in the back and icy green folds of material that swayed with her every movement; her bare feet were covered by smart, high-button shoes of kid. It was a startling—and to most of the men in the saloon a gratifying—change. Of course, Jordan reflected, very few of them had seen her before this metamorphosis, so they could not appreciate the full effect. She even smelled as delicate as a spring flower, and her hair had been swept from her neck into a lustrous twist on the back of her head.

It was Griffin who broke the silence between them as he said in a soft breath, "Jolie, you are beautiful!"

Her dimple appeared, and her eyes—was it possible they were even greener than usual?—shone with soft lights. "Thank you, Griffin," she said demurely. "So are you."

"Lord, child, you're prettier than anything I've seen in a long time," Amos put in with a wide, white grin. He rubbed at his sparse beard with a thumb and two fingers as he considered her for a long moment. "Yep, you're beautiful!" he agreed with Griffin.

Jolie waited for Jordan to speak, to say the words she wanted to hear, but he only tilted his chair back on two legs and regarded her with a faintly cynical expression.

"May I sit down?" she asked when it became apparent he would say nothing. She indicated an empty chair with a wave of her hand.

Jordan shrugged. "Sure. I'm not using it."

Faint spots of color stained Jolie's cheeks as she pulled out the chair, slanting him an appraising glance as she did so. *Arrogant beast!* she fumed silently. He was worse than the coyote!

Griffin leaned forward, admiration in his eyes as he said, "Hey, Jolie, this is no place for you. There ain't nothing here but men, rough men, so why don't we go on down the street? They're having some sort of town social, with tables of food and a big beef on a spit. We can get a steak and maybe drink some good wine, like my mama likes to do sometimes.''

Jordan's chair legs thunked forward. ''Nobody will bother her here. Sit down, Jolie.''

Defiant sparks glittered for a moment as she answered sweetly, ''But I like Griffin's idea, Jor-dan. I think I shall go with him, thank you.''

Amos pursed his lips, rolled his eyes, and lifted his drink. ''Mebbe we can all go,'' he said, nudging Griffin with the toe of his boot. ''Come on, Jordan. A steak would taste great after all this rye.''

Jordan refused to go along with the majority. His mouth tightened as he shook his head and declined rather ungraciously. ''No, thanks. I'll stay here.''

''Then the rest of us shall have a good time without you. This is so, yes, Griffin?'' Jolie said with forced gaiety.

''This is so, yes, Jolie,'' Griffin returned with a wide grin. Scraping back his chair, he rose and took her by one arm, winking broadly at Amos as he did so and ignoring his uncle. If Jordan wished to pretend indifference, it was fine with him. After all, he wasn't his uncle's keeper, was he? And he wanted to go with Jolie. She was fun—much less inhibited and restrained than the girls he knew back home, who were inclined to be a bit on the prim side. Not that Jolie was loose—just more liberated. She was a ''nice'' girl with none of society's restrictions binding her.

Amos swayed for a moment between drinking with Jordan and going with Griffin and Jolie; then he obviously decided that his best interest lay in being impartial.

''You know, I'm a lot more tired than I thought. Think I'll pass on another drink and that steak. I'm going back to the stable and bunk in with the horses," he said as he rose from the table. "See you in the morning, folks."

"Looks like it's just me and you, Jolie," Griffin said cheerfully. "Let's go." Deviltry danced in his blue eyes as he held out an arm for her to take, and she put her hand in the crook of his elbow.

Though she was well aware of Jordan's narrowed gaze boring into her back as she left, Jolie resisted the urge to turn around and look at him as she wanted to do. He was behaving badly toward her when she had done nothing to deserve it. Why wouldn't he at least tell her that she looked nice? She had chosen her garments very carefully from the secondhand store on the little side street of the main district, and had done quite nicely, she thought. Of course, the lady who owned the store had helped her pick out the bonnet and shoes and had even given her the perfumed soap free of charge. Her pleasure in the acquisitions had not been disturbed, even when another customer had looked down her long nose and made an unkind remark about heathens dressing up like white folks. Only Jordan was able to spoil her mood.

But she determinedly put his unkind comments to the back of her mind. Now was not the time to confront him. That could come later. Now it was time to be happy, and she set about doing just that with Griffin.

The night was sultry with heat and the sounds of music from a small band as they strolled down the wooden sidewalk to the end of town. Strains of melodies played by a banjo, fiddle, and guitar filtered through stands of cottonwood trees, and bright lanterns swayed from the branches like captured fireflies, illuminating the musicians. Thick aromas of sizzling beef mingled with the more subtle fragrance of hot biscuits and peach pies, and crowds pressed close to long tables set up near the musicians. Jolie drew in a deep breath, enjoying the scene to the fullest.

And the scene seemed to be enjoying the two newcomers also. Men slanted warm, curious glances toward the exotic creature in the green dress, apparently unable to decide if she was white or Indian but liking what they saw; the young women threw the blond youth with the angelic features promising stares from beneath flirtatious lashes. Griffin, of course, was accustomed to it, his looks having drawn the female gender to him all his life, but Jolie was more accustomed to the cruel jibes aimed at the Apache because of the color of her skin. Now, garbed in clothes that made her blend in with the other women, she knew instinctively that her French accent would give her credence in the white man's world. And would that be so bad? After all, her father *was* French, and it would not be a denial of her race. . . .

"Shall we eat, Jolie?" Griffin was asking, turning from the bold stare of a particularly lovely young woman. "It sure smells good."

"*Oui,*" she murmured, eyes sparkling as she skimmed the crowd with interest. But when Griffin brought her a plate piled high with juicy meat, corn on the cob, hot biscuits, small potatoes that had been cooked on the coals until they were so flaky they fell apart at the touch of a fork, slices of fresh fruit, and a glass of chilled wine shipped from France via Galveston, Jolie was too excited to eat. She held the plate for a moment, then set it down on a huge tree stump without tasting her food. When she began clapping her hands in rhythm with the music, Griffin knew what she wanted to do.

"Griffin, look," she said. "They are having such fun!"

"They sure are. Don't you want to eat?" he urged, eying her full plate. "Or at least taste the wine?"

"Wine? My father used to drink wine," she said. "He would take many furs to the trading post, and they would have special bottles just for him. It always made him happy."

"I can imagine," Griffin murmured, handing Jolie her wine. His eyes widened, soaking up the light from swaying lanterns as he watched Jolie down the tall glass of wine without putting it down. "Hey! This stuff is more potent than cider, you know..."

"I know. But it is not more potent than *tulpái*, the drink my mother's people make. It is made from corn, and very good."

"I'll bet," Griffin said, a little awed by the fact that Jolie drank corn liquor. He'd heard of it, though the whites called it *tiswin* instead of *tulpái*, and he knew it to be strong.

Leaning back against a long table formed by planks stretched across sawhorses and covered with a tablecloth, Jolie watched the dancers enviously. Her feet, encased in the unaccustomed pair of shoes that pinched her toes, tapped against the ground, causing puffs of dust to rise into the air. To make Griffin happy, she nibbled at the food, though her appetite was slight.

A brisk breeze blew, stirring the lanterns strung from trees, teasing soft tendrils of Jolie's night-dark hair into stray wisps that drifted into her eyes. She pushed at it impatiently, attention trained on the dancers, unaware of the gazes directed toward her. Griffin's—admiring and warm with affection—and others' more intent gazes watched as she clapped her hands and moved in tempo with the music. Restless, and wanting to join in, Jolie slanted Griffin an intriguing smile.

"Uh—do you want more wine?" he asked, uncertain what she wanted.

"*Non,* let's dance! Please, Griffin . . ."

"Can't we eat first? I've only had one helping, and this is pretty good food. . . ."

Jolie stamped an impatient foot, her hands resting on her hips. "*Mon Dieu!* Is food all you think of, *cochon?*"

"Aw, Jolie," he began, when another man stepped close.

"I'll dance with the little lady," the man said politely, removing his hat and smiling at Jolie.

Griffin set down his plate. "No. That's all right. I'll dance with her." His smile was cold, his eyes piercing, and the man nodded uneasily.

"Sure. Just thought I'd offer."

"That's real kind of you, but I can handle it." Griffin's cold smile never wavered, and the burly gentleman moved away rather swiftly.

Whispering, "You are not very friendly," in Griffin's ear, Jolie urged him to the wooden dance platform before he could change his mind. Brightly gowned women swung on the arms of men who wore neatly pressed white shirts and black string ties instead of their customary working clothes of denims and plaid shirts.

Laughing, Griffin allowed himself to be pulled along, pushing his hat to the back of his head as he took Jolie's hand. "Okay, okay, but you don't know what you're getting into!" he warned. "I just happen to be the best dancer west of the Mississippi River, Jolie. . . ."

Sets had already been formed, but a man standing by the musicians called out the figure, "All join hands and circle wide," and Jolie and Griffin were pulled into a group. To Jolie it was confusing as she tried to follow the instructions announced by the man on the platform, but she quickly followed Griffin's lead. There were strange phrases such as "allemande left" and "do-si-do," but she managed to catch on by watching the others and imitating their movements. The dance moved from the "Texas Star" to the "Arkansas Traveler," then into something the caller announced as the "Darling Nellie Gray."

"What strange names your dances have," Jolie whispered into Griffin's ear as they do-si-doed a circular path with the others.

Griffin agreed, swinging her in a wide pattern and releasing her to the next partner. He grinned as Jolie was clasped by a large man with a stomach that drooped over his belt, then swung in an energetic circle. The expression on her face was priceless—one of pained politeness as the man accidentally trod upon her foot—and Griffin was enjoying himself immensely. Jolie was a delight to watch, and he had already noticed that he was not the only man present who liked watching her. There were others who seemed captivated by her animation and exotic face, the big green eyes and perfect features that seemed as if they should belong to a painting in a museum.

Half-turning, Griffin's gaze flickered over her. It was too bad Jordan was such an insufferable idiot, or he could be enjoying himself, too, instead of sitting alone in a bar nursing a shot glass of rye.

The fiddle played, and Griffin's feet skipped across the wooden platform. The night air seemed warmer, swinging from one partner to another. Most of the men were hatless and none wore their guns, making Griffin feel slightly conspicuous since his .45s were still strapped around his waist. But it was better than being unprepared for trouble, he reflected, reaching out for another hand swinging toward him.

It was then that he found his shoulder gripped by an unrelenting hand. Surprised and tensing in readiness, he half-turned to see Jordan standing in the midst of the swirling dancers, a scowl creasing his face.

"I'll take it from here," Jordan said shortly, his eyes resting on Jolie as she skimmed across the platform like a green summer butterfly, laughing gaily.

"Hey!"

"Hey nothing. You're holding up the dance," Jordan said rudely, shoving Griffin aside.

"You gonna dance or talk?" a man objected as the set began to back up, and Griffin surrendered with a shrug, stepping from the platform into the dust.

Jordan slid smoothly into the motions of the dance, his gaze on Jolie, so that when she turned she would meet his eyes. She was swinging from one partner to the next, her skirts belling out to expose trim ankles, when she saw him.

Stopping so suddenly that the people behind her stumbled into her, Jolie's mouth drooped in surprise. He had followed her—he was standing there, hatless and handsome in his white shirt and dark cord trousers, his freshly shaved face creased into a faintly mocking expression that she had come to know so well. Her lips curved into a welcoming smile.

"Jor-dan . . ."

Deftly grabbing her hands as the caller announced the command to do-si-do, Jordan pulled her along with him, slanting her a glance from beneath his thick lashes and murmuring, "You gonna dance or talk?"

"Both."

"I knew you'd have an unusual answer," he shot back dryly.

"I'm an unusual woman," Jolie returned with a toss of her dark head. After her first start of surprise, a rush of pleasure enveloped her, and she realized that Jordan had deliberately sought her out. Why? He must have missed her, she reasoned. Perhaps he even realized that he was drawn to her, just as Gray Ghost had been drawn to Lozen. . . .

Jordan's eyes narrowed at the faint expression of feline satisfaction on Jolie's face. His gaze flicked over her body, taking careful note of the slim curves that seemed much more womanly in the form-fitting jade gown than they had in the shapeless buckskin dress and tight Levis he was used to seeing her wear.

"You bet, you are an unusual woman," he murmured thoughtfully. "You bet."

There was an odd note in his voice that caught her attention, and Jolie's gaze sharpened. Was he making fun of her again? But then Jordan was taking her hands and leading her from the dance platform into the crowd, pushing past a waiting Griffin to step into the shadows far beyond the stand of cottonwood trees.

"Hey!" Griffin protested, his piercing blue eyes narrowing at his uncle as he caught up with them under the spreading branches of a cottonwood. "Where do you think you're taking her?"

Jordan halted, swinging around to stare at Griffin with a raised brow. "When did I start having to explain myself to you?"

Griffin held his ground. "When you snatch Jolie out from under my nose, that's when! I brought her to the dance when you wouldn't . . ."

"Well, I'm here now, and she wants to be with me, don't you, Jolie?"

Biting her lower lip in consternation, Jolie gazed at Griffin's set face and sighed. "Griffin, you know what I want, don't you?"

"Yeah, but I know what he wants, too," Griffin growled in return. "Hell, Jolie, make him treat you like a lady! Don't jump every time he yells frog. Jordan's too used to getting his way, anyhow. . . ."

"Thanks, nephew," Jordan said sarcastically. "Any more words of advice you wish to offer before we leave your charming company?"

"Yeah, but you wouldn't like 'em, and she wouldn't listen, so I guess I might as well shut up."

"Might as well," Jordan agreed. "Stop acting like a mother hen with its only chick, Griffin. It don't suit you."

"Maybe not, but what I'm seein' lately don't suit you either, *Uncle* Jordan." The boy's eyes were as cold as his tone, impaling Jordan with unuttered accusations.

Before Jordan could respond with what could only be inflammatory words, Jolie stepped into the breach. "I want to go with him, Griffin," she said, putting out her hand to lay it on his sleeve. "Please understand."

"Oh, I do understand *you*, Jolie. I'm just not too sure about him right now. . . ."

Slightly confused because Griffin had never shown open animosity toward his uncle's treatment of her before, Jolie gazed at the blond-haired youth with troubled eyes. Guitar music trembled in the air and a soft breeze blew as she considered the situation, but then Jordan was tugging at her impatiently, pulling her with him.

"I'll be all right, Griffin," she assured him over one shoulder, trotting to keep up with Jordan's long-legged stride.

Griffin just watched as they disappeared into the night shadows, his perfect features creased into a worried frown. He had just ignored the basic rule of non-interference in another man's business, but he didn't spare a moment of regret. Somebody had to look out for a girl as innocent and naive as Jolie, and he had elected himself for the job.

Chapter
11

"I'm tired of playing games, green eyes. We need to talk," Jordan muttered to Jolie, wondering why he was bothering. Maybe it was the influence of his second bottle of rye that had prompted him to seek her out when he knew better. Griffin was probably right. Conversation with this woman-child was dangerous, he'd learned, so why was he even attempting it?

"But I want to dance," Jolie objected. Her eyes gleamed, and her heart was beating so quickly that it sounded like the drums of war. Even her breath was much shorter than usual, as if she had been running uphill. Why was it so easy for Jordan to affect her this way—to make her feel as weak-kneed as a newborn colt?

Jordan ignored her, steering her along with him away from the crowds toward the line of wooden buildings. Jolie began to sense something different about him, a tightly coiled tension that quivered just beneath the surface of civility, and recalling Griffin's words, she became vaguely uneasy.

"Where are we going? I wish to stay and dance," she

repeated, tugging at her arm. It was held fast in his harsh grip, and she felt the first, faint fluttering of alarm.

"Dammit, why do you always have to be so contrary?" he snapped. "Can't you ever just agree with me on something? On *anything*?"

"Yes, Jordan. I can agree with you. I agree that we should not quarrel." She put her other hand on his arm, feeling his muscles tense at her touch, and her lips curved into a placating smile. "I do not wish to quarrel with you. I would much rather do something . . . nicer."

"I'll bet you would," he commented, and she had the distinct impression that he was talking to her in the same tone he had used with the girl Hayley earlier in the day. Did he think of her like that? she wondered indignantly.

"Jordan, I do not wish for you to treat me like . . . like . . ."

"Like what?"

"Like—the girl you met earlier. I am not like her, Jordan."

"You're right. At least she's honest about what she wants. . . ."

"And I am not? Have I not told you what it is I want from you, Jordan?" Her lips thinned into an angry line, and she tugged earnestly at her captured arm. "Let me go. . . ."

"I will—when I'm damn good and ready."

Jolie briefly considered serious struggle, then rejected the idea. He would only overpower her, and who in this town, where she knew no one, would stop him? So she allowed herself to be pulled along, down the wooden sidewalks past closed shops and open, noisy saloons, then into the dusty streets.

He was walking much more swiftly now, almost dragging her as he headed away from the line of buildings. Jolie could see the faint, hazy outline of the mountains on the horizon, the thick sprinkling of stars that seemed to press close to the ground, and the half-moon poised on the tip of a peak. Her breath was coming more quickly, her shoes scuffing up puffs of thick dust and her skirts dragging the ground, and she put up one hand to grab at the pretty bonnet she wore. It eluded her efforts to keep it on her head and fluttered to the ground in a frenzy of satin ribbons.

"Jordan," she began, motioning toward her hat, but he cut her off.

"Shut up."

"But . . ."

He whirled, and his eyes in the dim light of the half moon were narrowed and angry. "You started this, green eyes, so don't think you can back out on me now."

"What do you mean?"

"This," he muttered, flexing his arm and yanking her close to press against his hard chest, his mouth only inches above her half-parted lips. His other arm circled her in a harsh grip, his spread fingers cradling the back of her head and loosing the carefully twisted knot of dark hair, letting it spill down over her shoulders.

In spite of the tiny thrill of fear and anger that tingled along her spine, Jolie felt a strange excitement. It was quiet in the street where they stood, with only the night moths as witness to their embrace, that hard melding of their bodies into a solitary shadow in the dark. Jordan smelled of tobacco, leather, and whiskey, and the dark angles and planes of his face were different somehow, harsher, so that when he finally kissed her, it was as if she were being invaded.

He crushed her to him almost painfully, his belt buckle pressing into her stomach, his mouth demanding and hard. It was an assault on her senses, and she closed her eyes, her hands curling into tight, helpless fists wedged between their bodies. Jolie felt as if she were being drawn into a whirlpool, sucked beneath the waves and carried along on a tide of desire that she couldn't control. There was a strange, unfamiliar fire in the pit of her stomach, curling upward, filling her with a languor she had never experienced before as she melted into his embrace. His mouth was hot and searing, pressing fevered kisses along the smooth arch of her throat, tilting her head back.

Her quivering lips were soft, pliant and untaught as she simply yielded to his caresses, and Jordan drew back slightly, teasing, "Can't you do better than that, green eyes?"

Her candidly honest response was a sharp, "How can I, when I've never done this before?" so that he laughed softly and held her even more tightly.

"Somehow, with your life experiences, I find that hard to swallow," he murmured derisively, capturing her mouth with his once more, muffling her indignant words.

Jolie spared a brief wish that Jordan would not be quite so good at sharpening his tongue on her feelings, seeming to know exactly what to say to goad her into reaction. He was also good at hiding his emotions, another irritating ability. Behind those sky-blue, inscrutable eyes were well-hidden emotions, and she wished she knew what he was thinking.

Then her own thoughts were disrupted as his mouth moved from her lips to the golden hollow in her throat, and she steeled herself against a response. She'd never been so conscious of Jordan's virility, nor her own vulnerability, and she didn't know where to look or what to do. Somehow, she felt a sense of detachment, as if this were happening to someone else and she was just an observer. Their embrace was certainly not as she had often pictured it would be, and she couldn't help a soft sigh.

Jordan felt her lack of response and isolation and lifted his dark head, gazing at her speculatively. He could feel the tenseness in her slim body and the cool indifference of her lips beneath his. Spurred to greater effort, he let his mouth roam from her lips to the softness of her shoulders, bare beneath the scooped neck of her secondhand gown, lingering, tasting and teasing with expert efficiency until she made a soft, sighing sound of surrender and wanting. Jordan smiled against the tiny pulse beating in the hollow of her throat, sensing triumph just ahead. But then Jolie was stiffening, trying to pull away, pushing at him with the flat of her hands as she attempted to avoid his mouth.

Solemnly, her breath coming more quickly now, her sense of detachment abruptly dissolved into resistance. Perhaps it was his pure, animal desire that frightened her; or maybe it was his calm expectance that she would permit any liberties without expectations of her own.

Why was she resisting now, when this sweet, wild surrender was what she'd wanted from the first moment she'd seen him? she wondered vaguely. Perhaps it was because she didn't want an angry Jordan; she wanted a loving Jordan to hold her tenderly, out of love, not anger.

Summoning a strength she hadn't known she possessed, Jolie shoved him violently, tearing her lips from his and jerking away to stare at him with wide green eyes, her chest heaving with her efforts, her mouth bruised and swollen.

"Dah!"

"What do you mean, 'no'?" Jordan mocked, snaring one of her arms with steely fingers. "You said you wanted to 'sit with me', didn't you? Well, I'm ready to sit with you now, Jolie, Gáadu, or whatever you want to call youself. Why back out on me now? You started this, prancing off with Griffin like that, flirting with big, innocent eyes and trying to seduce a kid! Do you think I don't know what you're up to? If you can't have one, you'll have the other, right? Well, I'm not as stupid as you'd like to think. . . .''

She sucked in a furious breath, stormy eyes glaring up at him, and her lips curled in disgust. *"Gúuchi!* You are worse than a pig, Jordan Sinclair! And you are wrong—you are even more stupid than I thought! Griffin is *shich'unné*—my friend—and I should have listened to him!''

Wrenching her arm from his grasp, Jolie took three steps away before he caught her again, whirling her around to face him, his fingers biting into her shoulders.

"You're not walking off. What's the matter, green eyes? Can't you take the truth?''

"Truth? You are not even on speaking terms with the truth! *Duu ñlíída!*" she added furiously.

"And what in the hell does that mean?''

"You are worthless,'' she translated promptly. "Now let me go.''

"And what if I say no? What will you do then?'' He drew her relentlessly forward in spite of her struggles, capturing her in an iron embrace and laughing at her futile efforts to free herself. "See? I have you, Jolie La Fleur, and there's nothing you can do.''

Bending slightly, Jordan lifted her as easily as if she were a sack of feathers, and flung her over his shoulder. The movement drove the breath from her lungs in a loud poof of air that required several moments of recovery. Jordan was stalking down the street with long, determined strides, but she had no idea where he was headed. All she could see from her upside-down position were their faint, distorted shadows wavering in the road. This final indignity was too much, and she beat on his back with her fists, kicking her legs and shrieking at him in French, Spanish, and Apache until he smacked her on the bottom with the flat of his hand, shocking her into silence.

"Be quiet. There will be plenty of time later for screaming at me, green eyes."

Almost sobbing with sheer rage and humiliation, Jolie subsided into indistinct mutters and threats, bobbing like a cork over Jordan's shoulder. Her head began to ache and her legs were entangled in her long skirts, and she felt utterly ridiculous dangling several feet above the ground. Then the ground changed from dusty street to wooden sidewalk again, and Jordan's boots thudded dully against the planks as he walked with a steady, measured tread. She could hear music and laughter and the clink of glasses, and bright swatches of light spilled across the walkway in uneven patches.

"Where are we going?" she dared to ask, trying to lift her head, but he ignored her. It was only when they arrived that she realized he had taken her to a hotel of sorts, with separate rooms and long, musty hallways. A man's voice growled an inquiry that Jordan answered, then there was the sound of a slamming door. For a brief moment Jolie was airborne, then she came to a sudden, stomach-churning rest in the middle of a huge feather mattress. She bounced once, then twice, pushing herself to a sitting position. She had a brief impression of gold-veined mirrors and a lacquered dressing screen in one corner, a small table and two or three curved-back chairs, and a cut-glass lamp burning on a wide chest of drawers.

"Comfortable?" Jordan mocked, grinning down at her, his thumbs hooked in his belt. He rocked back on his heels, waiting for the inevitable explosion, cocking a dark brow at the disheveled, tumble-haired girl sprawled on the paisley-patterned bedspread with her skirts flung up to her knees.

"You're drunk!" Jolie accused breathlessly, pushing at the snarls of ebony hair in her eyes and glaring up at him.

"You bet. So?"

Jolie scooted to the edge of the bed, pushing at the hem of her skirts with one hand and propelling herself forward with the other. "*Nadistsaa,*" she muttered, flinging Jordan a dark look when he grabbed her arm.

His eyes were cold and narrowed. "What does that mean?"

"I am going home." Pausing, she held his gaze, adding, "I no longer wish to stay with you, Jordan."

"Why not? Don't you want to 'sit with me' anymore?"

Jolie shook her head, strands of sable hair whipping across her face. "*Dah.* Not like this!" She pushed at him when he tightened his grip on her arm, one hand arcing toward his face in a wide swing that he caught easily. "I wish I had a knife!" she spat then, raging at him, kicking at his shins with her feet. She was furious, twisting and turning in his grasp like a trapped wildcat, biting and snarling at Jordan with the strength of all her pent-up emotions and wounded pride.

Pushing her back as easily as he would a small child, Jordan pinned her to the mattress with one hand gripping both her wrists over her head, a long, lean leg thrown across her twisting body to hold her down.

"Going somewhere?" he mocked, infuriating her even more. Jolie bucked and heaved in an effort to throw him off, but it was useless. He was too heavy and muscular, and she could not budge him.

"I should kill you for this!" she managed to say in between gasps for breath. Jordan only laughed, reaching out with his other hand to trace a path along her cheek and the line of her jaw.

"Really?" he drawled. "And how would you do that, little one?" His fingers tangled in the bodice of her gown and he jerked with a quick motion, ripping it down the front.

Jolie could not help a cry of dismay though she didn't want to give him the satisfaction. She clenched her teeth as he palmed her breast, glaring up at him and wondering why she had ever thought he would be gentle and loving. Then she retreated into the blank stoicism of the Apache, withdrawn and remote, refusing to react as Jordan explored the lacy confines of her undergarment called a chemise.

The chemise went the way of the green dress, pulled down to her waist firmly but more gently, leaving her bare.

White women wore such silly, restricting things, she thought distractedly, gritting her teeth when Jordan brushed his mouth across the dusky swell of a breast. Long lashes lowered to hide the smoky gleam in his eyes, but she could not conceal the slight quiver of her mouth at his touch. Forbidden fires began to burn in the pit of her belly, coiling upward like a rattlesnake, spreading sweet heat through her. *So this is what it's like,* she thought vaguely. Then Jolie steeled herself against the touch of his hand on her breast, against his mouth moving from the golden hollow in her throat up to her ear. She recalled his every angry, mocking word as armor against him, but it was useless. Helpless, feminine tears rolled down her cheeks.

Jordan tasted the salt of the tears on her cheek and lifted his head to gaze into her face. The sight of Jolie's pathetic attempt to hide her feelings sobered him as nothing else could have done. Propping himself on one elbow, Jordan released her wrists and gathered her into his embrace, holding her loosely.

"Ah, Jolie," he muttered, "I shouldn't have . . . I'm sorry. Here." Digging into his shirt pocket, Jordan pulled out a handkerchief and held it out, gently wiping her face when she made no move to take it. "I don't know what made me treat you this way. Hell, you're only a kid. . . ."

"No, I'm not!" she said then, fiercely, her eyes snapping open to glare up at him. "I am a woman, Jordan Sinclair! I am a full-grown woman who will know how to please my man. . . ."

To his surprise, Jolie flung her arms around his neck, pulling his face to hers, her lips clinging to his mouth and forcing a response. After the briefest of hesitations, Jordan was kissing her back, hungrily, holding her tightly against him.

The small fire Jordan had ignited a few moments before flared into a raging inferno as she kissed him, knowing instinctively how to touch her tongue lightly to his, teasing and withdrawing. She fenced as expertly as if he were not the first man she had kissed but the hundredth.

"Hey—Jolie," Jordan muttered when her deft fingers began to unbutton his shirt and slide inside to caress him, pushing aside the thin cotton material. He caught at her hand, wondering what game she was playing with him now. "I told you earlier about games, remember? I'm not in the mood to play polite gentleman," he warned roughly, "so if you know what's good for you, you'll get out of here right now. Because if you stay here, Jolie La Fleur, I'm going to forget all my good intentions of a few minutes ago and make love to you. Now go. . . ."

But she couldn't. Not when he was jerking her so close and kissing her again, his mouth hot and insistent, his hands caressing the warm flesh trembling beneath his touch.

Soft lights from the lamps on a table against the far wall flickered briefly, the rosy pools of light highlighting Jordan's hair as he bent over her, and Jolie closed her eyes. She was trembling all over even though she wanted to stay, frightened yet anticipating.

Then Jordan was kneeling on the bed, his weight sagging the mattress, his hands removing the ruined remnants of her dress, pulling it over her head. Jolie didn't help him. She lay quietly while he peeled the gown away and removed her chemise, the long white pantalettes, and the hot, annoying stockings and shoes.

"What? No petticoats?" he drawled, sitting back on his heels to stare hungrily at her sweetly formed body. His gaze lingered on the swell of her hips, tiny waist, and small, firm breasts before returning to her face.

She shrugged. "No. I ran out of money and patience for the silly things white women wear. I would prefer dressing as you do, Jordan, in pants and a shirt."

When he laughed, she pushed impatiently at his shirt, baring his wide chest furred with tiny swirls of dark hair. Reaching up, Jolie's fingers skimmed lightly over him, watching in fascination as his hair curled around her fingertips. Then her hands dropped to his gunbelt and fumbled with the buckle, her gaze returning to watch his face. Boldly yet delicately Jolie began to undress Jordan, sitting up and investigating him with hands and eyes and mouth as she pulled off his shirt and unfastened the buttons of his dark cord trousers, touching and tasting with a naive curiosity that amused him.

Jordan groaned when her tongue explored the shadowed region of his navel, flicking as lightly as the tongue of an adder. His eyes closed, opening only when she had removed his gunbelt.

"I'll take that," he said, cradling the holster and Colt .45 in his palm. He laid it gently on the table beside the bed, just within reach, leaning over Jolie.

"Do you expect trouble?" she asked curiously, circling his lean waist with both arms as he leaned over her.

"Always expect the unexpected," Jordan returned. One hand rested briefly on the top of her head as he reflected on the fact that Jolie was the most unexpected treasure and trouble he had ever found.

Jolie smiled against the hard band of muscles on his abdomen as if she knew what he was thinking. She twisted to a sitting position, and her fingers dipped into the waistband of his trousers to caress him. Then she paused, rocking back on her heels. Firmly but gently she pushed him back on the mattress until he was stretched out, his feet hanging off the end of the bed.

"Need any help?" he asked when she moved to tug at his dusty boots, but she shook her head, preferring to do it herself.

"*Dah.* I can do it." Both boots clunked to the threadbare carpet of the floor. "I like your body," she announced when his pants lay in a heap next to his boots and shirt. Perched on the edge of the bed, she gazed at him with a satisfied expression. "You are hard and lean, not soft like a woman."

"Well, I should hope so," he murmured dryly, reaching out to pull her close. "Are you through looking now, Jolie? Let's move on to touching. . . ."

"Do you mean like this?" she asked with a hint of mischief, quickly reaching down to run her fingers across the hard, flat planes of his belly and lower. He sucked in his breath and nodded.

"You bet—just like that."

Jolie smiled, her voice a husky whisper. "I like it, too."

Moving with startling speed, Jordan levered his body across hers, pushing her into the mattress again, his chest hairs tickling her bare breasts. Both hands grasped her wrists and held them out to the sides, his fingers meshing with hers while his mouth moved from her ear to her half-parted lips. Jolie could feel the heated length of him against her, his hard thighs against her legs, and another, umfamiliar, pressure against her belly.

"Do you like this?" he muttered in her ear, moving even closer. One knee slid between her thighs, gently yet firmly, nudging them apart, and his mouth moved from her ear to the wildly throbbing pulse in her throat. Jolie could only nod wordlessly as he found the peak of one breast, his tongue flicking against it with quick, rapid motions that left her breathless.

Jordan's hands moved to fondle her breasts, his fingers cupping the small, ripe swells possessively, teasing before his dark head lowered again, covering a rosy crest with his lips, sending lightning sparks racing through her body. When his teeth gently nibbled, Jolie moaned softly, writhing beneath him, her head thrashing back and forth in a silken ebony tangle. Jordan's hand moved between her legs, his fingers searching and finding, and she cried out in protest, her eyes snapping open to stare up into his blue gaze.

"It's all right, love," he said, covering her mouth with his, kissing her until she could only whimper, her back arching and heels digging into the print bedspread. He left her weak with wanting, needing him but uncertain how, and Jolie sobbed aloud.

While his fingers worked their magic, Jordan trailed a path of fiery kisses from her lips to her stomach, his tongue swirling, exploring the ridges of her ribs, then probing her navel. When he moved lower, to that silky ridge, Jolie gasped in shock and tangled her fingers in his hair.

"*Sacré bleu!* Jor-dan! What . . . what are you doing?"

"I was just . . . ah, never mind, love," he muttered,

catching himself. His body slid slowly back up over hers, belly to belly, chest to breast, and his breath tickled the damp tendrils of her hair at each temple as he murmured in her ear, "Maybe later . . ."

Feeling the hard strength of his body molded to hers, Jolie was suddenly impatient, tired of the waiting.

"Jor-dan," she moaned against his shoulder, "I've waited so long. . . ."

He understood what she meant and needed. "All right, love. Let's solve the mystery, then."

Poised above her, his knees between her golden thighs, Jordan moved slowly, inexorably, forward, cradling her in his arms. Jolie trembled, her arms around him as he kissed her, his mouth lingering on her lips. When he thrust forward with a sudden, knifelike plunge, she stiffened, heaving upward. It was so unexpected that she was shocked, her short scream muffled against his mouth.

She pushed at him frantically when he did not withdraw, but he ignored her, finally grabbing her wrists and holding them in a firm grip over her head. Jolie was panting like a wounded animal, her eyes wide and accusing as she stared up at him.

"It won't hurt again, love, I promise," he said in her ear, not moving, but remaining imbedded within her. "Lie still now. . . ."

"I can't. . . ."

"Yes, you can." He released his grip on her wrists, his fingers moving to tangle in her hair, holding her thrashing head still, then he began moving very slowly inside her again. Jolie discovered that he was right. There was no more pain. Jordan's body moved faster and faster against her in a primitive, driving motion that she tried to match. Instinctively, she curled her legs around him, her hands skimming over the smooth skin of his back, feeling his muscles flex beneath her fingers.

Closing her eyes, Jolie could feel his hot breath against his neck, hear his harsh breathing; then there was a wildly churning excitement in her, building up, curling from her belly and spreading to her loins. She was poised on the brink, waiting, then a wild rush flowed through her in a hot tide that left her weak and crying out. Groaning, Jordan slammed against her deeply, fiercely, his entire body tense, then he was still.

Jolie lay limp and exhausted beneath him, holding him in her arms. She could feel the steady pounding of his heart against her breast and reveled in their closeness. A smile curved her passion-bruised lips. Now Jordan was hers.

Chapter
12

Amos propped his booted feet upon the scarred wooden table in Pete McCall's saloon, only half-listening to the drunken rambling of a weathered prospector. The old man and his partner, a moon-faced young man who didn't seem quite right in the head, had spent the better part of the evening depleting Pete's stock of whiskey and were now sprawled in their chairs.

"Lissen," the old man slurred, pausing to belch loudly, "I kin tell ya' 'bout gold minin'! Why, I done been and seed things that most men never see in a lifetime!"

"Is that right?" Amos said politely, his mind only half on the old man. Ever since Griffin had found him in the stable and reported that his uncle had disappeared with Jolie, he had been worried about them. He felt partly responsible for the girl. Even for an Apache, or half-Apache, she seemed naive in certain matters that women of his acquaintance were well-versed in, and he didn't like the way she had been so taken with Jordan. It was only a matter of time, he supposed, until Sinclair either got mad enough to run her off completely, or took advantage of her obvious attraction to him.

Amos sipped at his drink, nodding distractedly at the old miner beside him, his thoughts lingering on Jordan and Jolie. Perhaps it would have been better if they had returned her to her camp immediately, but what was done was done. And, from what Griffin had related a few hours before, it was too late for any second thoughts now. And that was another thing—Griffin was too caught up with the girl. Maybe she appealed to his protective instincts, but it could only cause trouble between him and Jordan.

"... An' thar it wuz," the grizzled miner was drawling in drunken tones, "piles of it! I ain' never seed such gold a'fore! Why, if'n I could find it a'gin . . ."

His attention snared at last, Amos leaned forward. "What are you talking about, old man?"

"Gold, boy, gold!" Wiping at his unshaven chin with fingers that were dirt-stained and gnarled, the old man cackled. "I seed more gold than thar should be in the world!"

Careful to keep his tone calm and detached, Amos shrugged carelessly and said, "You're dreaming, old man."

Bristling, the miner retorted, "Hell no, I ain't! I seed it, I tell ya, didn't I, Charlie? He turned to his bleary-eyed companion and poked him in the ribs with a stubby forefinger. "Didn't we see gold?"

"'At's right, Sam." Bobbing his head in their general direction, Charlie seemed to be struggling for control of his head, then obviously gave up. He sighed softly, gave a helpless shrug, then slid gracefully from his chair into a heap on the dirty saloon floor, his eyes closed and mouth creased in a peaceful smile. Sam stared down at him for a moment with a thoughtful expression, then reached to tug Charlie's hat from under his head and place it over his face before he turned back to Amos.

"See?" he said. "I tole ya..."

"Well, if you really saw gold, where was it?" Amos asked.

"Hah! Ya think I'd tell? I ain' as crazy as I look, boy, no I ain'!" Sam wheezed loudly, and Amos was faintly surprised that the air in front of the old man didn't turn blue from the liquor fumes.

Nodding sagely, Amos agreed, adding, "Let me buy you another drink, Sam."

An hour later Sam was sleeping peacefully, with his head resting upon the table. Rising from his chair, Amos gave him a pat on the shoulder, then tilted back his head and downed the last inch left in the entire bottle of rye that he had bought for Sam. The empty bottle was clunked to the table top, and Amos stretched, loosening muscles cramped from long hours of sitting. It had been worth it, he decided with a smile, tugging his hat over his eyes and lifting the rifle he always carried with him.

As Amos made his way through the crowded saloon toward the swinging front doors, he reflected that it had been very worth his efforts and the long hours indeed. Now, to find Jordan and Griffin and share his news....

It was still dark when Jolie woke, snuggling close to Jordan, one arm across his chest. The lamp had burned low, with only a faint glimmer left to light the room. Shadows blanketed them, but she could still see Jordan's handsome profile, his thin, straight nose and the chiseled lips that had awakened such torrents of passion in her. Content, Jolie marveled at the flood of emotions he had released. Was it possible to feel such a strong emotion and emerge whole?

She sighed, her breath whispering across his chest and stirring tiny curls of hair. Unable to restrain herself, Jolie began to explore the hard ridges of his body. The pads of her fingers skimmed the pelt of chest hair and tested bronze muscles lightly, examining the hollow beneath his ribs and the taut, flat muscles of his belly. Jordan moved restlessly, still asleep, arms flung over his head.

"Jordan?" Her lips teased the vulnerable spot between his neck and shoulder. "Are you awake?" Edging even closer, Jolie laid one thigh across his legs.

Jordan opened one eye. "No." The eye closed, long lashes shadowing his cheek. Smiling now, Jolie began to nibble on his earlobe, her curious tongue occasionally darting into his ear in light exploration. Results were slow but satisfactory.

"Don't you ever sleep?" he grumbled, flexing his arms to pull her atop him. Jordan's mouth sought and found her lips, then her throat, before moving to the impudent swell of a breast. Arching her back, Jolie tangled her fingers in his thick mane of hair, pressing forward, her long legs straddling him. Jordan took her then, sweetly and fiercely, taking his time until she was crying his name aloud.

Panting from their exertions, the lovers lay entwined, forgetting the outside world for a time. Jordan gently stroked her damp hair back from her face, then traced the ripe outline of her mouth with his thumb, dragging it across her lower lip in a sweet caress.

Finally easing from atop him, Jolie lay on her side facing him, a contented smile curving under the pressure of his thumb.

"For once you aren't all questions," he teased, grinning at her.

"No, Jordan. I am your woman now," she said seriously. "Isn't that true?"

He held her close. "Yes, Jolie. You are a woman now," he answered.

"*Dah* . . . I am *your* woman now," she corrected, pulling away slightly to look into his eyes. "I belong to you."

Jordan began to wish he had not drunk quite so much rye so that he could understand the fine distinction she seemed to be making, but giving in to the gentle haze in his brain that demanded he either agree or sleep, he nodded. "Yes, love. You belong to me," he murmured, pulling her close again. "Now let's sleep a little more."

It was well past noon when a pounding on the door of their room jerked Jolie and Jordan from an exhausted sleep. They had awakened several times to re-explore one another's bodies, then fallen back asleep, and this intrusion in their privacy was very unwelcome.

"Who the hell is it?" Jordan shouted irritably while Jolie pulled the paisley-patterned bedspread over her naked body. Swinging his long legs over the side of the bed, he grabbed his pants and stalked to the door when he heard Griffin's voice. "What do you want?" Jordan muttered, holding up his unbuttoned pants with one hand and opening the door a crack with the other.

"Don't worry—I'm not on the town morals committee," Griffin flashed back from the hallway, "and I don't want to come in. You and Jolie meet us in the lobby of the Fairmont in a half hour. Amos has something he wants to tell you over lunch—or breakfast, as the case may be."

"Like what?"

"If you really want to know, be there," was all Griffin would say. The sound of his bootsteps faded away as he turned and left, and Jordan shut the door.

Jolie's voice came to him softly from the mound of bedspread, tawny skin, and ebony hair. "Jor-dan? Griffin is angry with us, yes?"

Shortly, "Yes."

"Why?"

"Oh hell, Jolie! Why do you think? He's used to getting his own way, that's why, and he . . . forget it," he ended abruptly. "It doesn't matter anyway. He's only a kid."

"But he's my friend," Jolie said quietly, "and I don't want him to be upset with either one of us."

"Too bad, then, 'cause he is. He'll get over it." Jordan shrugged into his shirt and picked up his boots and gunbelt. "I'm going downstairs to get a bath. Meet me in the lobby of the Fairmont Hotel in a half hour, like Amos wants. We'll find out what he's got on his mind."

A little startled by Jordan's coolness, Jolie just nodded stiffly, her eyes never leaving his face. Almost as an afterthought, Jordan paused, turned, and returned to the bed, grasping her chin in the palm of one hand and bending to kiss her hard on the mouth. The kiss left her breathless and Jordan breathing more rapidly.

He seemed about to say something then caught himself, muttering, "Don't leave town," before he straightened and strode from the room without looking back again.

Jolie sat in thoughtful silence, staring at the closed door. Things had changed between Jordan and herself, and it wasn't quite as she had pictured. Where was the closeness she had expected? Ah, perhaps she was expecting too much too quickly, she admonished herself. After all, it had been only a few hours.

Swinging her legs over the side of the bed, Jolie stood up and stretched lazily. She wasn't sure where the Fairmont Hotel was, or even where she was at this moment. Jordan should have given her directions, but since he hadn't, she would need to hurry.

The green dress lay in a torn heap on the floor, and when

she lifted it to gaze critically at the rips, Jolie heaved a soft sigh. It could be repaired if she had a needle and thread, but she did not, so she considered for several moments before she hit upon the idea of using the ribbon trim to tie the bodice where Jordan had torn it. Time flew as Jolie worked on her dress, so that she had only a few minutes left to wash, dress, and find her way to the Fairmont. Shrugging fatalistically, she decided they would just have to wait on her. It could not be helped, so there was no sense in worrying.

By the time she had dressed, clubbed her long hair into a fairly neat bun on the back of her neck, and descended a short flight of stairs that she didn't remember from the night before, Jolie was not only late, she was starving. Hunger pains rumbled in her stomach with a noise that was embarrassingly loud. Pressing the flat of her hands to her stomach as if to stifle the noises, she asked directions to the Fairmont from a rough-looking man lounging in an open doorway.

Surveying her for a moment, his gaze lingering on the clumsily tied bodice that revealed almost as much as it hid, he replied shortly, "Down the street three blocks, turn right, it's on the next corner."

"*Merci*," Jolie replied, backing away from the heated gaze trained upon her bodice. Were the ribbons untied? She dared a glance down and winced at the sight of an inch of bare flesh peeking from between the gaping edges of her bodice. Drawing the edges together with as much dignity as possible, she retreated out the front door, across the wooden sidewalk, and into the dusty street.

Dodging wagons and horses and pedestrians, she crossed the street and walked the three blocks to the Fairmont Hotel with her fingers tangled in the ribbons of her dress. It looked rather odd to be clutching herself, but that was better than having strangers gawking at her bosom.

The lobby was not crowded at all when Jolie arrived. In fact, it was deserted except for Griffin, Amos, and Jordan, who sat watching the front door as if waiting for the arrival of a bevy of millionaires. Three faces lightened considerably when she stepped into the lobby, brushing dust from her face and neck with the backs of her fingers.

Griffin was the first to reach her. "We're sittin' over here, Jolie. Where have you been? I was beginning to think you'd gotten lost—or was hurt." This last was directed at Jordan, who ignored his nephew and Jolie.

Amos smiled at her, politely rising from his chair as Griffin seated her, an act that startled Jolie into wondering if she had changed that much during the past twelve hours. Did feminine clothing always bring out this reaction in men? Perhaps it would be worth the discomfort to continue wearing it. Slanting Amos a skeptical glance, she took her seat without a word and folded her hands in her lap, forgetting all about her torn dress.

Jordan's voice was tight and gruff as he demanded, "Why didn't you repair your dress? Or do you like showing bare skin to the world?"

Jolie flushed and grabbed the frayed edges of the pretty green dress. Thin satin ribbons slithered between her fingers as she met Jordan's cold stare. "I could not find needle and thread, and you said a half hour, so I did the best I could."

"You did a great job, Jolie," Griffin put in. "Here. Let me help you out a little. I happen to have some pins."

"How convenient!" Jordan snapped, lifting a dark brow at his nephew. "And how did that come about?"

"I've got a great imagination," the youth answered

imperturbably. "I kinda figured out what might happen if the fox was left alone with the chicken . . ."

"You've got a pretty smart mouth for a kid . . ."

"I'm pretty smart, period." Griffin pulled out a paper of pins and held them out to Jolie, instructing her how to repair her torn dress in a calm tone as Jordan glowered. It took only a moment until the dress was much more modest.

" *'Ixéhe,'* " Jolie said politely, tucking her chin into her neck to peer down at the dress.

"You're welcome," Griffin answered as if he'd understood her perfectly, earning a sharp glance from his uncle.

"Are we all through with our sewing lessons? Good. All right, Amos," Jordan said, leaning back in his chair, "let's hear what you've got to say. All this mystery has me kind of intrigued."

Jolie's gaze shifted from Jordan's handsome face to Amos's as he shrugged and said, "Not much mystery, Sinclair, just a few facts I picked up last night. Thought they might interest all of us." Emphasis was placed on the word "all," as if one of them might disagree, and Amos continued, "I got restless last night and decided to have a few drinks at the bar where I met you, Jordan. While I was there, a couple of crusty old prospectors wandered in and ended up sitting down with me. Probably because I was the only man there who'd let them," he added with a wry smile, "but anyway, Sam and Charlie had a recent find kinda like ours. I found out something else, too." He leaned forward, clasping his hands and staring at each of them in turn, his gaze intent, his tone serious. "There's another cave in a sister peak like the one we just re-found—and there's an underground tunnel leading from one to the other . . ."

"Bull!" Jordan said mildly. "The closest peak around is a mile away."

"So?" Amos levelled a steady gaze at his partner. "You ain't never seen a tunnel a mile long?"

"Of course . . ."

"Then what's so unusual about an underground tunnel? Hell, Sinclair, I've seen caves that run for miles under the ground!"

"So have I, but don't you think it would be too much of a coincidence for two caves filled with gold to connect? If that was the truth, then somebody would have found the gold long before this, Weatherby!" Jordan sat back in his chair and swept the group with an irritated glance. "It just sounds too farfetched for me."

"I say we take a vote," Griffin put in calmly. "Ain't that what we agreed on when we first started out—to do this democratically?"

Jordan grunted in exasperation. "What do you know about democracy, kid? You're still wet behind the ears . . ."

Griffin's eyes narrowed. "I may be, but I'm dry enough to know right from wrong, *Uncle* Jordan."

"And what's that supposed to mean?"

"I think you know damn good and well what it means! Some people may be too innocent and naive to know what's good for 'em, but as young as I may be, I can still see what's happening. . . ."

"Whoa," Amos interrupted, bringing the flat of his hand down on the table top and startling all of them. "This is getting away from the subject, and too damned personal. Whatever beef you two got between you shouldn't interfere with business. Right? Now, let's get back to the gold before we all end up madder than a bee-stung bear."

Griffin subsided sullenly, while Jordan glowered in silence. Jolie, sensing that their argument was about her, remained discreetly silent for a change. The gold meant little to her. Griffin's friendship meant a lot, while Jordan meant the most.

"Did he have proof of the tunnel and gold?" Jordan wanted to know, directing his attention to Amos.

"I didn't see any, but he had enough description that I know he was there. The old man, drunk as he was, was fairly crafty, and his partner passed out early." Amos grinned. "I helped the old man on his way, and he was sleeping peacefully the last I saw of him."

"So how many gold deposits do you think there are?" Griffin asked. "It sounds like Jolie's French padre had enough energy to leave piles of gold in every crevice he ran across."

"Almost. If we looked real hard, we'd probably find bits of gold in fifty different places, but I think there's only three main deposits. Now, what we have to do is go prepared to get all we can in one big haul. Once word leaks out that we've struck gold, every prospector, carpetbagger, and bandit in three territories will be after our asses. What do you say? You guys—and lady—game to try for it?"

Jolie was conscious of the sun streaming through the thick leaded window panes, warming the back of her neck and lighting the table, tiny dust motes swimming in the beams as if fish in water. She concentrated upon the light and the backs of her hands, frowning. To search for the gold meant that she would be with Jordan, but it violated the beliefs of her mother's people. Not that she adhered to all the Apache customs, but it was never wise to flagrantly ignore them.

There was a loud rumble in the vicinity of her stomach again, and Jordan's head jerked around to look at her.

Jolie's direct gaze rested upon his inquiring face. "I have not eaten," she explained unnecessarily. It did not embarrass her that her stomach rumbled, but it was inconvenient that everyone at the table should be informed of Jordan's lack of hospitality in providing her with food. It was a serious breach of etiquette.

"Let's vote and eat," Griffin said promptly. "I'm hungry, too." His warm gaze rested kindly upon Jolie, as if to assure her he would see to her needs.

"Eatin' again?" Amos asked. "Hell, boy! How much more can you eat after all those eggs and . . . ouch!" Amos flinched, stared reproachfully at Griffin, and bent to rub at his shin as the boy explained that he hadn't been able to eat all of his breakfast and was hungry again, and he voted yes to get the gold, so could they get on with it?

"Uncle Jordan? Jolie? What are your votes?" Griffin asked.

After a moment's deliberation, Jordan mutttered, "Aw, what the hell! We can't lose anything but time, I guess. And it sure beats digging in hard dirt and rocks. Yeah, I'm for trying that other peak. We might get lucky, after all."

"*Oui*," Jolie said promptly when Griffin's gaze moved to her. "I will go with you."

"Not this time, green eyes," Jordan said before Griffin could speak. "It's too dangerous. You might get hurt. Don't look at me like that," he added when her gaze frosted with an expression of hurt and shock. "I'll be back when we find it, and I'll leave you enough money to stay here until I do."

"I'm a partner," Jolie said quietly. She tossed back her head and leaned forward, small hands clenching into fists on the table top. "You made me a partner, remember? And this partner wishes to go with you."

"Now Jolie, be reasonable . . ."

"I'm being reasonable, and I'm going with you," she said stubbornly. Her eyes didn't move from his face. They rested, great green orbs shining like bits of bottle glass, seeming to pierce his mind and soul with unspoken reproach.

Giving an exasperated shrug, Jordan muttered, "Suit yourself."

Chapter
13

Jolie did suit herself. She trailed along with Griffin from store to hostler, buying supplies and animals equipped to carry heavy loads. It would be a much better prepared convoy that left Franklin for the San Andres mountain range this time.

"Have you ever heard about this other cache of gold, Jolie?" Griffin asked her while they were waiting on Mr. Barlow, the owner of a store filled with dusty shelves and black iron pots, pans, skillets, and cooking implements.

"*'Au*," she nodded. "But I forgot about it. The stories were told so long ago, and I wasn't really interested at the time. I was thinking of . . . other things."

Griffin grinned. "Like a certain young man, perhaps?" he teased.

Jolie shook her head. "*Dah*! Jordan has been the only man who turns my thoughts his way. There has been no other. I waited—like Lozen—and now I have found him."

"Your Gray Ghost," Griffin muttered. "Yeah, I remember you tellin' me about that legend a while back. Look, Jolie, have you ever considered the fact that you're not

Lozen and Jordan may not be your Gray Ghost? I know you're all caught up in this romantic fairytale, but look how Lozen's romance turned out. Did you ever think that maybe your fairy tale may not end with 'happily ever after'?''

Concentrating on a picture she was drawing with the tip of her finger in the thick dust on the countertop, Jolie chose to ignore Griffin. Her eyes narrowed at the faint outline of sketched mountains, her fingernail scratching out a huge round sun and a wisp of clouds over the peaks. She seemed totally absorbed in her dust art.

"Jolie, I hate to be the one to tell you this, but Jordan has never been one to hang around a woman long. He's always had a way of treating women!" Griffin snapped.

"I don't understand . . ."

Shrugging, half-wishing he hadn't begun this futile conversation, Griffin explained, "Let me put it to you pretty plain, Jolie: Jordan's philosophy about women is find 'em; fool 'em; and forget 'em. Now do you understand? He'll do the same to you. Your Gray Ghost has a heart of stone, not gold, Jolie."

"Not with me. Anyway, gold is a stone, is it not?"

"Okay, Jolie. Have it your way. Don't listen. But I don't want to be around when you find out life ain't half as romantic as you seem to think. . . ."

The edge of Jolie's palm swept away the countertop mountains in a broad sweep as she turned to Griffin. "Do you think I do not know about the realities of life, Griffin? Do you think I have never seen death or known hunger? *You* are the one who does not know! You have never been run from your home by howling, butchering soldiers, nor have you seen your mother die in your arms because of cholera-infected blankets given to us by white soldiers! And you have not heard the thin cry of babies in the night, needing a mother who will never come to them again. . . ."

Catching her breath, Jolie struggled for composure, her lips quivering with the effort. Griffin reached out to touch her on the shoulder, shaking his golden head.

"No, Jolie, I have not seen those things. Maybe my life hasn't been as . . . precarious . . . as yours, but I can still worry about you, can't I?"

Immediately forgiving him and flinging her arms around him, Jolie said into the thin material of his shirt, "I am worse than the coyote, Griffin. I did not mean to shout at you or say those things. I know you like me and only want to shelter me from being hurt, but Jordan would not hurt me. I do not know why you think he would, but we are one now." She pulled back and gazed earnestly into Griffin's doubtful blue eyes. "I am his woman now," she said softly.

"Yes, Jolie, I know. . . ."

"Then you know that he would not hurt me."

"I wish I was as sure of that as you seem to be," Griffin muttered tightly. "Look, here comes old Barlow with our stuff. We'll talk about this again later. There's a few more facts of life I think you ought to know."

The storekeeper's derisive snort caught Griffin's immediate attention. Placing the paper-wrapped bundles on the countertop, Barlow sneered, "Injun squaws know a lot more about the facts of life than you seem ta think, boy! Why, I bet this purty li'l squaw could teach you things you ain' never dreamed of!"

Griffin's ice-blue eyes flashed dangerously, but the storekeeper was looking at Jolie instead of the seemingly callow youth beside her, licking his thick lips and grinning in a way she didn't like. She took a step backward, away from the counter and Barlow, recognizing that feral gleam in his watery eyes.

"Tell you what, boy," the man said, still looking at Jolie, "I'll give you a dollar while I take your brown-skinned li'l gal in the back room for a romp, an' you keep a sharp eye out for..."

That was as far as he got before Griffin's hand had magically sprouted a lethal Colt that was nudging Barlow's chin with the cold barrel.

"I think I've heard enough," Griffin said softly, and the barrel jabbed viciously against Barlow's throat. "You owe the lady an apology..."

"What?" Barlow's voice was a frightened screech. "Apologize to a dirty Injun squaw? That ain't natcheral..."

"Neither is living with a bullet in your craw," Griffin snarled. "Now do you want to apologize?"

"Griffin, no!" Jolie urged, tugging at his arm. "It doesn't matter—let's go."

"Not until he apologizes," the boy answered, shaking free of her hand. "And what do you mean it doesn't matter? He insulted you, Jolie."

"I've heard them all before," she said. "Do you think this pig is the first man to ever say or think those things? He's only one of many, Griffin. Now please—let's leave before someone comes in."

Slowly relaxing his tensed muscles, Griffin lowered the barrel of the Colt, and Barlow drew in a long, deep breath. "She's got more sense than you do, boy," the storekeeper said, hiding his shaking hands behind the counter. "No one 'round here's gonna take up fer an Injun or a squaw-man. In fact, you might find yerself mighty unpopular..."

"If the rest of the citizens are like you, I'd consider that a compliment," Griffin returned coolly, scooping the packages from the countertop. His Colt was still cradled in his palm as if he expected trouble, and with Jolie behind him, he backed from the General Store and out into the hot, dusty street.

They walked back to the stable in a silence that was as heavy and oppressive as the heat pressing down on them. For the first time, Griffin noticed the sidelong glances flung toward them as unfriendly and hostile, regarding Jolie more as a hated savage than simply as a pretty woman. She walked proudly, looking neither to the right nor to the left but straight ahead, ignoring the looks she received with a calmness that he could not help but admire.

"Has it always been like this, Jolie?" he asked when they neared the stable at last. "Don't you hate it when people do that?"

"'*Au*," she answered sadly, "but it is the way it is, Griffin. I cannot change it. And not everyone feels the way Barlow feels." She smiled suddenly, which had the effect of sunlight breaking through a mask of clouds, and said, "The Apache feel the same way about the '*indaa*', you know! White men are stupid and rude, and do not have good manners. . . ."

Griffin laughed, juggling the packages in his arms. "I guess people have their prejudices no matter what race they are, huh, Jolie? Maybe you can tell me what else the Apache think about us rude white men sometime. . . ."

But the opportunity didn't come again for a while. There was too much to do, and all four of them were kept busy preparing for their trek into fame and fortune. It took several days to gather all their supplies, as they were being as discreet as possible.

"Don't need nobody guessin' what we're up to," Amos observed sagely. "We're gonna have enough troubles tryin' to get through Apache land again without invitin' even more guests along for the ride."

"No kidding," Jordan returned shortly. They were all

sitting in the lobby of the Fairmont Hotel again, grouped around a small round table in the corner. "Buying supplies separately shouldn't alert anybody, even those old miner friends of yours, Amos. What happened to Sam and Charlie anyway?"

Grinning, Amos shook his close-cropped head. "Last time I caught a glimpse of Charlie, he was still at Opal's Crystal Palace, lyin' acrost the lap of one of the biggest women I've ever seen!"

Jolie, leaning her elbow on the tabletop, could hardly keep her attention on the conversation. All she could think about was Jordan, wondering why he continued to treat her just the same as he had before. It had been three days now, and still he had not mentioned their new relationship in more than casual terms. They still had their room in the tiny house on the fringe of the business district, and they still spent the hot, sultry nights together, but other than that, it was as before. Only the nights had changed. Now they spent the dark hours wrapped in tangled sheets and heated air, as close as a man and a woman can be, flesh to flesh, whispers mingling in the night. The hours were sweet, filled with soft sighs and husky breath, gentle caresses and surging passions. Jolie surprised even herself with her responses to Jordan, to the touch of his hands on her breasts, belly, and thighs. And she surprised him with her abandon, with a sweet, wild surrender and tempestuous ardor that took away his breath. But still, there were no words of love, and no promises made.

Sensing Jordan's reticence, Jolie was also reluctant to bring up the subject of the future. Though she'd long ago learned patience, waiting was foreign to her more volatile nature; she waited impatiently, certain Jordan would finally say what she wanted to hear.

Griffin, however, had no illusions about Jordan. He frequently watched his uncle with narrowed eyes, wondering how long it would take before Jolie exploded with her impatience. She reminded him of a bird, swelled up with song and waiting for the first blush of dawn to burst into melody. Griffin smiled grimly at the mental picture and Jordan's possible reaction. Did he even realize the temperament of the girl? Griffin wondered. Or did he just assume that Jolie was like other girls he'd known, accepting and docile and willing to wait? And how long would it take for Jolie to show him the error of his ways? The answer to that question should be very interesting and quite entertaining, Griffin reflected with a grin. And he didn't feel the least bit compelled to tell Jordan what was in store for him. If his uncle could not see that Jolie was different, was not like the other women he'd known, then why should he be the one to explain to him? Let him find out on his own.

So while Jordan and Jolie spent their nights in the small, closed room at the edge of town, Griffin and Amos spent the hours in one saloon after another. While Amos was usually the first one to depart for a bed of hay, Griffin often lingered until the daylight hours, arriving drunk and staggering at the stable loft he shared with Amos.

"I'm gettin' too damned old for this foolishness," Amos grumbled aloud one evening after Griffin had fallen the third time from the ladder leading to the loft. He hauled him up by his belt and the seat of his pants, puffing, "I'm glad we're leavin' town tomorrow, boy. You don't need to be getting so drunk and making such a damned nuisance of yorself."

"I ain' no new...new...what'd you call me?"

"Nuisance."

"Yeah. I ain' no nuisance, Amos. An' I ain' drunk."

Griffin smiled, his angelic face as sweet as a babe's and leaving Amos to shake his head and wonder how such a hell-bent boy could look so innocent.

"You're drunk as a rat at the bottom of a beer barrel, Griffin. Why do you have to go and drink so much?" Amos complained, heaving Griffin's inert body onto a pile of hay in the corner.

Griffin's right hand flopped aimlessly. "Gotta drink to forget," he muttered, his ridiculously long lashes drooping over his eyes, shutting out the sight of Amos's blurred face swimming over him. "Gotta forget..."

"Forget what?" Amos snapped. "What have you got to forget in your young life, boy? Too many sugar tits, maybe?"

Too drunk to take offense at Amos's tone or his words, Griffin just shook his head. Straw bristles stuck in his pale hair, blending with the silky strands as if they belonged. "Naw. Not that. Jo...Jolie...she's too young...too innocent...she don' even know or care what he's doin...." His mumbled words subsided into hiccups.

Sinking into the hay beside him, Amos pondered the young man's words for a few moments as he knelt beside Griffin with one knee in the straw and his forearm resting across his other leg. The situation was sticky, and he wished he hadn't gotten involved and that they hadn't taken the girl, or at the least, kept her, and that Griffin hadn't decided to take her under his wing like a mama eagle with her only egg. Hell, he didn't know how long he could remain neutral, and he certainly didn't want to get in between Jordan and Griffin, no matter how he felt about Jolie.

Amos stuck a wisp of straw between his teeth and chewed vigorously. There was no point in arguing with Griffin now because he'd already passed out, his youthful countenance peaceful and benign as he slept dreamlessly. And there was no point in arguing with Jordan—ever—because he would only point out the inescapable fact that it was none of Amos's business to butt into his relationships with Jolie and Griffin. So Amos rose from the straw and returned to his pile of blankets to try and sleep for the last hour before dawn. Things would sort themselves out eventually, and he could only hope that once they were on the trail all this nonsense would be forgotten in the search for gold.

Jordan was hoping the same thing. He lay beside Jolie with his eyes open, staring blankly at the shadowed ceiling of the room, wondering how much longer he could hold off the inevitable. It was only a matter of time before she began to nag him—as females always seemed to do—and he would have to drag out the glib answers and kind lies as he always had before, and why had he even started this anyway? It had been a moment of weakness when his guard was down, and he'd regretted it almost immediately, but what was done was done. Now he was faced with retribution for getting drunk and taking what was so freely offered. Only—Jolie was different.

That sounded suspiciously like a remark she was supposed to make to him instead of his own observation, but it was uncomfortably true. She *was* different. There was none of the subtle subterfuge practiced by the other women in his life, none of the matter-of-fact performances by the experienced women of the saloons and houses he'd frequented. Jolie was artless, naive, honest.

"Dammit," Jordan swore aloud, rousing Jolie from her light, satisfied slumber.

"Hmmm?" she murmured sleepily, rolling over to face him, one arm sliding across his bare stomach. "*Hiyaa . . .*"

"Which means?" Jordan grumbled. "I wish you'd stick to one language, green eyes..."

"It means that I'm tired." Jolie's fingers drifted across Jordan's chest in light tickles, dark hairs curling around her fingertips as her lips nuzzled his neck. "Are you tired?" she whispered suggestively, trailing her fingers across the flat, muscular plane of his belly and lower.

"'*Au, hiyaa,*'" he answered, startling her with his knowledge of Apache words. "Did you think I couldn't remember a few simple words?" He grinned down into the wide eyes looking up at him. "I *can* listen—maybe even as good as you can."

The dim moonlight filtering in through the slatted wooden shutters over the double windows illuminated Jolie's face in hazy streamers, striping her with light and dark lines. All Jordan could see were her eyes and the smiling curve of her mouth outlined in the bars of moonlight.

"You look like a zebra," he commented idly, reaching out to flick back a lazy curl of hair that had drifted into her eyes.

"What is a zebra?"

Gazing into her curious eyes, Jordan was once more aware of the wide gap between their cultures. Maybe he'd never actually *seen* a zebra, but at least he knew what one was, while Jolie... well, she knew about coyotes, badgers, and eagles, maybe, but not about things like zebras, pink champagne, finger sandwiches, or crystal chandeliers. Not that he knew a lot about them, but he had been exposed to a society where those things existed and had known how to deal with them when he had to do so. He had a sudden mental picture of Jolie confronted with a silver tray of finger sandwiches and smiled.

"Well?" she prompted, laying her fingertips across his lips. "Why are you smiling? What is a zebra?"

"I'm smiling because I wonder if you would like finger sandwiches, and a zebra is . . ."

"*Finger* sandwiches?" Jolie echoed in a horrified tone. "And the '*indaa*' claim the Apache are savages? At least we do not devour our own kind, like the *tseeshuuye*. . . ."

"Like the what?"

"Buzzard . . . how can you eat finger sandwiches, Jordan? I did not think you so . . . so uncivilized."

"A finger sandwich is not what you think, Jolie. It is only meat filling like chicken, beef, or turkey between two slices of bread *shaped* like a finger." He held up a finger. "See? Short and slender, like a finger—that is all."

"Oh. Then what is a zebra?"

"A wild horse with black and white stripes like a tiger— oh, you probably don't know about tigers either—like a striped cat."

Jolie lay quietly trying to imagine a horse with the stripes of a cat but could not summon the proper image. It must be an odd looking creature indeed, she decided, then remembered the armadillo. Perhaps a zebra was as different as that creature with the head of a pig, the tail of a rat, and the armor of a turtle.

Cuddling closer to Jordan, she murmured, "Perhaps one day you shall show me a zebra. Where is your village, Jor-dan, your mother's village?"

"Why?"

"I just wondered where we would stay after we find this gold you search for . . ."

"Uh, Jolie, my mother is dead."

"Oh, I know. But she must have people who are still alive. Do you not have a sister? Griffin's mother?"

"Yes . . ."

"Then I suppose we shall go there. Do you like babies, Jordan?"

Weakly, "Babies?"

"'Au—'élchiné—you know, small people . . ."

"I *know* what babies *are*, Jolie! I'm just not sure I know what you want me to say. . . ."

"The truth, of course. One always expects the truth from *kághasstí* . . ."

"From who?"

"One's husband. You need to learn the Apache word for this, Jor-dan, if we are *dziike*—where are you going?"

Slinging his legs over the side of the bed, Jordan groped in the dark for his pants. "I'm going . . . somewhere. Opal's Palace, maybe. The Last Chance Saloon. Hell, California! I don't know where."

"Was it something I said?"

"No. Yes."

There was a metallic clink as he picked up his gun belt and drew it around his hips, buckling it and shifting the holster into place. Jolie strained to see him in the dark, squinting at his shadowy form and feeling bewildered.

"*Yáá*'? What . . . what did I say, Jordan?"

There was silence, then a soft sigh, and she felt the mattress dip beneath his weight. "Ah, Jolie, I don't know how to say what you're wanting to hear. I don't even know if I *want* to say it. See, I'm used to riding alone. You know, without anyone else with me. I'm not used to having a woman along . . ."

"I know," she interrupted softly. "Griffin told me. You . . ." She strained for a moment, trying to remember, than said, "You find women, then forget them; but that is all right. I know . . ."

"I *what*?" Jordan demanded, narrowing his eyes. "What has Griffin been telling you now? Damn him—I should have had a long talk with him already—what did he tell you?"

Cautiously, sensing his anger, she said, "Only about the . . . the way you have about women. And about your stone heart, that is all."

"I'll beat him senseless—no, he's already senseless," Jordan muttered through clenched teeth, then, to Jolie, "What is this stone heart Griffin says I have?"

Jolie explained quickly and quietly, watching Jordan's face grow dark with fury. "It's all right," she added hastily, "I do not mind. I know that I am different."

Though he'd been thinking the same thing only moments before, Jordan shook his head. "No, it's not all right. You may be different, but . . . hell, how can I explain it when I'm not quite sure what I want to explain?"

"I know what you are trying to say, and it is all right."

Skeptically, he asked, "You do? No, I don't think you really do." He hated scenes, especially with females, who were prone to copious weeping and violent tantrums.

"'*Au*—of course it is all right. I will ride behind you as is my people's custom, and ask little of you. After all, when . . . *niijít'e* . . .'"

"When what?"

"When one is to marry, one must be a good wife, and learn to cook as you like it, and to sew your . . ."

"No! You don't understand, Jolie! I never meant that we should . . . that I would . . . hell, I never thought about *marrying* you and having babies and settling down to raise crops of dust and tumbleweeds. I'm a wanderer. I stay in a place for a while, then I want to move on. It's my nature. I can't stay in one place with . . . with one woman." Jordan, who would ordinarily not quail at facing a fully armed man at ten paces, found himself flinching at the soft sheen of tears glittering in Jolie's eyes. "Aw, that's not fair," he muttered uneasily, reaching out to take her hand. He gave it a slight squeeze and looked at the opposite wall, examining the patterns of moonlight and shadows with great interest.

It was quiet in the room, the dark pressing down like a smothering banket, and he began to wish he was a hundred miles away. Why in the hell did he feel so guilty? He'd done nothing. It was Griffin's fault. Griffin, who had taken her under his wing and opened his big mouth to say things he had no business saying, had made a misunderstanding even worse. Now what was he going to do?

Turning his head, he chanced to meet her steady gaze, and Jordan signed audibily. An active conscience was damned inconvenient at this stage of the game, he decided.

"Look, Jolie, I think maybe it'd be best if I spent the rest of the night in the barn with Amos and Griffin, okay?"

She remained silent, but her eyes spoke volumes. Jordan shrugged and turned away, releasing her hand and rising from the bed.

"See you in the morning," he muttered. "We'll talk about things then."

Lying on her side, Jolie heard the door click softly shut, and she was alone in the moonlight and shadows. One hand slid across the sheets to the spot where Jordan had lain. It was still warm from the press of his body, and she could smell the faint fragrance of his tobacco. She closed her eyes, steeling herself against the surge of pain that rose in a wave to envelop her. No. She would not cry, would not believe that he meant what he said. He was only fighting a battle within himself and did not mean it. Griffin was wrong. Jordan's heart was not made of the hard stone, but the softer metal of gold. And like gold, which could be easily carved and shaped, his heart would soon bear her imprint.

With this small comfort, Jolie drifted into an uneasy slumber marred by dreams of being lost and alone on a mountain of impregnable granite.

Part Two

*

Chapter
14

Griffin woke to find Jordan snoring beside him. The sun was just coming up over the purple hills, sending curious fingers of light flooding over the town and through cracks and crevices in the wooden boards of the stable, highlighting the loft with an ethereal, dusty shimmer. It was still early enough to be cool, and sometime during the night—Griffin had been too drunk to remember—Jordan had come in and commandeered his thin blanket. He lay wrapped in it now, sleeping peacefully as if he hadn't a care in the world. That irritated Griffin to the extreme.

"Jordan?" He nudged him with the heel of his hand, then curled his fingers into the edges of the blanket and tugged hard. "Hey, what happened? Jolie kick you out of bed? If she didn't, she should have."

Spitting out a stray wisp of straw that clung to the side of his mouth, Jordan barely opened one eye to glare at his intrepid nephew. "Shut up." The blanket was pulled over his head to close out Griffin and the daylight.

"Why? Don't you like the truth?"

"Not at five in the morning."

"So—*did* she?"

"Did she what?" Jordan snapped, rolling over on his stomach and peering from beneath the blanket to regard Griffin with all the warmth of a lizard inspecting its next meal. "Do you always wake up so inquisitive?"

"Not always. Sometimes I wake up with nicer bed partners..."

"Bragging again?"

"... like rattlesnakes," Griffin continued blandly, earning a sharp exclamation from Jordan.

"Dammit, Griffin! What's eating you?"

"What do you think?"

"I took your blanket?"

"That, too, but Jolie is my main concern."

"I don't know why," Jordan began, but Griffin cut him off.

"It irritates me to see innocent women betrayed and misled, especially one who is so obviously in love with you!" the boy snapped.

Jordan propped himself on his elbows and glared at his nephew. "You're crazy. I did everything I could to discourage her, and you know it! Every time I turned around, the girl was right on my heels, so what else did you expect from me?"

"From you? Much better," Griffin muttered.

Amos, long awake but unwilling to admit it, gave up at last and sat up, shaking his head and muttering, "We might as well all get up and fight."

"We're not fighting," Griffin interrupted, half-turning his tousled blond head in Amos's direction, "we're only discussing."

"*Dis*cussin'?" Amos's brows rose. "Sounds more like cussin' to me."

"That, too. Tell Jordan he should leave Jolie alone or marry her, Amos."

Amos stood up and reached for his boots and rifle. "I ain' about to butt into his business, Rooster, an' maybe you should think about easin' out yourself. Did Jolie ask you to defend her?"

"Well . . . no, but she needs somebody to take up for her if he's gonna . . ."

"What she needs she'll ask for," Amos cut in. "Look, it's early, and we need to get out of here sometime today. Now's as good a time as any, so I suggest we saddle up, load our gear, and head for the San Andres while we ain' got no unwanted company tagging along."

Suiting action to words, Amos descended the rough wooden ladder to the floor of the stable and began saddling his mount. Griffin, left alone with an irritable Jordan, slid his uncle a glance and shrugged. Maybe he should take Amos's advice. But then again—maybe Jordan should take *his* advice. Dammit, why did he feel obliged to get involved, anyway? This had all started out as a lark, and now he was caught between a rock and a hard place, trying to be a go-between for Jordan and Jolie when he should be minding his own business. It wasn't *his* fault he'd gotten the wrong girl—well, not *all* his fault. It had been Jordan's idea so he should take most of the blame. Who'd have thought the wrong girl would be so . . . so . . . *vulnerable*? If she'd been as bitchy as she'd started out, maybe he wouldn't feel some sort of obligation to her, but she wasn't. And she was so foolishly, hopelessly in love with Jordan—who didn't give a damn about most women—when it was as plain as the nose on her face that he wasn't her type at all. Hell, *he* was more her type than Jordan.

Griffin's thought processes halted abruptly, shocked by this new revelation. Dammit—who'da thought it? He was sweet on her himself. His brows drew into a fierce scowl as Griffin wondered irritably what in the blue hell Jolie was thinking of.

Jolie was thinking of Jordan, and reassuring herself that he would realize how silly he was being. What was it Griffin had told her? Something about never knowing what one wanted until it was gone. Maybe Jordan would realize how empty his arms had been without her during the long hours of the night. But what if he didn't? What if he'd gone to visit that *'indaa 'puta,* Hayley, who had attached herself to him when they'd first arrived in town? But that was foolish. He would not do that. Would he?

She sat straight up in bed, frowning at the slatted wooden shutters where daylight was beginning to thread its way into the stuffy little room. Flinging back the paisley bedspread, Jolie reflected that tipis were infinitely preferable to such a dwelling as this. At least in a tipi one could breathe, and there was proper ventilation under the lifted flaps at the bottom, where in a white man's dwelling one had to depend upon a wandering breeze to find this one little square opening to cool the room. Would Jordan consent to living in a tipi?

Jolie began to dress, ignoring the green gown and step- ping into the snug Levis that Griffin had given her. She tugged on a loose shirt donated by Jordan, then stuffed her long hair up into a battered felt hat that Amos had decided should be hers. Disdaining the tight pair of boots that Griffin had tried to coax her into wearing, Jolie quickly packed the rest of her gear in a blanket, bound it with a belt that someone had intended she wear but was too large to fit around her small waist, and left the tiny little room without a backward glance.

When she reached the stable, she discovered that Jordan, Amos, and Griffin were almost packed. The mules they'd bought were already loaded with supplies, and the horses were saddled. Her blanket-wrapped bundle dropped to the ground as she surveyed the dim interior of the stable.

"Were you going to come after me?" she couldn't help asking, hands resting on her hips, standing in the open double doors of the stable. Her shadow preceded her, falling across the straw-littered floor like an accusing finger to point at Jordan.

"Sure," Jordan answered without looking up. He was bent over, buckling the back girth on his saddle, reaching under the belly of his gray. His voice was muffled against the animal's side.

"When—in a month?" Jolie couldn't help snapping. Her instincts warned her that he had considered leaving her behind, and her hands clenched into small fists at her sides. Bare feet scuffed through the straw dust as she stepped closer, so that when he lifted his head from buckling the girth, she was standing right beside him, her eyes boring into him accusingly.

"No," he answered, "in just a little while. I was letting you rest . . ."

"Stow it!" she retorted, repeating a phrase she had learned from Griffin. "You had no intention of coming back for me."

Jordan straightened slowly, towering over her, his eyes dark with exasperation. "Probably not, if it was just up to me, but your knight in shining armor here"—he gestured to Griffin— "would have skewered me on the lance of chivalry if I had tried to leave you behind. Don't worry, green eyes. You're going with us.''

This reassurance did nothing for Jolie's sense of security where Jordan was concerned. She sighed. It seemed that he was not yet convinced he was her man.

''Jolie,'' Griffin was saying, leading her saddled piebald forward, ''Where are your boots?''

Still distracted, she waved in the general direction of her small bound packet of possessions. ''There. I do not wear them.''

''But . . .''

''They pinch my toes, Griffin. I do not see why you insist upon binding me with rules and shoes!'' she flared. ''I cannot wear them.''

''Okay, okay,'' he said hastily, putting the leather ends of her horse's reins in her hand. ''Don't bite my head off. I just thought I'd ask.''

Guiltily, half ashamed that she had snapped at Griffin, who had, after all, been a true friend, she said, ''I will find something to wear on my feet if it bothers you. I just don't like the boots.''

''Fair enough,'' Griffin answered gently, fully aware of Jolie's distress. ''Hell, I don't care if you wear boots or not. It's just that I don't want your feet scratched up when we ride through the brush.''

''I know.'' Jolie could feel Jordan's gaze resting on her, but she refused to look at him. She couldn't. If she did, he would know how she felt—would know that she was waiting for him to give her a sign that he cared. Surely Griffin had been wrong about him. Jordan did not have a heart of stone, did he?

Shuffling her bare feet in the dusty straw of the stable floor, Jolie concentrated on the flies swarming over the spilled horse feed instead of looking at Jordan. She looked at the neat rows of bridles and harness hanging from pegs along the unevenly boarded walls; she found the tiny cracks between the pine boards fascinating, and counted sixteen of them before her attention was distracted again.

"If you're going with us, green eyes," Jordan was saying, "you need to tend to your own horse. Remember?"

"I remember," she said without looking at him, tugging at the piebald's reins in a light, sawing motion. "I remember a lot of things."

"Do you?" Jordan asked, pausing beside her, gazing down at Jolie with a faint flickering of regret in his eyes that was gone so quickly she never saw it.

She flung back her head to look at him then, her mouth a tight line, eyes remote and unreadable. " '*Au*—I do."

Amos broke the tense silence that surrounded them, coughing discreetly and saying, "All this talkin' ain't gitting us on the road, folks. Why don't we head out before it gets too hot?"

"Sounds good to me," Jordan said easily, his eyes still locked with Jolie's.

"Sounds even better to me," Griffin muttered, tugging the brim of his hat lower. "It's smelling pretty bad in here. I think I need some fresh air."

Constraint dogged their heels as they rode away from Franklin. Jolie didn't speak to Jordan; Jordan didn't speak to Jolie; Griffin didn't speak to Jordan; and Amos gave up on speaking to any of them. For a long time there was only the sound of the horses' hooves clattering on the rock-hard trail, the jangling of metal bits on the bridles, and an occasional bray from one of the well-laden mules. Heat pressed down on them with an iron hand, and all were grateful for the sparing sips of water from their leather pouches.

It was Jolie who finally broke the tension between them, nudging her horse close to Jordan's and saying, "*Gostood' né?*"

Irritably, slanting her a wary glance, he snapped, "What?"

"It's hot, isn't it?" she repeated in English, a wide smile curving the soft line of her mouth as she gazed at him.

Jordan stared back at her for a long moment, his face registering disbelief and exasperation. Then he grinned and shook his head. "Like I've said before, green eyes, you sure don't carry grudges long."

"No. Life is to short to bear ill feelings, and it only hurts the vessel that carries such poison, not the ground it's poured upon."

"Very profound," Jordan observed, tugging at the brim of his hat to shade his eyes from her view, "if a little inaccurate. What made you so wise so young?"

Sensing a thread of derision in his tone, she shrugged and said, "I only watch what happens, Jor-dan, that is all. And I try to learn from it."

"And what happened to teach you this particular lesson? It's hard for me to believe that you've experienced so much yourself."

"As I told you, I watch." Jolie swept her hat from her head and shook her hair free, letting it spin in the air for a moment, then lifted it from her neck to allow a drift of wind to cool her heated skin. Ebony skeins spilled across her arm in tangled threads, capturing Jordan's attention.

For some reason, he was remembering those same streamers of hair flowing across a pillow, a sable cushion for Jolie's small, exquisite features, her expression one of love and passion as she gazed up at him, and he shook his head to clear the memory.

"What happened?" he repeated. "How'd you become an authority on hate, green eyes?"

"From watching Little Bear and She-Who-Laughs together. Little Bear loved She-Who-Laughs, but She-Who-Laughs loved Spotted Tail. Day after day, Little Bear would follow She-Who-Laughs—who was very beautiful—and watch her flirt with Spotted Tail. Little Bear grew to hate them both after a time, even though he had loved She-Who-Laughs," Jolie explained. "It ended with Little Bear challenging Spotted Tail to a duel of warriors that Spotted Tail won. Then Little Bear had to slink off like a cur while all the village laughed at him. He was so unhappy, so miserable with his hate, that he threw himself from a high rock. Now it is said that his unhappy spirit will roam forever."

"He was probably much better off without the girl," Jordan observed dryly. "Too bad he didn't realize it."

Jolie slanted him a curious glance. "Do you truly think so—that he would be better off without the one he loved, Jordan?"

"Maybe yes—maybe no. It all depends on how you look at it, I guess." A dark brow lifted as he returned Jolie's steady gaze. Little minx. She was trying to tell him something with that ridiculous story, of course, but he was damned if he'd let her get away with it. Did he need a girl fresh out of the nursery relating fables to him? He was a little bit older and a lot wiser than she thought.

Smiling, Jordan let his gaze move from her thoughtful eyes to the gentle swell of her breasts beneath the thin cotton shirt she wore. Damned thoughtful of Griffin to provide her with such an article of clothing—or was it his? He couldn't remember. And right now all he could think about was how tempting she looked in the tight Levis and loose cotton blouse. Why did sex have to interfere just when he was getting used to thinking of her as a nuisance again? Jordan wondered irritably. He spurred his horse into a brisk trot, leaving Jolie behind breathing clouds of his dust. It'd be good for her. She was too confident, too certain that he would marry her. Hell, he'd never let a woman lasso him before and wasn't about to do so now. Not even Jolie.

"Don't let him get to you, Jolie," Griffin was saying quietly, having ridden his bay close to her. She sat her horse easily, staring ahead at Jordan's back as if he were merely one of the yucca plants dotting the landscape. Managing a careless shrug, she turned to the youth.

"He does not bother me," she said. A small smile curved her mouth into a bow. "He only fools himself."

Griffin couldn't help a wide grin. "For a gal who keeps getting shot down, you sure are certain of yourself. What makes you think Jordan will ever marry you, Jolie?"

She turned to look at him with a serious expression. "It is what you call fate, Griffin. Our eyes met across a ground crowded with warriors and hate, and I saw something in his eyes. It is still there, though he tries to hide it from me."

Carefully, Griffin suggested, "Are you sure it ain't something else you're readin' in his eyes, Jolie? Like *wantin'* instead of love? There's a big difference, you know."

"I know. He feels that too, of course, as I do. But he loves me, Griffin, I know he does."

"I hope so," Griffin muttered, reining his horse away from a hole in the trail. The hot wind offered little relief from the broiling sun, and he wiped his forehead with a sleeve. The string of pack mules plodded wearily behind him so that he couldn't even take a brief run and feel the wind against him; not that he could have anyway. In this heat, it would have ruined his horse.

Amos, leading the rest of the mules, caught up with their slow pace. "Even my eyeballs are parched," he grumbled to no one in particular. The bright red bandana he wore beneath his hat flapped around his ears as his horse jogged slowly beside Jolie's piebald. Sweat had drenched his shirt in huge dark patches under his brawny arms and on his chest and was streaming down his face to drip from his chin.

"You look as if you just stood under a water spout," Griffin observed.

"You don't look much better, Rooster!" Amos shot back. "In fact, Jolie's the only one who don't look like she's been in the middle of a river. How do you stay lookin' so cool, gal?"

Jolie, who was uncomfortably aware of how her shirt stuck to her clammy skin and her hair was wet at the nape and temples, clinging to her forehead in limp strands, shook her head. "I do not *feel* cool! I feel like the cooked prairie dog instead."

"Cooked prairie dog?" Griffin, who had never experienced the hardships of a trail as Amos had done, made a face. "I think you're making that up."

"No, she ain't. I've eaten 'em that way. You leave the skin on and bury it in the embers of a fire, then when it's done, you skin it and eat it," Amos said, enjoying himself. "Hell, I bet you ain't never eaten bear either."

"No," Griffin said faintly, "I sure haven't. And I don't intend to."

"Get hungry enough," Jolie said, "and you will eat anything, Griffin, even a *tseeshμμye*."

"A what?"

"Buzzard," Amos answered for her. "And they ain't half bad either if you cook 'em real done . . ."

"Enough!" Griffin cut in. "I know what you're trying to do—get me sick enough so you can have my share of lunch today. Well, you can just forget it! I'm eating all of it!"

But when they finally stopped for the noon meal, Griffin was too sick from the heat to take a single bite of the beef jerky in his pack. He did manage his ration of water, but that was all. He sat slumped on a hump of rock, staring morosely at the undulating landscape of mesquite and yucca, the mountains that were their destination still a purple haze in the distance.

"How far you reckon we have to go?" he asked Jordan, who was close to him, lying back on the flatter part of the rock with his hands behind his head and his hat over his eyes. "This mountain we're looking for isn't too far from Hembrillo Peak, is it?"

"Not according to Amos. Or rather, Amos's miner friend. If he's to be believed, it's only a few steps away."

"You don't believe him?"

"It's not that I don't believe him, but sometimes it's hard to tell distance out here, and the old man was—by Amos's expert observation—roaring drunk. I remember seeing another peak, but as for a tunnel between the two—I'll believe it when I see it," Jordan said from beneath the shade of his hat.

"But even Jolie remembers something about a twin peak," Griffin persisted.

"Jolie seems to have a convenient memory," Jordan retorted. "She forgets what she doesn't want to remember, and remembers what suits her."

"So?"

Jordan pushed back his hat, peering at his nephew from

beneath the brim. "So, she'll say anything you want to hear, that's *so*."

"That's not so," Jolie said indignantly. She was sitting cross-legged on the ground not far from Jordan and Griffin's rock. Though it had been wandering moments before, her attention had just been snared by the mention of her name, and now she gazed up at the two on the rock with irritation. "I say only what I feel, Jor-dan. You are shoving words in my ear..."

"You mean, putting words in your mouth," Griffin corrected gently.

She waved an impatient hand. "That does not signify. He knows what I mean."

"Sure I do, but my statement still stands," Jordan said. He sat up, pushed back his hat and draped one arm over his bent leg, then squinted at Jolie with a critical gaze. "You can't argue with the truth, green eyes."

"I don't intend to. I argue with the...the..."

While she fumbled for the lost word, Griffin leaned forward to whisper loudly, "Lie," and Jolie promptly finished, "the lie!"

Jordan snorted. "You can't even defend yourself without help! How can you expect me to swallow every tall tale you happen to pass along as truth? And anyway, what does all this matter when it comes down to it? If the gold is there, it's there. If it's not..." He shrugged. "I go to Mexico as broke as I was before I ran into Amos, that's all."

On her knees now, Jolie leaned forward to stare at Jordan intently. He shifted uncomfortably beneath her steady gaze, knowing her doubts. How could he tell her what she wanted to hear? He couldn't.

"You never meant to take me with you, did you?" Jolie

said, stating it as calmly as if remarking upon the weather. "I see I've been very wrong."

"Look, Jolie, I didn't make any promises, did I? I never meant to mislead you or make you think I'd do something I knew I wasn't going to do . . ."

"Bullshit," Griffin was heard to mutter, but when Jordan sliced him a narrowed glance, the youth was looking off into the distance.

Jordan turned his attention back to Jolie, who had risen to her feet and was standing in front of him, her gaze level with his and piercing him like a knife. Her dusky skin was flushed, and her full lips quivered ever so slightly, but there was no trace of tears in her eyes. "The padre at the mission used to speak of the sin of omission as well as the sin of . . . of . . . well, I can't remember the word, but he meant that what one does not do can often be as bad as what one does," Jolie answered softly, still staring at Jordan.

Amos, who had remained quietly listening and neutral as usual, coughed loudly. "I hate to interrupt this tender, emotional little scene, but if'n I don't, we may be decoratin' some lodge pole somewhere this time tomorrow."

Three heads swiveled to look in the direction he was pointing. A faint haze of dust rose over the hill they had just crossed, and Griffin correctly observed that it must be horsemen.

"At least four or five of them, judging from the amount of dust," Jordan said, leaving the rock in a fluid movement like a cat, tightening the buckle of his gunbelt in the same motion.

"They might be friends," Jolie ventured, frowning at the brown haze of dust.

"Friends? Like whose? Yours, maybe?" Jordan snapped. "That's all we need. That, in fact, green eyes, is why we brought you along in the first place. If they're *your* friends, you keep 'em happy. You're our T.O.H.—ticket outa here.''

''Not with these guys,'' Amos muttered, squinting through an old Army field glass. He lowered it and looked at Jordan with a solemn expression. ''These guys look like Mexican bandidos and loaded for action, partner.''

''How many?''

''At least five, maybe more.''

''And there's three of us,'' Jordan murmured, thinking out loud.

''Four,'' Jolie corrected.

''Three,'' Jordan returned firmly. Stepping forward, he lifted her easily and sat her on her horse. ''Don't do anything we don't tell you to do.''

''So what are we gonna do?'' Griffin asked. ''We sure as hell can't outrun them unless we cut the pack mules loose, and I ain't real crazy about that idea.''

''Maybe they're just curious about us. Or maybe they just happen to be ridin' this trail,'' Amos added. ''We could be gettin' ahead of ourselves here.''

''You think so?'' Jordan drawled, watching the cloud of dust draw closer. ''Then tell me why those men are riding so hard in this heat. I'd say they were chasing somebody, and I haven't run across anybody else today.''

''Good point,'' Amos returned gloomily. ''Let's ride on real casual-like and see what happens. If we can get to that big pile of rocks in the foothills, we can make a stand—just in case we have to fight.''

Chapter
15

It seemed that Jordan's caution had proved useful. The cloud of dust stayed just far enough behind them to keep from being easily seen. Each time they stopped, the cloud of dust stopped; when they struck a faster pace, the dust cloud was not far behind; when they slowed, the dust cloud hovered in a lazy haze. Now they'd halted once more, finally reaching the protective cover of the rock pile Amos had mentioned earlier. The men behind them had halted just over the next ridge and waited, like hopeful birds of prey, their intentions a mystery that was the main topic of conversation in the pile of rocks as dark fell.

"Who do you suppose they are?" Jordan wondered aloud for what was probably the eleventh time. "You got any posters out on you, Amos? Griffin? No? Then who are those men?"

Lying stretched out on his belly on the flat surface of a boulder, Jordan squinted into the dark, trying to sort one shadow from the next. The rock was still warm from the sun's rays during the day, and he could feel the heat seeping in through his cotton shirt, warming his belly. There were the usual night sounds, and silence from beyond.

"Who are those men?" Jordan muttered again, perplexed. He couldn't figure out who might be following them. They weren't Apache, which would have been more logical, but from their gear they seemed to be cowboys. Now why, Jordan wondered irritably, would ordinary cowboys be following a ragtag caravan like theirs? It didn't make sense.

He didn't realize he'd spoken the last few words aloud until Amos commented softly, "Could be they know where we're headed, but I'm damned if'n I know how they'd know. You tell anybody what we's up to?"

"Of course not," Jordan growled. "How about you, Jolie? Did you tell anybody about the gold or where we're going?"

A sliver of moon lent a pale light to the night, and she was barely visible as she answered, "*Dah*. Who would I tell, Jor-dan?" He could hear her shift on the rocks, her shadow blurred and unrecognizable as she turned to face him. Pebbles rolled down the incline in a pattering slide as Jolie said, "I have no use for the gold—it is not my search but yours—yet I still would not speak of it to anyone."

"Well, if you didn't say anything, and I didn't say anything, and neither did Amos or Griffin—who the hell are they?"

A night hawk's cry sliced through the air, shrill and searching, followed by silence again, and Jordan could have sworn he heard the beating of the bird's wings against the wind. After a moment Griffin quietly said, "They're some guys I played poker with one night, Jordan."

Silence, then, "What the hell are you talking about?"

"I'm talking about those guys who are following us. I know them."

"Wait a minute, Rooster," Amos began, "you need to explain that a little better. I knows it can't be like it sounds . . ."

"Aw, you know it ain't like *that*, Amos." There was a brief lifting of Griffin's shoulder, more heard than seen as he explained, "I was sitting around a table at the saloon one night, see, and these two guys came up and invited me to join in a friendly little game of poker. Now, you know how bad I am at poker, but I was feelin' kind of low that night and so I said 'Yeah.' Soon it was about six or seven of them, and they all seemed to know each other. Every time I turned around my whiskey glass was full, and I was steady pullin' at it, so I know they kept it that way for me. Or rather, for reasons of their own. Hell, it wasn't long before I was too drunk to spit!" Griffin's voice grew sheepish, and he took a long pause before continuing, "I ran out of money quick, so I threw a small chunk off that gold bar we found in the cave onto the table." He waited out the sharp expletives that followed that remark before he said, "The last thing I remember is tellin' 'em some kind of story about a hidden mine. I recollect trying to confuse 'em, but they must've seen through me."

"Must have," Jordan agreed harshly. "At least we know who they are now. What kind of guys were these? Drifters, gunslingers, cowboys, miners?"

"Hell, Jordan, I don't know. Drifters, I think. Pretty good poker players, anyway."

"Well, great! Got any cards with you? Maybe we can invite them to sit in on a game."

"Why don't we save our energy for figurin' out how to lose 'em?" Amos asked quickly. "That makes better sense than wastin' time arguing about whose fault it is they're following us. Once we get away, we got plenty of time for that."

Jolie was sitting close to Griffin on the ground and reached out wordlessly to put her hand on his shoulder. His fingers curled around her wrist in a grateful clasp.

"Thanks," he whispered. "I've sure made a mess of things."

"What's done is done. One can only go forward," she whispered back.

A comfortable silence stretched between them, interrupted only by Jordan's muffled movements on the rock and Amos's muttered comment that at first light they needed to make their move.

"We can make a run for it or fight it out right here. I think we should provoke 'em into a fight here," Amos said. "What do you think, Jordan?"

"I agree. It'd be in our favor then."

"How do you suggest we provoke them?" Griffin wanted to know. "Throw rocks?"

"Let's try something a bit more mature than rock throwing or bragging," Jordan drawled.

"I didn't know you could think of anything more mature than that, especially with the way you treat Jolie . . ."

"Why don't you both quit sniping at each other for a change?" Amos cut in. "I like her, too, but hell—you two are getting on my nerves, tangling like a couple of randy wildcats! Forget fightin' over what's good or bad for Jolie, and let's figure out how to get those guys."

The plan was simple. Or it would have been if the mules hadn't balked. What should have been a smooth operation turned into a fiasco and almost a disaster.

The southernmost tip of the Jornada, that trackless waste of burning sand and deep arroyos, stretched along their west side, with the thrust of the Organs on the east. The plan was to pretend to leave the safety of the boulders and head into the open, then double back through one of the arroyos to come up behind those following and surprise them. It was simple, so simple it should have worked without a hitch, and it almost did.

Unfortunately, the mules, cranky without their shaded stable and plentitude of hay and water, descended into the arroyo and refused to go any further than halfway. It wouldn't have been so bad if Griffin, Jordan, and Jolie hadn't been stuck behind with no way to get around in the narrow cut. Only Amos rode ahead, trying to coax the mules up the steep ravine and failing miserably.

"So what the hell do I do now?" he wanted to know, hissing his demand as quietly as possible. "It ain't gonna be long before those guys figure out we ain't just ahead of 'em no more!" He tugged furiously at the rope attached to the lead mule, and the animal responded by promptly sinking to its haunches and braying in a loud, offended voice.

Time was critical, and Jordan decided that surprise was still their best bet. Pulling his feet under him, he stood up in his saddle and half-leaped, half-walked from his gray's back to the back of the nearest mule. The animal wheezed with surprise but, wedged between the high sandstone walls and the mule in front of it, it had little option but to submit. Jordan stepped gingerly from one mule back to the next until he had traversed the entire train of seven mules and was standing in front of Amos.

"Well?" Jordan said impatiently, motioning to Griffin to do the same. "Come on!"

Grinning, Griffin leapfrogged from his horse to Jolie's piebald, urging her with him as he made the same trip Jordan had just made. He held her by one hand as he balanced himself among the packs attached to a protesting mule. "This reminds me of school," he said with a laugh. "We all used to play leapfrog every day at lunch. In fact, this particular mule kinda reminds me of Tommy Simmons, with that dumb look on his face and the floppy ears.''

''Well, recess is over and this ain't school,'' Jordan said grimly. ''And the only two-legged jackass I see right now is you, so let's *go*.''

And go they did, crawling up the hard, sun-baked walls of the arroyo like agile spiders, their guns bumping against the rock walls with a muffled clatter. Tiny showers of red dust sprayed over those below the first climber, and heads were bent to keep it out of their eyes. Amos went first, Griffin second, then Jolie, and finally Jordan bringing up the rear.

It was a most interesting view, Jordan decided, looking up to see Jolie's enticing bottom just above his head. The snug Levis fit her rounded curves perfectly, and his imagination supplied the details the denims hid, so that he was grinning in spite of himself. It was playing with fire even to think of her in those terms, he scolded himself, but how could he help it? Damn, if she wasn't so young and innocent, expecting him to be some white knight or something, maybe he could stay with her a while. But it would be cruel to stay with her any longer than he already had when she was expecting so much more. And cruelty now was a lot kinder than later.

Turning his attention back to the business at hand, Jordan observed Jolie's bare toes curl around a fragment of rock that immediately crumbled beneath her step, and he reached up a hand to keep her from falling back. The brief, warm pressure of her behind resting in his open palm left him with a tingling that lingered long after she had pulled herself over the top, an event that made him impatient and irritable.

Once atop the crevice, they snaked their way along the brush-stubbled ground back to the rocks they had abandoned only a half hour before. Amos, the first over the lip of the crest, made an admirable imitation of a rattlesnake as he snaked his way along, belly down, with his rifle in one hand, his sidearm crushed against the leg of his army blue-and-yellow striped trousers, and a peculiar rattling noise in his throat.

"You okay?" Griffin asked in a loud whisper.

"Yeah, I guess. I mean, I've heard of gittin' down to earth, but this is damned ridiculous," Amos muttered around a mouthful of red dust. His face was thickly coated with a grainy layer of New Mexico, and he tried to cough out the generous portion lodged in his throat. When he half-turned to look back, Griffin laughed, muffling the sound in his palm. "What's so damned funny, Rooster?" Amos wanted to know.

"Oh nothing. You just kinda remind me of a raccoon, with a black mask and nose and your face all brown and whiskery..."

"Hell, you wouldn' win no prize for beauty yourself!" Amos returned. "You look worse than you did with that nutberry juice all over your face."

"If you two are through trading compliments, could we move on?" Jordan asked, nudging closer to them. "Come on, keep up, Jolie," he said over his shoulder when she lagged behind. "I still think you should have stayed with the mules."

"And be drowned if there's a sudden flood? Not on your life," she retorted, repeating another phrase learned from Griffin.

"There's not going to be a flood within the next hour, is there?" Griffin asked in alarm. "I'd hate to think about losing our mules and packs."

"Get on up here," Amos was urging from a few yards

away, beckoning impatiently to them with one hand. "I think our buddies just passed the rocks."

Conversation ended abruptly as they threaded their way through beargrass and rocks to the huge pile of granite where they had spent the previous night. A cloud of dust just beyond verified Amos's suspicion that their followers had passed, and they quickly positioned themselves behind the security of two-ton boulders.

"Now?" Griffin asked Jordan, easing one of his .45s from his holster. When Jordan gave a brief nod, Griffin grinned. "All *right*!" he said, thumbing back the hammer of the Colt.

The explosion echoed among the rocks in an eerie, ear-splitting whine as the bullet left the barrel. A moment later its destination was evident as a felt hat spun wildly in the air like a wounded bird before floating almost gracefully to the tangled branches of a mesquite.

"That's very good, Griffin," Jolie approved.

"Thank you," the boy said modestly.

Reaction from the target was immediate. Startled yelps followed the shot, and the men in long coats and big hats dived from their horses to the nearest available cover. It was obvious they hadn't expected such an action, and they bunched in a tight knot behind a stand of stunted mesquite trees to confer with one another, firing an occasional wild shot in the general direction of the rocks.

"Let's not give 'em time to think up a plan or see our mules still in the gully," Amos suggested. All agreed to this. Amos pumped his Winchester with enthusiasm, spacing his shots effectively so as not to waste ammunition, while Jordan squeezed off careful shots to keep them pinned down. It was Griffin, however, with his expert marksmanship, who caused pandemonium.

Griffin's skilled shot severed the tightly held reins of one man's horse, loosing the animal to run wildly across the sand to an unknown destination; another shot plucked the hat from a man's head again, while still another bullet punctured a leather water pouch hanging from the saddle of a plunging horse without injuring the animal.

"Hey, damn good shootin'," Amos said admiringly, squeezing off another random shot. "You'd be a hell of a gunfighter if you had to be."

"Yeah, guess I could be, couldn't I?" Griffin admitted without a trace of modesty this time. "Thought about it for a while, but there's always somebody who's a shade faster, or who gets the drop on you—hey!" He ducked as a wild shot found the crown of his new brown hat, sending it flying from his head and into the dust and rubble behind him.

"You were saying?" Jordan drawled, and Griffin's mouth curved in a reluctant smile.

Jolie, sitting with drawn-up knees and arms curled around them, reached over to pick up his hat. One slender finger poked experimentally through a small, neat hole. "*Ghá-da'ii'áne*," she observed, turning the hat over to discover the point of exit for the bullet.

"He's lucky it ain't his head that's holey," Amos remarked sourly. "Keep down, dammit, Rooster! Them guys are gonna fight back, you know."

"Yeah, it looks that way."

"Could you see how many there are?" Jordan asked Amos, squinting across the flat top of the rock he had chosen as cover.

"Seven, I think."

Crouching on her knees, Jolie shook her head at Amos as she handed Griffin his hat. "*Dah. 'Áashdlai'.*"

Amos's head swiveled around to stare thoughtfully at her. "Five? Did you count 'em?"

"'*Au*. One of them is *t'eeshínde*, like yourself."

"How can you see with all that dust?" Griffin asked with a trace of awe. "I'm having trouble picking out a target I can see, much less figure out the nationality."

"Why don't you tell us the color of the eyes while you're at it," Jordan commented cynically, "and which foods they prefer?"

"You're making me the joke again," Jolie said with rising irritation. "Why do you always do that, Jordan?"

A spate of bullets precluded any answer he might have given, and they all flattened themselves close to the ground while lead flew over their heads with the sound of a swarm of angry bees. It seemed that their target had recovered sufficiently to devise some sort of counterattack and defense. Several minutes passed while they hugged rocks that were already hot from the early morning sun, almost burning the unprotected skin on their hands and cheeks.

As soon as there was a lull in the shooting, Griffin popped up and fired off a quick shot, grinning at the distant curse barely audible over the fading echo of his gun's report. "That ought to show 'em who they're dealing with," he murmured.

"Sure. Too bad *we* don't know who we're dealing with," Jordan said, busily reloading both his pistols. He shut the chambers with a click and glnaced up at his nephew. "Do you think they're after what gold we've got, or information?"

Griffin shrugged. "I don't know. I figure—since they didn't ambush us as soon as we were far enough away from Franklin—that they want to know the location of where we found that gold bar as well as where we're headed. What do you think, Amos?"

The red bandana tucked beneath his cap flapped with the nod of his head as Amos agreed. "Yeah, that sounds more logical than all this fuss for one gold bar. Split between five men, it wouldn't be a fortune. Of course, we could always agree to parley, then give 'em wrong directions. That might work."

Jordan disagreed. "No, that's inviting trouble."

"Then what do you suggest? That we pick them off one by one like a turkey shoot?"

"That's probably safest, but I'm not sure I want to hang for murder. After all, we don't have any proof that they want to jump us, just Griffin's confession that he ran his mouth too much. Any survivors would be sure to rely on that point." Jordan pushed his hat back, fingers spread as he raked through his hair. His glance moved to Jolie and lingered, as it did entirely too much for his liking, before he turned his attention back to Amos. "You want to try talking to 'em?"

There was a long moment of silence, broken by erratic bursts of gunfire from across the rocks before Amos shrugged and said, "Sure. It's a good day to die."

The old Indian saying sparked a responsive chord in Jordan, and his eyes met Amos's with that empathy that only two men who've shared the same life-threatening experiences can possess. But all he said was, "I'll try to cover you, and even better, Griffin will be watching."

Amos grinned. "I like you, Jordan, but I do prefer Griffin watching out for me over you. No offense, now . . ."

"No offense," Jordan returned with a grin.

"But that can be dangerous!" Jolie protested, appalled that Amos would even consider such a rash act. "You must not trust those men, my friend!"

"Oh I don't, gal. I trust Griffin's shootin', though."

Amos was busily affixing the scrap of white material that was all that was left of his linen handkerchief to the end of his rifle barrel. "And I trust old Bess here," he added, patting the smooth wooden stock of his Winchester. "She's seen me through a lot, and I reckon she'll see me through a lot more."

Scrambling down from the protection of the rocks, Amos crouched behind a stunted bush for a moment before stepping out into the open.

Chapter
16

Jolie waited tensely, scrunched down against a rock, her eyes fixed upon Amos's tall, muscular frame as he walked slowly toward the stand of mesquite. It was an agony of suspense for her, and she realized how fond she had grown of the calmest member of their little group. Amos was the mediator, the one who remained coolest under pressure. Jolie bit down on her knuckles, heedless of the pain as she kept an eye on the scene unfolding before her.

Amos walked with a slow, measured tread, holding his rifle high, the white handkerchief waving with each step he took. The red bandana underneath his blue Army cap covered his ears and the back of his neck, and sweat trickled from beneath the cap down the sides of his face. The close-cropped beard he wore glistened with it in the morning sun. Heavy silence greeted his approach across the hot sands. A deep cut angled between the mesquite and the rocks where Amos's group was hidden, and he paused at the edge and called out a request for a truce. Not a branch moved among the mesquite, but there was a brief glint of sun along the smooth barrel of a rifle poking from the low shrubs and flashing across the space between Amos and the trees.

When Jolie would have called out a warning, Jordan's hand clamped over her mouth. "Don't," he warned softly. "Let's not spook anybody into reacting too fast."

Her head fell back against his shoulder, and she took comfort from the fact that Jordan was so close to her. She could feel the steady rhythm of his heartbeat, and the flex of his muscles as his arm tightened around her. Jolie's lashes fluttered shut, and she gave a contented sigh that was somewhat surprising considering the situation.

"You okay?" Jordan muttered in her ear, pushing her slightly away to peer at her with a frown.

"*Oui*. I just made the noise—aahh—that is all," she said with a smile. "I like for you to hold me."

"Oh, for Christ's sake!" Jordan exploded, shoving her roughly away. "Do you have to do that now? We're in the middle of a battle here, and you want to go and get romantic!"

A sharp rifle report cut across his angry rebuff, jerking both heads around just in time to see Amos fall to his knees, his rifle pitching forward. It hit the dust, the white handkerchief falling limply beneath the barrel and Amos falling across his rifle.

"Oh, damn!" Jordan and Griffin both said at the same time. Their weapons fired simultaneously, holding down the men in the mesquite for a few moments.

"I'll go after him," Griffin said grimly, rising to his feet, half-crouched behind a rock.

"The hell you will," Jordan argued, also rising.

"Look, hero, why don't you just forget about what you want for a few minutes? One of us has to go out there, and the logical choice is me."

"Do you want to depend on *my* accuracy with a gun to save your life?" Jordan pointed out reasonably. "You're a much better shot, Griffin. Cover me while I go. Anyway, I'm a lot bigger than you and can carry him easier."

Common sense won over loyalty without a struggle, and Griffin nodded. "Okay. You go."

Pausing, Jordan flashed Griffin a reasonable facsimile of his former easy grin and said, "Why do I feel like I've just won the door prize? It's *my* ass they're going to be shooting at!"

Griffin grinned, too. "Because you're not too bright," he said. "Now go before they get up enough nerve to stick their heads up again."

"Jordan!" Jolie cried, flinging herself forward to grab him with a frantic hand. "Be . . . be careful."

"I will, green eyes. You back Griffin up with the extra rifle. We can use all the help we can get."

Obediently, Jolie picked up the extra rifle lying at Griffin's feet, though she had only a vague notion how to use it. It was not at all like her papa's rifle, which was an ancient but highly valued Hawken.

"No, this way," Griffin instructed, turning the rifle in her hands and showing her how to pump the lever. They positioned themselves on the flat surface of a rock near the crest, then gave the nod to Jordan to go.

The first time Jolie fired she was knocked backward, landing on her posterior in the similar position of a turtle on its back. She scrambled up quickly and slanted Griffin a glance to see if he was laughing at her, but he was too busy firing to take notice.

"One, two, three," the youth counted, squeezing off a shot that must have hit its target because there was a distant scream from the mesquite. They both fired rapidly and steadily as Jordan crept from the safety of the rocks, running in a crouch toward Amos.

Amos had somehow managed to wriggle across the ground like a snake, taking cover under the scant security of a bearberry bush. A crimson trail of blood marked his path, and Jordan grimaced. From the amount, it appeared that Amos had been hit pretty badly. He was trying to fire his rifle, but his hands were slow and clumsy, so that by the time Jordan reached him, Amos had still not managed to get off a single shot.

"They got me in the side," Amos grunted, wheezing badly as he half-rolled toward Jordan.

"No time to look now. Just bear with me while I get you out of here," Jordan said, reaching down to slide one arm underneath the brawny Negro and lift him from the ground. "You've got to help me, Amos," he said when he met resistance, "or I'll never get either one of us back to the rocks alive."

"Yeah," Amos puffed, gritting his teeth and pushing hard against the ground with both hands. Jordan just succeeded in lifting him up, half-staggering under his weight as Griffin and Jolie kept up a steady bark of fire at the men in the mesquite. Even with their cover, a few bullets whizzed uncomfortably close as Jordan half-carried, half-dragged Amos to the safety of the rocks only a few yards away. Griffin was at their sides almost immediately while Jolie continued a rapid patter of rifle fire.

She had discovered a system that allowed her to fire without being knocked backward, but her entire shoulder was numb from her efforts. Guns hadn't been a way of life for her in the past, but she was quickly discovering their usefulness as she kept the unseen men pinned down. The rifle barrel rested on the surface of the rock just ahead of her, and she was safely wedged between two others so that the brunt of the Winchester's recoil rested chiefly on the rocks. Jolie did not cease firing until Amos was lying safely among the rocks and brush behind her.

Sweat streamed down his face as Amos attempted to smile at her around Jordan's broad shoulders. All Jolie could see of him as Griffin wadded up a shirt and stuffed it under his head was a slice of white teeth and a broad wink.

"Let me look at him," she insisted to Jordan, "while you go back to the rocks and fire at those men. I can take care of his wound."

"Don't be ridiculous! You'd kill him . . ."

Anger flared in her eyes, and Jolie resisted the urge to give Jordan a good, swift kick in the seat of his pants. "I am used to tending wounds, Jor-dan, while I am not used to firing a rifle."

He glanced up at her with a frown, then apparently decided there was something to what she was saying, because he shrugged and relinquished his examination of the patient.

"Okay, if you think you can do it, go ahead. But if you can't, don't do it just to irritate me."

"What kind of person do you believe me to be?" she couldn't help asking as she pushed him aside and knelt beside Amos. "Do you think I do not care for Amos?"

Jordan's answer went unheard as she became quickly absorbed in discovering the extent of the injuries. The wound was raw and bleeding, but in places the flow of blood had already begun to slow. That was good. His heartbeat was strong and steady, and he had never lost consciousness, which all worked in his favor.

"*Ndiih né?*" she asked, and Amos shook his head.

"No, it's not that painful. My hand hurts the most . . ."

"Your hand?" Griffin cut in, worry creasing his brow. "Did you get shot in the hand?"

"Naw, I fell on it."

"*Nigan ndiih née*?" Jolie quickly examined his hand, turning it over and feeling the bones with a delicate touch. "Nothing is broken, so it must just be bruised. Go and get me some clean cloths," she instructed Griffin, "and I will search for some salve for his wound. We must get him in the shade first and cover it from the sun."

They half-pulled, half-carried Amos to the scant shade of a rock shelf, then Jolie ventured as far from the boulders as she dared to search for a particular plant. She could hear the occasional shot as Jordan and the men in the mesquite traded fire, and she had the uneasy feeling that those men had devised some sort of plan to conquer them. She had to hurry. . . .

There was only one plant that would suffice, and it was a small one, with the characteristic sharp, bladed leaves and cluster of unpleasant-smelling blossoms. She broke off several stems and gathered them in the tail of her shirt, then returned to Amos.

He was resting more easily, sipping at a small brown bottle of whiskey that Griffin had thoughtfully provided.

"Gettin' shot ain't quite so bad when you got a bit of joy-juice," he commented with a wink.

"My people make a drink you would like," Jolie said, kneeling beside him and swiftly rolling out the precious leaves onto a white cloth. Griffin had left a small bundle of medical supplies in a nest of clean white rags: water, a knife, and a jar of foul-smelling ointment. She carefully washed the wound with their precious water. Gunfire ricocheted above them, and she flashed Amos a soothing smile as she lifted the bone-handled knife. She took the whiskey from him and poured it generously over the blade, then handed back the bottle. "This will hurt," she said cheerfully, and flicked back his bloodied shirt to expose the wound.

Amos took a hasty gulp from the brown bottle. "What kind of drink do your people make?"

"*Tulpái.*" Her fingers gently probed the wound and found the bullet. Fortunately, it was close to the surface so she would not have to dig deeply to remove it. "*Tulpái* has a bite like a rattlesnake and burns like winter fire," she said, and the knife slid into the rough-edged wound.

Amos sucked in a deep breath, air hissing from between his clenched teeth. "So," he gasped, "when do I get to try some *tulpái*? I sure could use some right . . . now."

Forcing her trembling fingers to be steady, Jolie deftly found the bullet and forced it from his flesh, hoping her nerves would not falter on her now. True, she had tended many wounds before, but only as an assistant, never as the surgeon.

"Soon you will try *tulpái*," she promised, dropping the knife and staunching the fresh flow of blood with a clean rag. She held it to his side for a moment, then took the leaves she had gathered and squeezed the soft, jellied juice from them onto the open wound. There was no time to make a proper salve, as the gunfire had resumed a steady, frenetic pace, and she bandaged him as quickly as possible.

Sitting back, she dragged a weary hand across her forehead, smearing traces of blood, and managed a bright smile. "How do you feel?"

"Like I've been draggd through the briars and hung out to dry," he muttered, fine pale lines bracketing his mouth. "But I'm mighty grateful to you, Jolie. Jordan has less than a gentle hand with the wounded." He reached out and took her hand in his and gave it a gentle squeeze. "Thanks," he whispered.

"Perhaps, one day, you will do the same for me or one of my people," Jolie whispered back.

Amos nodded and closed tired eyes. He was resting quietly when Jordan returned to check on him.

"He going to be okay?" he asked Jolie, crouching down beside Amos.

"Yes. It was not a bad wound, and the bullet was not very deep, but he did lose a lot of blood." She sat with her legs drawn up and her arms curled around them, regarding Jordan with a steady gaze that he found most disconcerting.

"What's the matter?"

"Nothing. I still hear those men shooting at us. Can we not do something?"

"Like what? We're almost out of ammunition, and the supply mules are still down in that damned arroyo, waiting like sitting ducks for somebody to come along. What do you suggest we do?"

He sounded angry, but Jolie knew it was not with her. "I don't know. What does Griffin say?"

"Griffin! What can that pup say? Hell, he's never been away from home before. Just what is it between you and him, Jolie?" He regarded her with narrowed blue eyes for a long moment. "Maybe I've been wrong in thinking you're only friends. Maybe there's a lot more to it than that . . ."

Eyes flashed with anger as she surged to her feet. "*Chúúné*! No, you are worse than the dog! How can you say such a thing about Griffin—about *me*? *Haashkéń—duu ńlíída*."

"Look!" He interrupted her tirade, rising to his feet and grasping her by both arms. "Maybe I didn't mean that, but I still wish you'd just . . . just . . ." He halted, not quite knowing what he wanted her to do. Dammit, just when he got everything all straight in his mind again, she did something to confuse him. It was a lot easier when he could think of

-219-

her as just a nuisance, a pretty child who had formed an attachment to him; but then she would do something to force him to remember that she was not a child but a strong-minded, poised young woman of considerable beauty. How could he even consider falling in love with a girl whose people had massacred his friends? It went against his grain, against everything he'd believed in for so long.

Jordan released her arms abruptly, staring angrily into her flushed face. This was ridiculous. She still had blood smeared across her forehead, testifying to her skill in performing surgery on a wounded man. Her ebony hair was bound in a knot on the nape of her neck and dirt marred her fine features, and yet he felt a surge of desire that made him want to take her in his arms and carry her to some spot on the rocks and make love to her until they were both exhausted.

Something of what he was feeling must have shown in his eyes, for Jolie suddenly smiled, a mere lifting of the corners of her mouth into an enchanting tilt that mystified as well as charmed him.

"Dammit," he muttered, "don't look at me like that."

"Like what, Jor-dan? Like this?" she was murmuring softly as she stepped close. She had recognized the gleam of desire in his eyes.

"Yes," he growled, catching her hands before she could reach out to touch him, "like that. You know what you're doing, you little minx . . ."

"Mink? Do you mean, like the otter?"

"No, I mean like saucebox, flirt, coquette . . ."

"Ahh," she said. She knew what coquette meant, and agreed. "Yes, I am, aren't I? But only for you, Jordan."

Warm fingers curled under her chin to tilt her head back

so that he could gaze into her eyes. "Promise?" he asked in a light, teasing tone.

"I have eyes only for you, Jordan . . ."

"And those guys in the bushes have eyes only for us and our mules," Griffin snapped, descending upon them in a shower of gravel and youthful irritation. "Do you mind? I mean they *are* still shooting at us, and I'm almost out of ammunition, while you guys are standing here making sheep's eyes at one another!"

"Sheep's eyes?" Jolie echoed with a puzzled frown when Jordan released her chin and turned to Griffin.

"Sorry. I came to check on Amos."

"And how is he?" was Griffin's sarcastic query.

"Resting," Jolie supplied quickly. "What shall we do now?"

"Figuratively speaking, we need to get the hell out of Dodge," Jordan said, removing the last of his cartridges from his gunbelt and loading his pistol. "How's our water holding out?"

"Gone." Griffin affirmed the worst.

"There's only a little bit left for Amos," Jolie said with a worried frown.

"Damn!" Jordan tugged at the brim of his hat, as he often did when confronted with a situation he didn't like. "We need to get to those mules," he said as Griffin climbed back up the incline to take up his position with a rifle.

"I'll go," Jolie volunteered, but Jordan shook his head.

"No, ma'am, green eyes. You're going to stay right here with Amos while Griffin and I figure out something."

"But . . ." she began to protest when Jordan lay his fingers across her lips.

"Hush. For once, do as I ask. This is no time to argue,

Jolie. If you have any suggestions that might help, let us know. Otherwise, just follow orders."

A groan from Amos preempted any comment she might have made, and Jolie slanted the retreating Jordan a last glance as she returned to her patient. Fine beads of perspiration dotted his forehead, and his face was a gray, chalky color that worried her. He needed water and more shade than he now had, but there was nothing she could do.

Breaking a branch from the stunted bush jutting from the ground beside the rock, she waved it in an effort to stir air, but it was a futile act. Gunfire barked and spit above her, and she could hear Griffin and Jordan's muttered worries about the ammunition. Jolie slid a glance toward the lip of the arroyo they'd climbed earlier. Just beyond that crusty edge there was water and ammunition. It was just out of reach . . .

It didn't take long to decide. Griffin and Jordan were busy spacing careful shots at the men, who had stepped up their attack, and Amos was unconscious. If she crept to the shelter of that rock not far from the edge, perhaps she could make it to the ravine before their attackers noticed her. If not—well, she'd think about that when the time came.

Years of living in an Apache camp had trained her in the art of walking quietly, on silent feet like the mountain cat, and Jolie used that training now. No rock betrayed her, nor snap of a dry twig as she moved as silently as a shadow across the space between the boulders and the small shelter of a lone rock not far from the edge of the arroyo. In fact, if Griffin hadn't just happened to look around, neither one of them would have noticed what she was doing.

But Griffin did look around, and his snarled, "Dammit!" alerted Jordan to Jolie's actions. Sunlight glittered from his blond head as Griffin swept off his hat and hit the rock with it in frustration. "Just lookit!"

Jordan looked, and his dark brows swooped down in an ominous frown. At that moment, if she'd been within range, he would have taken her slender little neck between his hands and cheerfully strangled her. Had she no regard for her own safety? he wondered savagely even as Griffin was asking the same thing.

"Don't yell at her," Jordan said quickly, "or they might see her."

"Do you think I'm stupid?" the boy snarled.

"Never ask questions you don't want answered," Jordan shot back, "but I only meant that I was tempted to call her back myself. We'll just have to let her go now. She's too far for us to help."

So they watched in an agony of suspense as Jolie waited behind the rock for the right moment to run. Using the last of their precious ammunition, Jordan and Griffin fired a barrage of shots that effectively held down the men in the mesquite long enough for Jolie to make it to the edge of the cut. Only when her dark head disappeared over the lip did they cease firing.

"Let's hope she comes back," Jordan muttered under his breath, slamming the last of his cartridges into his pistol and shapping it closed.

"Oh, she'll be back," Griffin said. "She's probably more worried about your neck than you are. So what do we do now?"

"Wait."

Chapter
17

Jolie would never have admitted it, but she was terrified. Where were all her brave words about death—the calm acceptance that she was supposed to feel? Carried away on the hot drift of wind that was filtering down the arroyo, probably, because she was feeling nothing but stark terror.

Trembling fingers gripped the crumbling red rock as she descended the steep side of the ravine, and her bare feet scrambled for a footing as she half-slid, half-crawled like a spider down the walls. The mules had—contrarily or perhaps because they had been frightened by the gunfire—wandered further down the length of the ravine, so that she was obliged to follow them.

Letting go of the rock, she leaped the last four feet from the walls to the arroyo floor, landing on a rock and bruising her foot. She hobbled several feet, grimacing painfully as she forced herself not to pause and rub her injured instep. Water and ammunition were needed most desperately, and hesitation might be fatal.

Their horses had vanished, wandering off to better pastures, no doubt, but the mules were still in the arroyo. The lead mule had found wider and better space, and the other mules trotted behind him with an enthusiasm and energy they had never displayed when being led by Amos, so that by the time Jolie caught up with one of them she was quite winded. She had begun wishing that she had been trained as Cháa had been trained in his youth, to run up the side of a mountain with a mouthful of water, exhorted not to swallow or lose a drop of the liquid. It had been an excellent training process for young Apache boys, enabling them to run miles without becoming winded. Apache girls, however, were given no such training, so Jolie sucked in deep, struggling breaths of air as she wrestled with the mule she had caught.

"Jǫ'e," she addressed him politely by his name, "I must ask you to be still so that I may search through your packs." But Mule had different ideas. He bucked; he lunged; he brayed loudly, and his eyes rolled indignantly.

Jolie firmly but kindly hit him between the eyes with her clenched fist. Mule quieted. *"'Ixéhe,"* she thanked him as she quickly explored the packs on his back. No water and no ammunition were among the shovels and picks, and she gave a sharp exclamation of frustration. Surrendering to necessity, Jolie led the now docile beast closer to the others. They had wandered some distance from where they had been left, which was to be expected, but it was time-consuming and irritating to have to chase them.

The sun was scalding, beating down with a vengeance, as Jolie and her mule chased the pack train down the arroyo.

"Where the hell is she?" Jordan muttered to no one in particular. "I'm willing to bet she headed for home."

"You know she wouldn't do that. I don't know what's keeping her, but I hope she's okay," Griffin said, worried.

"Hah. She's just like a damned cat, always landing on her feet," Jordan returned gloomily. His narrowed eyes were trained on the mesquite, where it was obvious the men below them were intent on some sort of plan of attack. "We're about to be hit from two sides, Griffin. Look!" He pointed to the men snaking out to one side. "It looks like they've got two men down in the mesquite, two going to one side, and one to another. I've got three shots left, how about you?"

"One." Griffin exchanged a long look with his uncle. "Unless Jolie gets back pretty quick, we ain't got a prayer."

"Yeah." Jordan's gaze flicked to Amos, still unconscious below them. "Who knows?" he murmured hopelessly. "Maybe we'll get a miracle." He rolled onto his back and contemplated the blue, blue sky overhead. The mountain peaks fringing the Jornada loomed behind them, promising safety, but were too far away to reach safely.

"Those men are moving closer," Griffin said softly. "All of them are hiding in that arroyo just below us. I think they're trying to figure out if we've got any ammunition left."

"That shouldn't take long," was Jordan's dry rejoinder, and Griffin managed a weak grin.

" 'Bout two shots, I'd say."

Rolling back to his stomach, Jordan contemplated the scene below them, the short stretch of hard-baked earth and the narrow cut that was no more than six feet across, fringed on the other side with the mesquite. The ravine angled sharply, so that the men could easily bypass it instead of going through it, but it seems that they chose to hide in the cut as if it was a natural foxhole. It did provide shelter of a sort, and Jordan cursed the fact.

"Think they might bargain?" Griffin asked.

Jordan shrugged. "Why should they? They've got time on their side, while we don't. If we try to backtrack, they've still got easy access to their horses and can run us down in a few minutes. We can't fight them with no bullets, and I've no desire to try and club them to death with the butt of a rifle. Once they figure out we don't have any options left, they won't need to talk. They'll just politely tell us what they want, and we can be prepared to talk or die. It's as simple as that."

"Sorry I asked," Griffin muttered. "I sure hope Jolie don't come back. I hope she finds our horses and rides out of here as fast as she can."

"I do, too," Jordan surprised him by agreeing. Noting Griffin's expression, he said testily, "Well, you didn't think I *really* wanted her hurt, did you? Never mind."

"No, no," Griffin said hastily. "I didn't *really* think you wanted her hurt. Not bad, anyway."

"Look, it's just that . . ."

An ominous rumble sounded, interrupting Jordan's explanation and train of thought. It jerked both their heads around to see what was happening. Jordan's first thought was that the noise sounded like the distant rumble of cannon fire. Then he recognized it: the chilling memory of that day weeks before when a wall of water had washed down a gully returned, and he knew it was one of those sudden floods.

"Hey!" he yelled, leaping to his feet and waving his arms over his head. "Flood!"

A shot rang out in answer, sending his hat flying from his head and his body diving for cover.

"You crazy?" Griffin wanted to know. "What'd you do that for?"

"Sudden flood," Jordan explained tersely.

"So? Those guys want to kill us," Griffin half-laughed in amazement. "Do you really want to warn 'em . . . ?" He stopped, and his thick-lashed blue eyes widened, absorbing

-227-

light like a mirror. 'Jolie!'' Griffin and Jordan said at the same time.

Both stared in horror at the wall of water rushing down the arroyo, filling it to the brim and carrying away everything in its path. Storms in the mountains often sent water tumbling down to fill the riverbeds that were bone-dry and rock-hard most of the year. Griffin and Jordan could hear the faint, helpless cries of the men being swept away but were powerless to help. All they could do was hope that Jolie had heard the flood in time to avoid it.

The silence that followed the flood was oppressive. Only Amos was spared the mental anguish of uncertainty as he slept on. Slumped against the hard, hot rock, Griffin gazed at Jordan with bright, unashamed tears in his eyes.

"I'm going to look for her, Jordan."

"No. You stay here with Amos. I'll look for her..."

"No!" Griffin said savagely, surging to his feet in a lithe motion, his young body hard and tensed like a half-grown wildcat. "You don't love her. Let somebody go who cares..."

"Whether I love her or not isn't the point. *She* loves *me*," Jordan said. "I should be the one... be the one to look for her. Besides, if I do find her... like that... I can take it better than you can." His voice softened. "And it'll be hard enough on me, Griffin."

"Go, then," Griffin said, his voice half-breaking. "I'll stay with Amos."

It was almost an hour before Jordan found her, and when he did, his face registered disbelief. Jolie had draped her blanket over the knobby stump of a tree that stuck up from the ground and was shaded by spindly branches of a young mesquite. Behind her, arrayed in a half-circle, were all their horses and the pack mules. Stunned, he stopped within inches of her and stood slack-jawed and loose-limbed, gazing at her as if she were made of moondust and air instead of flesh and blood. He was not, Jordan was to reflect later, at his most articulate.

"Uh . . . where . . . why . . . how . . . how did you do that?"

"Do what, Jor-dan?" Jolie asked, busily knotting her red scarf around her foot.

"Do . . . *that*! Herd up all the horses and the mules and . . . and why didn't you come back? You knew we were waiting on water and ammunition, damn you!" Inexplicable rage at seeing her unharmed banished the concern he had voiced earlier, and he stalked toward her with grim purpose. "Were you hoping we'd buy a one-way ticket to hell, maybe, so you could get the gold all by yourself? Well, too bad!"

Jolie's eyes flashed dangerously, but Jordan was too incensed to notice. "*Dah*," she said shortly, keeping her eyes on her hands and her hands busy with the red bandana.

"Yeah, I'll bet," he sneered, halting in front of her with his thumbs hooked in his belt in an insolent mein that Jolie disliked. "Those guys sure could have made it a lot easier for you by killing us, couldn't they, green eyes?"

Finishing the last knot, Jolie shook back her mane of sable hair and stood up, gingerly lowering her wrapped foot to the ground and testing it with her weight. She immediately crumpled to one knee with a soft cry of pain.

Jordan frowned as he reached down to lift her. She slapped away his hand and gave her arm an angry shake. "Leave me alone! I made it this far without you, worthless one, so I can make it back to Griffin and Amos."

"What—are you hurt or something?"

She flung back her head to give him such a look of scathing contempt that he actually flinched. "Does that matter to you?'' she stormed. ''Or were you more worried over your mules? They are all unharmed, as you can see, and I even found the horses. Or, they found me once we got out of the *gun'a*—arroyo. I think they are hungry, so you need to feed them when you get back.''

''Aren't you even going to ask me what happened back there?'' Jordan snapped. ''Aren't you worried about Griffin or Amos?''

''No. You are here, and you are too busy being angry with me. If Amos and Griffin were hurt, you would not waste time with such a trivial emotion as anger...''

''Trivial! You leave us to be massacred, and you call that trivial?'' He grabbed her by the upper arms and yanked her up, giving her a rough shake.

''I...did...not...leave...you,'' she managed to say between snaps of her head back and forth. When Jordan released her she stumbled backward and put out her hands to steady herself against the slender trunk of the mesquite as she replied in a calm tone, ''I went to get water and bullets because you could not.''

''That still doesn't explain why you were just sitting here on a blanket instead of bringing us the water and bullets, now does it?''

Jolie's eyes widened a fraction, then narrowed, and her expression was one of impatience and irritation as she said, ''I have a broken *shikétsíne'*, and I cannot very well...''

''Broken what?''

''My ankle—and I cannot very well manage all the animals and travel back on one leg,'' she finished, pointing to the red bandana wrapped around her foot and ankle.

Jordan's sardonic gaze skimmed the length of her slender, Levis-clad leg, then rested on the carefully wrapped foot and ankle. He was well aware that anyone could wrap an ankle and pretend it was broken. "No, I suppose you can't," he agreed smoothly. "How convenient. Maybe I should just take a look at your ankle, green eyes."

He was already bending and taking her foot in his big palm, cradling it gently for a man who was furious, his fingers untying the knot she had just tied. In spite of her irritation, she longed to take the hat from his head and run her fingers through his thick, dark hair that held hints of sunrise in the strands. Her throat tightened with the memory as she recalled their nights in each other's arms, and how closely he had held her, whispering words of love that he obviously had not meant. Perhaps there was a difference in the way men and women expressed their love that had nothing to do with race, with whether she was Apache or French and whether Jordan was an *'indaa'*. He was still *bika*—her lover, but did he love her?

Hunkering down on his heels in front of her, Jordan pushed back his hat with one hand, still holding her foot with the other, and looked up at Jolie. "You're right, green eyes. It's broken. How'd you do that?"

"I stepped into a hole while chasing the mules up the gully," she answered. A faint smile curved her mouth at his expression of apology, though no words of apology could be heard. It was, she supposed, the closest he would go to admitting he'd misjudged her.

Rebandaging her foot, Jordan let it rest gently on the ground and straightened in a lithe movement, uncoiling his lean body as effortlessly as a panther. An answering smile slanted the usually harsh line of his mouth as he removed his hat, raking his spread fingers through his thick hair and sighing. "Guess I'll get your horse for you. We can both lead the mules back."

"'*Au*," she agreed softly. "That would be good." Jolie's

eyes lingered on Jordan's face. He was only inches away, so close that she could almost hear the beat of his heart. Why was she in love with a man who did not love her in return? And why did her pulse race as swiftly as the fleeing hare when he was so close?

"Can we not . . . rest . . . for a few minutes before we go?" she suggested shyly. "The sun is so hot, and there is shade here beneath the branches of the trees. We have water, and the horses will not run away again."

Meeting her eyes, Jordan felt the same small shock of electricity that she obviously did, because he was moving toward her then, giving her no chance to protest, lifting her into his arms and placing her beneath the sheltering branches of the mesquite. Here the trees did not grow as tall as they did in other areas, but the branches were as widespread, forming a leafy canopy that hid them effectively from the world.

Jolie's blanket cushioned her weight as Jordan lowered her to the ground, his hands hot and insistent on her body. Only earth and sky and trees surrounded her—and Jordan. He rose to his knees, blotting out the rest of the world, shedding his guns and shirt before lying down beside her. They were both caught up in a powerful surge of desire that neither could deny.

Gasping as Jordan rained hot, scalding kisses on her mouth, his lips searing along the sweep of her jaw, Jolie held him tightly. Jordan's hands tunnelled into her hair, pulling the loose braids free to spread a cape of sable silk over the woven blanket beneath them. Bunching a fistful in one hand, he pulled her head slowly back so that she was looking into his eyes. Jolie was trembling with reaction. There was no gentleness in his hot gaze, nothing in the deep blue of his eyes that indicated love instead of wanting, and she shivered.

"Afraid, green eyes?" he asked softly, the whisper somehow seeming loud in the heavy silence around them.

"No. I am not afraid of you, Jor-dan . . ." She wasn't afraid of him, not the way he meant. She was more afraid of herself and her own reaction to him. Jolie tingled with excitement as Jordan's mouth moved to scorch a path from her lips to her temple, then the small whorls of her ear. Burying his face in her hair, he muttered love words, sex words that brought out a primitive instinct in Jolie to respond, and she did.

Her hands moved boldly along his chest, her fingers sliding beneath his belt and buckle, undoing it with swift, deft movements that took away his breath. When her hands slipped inside his pants to caress him, he gave a rough groan that was immediately lost in fevered response. Impatient with the buttons of her shirt—his shirt—Jordan jerked sharply and they popped off, baring small firm breasts with buds that were already hardened in anticipation.

Shoving aside the open edges of the shirt until it slipped from her shoulders and down her arms, Jordan found and held her breasts in cupped palms. Her dusky skin was lightly beaded with perspiration, the deep rose of her nipples tempting him. Bending his head, he covered a rosy crest with his lips, sucking gently, sending lightning sparks tingling through her as his tongue swirled in teasing caresses.

Jolie arched her back, straining closer, her arms curled around Jordan's neck, her fingers combing through his thick hair. She was only vaguely aware that he was tugging at her Levis, pulling them away until she lay bare before him. His knee was wedging between her thighs, forcing them apart. When his hand sought the downy curls covering her mound, brushing gently against her in an intimate way, she cried out in protest. But Jordan covered her mouth with his own, muffling her whimpers as he continued stroking the soft folds of her body, pulling at the tiny black curls and satiny swells. It was torture, sweet torture, and her head thrashed back and forth on the rumpled blanket as she moaned.

She cried out in French, Apache, and Spanish, finally pleading, "No, Jordan! I don't know... I can't..."

"You're not supposed to do anything, love. I won't hurt your ankle. Just lie there and let me love you," he said against the swollen pout of her mouth. "That's all you have to do."

Then he was moving lower, sliding his sweat-slick body down over hers, his buckle rubbing harshly against her bare skin, his mouth nipping at her in teasing nibbles. Jordan seared a path between the valley of her breasts, tasting and taunting, his tongue flicking like a snake's over the ridge of her ribs and down to her navel, then lower. Jolie almost shrieked when he kissed that small, dark mound between her legs, and her thighs instinctively clamped shut on his head.

Gently but firmly, Jordan pushed them apart. "It's all right, love. You're as beautiful there as everywhere else, and I won't hurt you."

"*Sacré bleu,*" she moaned, writhing and straining against his tongue, shocked in spite of herself. It could not be right, but it felt so good, and nothing in her experience had prepared her for this. She was burning inside. It was as if the scorching sun had been swallowed and was glowing deep in the pit of her stomach, sending out tremors to rock her from head to toe. Yet when the waves finally overtook her, drowning her in a series of throbbing pulses that she wanted to last forever, Jolie thought she could never experience such an exquisite feeling again.

Eyes smoky with repletion found and held his, and she managed a tentative smile.

"That wasn't so bad, was it?" Jordan teased softly, nuzzling her ear, and Jolie shook her head. His breath was warm, curling over her cheek and stirring tendrils of sable hair as he whispered, "I'm glad you liked it—wait 'til you see what comes next."

Rising to his knees, Jordan began unbuttoning his pants with his eyes resting on Jolie's face, his mouth slanted in a tender smile. Her heart beat faster as she watched him, a dark shadow against the bright sunshine outside their leafy cocoon, his motions swift as he slipped out of his pants and stood before her tall and proud and as bare as the day he'd been born.

Jolie lifted her arms to him and Jordan took her hands. He pulled her slowly up until she knelt before him, and his palms gently cradled each side of her face. Sliding her hands over his body, Jolie's fingers skimmed over the dark mat of hair on his chest as she explored the hard ridges of his ribs, then the flat band of muscles on his stomach. She carefully watched his reaction, his tension as her hands slipped lower to caress and hold him; then—growing bolder than she'd ever been—she took him between her lips, her tongue imitating the flickers of lightning often seen in the hot summer sky. Jordan sucked in a deep breath and seemed to hold it, his fingers reaching blindly out to tangle in the wealth of her hair and hold her head still, but she refused to be held. She shook free of his hold and continued, until finally he could stand it no longer and shoved her back against the rough folds of the blanket. Poised above her, his eyes were pinpoint blue flames of desire, as searing as the hottest part of a fire, stabbing into her as he slowly lowered his lean body over hers.

In spite of the urgency of desire pricking him, Jordan took his time, coaxing the response he wanted from Jolie's willing body. Soft, heated caresses and deep kisses sparked her desire into a raging flame, until she was arching against him. Surging forward, Jordan pushed deep inside her with a single lunge, and Jolie's arms wrapped around him to hold him close.

"Now wrap your legs around me," Jordan rasped, and she did, trembling violently, half-dazed with the force of emotions inside her, the turbulent reaction to Jordan's hard, driving motions. Even though the sun was shining brightly she felt as if she was in the middle of a thunderstorm, with dark rolling clouds and blinding flashes of lightning crackling in the air. The storm built slowly to a peak as Jordan moved against her, until release came in a shattering explosion.

At almost the same instant, Jordan thrust himself into her so fiercely that she cried out, his body pulsing with the juices of life, then he was still.

Still holding him, Jolie felt weak and drained, depleted of energy though her pulses were still throbbing and her heart still racing. The steady thump of Jordan's heart thudded against her breast, and their hot, moist bodies were joined at thigh, hip, and shoulder. His mouth moved against her ear, nibbling lightly, then whispering, "See? I told you it got better."

Jolie smiled weakly, opening her eyes to gaze up at him, then rubbing her forehead against the dark stubble of his day-old beard.

"How do you know it got better?" she murmured. "Maybe I do not think so."

Blue eyes narrowed down at her. "Didn't it?"

Now she laughed aloud. "*Oui*—I feel as if I have touched the sky," she admitted. "You are different out here with the sky and sun and wind than you are in a small room where one cannot see the stars or the moon. I think I shall never like coming together with you unless we are like this." She pushed at a damp strand of hair in his eyes and traced the line furrowed between his brows. "Do you not agree, Jor-dan?"

"In a way," he answered slowly. "With you, it feels more . . . right . . . on a blanket under a tree than in a feather bed. Maybe because of who you are."

"And who am I? Am I someone you like, Jor-dan?"

Twisting a strand of her sable hair around his finger, Jordan studied it silently for a moment as if it held all the secrets to life in the gleaming depths. Then he said, "Yes, Jolie. You are definitely someone I like, but I'm damned if I know why."

Drawing back slightly, her eyes widened at his answer. "What do you mean by that?"

A half-smile pressed against the corners of his mouth. "Not what you think." He rubbed his belly against hers and lowered his head to give her a lingering kiss, then murmured against her lips, "Maybe I just like you too much, Jolie . . ."

"*Dah*," she replied. "There's no such thing as too much, Jor-dan."

Chapter
18

Griffin, perched morosely on the hump of a rock, looked up when he heard the faint clatter of hooves on hard-packed ground. Thick-lashed blue eyes widened in glad surprise as he saw Jordan and Jolie.

"Hey! God, am I glad to see you," he called, sliding from the rock and running to meet Jolie. "I thought for sure that you'd been carried away by the flood. Amos is still asleep, and I've just been sitting here, waiting and worrying—what's the matter with your foot?" he asked, noticing the red bandana around Jolie's ankle.

"It's broken," Jordan answered for her, tossing Griffin the lead lines to the mules and dismounting from his weary gray.

"You sure?"

"No. I'm no damned doctor, but it's all swollen and bruised."

"Let me have a look at it," Griffin said, reaching up to swing Jolie down from her horse. The red bandana had been loosely retied and now was drooping around her ankle. Griffin cradled her against his chest and carried her to the rock he had just left. Lowering her to perch on the rough, flat surface, he knelt at her feet and untied the makeshift bandage. "Bruised, sprained maybe," was his verdict several moments later.

"You sure?" Jordan asked. "It felt broken to me."

"Naw, it's just sprained real bad," Griffin insisted. "If we had some ice, when the swelling went down she'd be able to walk on it."

"Where'd you go to medical school?" Jordan wanted to know as he gave Jolie a wink and a smile. Smears of pink stained her cheeks as she returned Jordan's lingering look, her soft lips curved in an answering smile.

Griffin's attention narrowed on the girl's flushed face, and he pulled at his bottom lip as he looked from one to the other.

"Something goin' on here that I don't know about?" he asked his uncle, but Jordan feigned ignorance.

"Why, no. What do you mean by that, Griffin?"

"Just that you and her are lookin' at each other like you . . . like you . . ." He stumbled to a halt, eyes narrowing suspiciously when Jordan grinned.

"Like we were what?"

"Like you had a bellyache or something!" Griffin snapped irritably. He stalked away from the rock where Jolie was sitting, going to his horse and pretending to rummage through his packs.

Pushing back his hat, Jordan stared after Griffin for a long moment. "Hell, he nags at me to be nice to you, and now that I am, he doesn't like it," he said to Jolie. "I can't figure that kid out."

Pushing up from her hard perch, Jolie said, "Don't try, Jordan. I do not think Griffin wants you to 'figure him out.' I think that would only make it worse." She limped close, and Jordan lifted her from her feet into his arms.

"Well, just the same, it'd be nice to know what it is he thinks I'm supposed to do," he muttered against the top of her head.

"Don't do anything," she repeated, snuggling into his chest and tucking her head beneath his square chin. "All things will be resolved with time, just as we have been."

"We're resolved?" Jordan inquired. "Since when?"

"Since this afternoon." She angled her head and looked up at him. "Aren't we?"

How could he deny the naked appeal in those luminous green eyes that were gazing at him with the trusting confidence of a child? He couldn't. And he knew he couldn't. And worse—*she* knew he couldn't.

"Sure, baby," he said with insincere cheerfulness that didn't fool Jolie for a moment, "we're resolved."

"I thought we were," she answered, snuggling close again with a resigned sigh.

Jordan gave a mental groan and wondered how he was going to deal with this situation. Jolie wasn't just an ordinary girl he could leave behind without a qualm. Somehow—maybe because he'd been her first man—he knew he'd never forgive himself if he did that. But he didn't want to be tied down, either. So what was a man to do?

Jolie was thinking the same thing, only from her point of view. They were resolved as far as their affection for one another was concerned, but she wasn't at all certain about the direction of their relationship. She did not like the small, stuffy room she had occupied with Jordan in Franklin, and she wasn't at all sure that she could spend the rest of her life in a confining wooden house. At the same time, she did not intend to let the choice of a dwelling come between her and Jordan. And, too, what would her father say when she returned to her people with a husband? Henri La Fleur was no small obstacle to overcome if he objected, and he'd never been a predictable parent.

So it was with some trepidation that Jolie considered her choice of a mate, but only the manner in which to introduce him to her parent and the joys of living in a house that breathed instead of keeping out the elements.

"Well," Jordan was saying to Griffin, his voice lightly tinged with sarcasm, "what do you suggest we do now that your friends are disposed of? Amos is hurt, Jolie is hurt, and one of our packs fell off the lead mule, so if you have any ideas . . ."

Griffin shrugged carelessly, his attention trained on the leather lacings of the pack he was retying. "Suit yourself, Jordan. You always have an idea."

"Fine. Las Cruces isn't that far away. Let's try to make it there so we can get Amos a doctor and let him rest for a little while."

Las Cruces wasn't very far, but it still took them a day and a half to get there. They had to ride slowly because of Amos's injury, for each jolt shook him painfully and often reopened his wound.

They stopped for fresh water at a grove of cottonwoods and a small spring late in the afternoon. Jordan took the leather pouches to the spring and began refilling them while Jolie tended Amos and Griffin checked their animals. Amos was weak from the loss of blood, and weary, but still as calm as always. He waved Jolie away with a cheerful smile, insisting he was fine, and she finally gave in and left him alone.

The sun was a gigantic ball of fire in the western sky, sinking slowly over the lip of the earth, shooting daggers of light across the flat, verdant tableland ahead of them.

Covering her eyes with one hand, Jolie squinted into the distance.

"Where is Gudúudsis—the town we go to?" she asked Griffin, and he pointed west. He was squatting down and inspecting his horse's front hoof, digging at it with a pocket knife to remove a small rock that had been wedged between the shoe and the soft part of the hoof. Wiping his forehead with the back of one arm, he rocked back on his heels.

"It's not too far, I think. Jordan said it was about four miles northwest from here." Griffin grinned. "Why do you ask—thinking about going on without us?"

She made a teasing face. "Would any of you care if I did?"

"*I* would," he answered honestly. Griffin tapped the knife handle against his open palm, gazing at her with a speculative gleam in his eye. "And I think you know how Jordan feels better than I do."

"Sometimes I wonder," Jolie muttered. Limping close to where Griffin still crouched on the ground, she knelt beside him and rested her chin in the cup of her palm and fingers. The red bandana had been moved from her ankle to her head again, holding back the straight wings of dark hair from her eyes. Biting her bottom lip, she attempted to express her doubts to Griffin. "He is very gentle at times, very . . . loving . . . yet he has never *said* he loves me, Griffin. Do you think he does?"

Griffin looked away, staring back at the blue and emerald haze in the distance, the faint, blurred peaks of the mountains that brooded in silent wreaths of cloud and mystery. Shiny clusters of blooms on a yucca plant swayed in a gentle breeze, and slender stalks of flowers dipped their graceful heads. He gazed at the line of mules and gurgling spring and thin, drooping branches of the cottonwood trees. In fact, Griffin looked everywhere but at Jolie.

"Is that so hard to answer?" she prompted finally, and he gave a helpless shrug.

"How can I tell you what's in another man's mind or heart, Jolie? I can only tell you how I feel."

"But I asked you what you *thought*, Griffin. Do you not have an opinion?"

"Yes, but I don't want to share it with you right now."

"I see." Folding her arms around her drawn-up legs, Jolie grew still and quiet. Griffin's reluctance to answer could mean only one thing.

"It doesn't really matter what I think, you know," he said quietly a few moments later. The bone-handled knife he held slapped rhythmically against his open palm. "What matters most is what you think, and how you feel. That's all that should count."

"You are right," she agreed, pushing herself up to stand over Griffin. She gazed down at him with an enigmatic smile that made him frown. "I am a very determined person, Griffin Armstrong."

"Yes, Jolie La Fleur," he said, "I think you are. If Jordan is what you want—you'll get him."

"*Getting* Jor-dan is not the problem," she disagreed. "*Keeping* him may not be so easy. I don't want an unhappy man in my life."

"Smart girl," the youth approved.

A shadow fell across the pair, and they looked up to see Jordan sauntering in their direction. "What's the important conversation about?" he asked in the idle tone people use when they don't really care about the answer. "We ought to be getting into Las Cruces about noon tomorrow if we take it easy and don't bang Amos around too much. How's he feeling, Jolie?''

"Well enough to argue with me that he doesn't need a doctor,'' was the answer. "I told him the doctor was for my ankle, not his wound, and that made him more happy. He told me to go away then, and let him sleep.''

"Great. He's doing a lot better than I'd even hoped. If he's feeling well enough to argue with *you*, then he's feeling well enough to continue our little expedition.'' Jordan's gaze flicked over Jolie's face, then Griffin's. Though his first question had been offhand, he'd noticed how serious their conversation had seemed; he surmised that it had concerned the relationship between himself and Jolie. Not surprising, considering Griffin's infatuation with the girl. His own infatuation he could handle, but what could he do about this half-grown boy who was so quick to judge by inexperienced standards?

"Jordan,'' Griffin was saying, "do you really think Amos will be able to go on?''

"Sure. He's got a strong constitution and an even stronger mind. He'll probably outlast all of us.'' His gaze flicked to Jolie. "Except maybe her,'' Jordan added. "Somehow, I've got this strange feeling she is stronger than all of us put together.''

Lifting a dark, delicately arched brow, Jolie just smiled. She didn't feel stronger, but she did know what she wanted. Maybe that was the important thing. . . .

It was late at night, and Amos and Griffin were already asleep, rolled up in their blankets across the campfire. Jolie couldn't sleep. A hundred different thoughts chased through her mind like night moths flitting aimlessly about a flame, and each time she shut her eyes she was assailed by a new, even more disturbing thought. She thought of her father, her home in the Organ Mountains, her dead mother, and even Cháa, her childhood friend. She thought about the war raging between white settlers and the Apache, and she considered its effect on her relationship with Jordan.

Turning her head on the hard pillow of her saddle, Jolie gazed at the glowing embers of the campfire and the slender threads of smoke winding upward. The smoke drifted on the slight breeze blowing eastward toward the mountains and their ultimate destination, and she wondered about the gold lying somewhere ahead of them. Would it make a difference to Jordan? She had seen the avaricious gleam in men's eyes when it came to gold, and she hated the thought of Jordan being the same.

To the Apache, riches were in the meadow, sky, and trees. Wealth was horses, an abundance of food in the cooking pots, and good weapons with which to hunt—that was the mark of a well-to-do man. This passion for gold, which admittedly made pretty ornaments, was frowned upon by the Apache yet coveted by the *'indaa'*. Henri La Fleur had often told Jolie the stories of his youth, how he had scrounged in the Paris streets for bread and dreamed of a day when he would be free to roam the wilderness and hunt for his food. At the time, young Henri had not dreamed of coming to America, but a chance encounter with an Englishman had brought him to the American shores at the tender age of seventeen. He had gone West and remained to make a new life for himself, one where there was little use for gold or silver, where a man lived by his strength and wits. He had tried to convey that sense of freedom to his daughter, and she had listened well. Yet Jolie had more understanding when it came to gold than her father had. She knew its limitations, but she knew its power and understood the motives that spurred Jordan to risk his life in the search for gold.

Tilting her head, she bent a thoughtful gaze on Jordan. He was lying only a few feet away, separated from her by his rifle and a pack. His profile was outlined against the sullen embers of the fire, the straight nose and contour of his brow, and the strong, square jaw with its stubble of beard illuminated by the tip of his glowing cheroot.

"Jordan?" she whispered, and heard him sigh.

"Yeah?"

"You are not asleep . . ."

"Are we going to play this game again? I know it's one of your favorites, but a man does get a little tired of it now and then."

"You are funning me again," she said, borrowing another phrase from Griffin.

He laughed and said, "No, green eyes, I'm dead serious. But never mind. Go ahead and say whatever it is that's bothering you."

"How do you know something's bothering me?"

Even in the dim light she could see his grin. "Because you always start off this way when something's on your mind, love. What is it?"

She rolled over on her stomach and propped her chin in her hands. "Is the gold we seek more important to you than anything, Jor-dan?"

His answer was slow in coming, his words measured and careful. "Well, it's pretty damned important, but I don't know about being the *most* important thing. Why?"

"Because . . . because *I* want to be the most important thing in your life," she blurted, then stopped and bit her lip. Why had she confessed such a thing? She should have waited and let him say it first.

But Jordan was silent. He did not laugh at her, but he did not agree either. The coals within the stone-ringed campfire shifted and sparks flew upward, a brief, tiny meteor shower that quickly faded. He realized with a faint sense of surprise that Jolie was very important to him, yet he was loath to admit it. He'd not been really close to a woman since his sister, and of course, that was quite different. Female companionship was a charming, casual, infrequent commodity, wedged in between wars, poker games, and bouts of hard drinking, not something he'd given much planning or thought. But since meeting this bright-eyed, slender child/woman who had taken such an unwarranted liking to him and even seemed to consider him a romantic hero of some kind, he had begun to revise his thinking. Now it wasn't such a bad idea, having a woman around, even one who drove him to distraction the way Jolie did.

"You know," he said softly, his words seeming to float on the tendrils of smoke from his thin brown cheroot, "I *do* think you're kinda important—maybe even more important than gold, green eyes."

For Jolie, it was as close as she'd come to getting a commitment, and she gave a soft, satisfied sigh. "Let me know," she said softly, "when I become *more* important than gold, Jor-dan."

A chuckle rumbled from deep in his chest, and he promised, "Oh, I will, green eyes. I will."

The Rio Grande was just beyond Las Cruces, a flowing ribbon of water that widened and narrowed at intervals, winding past Las Cruces and its sister town, Mesilla. The caravan of three men, a girl, and seven mules plodded wearily down the dusty street under a hot, burning sun.

"No girls came out to meet you here, Jordan," Jolie

observed, nudging her horse close to his. A faint smile curved her mouth, and she put out the tip of her dry tongue in an attempt to wet parched lips as she recalled their last visit to a town and the girl who had rushed out to meet him. "Have you not been to Gudúusis—Las Cruces—before?"

Jordan grinned. "Jealous, green eyes?"

"*Dah!* I just like to know who might be following us."

"Witch," Jordan commented without glancing at her. He was juggling the lead lines of the mules with the reins to his fractious gray, who had taken a decided dislike to the presence of the lead mule. The mule obviously felt the same. Long yellow teeth nipped at the gray's flank, and the gelding squealed and lashed out with wicked hooves, catching the mule in the chest. Pandemonium erupted as the mule brayed loudly, long ears laid back and teeth gnashing, and the entire line of mules began plunging about madly.

The townspeople of Las Cruces displayed only a mild interest in the fracas in the middle of the street, as this sort of thing was not uncommon. Griffin, riding just ahead with the listing Amos on his mount, was convulsed with laughter, and Jolie's skittish piebald had shied away and was dancing down an alleyway between two wooden buildings. It was left to Jordan to calm the enraged animals, and this he did with well-placed kicks, curses, and the rough end of a rope. It took several minutes, of course, and if the mules hadn't been so tired and hot and thirsty, it wouldn't have worked so well, but Jordan's efforts were finally rewarded with sullen silence from the rebellious beasts.

"Well done," Griffin approved between snorts of laughter, earning a hot blue glare from his uncle. "I couldn't have done better myself," he added.

"You couldn't calm an enraged cockroach!" Jordan snarled

in reply, but Griffin had already nudged his horse forward to join Amos and was ignoring his uncle.

Jolie's horse was still rolling its eyes and prancing, but she pulled him close enough to apologize, "I'm sorry I couldn't help, Jordan. But you did it so quickly, you didn't need anyone else."

Only slightly mollified by her efforts to placate him, Jordan muttered a thanks and concentrated on keeping his gelding well away from the lead mule's teeth. It was only a few more yards down the street to a rough corral and leaning stable, and then he could relax.

But relaxation was not in the cards for the intrepid adventurers. Instead, a poker game and Griffin's quick temper and quicker trigger finger created problems.

It wasn't his fault, really, that the overbearing man who had been in Franklin, Texas, only a month before was now in Las Cruces. The man—Cooke was his name—was still belligerent and still remembered the cocky youth who had outplayed, outtalked, and outdrawn him. Pride demanded a confrontation.

"You still cheatin' at cards, Cooke?" Griffin asked jauntily when the bellicose gambler directed disparaging remarks about his youth and size toward the boy, who was leaning on the bar drinking a beer. "I seem to remember an ace in a coat sleeve."

Backing away, his hands spread at his sides, the beefy Cooke's upper lip curled in a sneer. "An' I seem to remember getting interrupted the last time we were going to settle this, kid."

"Don't let that stand in your way now," Griffin returned in a soft, menacing tone. He stepped away from the bar, a slender, youthful figure in dusty, wrinkled clothes with a lethal, long-barreled Colt hanging ominously from his hip.

The atmosphere in the saloon, fancifully named "The Hanged Man," changed immediately. Bystanders backed away or took cover behind scarred wooden tables, while the balding bartender protested vigorously.

"Hey! We don't like that kinda stuff here," the bartender snapped. "Go outside if you gotta do that."

"Suits me," Griffin said, and slanted Cooke a glance from beneath the brim of his hat. "How 'bout you?"

Cooke, peering at the youth, who betrayed no sign of nervousness whatsoever, had the belated thought that this boy might just be as good as he apparently thought he was, while he was better at cheating and bluffing than trading shots in the street. There was his pride, however, and then too, maybe this cocky kid was bluffing. After all, hadn't he managed to be rescued by his uncle that time in Franklin? Cooke reasoned, so he nodded.

"Yeah, kid. Let's go outside."

It was almost dark, and Griffin had wandered into The Hanged Man out of sheer boredom, not wanting to be around Jordan and Jolie in his present mood. This fight was an excellent way to vent his frustration.

So he stood, loose-limbed and waiting in the dusty street, the setting sun still high enough that it cast long shadows along the ground. Griffin instinctively chose the side that put the sun in Cooke's eyes instead of his own, and a thin smile curved his angelic mouth in a bow as he noticed the older man's consternation.

"Ain't quite fair this way," Cooke objected. "Let's stand sideways to th' sun, boy."

"Fine with me," was Griffin's cool reply, and he took several sideways steps, his boots scuffing up puffs of dust that hung in a brown haze over the ground. There was a hum of conversation among the men watching, and women and children scurried for cover from stray bullets.

"Wait'll the dust settles," Cooke said from several yards distant. Sweat was streaming down the sides of his face from under his wide white hat, and his natty suit coat with the jaunty handkerchief in the pocket had damp rings under the sleeves. He hooked a finger in the high collar of his stiffly starched shirt and pulled it away from his neck as if to cool himself off, and Griffin began to smile.

That sweet, cherubic face that any mother would have been proud to claim as her own creased into a sweet smile that fairly dripped sugar, and the wide, innocent blue eyes with lashes so thick they were coveted by every female who saw them gazed at Cooke with insincere concern.

"Gettin' too hot for you, Cooke?" he asked sweetly.

"Yeah, it's pretty hot for somebody who ain't a damn cold-blooded sidewinder!" the man snapped back. "We'll see how you like it in hell!"

Tensing, Griffin's muscles coiled in readiness, his fingers barely brushing the side of his holster where it hung low on his thigh, and his palm was turned inward.

"I'm ready anytime you are, Cooke. You go first, and I'll catch up."

Cooke cleared the dust from his throat and spat on the ground, well aware of the onlookers and the sick feeling in the pit of his stomach. This kid wasn't natural, he reflected. He was too cool, too sure of himself. Pale eyes flicked toward the avid faces watching, and he hesitated. Hell, he didn't want to die just to save face. Maybe this kid was as good as he thought he was—and maybe he wasn't.

Spurred by a faint snicker from the crowd, Cooke's hand flashed downward toward his gun. He never cleared leather. Griffin's shot tore through the tendons of his right hand, passing cleanly through and imbedding itself somewhere in the front of the building.

Unfortunately, the building happened to be the local sheriff's office, and the sound of the shot and the thunk of the bullet striking wood prompted the law enforcement official to rise from his creaking old chair and investigate the cause. In less than a half hour, both Griffin and Cooke—with a bandaged hand—were sitting morosely in separate jail cells kicking their respective heels.

No amount of explaining had deterred the man who was acting sheriff in the real sheriff's absence from his official duty. His adamant reply, repeated over and over, was that he didn't allow gunplay in his town.

"It endangers my peaceful evenin's," Sheriff White insisted. "And it doesn't make my dinner sit so good. You boys can stay here till the elected sheriff comes round, then he can decide what to do with you."

"What?" Griffin almost shouted, catapulted from his hard bunk by this information. He gripped the cold iron bars with both hands and pressed close, asking, "When will that be?"

White shrugged. "Don't know. Could be tomorrow. Then again," he added with a complacent wink, "it could be next month. He ain't always on time. But don't worry. My wife does the cookin', and she's the best cook in these parts."

"Great," Griffin muttered. "I was worried about that."

"What about my hand?" Cooke whined from the next cell. "I want to press charges! This kid has ruined me! I won't even be able to play cards like before . . ."

"You mean deal from the bottom . . ." Griffin put in.

"And I won't be able to shoot right . . ."

"You call what you did out there *shooting*?" Griffin

asked incredulously, then whooped with laughter. "I've seen babies do better!"

Cooke lunged at Griffin through the bars of his cell, his good hand groping furiously while the youth stepped just out of reach. "You little bastard! I should have just killed you!"

"You'd play hell killing a cockroach," Griffin returned coolly while Sheriff White shook his head with an amused smile.

"Glad to see you boys are getting along so well," the sheriff commented. "You'll have plenty of time to talk things over, though." His tall, portly frame lumbered back down the dimly lit hallway, and the keys in his hand clinked with an ominously final sound.

It was only when the door to the office shut behind him and shadows flooded the cells that Griffin began to reflect upon the results of his impetuosity. Amos would be so disappointed in him. Jolie would be distressed, maybe she'd even cry about it. And Jordan would be furious.

Chapter 19

Griffin was right. Jordan was furious. He'd hunted high and low for his nephew, searching in every saloon, boarding house and even the local house of ill repute. It was only by chance that he discovered Griffin's whereabouts.

Stopping in one of the saloons for a quick beer and a few minutes of contemplation as to where a sixteen-year-old might wander, Jordan happened to overhear two men discussing the recent confrontation between the gambler and a "cocky kid who was quicker on the draw than a bolt of lightning."

"Excuse me," Jordan said politely, "but did I hear you say something about a quick-draw kid?"

"The Quickdraw Kid? Is that his name?" one of the men said. "Yeah, it figures. He's fast, sure enough! Of course, Cooke was so nervous my horse could have outdrawn him, but that kid had cleared leather before Cooke could blink twice or even think about it. Why..."

"Where's the kid now?" Jordan interrupted, silently damning Griffin's temper, cockiness, and lack of prudence. "Is Cooke dead?"

"Naw, just wounded," the other man answered, gulping down his drink and wiping his mouth with the back of one hand. "I don't think the Kid really wanted to kill him or he could have. Hell, this boy's got the reflexes that'll make him more famous than Billy the Kid!"

"Not if I have anything to say about it," Jordan muttered grimly, then repeated, "Where's the kid now?"

"In jail," was the not unexpected answer. "Our sheriff don't like gunplay in the streets."

Flipping a coin on the bartop to pay for his beer, Jordan tipped his hat to the two men who had so enjoyably answered his questions, and strode from the saloon with firm purpose. Griffin in jail—Jassy would never understand why he hadn't taken better care of her son. And he only hoped that the sheriff would be reasonable.

Sheriff White was reasonable to a certain extent. "No," he said, leaning back in his chair and propping his booted feet on the surface of his cluttered desk, "I don't think the boy'll get in that much trouble since Cooke provoked the fight. But I still don't allow that sort of thing in my town."

"He's a hot-headed youngster," Jordan said smoothly. "If you will release him to my custody, I'll see that..."

"Oh, I don't think I can do that," White said with a smile. "He shot a man, you see, and while I agree that this particular varmint probably *needed* shootin', I can't have just anybody who wants to pull their gun doin' it. Makes for a mighty noisy town after a while, you understand."

"I understand that, but..."

"But the boy stays in that cell until the reg'lar sheriff comes 'round again, and afore you can ask me when that'll be, I'll tell you same as I told the boy—ain't no tellin'. He ain't always punctual, you understand."

Jordan's eyes narrowed in a way the sheriff didn't particularly like and gazed at him in an assessing manner that made him slightly nervous. This gentleman didn't seem at all the usual sort of man who was a drifter or looking for trouble. In fact, Sinclair had an air of quiet menace about him that was disturbing, and White had known men like him often enough to beware. He cleared his throat and shifted uneasily in his wide chair.

" 'Course, I might can do something about it since the boy will be in your care, Sinclair," he offered, peering from beneath bushy brows at the tall man in front of him.

"It would certainly be appreciated," Jordan said. Thin lines bracketed his turned-down mouth as he regarded the sheriff closely. "What, exactly, do you think you could do, Sheriff?"

"I suppose I can turn him loose after a few days. I have to check my posters first, and it don't look so good to let a man go so quick after a shootin'. Then the town don't quite understand why I ain't doin' my duty, you understand. Your nephew's a right impetuous lad, Sinclair."

"I know that. But we really didn't intend to stay here longer than a day or two, Sheriff."

The sheriff made a steeple of his hands and nodded wisely, asking, "If you don't mind me askin', why are you in Las Cruces?"

"My partner got hurt on the trail and we brought him in to see the doctor."

"Oh. That was you Doc Partridge was tellin' me about, huh?" Sheriff White frowned. "How'd he get shot, if you don't mind me askin', of course?"

Jordan took a deep breath in an effort to clear away the cobwebs of frustration and said, "Ambush. Five men hit us in an arroyo."

"Kill 'em?"

"No. Flood got them, and we got away."

"Kinda convenient, wasn't it?" White persisted with a nasty smile.

"No, it was *extremely* convenient, Sheriff," Jordan replied coolly.

"Don't you want to file charges?"

"Against dead men?" Jordan's expression was slightly incredulous. "What good would that do?"

"How can you be sure they're all dead? Who were they, and why did they want to ambush you?"

Indicating an empty chair, Jordan said, "Since this promises to be a long conversation, do you mind if I sit down?" He didn't wait for a reply before he jackknifed his long legs and sat down in a wooden chair just as rickety as the sheriff's. Then he waited until he'd pulled out a thin cheroot, lit it, and took a long satisfying draw before he answered White's questions. "I can't be sure they're dead, since I never saw them again after the water came down that ravine, and since I have no idea who they were, I can't imagine why they would want to ambush any of us."

"That's downright peculiar, I'd say."

Jordan shrugged. "The world's full of peculiar people, Sheriff."

"I'd heard that." Chair legs thunked loudly on the floor as White tipped his chair forward and pulled his feet off the table top. "Check back with me in a few days, and I'll let you know about your nephew. We'll keep him warm and dry 'til then."

"I'll be back tomorrow. Maybe you will have decided on the amount of a fine by then."

"You tryin' to bribe me, Sinclair?"

"No, I'm trying to get my nephew out of jail so we can leave your fair town. That's all."

White's brows lowered over his eyes. "That's the best offer I've heard yet. I'll think about it."

* * *

But in the end, Jordan, Jolie, and an almost recovered Amos had to wait three days on the sheriff's decision. The jail was in a squat adobe building perched on a corner of the street a little apart from the town. Jails in the new, raw West were, at best, a primitive affair. There were times when the local law officer was forced to do no more than position a felon under a large piece of cowhide pegged down to hold him into place. Some jails were large trees to which the accused would be tied, and some were one-room huts with no bars but a good, sturdy locked door. This jail was larger than a hut, but not by much. It had three cells and a front office separated by a thin partition of wood and a locked door. Judging by the standards of the day, however, the jail was quite impressive.

Griffin, close to despair and just discovering that he had a firm hatred of tiny dark holes, was banging his tin water cup on the bars to get the sheriff's attention when Jordan returned to the jail. A faint, amused smile curled Jordan's mouth when he heard his nephew's frustrated effort to snare White's notice.

"Noisy young feller," White commented, cocking a thick brow at Jordan.

Jordan's reply was equally casual. "Yeah, he sure is. Why don't you let me rid you of him now?"

White leaned back in his chair and studied Jordan for a moment, lacing his fingers over his ample belly. A matchstick protruded from one corner of his mouth, and he chewed vigorously, like a ruminating cow, while he thought about the situation.

"Cain't rightly do that," he said at last. "I sent a wire to the next town looking for the sheriff late yestiddy, and he's ain't goin' to be back here 'til next week. He gets a fee, you understand, for all prisoners he holds, so natcherly, he's kinda insistent about me holdin' these two fellas. You understand," he added again as if just saying it would make it true.

But Jordan disagreed. "No, I don't understand. If there's a fine, I'll pay it, but I need my nephew out of your jail as quickly as possible. We've already wasted enough time in this town as it is."

"I understand your bein' annoyed and all," White said, "but it won't do you no good to get ugly with me. I'm still the law, and I say the boy stays put until the sheriff gets back." His chair creaked loudly as he shifted forward, fixing Jordan with a steady gaze. "If you can't see it my way, then you can rest alongside your nephew until the sheriff gets here, Sinclair."

"That won't be necessary," Jordan said in a soft tone that didn't hide his dislike. Wheeling, he strode toward the door then paused and turned back around. "Do you know a man by the name of Albert J. Fountain?" he asked.

White's brows rose. "Who don't? He's the most prominent man in the territory, a Union Army hero, artillery commander in the revolutionary army for Juarez, and been a president of the Texas state Senate. A.J. Fountain ain't a man to mess around with—how do you know him?"

"I didn't say I did. I just asked if you did," Jordan replied in a cool, deliberate voice before he walked out the door.

Acting Sheriff White stared long and thoughtfully at the closed door for several minutes after Jordan's departure.

Later that afternoon, Griffin was inhaling the fresh air of freedom and listening to the sharp side of Jordan's tongue.

"Do you know what could have happened if I hadn't known someone to pull some strings?" Jordan demanded, glaring at Griffin's downcast face. "We could have been delayed until some time next week because of your hot temper."

"But we weren't," Griffin defended himself. He looked around the crowded hotel lobby to see if anyone besides Amos and Jolie was listening to their conversation, and shifted uncomfortably in the seat of his chair. "We weren't delayed long at all," he muttered again.

"No thanks to you!" Jordan snapped. "That wasn't quite the way to keep a low profile, you know. Here we are, hot on the trail of several million in gold, and you go and call a lot of attention to us. White was damned curious as to what we were doing here, and he checked up on our buying habits and the mules we've got, too. I had to come up with some pretty good reasons for Fountain, too. It's a damn good thing he remembered me from our old army days, boy, or you'd still be cooling your heels in that cell." Warming to his tirade, Jordan fixed Griffin with a scalding blue gaze and his mouth tightened ominously. "With Amos wounded by anonymous gunfire, any three-year-old could guess that we're looking for something profitable! Hell, we might just as well have taken out an ad in the *34* . . ."

"What is the *34*, Jor-dan?" Jolie wanted to know.

"A Doña Ana county newspaper from Mesilla. The editor, Sam Newman, is well acquainted with Albert Fountain, and both men can smell a story—especially about gold—in an instant. Dammit, Griffin, you've stirred up a hornet's nest with this escapade," Jordan grated harshly. "I ought to put you on the first train to Texas!"

Griffin gave a guilty start, and looked down. His eyes were shaded by girlishly long dark lashes tinged with gold so that Jordan could not see his chagrin. "Yeah, maybe you should," he muttered in resigned agreement. "We don't seem to be getting along too well, and I did mess things up."

"Look," Amos put in, "it's turned out all right in spite of the fact that the boy didn't stop and think." Amos's dark eyes rested on Griffin as he shifted his bandaged shoulder, resting the elbow of his injured arm in one palm. "I reckon he just ain't as grown up as we all thought he was."

An irate Jordan was not as bad as Amos's cutting summation, and Griffin found himself flushing to the roots of his pale hair. Lifting his head, he slanted a glance toward Jolie, who was looking away. Her dark hair was tucked into a sleek streamer hanging down her back, brushing her slender waist, and she was wearing a dress again. The flowing gown was a deep blue cotton, nipped in at the waist, with short puffed sleeves and a scooped neck. It was surprising how a dress changed Jolie's appearance so dramatically. In Levis and shirt she was still beautiful, but in soft, feminine folds of material she was alluring as well. Did this lovely, self-possessed young woman regard him as a callow youth also? he wondered with a regretful pang.

But then Jolie was turning to look at him, and her eyes were not condemning but understanding, and Griffin smiled. At least she didn't judge him badly.

"You're both right," he admitted candidly. "I did act without thinking, and I'm sorry. I'll try not to do it again."

His candor effectively spiked Jordan's ire and Amos's sarcasm. Jolie's smile and comforting squeeze of a hand on his arm also did a lot to ease his discomfort.

"You deserve a sound thrashing," Jordan muttered, but

his half-smile lessened the sting of his comment, and Griffin heaved a sigh of relief.

"I agree," he told his uncle, "but I'd just as soon you didn't try."

Jordan lifted one dark brow. "I didn't plan on it, but it did cross my mind."

"Well," Jolie interrupted, "now that we have it all settled, when do we leave?"

Dawn found them already on their way. The sky was still dark when they left Las Cruces, the promised dawn just a faint, pearly mist on the horizon. Even the animals were still sleepy, plodding mechanically along.

Griffin was unusually quiet, and Jolie knuckled sleep from her eyes as she rode her dependable little piebald beside him. "This is a great adventure, yes, Griffin?" she said when his silence stretched well past sunrise.

'Yeah."

"Jordan rides far ahead of the mules so he does not have to breathe their dust like we do," she commented a few moments later. "It makes me thirsty to ride behind them like this."

"Uh-huh."

"And I'm hungry, too. Are you?"

"Yeah. . . ." he muttered before lapsing into silence.

"Have you ever eaten *'iigaa'f*?"

"Icky?" Griffin stumbled over the translation. "What is that?"

"Apache cabbage—yucca blooms," she explained. "They are good if you know how to eat them."

Griffin gazed doubtfully at the lethal-looking yucca plants dotting the grassy landscape. The sword-shaped leaves often grew well up the stalk of the plant, and the waxy, white, bell-shaped clusters of berries didn't look at all appetizing to him.

"No," Jolie said in response to the skeptical expression in his eyes, "you eat the fruit of the plant. It is sweet and juicy. You would like it."

"Maybe," Griffin relented. "I guess the Apache know how to live off the land pretty good."

She shrugged. "Sometimes. The mesquite tree provides us with *nanstáné*—beans—and *hishtlishe*—mesquite bean pudding. There are *niishch'i*—piñon nuts—to eat, and, of course, meat from the elk or the antelope and jackrabbits and whatever our hunters can provide. Some years are good; some years are bad. Some winters we have gone hungry, and the children cry and the old and weak die; but other winters we have enough dried meat or plants to last until late *dąą*, or spring. It is the way of life."

Griffin thought of his mother and the delicious smells that always seemed to be in their homey kitchen. Freshly baked bread and cakes and pies, and the savory odor of frying chicken, bacon, or a lean roast had often lured him from the yard into the comfortable farm house for meals. It had never occurred to him to wonder if he would be able to eat the next day. The stark reality of an existence where the food supply was erratic was beyond his ken.

"You know, Jolie, you're not much older than me in years, but sometimes it seems like you're a whole hell of a lot older in other ways," he said thoughtfully.

Jolie smiled. "I am, but only because I was forced to be. If you had been born in a tipi or wickiup instead of a house, perhaps you would be old in experience also."

"Yeah, maybe. There are times when I feel pretty dumb next to you, Jolie."

"How smart you are often depends on where you are,

Griffin," she said. "I would be stupid at your home, and not know what things were, or what to say, or how to cook on a *bésh ye'ákµ'í* as you probably do."

"Stove?" Griffin guessed, and she nodded.

"'*Au*. That metal box with fire inside that one cooks on. See? I cannot even remember the name for it at times. I forget, and try to sort out the different words in my head. It becomes very confusing."

"And that's another thing," Griffin said, nudging his horse closer to hers. "I can only speak English, and I don't even do *that* well, while you can talk in French, Apache, and Spanish."

"That does not mean you're not smart. I cannot do sums like I've seen you do, figuring up how much is owed at the store, and I know nothing of places across the big water." She smiled. "See?"

He grinned. "Yeah."

Jordan, wheeling back to them, tugged at the brim of his hat and said, "You two look as pleased as a couple of grain-fed hogs. What's going on?"

"Nothing," Griffin replied, still grinning. "We've just both figured out that we're not *really* as dumb as we thought we were."

Jordan's lip curled in a derisive smile. "Oh? Who's been misleading you into believing that?"

"We thought of it ourselves," Jolie put in, and he laughed.

"I can believe that," he teased, his eyes lingering on her flushed face. Even wind-whipped and slightly pink from the sun, with wild tangles straying from the two braids she had tied in her hair, she was the most fetching sight he had ever seen, and he knew he was lost. "Ride with me, green eyes?'' he asked. ''Griffin can handle catch-up for a while without you.''

Jolie's heart thumped faster, and she barely managed to keep her delight from being obvious. She was trying to remember Griffin's advice—given in a moment when he had resigned himself to her love for Jordan—and so she gave a cool nod of her head after appearing to think it over, and said, ''Well, I *am* tired of eating dust.''

''I'm flattered that you're so thrilled at the prospect of riding with me,'' Jordan said dryly and wheeled his horse back around to follow Jolie, who had urged her piebald ahead.

''Not nearly as thrilled as you should be,'' Griffin mumbled to himself, watching as Jordan caught up with Jolie a few yards ahead. ''You should be grateful she even looks at you when you treat her so badly,'' he said to Jordan's back. He tugged hard at his hat brim, shading his eyes. ''And one day I'll tell you *every*thing I think!''

Then, noticing that Amos was looking at him rather oddly, Griffin grew silent. He returned his attention to a lagging mule, flicking him lightly on the rump with the end of his rope to spur him on.

Chapter
20

Night came again, and with it the different smells and sounds that belonged only to the dark. Coyotes howled plaintively, their wails hanging shrilly in the air before fading away, and there was the occasional scuffle of tiny feet scrabbling on rock and through the dirt. Jolie lay quietly watching the stars, which seemed almost as bright as the slice of moon that brilliantly illuminated the sky. She was thinking of Jordan and wondering if he was thinking of her. He lay only a few feet away, and she could tell by the glowing tip of his cigarette that he was still awake.

A soft smile flickered for a moment as she recalled his words earlier, and how he had ridden beside her for a long time. There had been no words of love, of course, but that would come in time. She knew he cared. Instead of love, Jordan had talked about the land, his life in the army, his sister—Griffin's mother—and his plans for the gold. In spite of the fact that he had not mentioned marriage in his future, Jolie was confident that he would. It was inevitable when one was in love.

She was so lost in her reverie of pleasant dreams that

Jordan's deep baritone startled her when he said, "What are you thinking about, green eyes?"

"Oh! I was thinking about you," she returned promptly and earned a chuckle from him. "It's true. I always think of you, even when I should not, Jor-dan."

"And when is that? What are the right times to be thinking about me, *chérie*?"

"You speak French well?"

"A little. I once knew a . . . girl . . . who taught me a few words here and there. I can understand it better than I can speak it, though."

An impish smile curved her lips as Jolie asked, *"Voulez-vous couchez avec moi?"* and Jordan laughed.

"That is understood by every sailor between New York and San Francisco, sweetheart! It's a standard phrase, and the answer is *'oui.'* I will lie down with you."

Suiting action to words, he rose from his bedroll and stepped to hers as she held up the edges of her blanket for him to slide in. When he had unfolded his long body next to hers, Jolie drew the blanket over them as if shutting out the world. She forgot about Amos, asleep and exhausted on his blanket placed well beyond the smoldering ashes of the campfire, and ignored the solitary figure of Griffin, who was standing watch on a distant hump of rock. All she could think about was Jordan, his lean body and hard muscles, the heated sweetness of his mouth on hers, and the solid length of him pressed close to her pliant curves.

Moonlight and cloud wisps flickered pristine shadows across the ground, weaving a canopy of pale magic to enshroud them. Jordan gently cradled Jolie's face in his palms and lowered his head so that his lips brushed lightly across her mouth. Holding her breath, Jolie did not move. She didn't want anything to spoil the moment, the tenderness that Jordan was showing as his fingers combed through the hair behind her ears.

His hands were warm and familiar, tugging gently at the ebony strands to turn her head, his tongue lightly exploring the tiny ridges of her ear while his thumbs dragged across that small spot just below. Then his lips found the spot his thumbs had just massaged, moving as softly as the flutter of a butterfly, making her shiver.

Turning into him, Jolie pushed his unbuttoned shirt aside and slid her hands over his bare chest. Her long fingers skimmed through the nest of dark hairs curling over his taut muscles, caressing and touching, exploring the ridges and scars. *C'est magnifique,* she thought, admiring his body that reminded her of the sleek form of a mountain cat, with well-toned muscles and perfect proportions. She still felt inept and shy, emboldened by his touch yet not quite sure what he wanted or how to please him.

Fortunately, Jordan solved her problem for her, murmuring into her ear, "Like this, sweetheart . . . yes, that's right. . . ." His breath whisked across her cheek and ear, warm and caressing like his hand as he guided her fingers to curl around him.

Awed by the response she could evoke with her touch, Jolie exulted that she could affect him as he did her. Each time they made love it thrilled her anew. Her mother, Nandile, had never told her it would be like this.

Then, somehow, their clothes were gone, piled together in a tumble outside the blankets, their bodies pressed close in the hot, moist cocoon of dyed wool and passion. Jordan held her tenderly in the cradle of his arms, and in spite of the driving urgency of his body, he took his time.

His hands, lean and tan, were pale against the darkly

burnished hollows and curves of her body, exploring until she arched blindly upward, aching for his touch. Warm fingers dragged in deliciously slow movements over the curve of her spine, then gently kneaded the smooth flesh of her buttocks. Jordan traced the hard curve of her hip, his hands cutting with the sureness of a scythe over the ridge of ribs and back to her breasts, those small, firm mounds as dusky and sweet as the golden fruit of a peach tree.

"Even your body is flushed with love," he murmured, and she smiled against his chest.

"Love, Jor-dan? Do you use that in the literal sense, or just as . . . as description?"

"Mmm, your vocabulary is improving rapidly, sweetheart. Both. Literal and descriptive. Wait—do that again— yes, just like that," he whispered with a catch in his breath. "Did I ever mention that your lips are sweeter than honey?" he asked when he could speak again.

"Not lately," she answered between thick waves of response. Long lashes shadowed her cheeks like the wings of a hawk, dark and fluttering, and her high cheekbones glowed with a pearly sheen as she arched upward again.

Jordan breathed heavily, fighting for control of his own body as Jolie writhed beneath him. His hands coasted over the gentle swell of her belly to the downy nest of sable curls below, seeking the damp satin softness between her thighs.

Jolie's quickly indrawn breath signalled her response to the expert motions of his hand and she gave a soft moan, biting her lower lip between her teeth. Almost feverishly, she reached down again to take the velvet heat of him in her hands, holding him. It was too much for Jordan, and with a thick groan he slid up and over her, his mouth capturing her lips as he pressed close.

She rose to meet him, arching her back and sighing, longing for an end to this burning desire that pricked her.

"Now—Jordan, please," she said against his mouth, and he obliged.

Jolie's heels burrowed like field mice into the thick folds of the blanket beneath them as she strained upward to meet him. Her hands cupped his broad shoulders, fingers digging into his smooth flesh to hold him as he buried himself within her velvety folds.

She plunged from crest to crest, as if she were caught up in the maelstrom of a raging river and was being carried helplessly downstream. Jolie had vague memories of mountain streams she had swum in, and how she had felt the same way, as if she were drowning.

Shivering with fierce intensity, Jordan slammed into her in a hard, driving motion that took them both to the peaks they sought. Finally, with a single, last shudder, release throbbed from Jordan into Jolie and she cried out, finding her own exquisite pleasure with him.

Drained at last, they lay silent and still, wrapped in the soft shrouds of night and blanket, damp with satisfaction. Slowly, they became aware of the night sounds around them, the coyote's howl, the hawk's cry, the badger's peculiar snuffle, and the rasping cough of a bobcat. It was a desert symphony serenading two lovers.

"This feels right, doesn't it?" Jordan murmured against the damply curling tendrils of hair over Jolie's ear, and she gave a languorous nod of her head.

"*Oui*. It feels just right, Jor-dan." Sighing softly, she cuddled even closer, curving one arm across his wide chest and nibbling thoughtfully at the springy mat of curls tickling her nose. "We are like the coyote and the badger."

"Ah—what?" Jordan drew back slightly and peered at her with a puzzled frown.

"The coyote and the badger. They travel the desert together, the coyote lithe and quick, his head up and eyes alert, and the badger, stolid and shuffling along slowly, but with powerful, dangerous claws," she explained. Then, seeing that he apparently didn't make the obvious connection, she continued. "The badger raids the burrows of the prairie dogs and mice and chases them out. Then, the quick coyote runs down the prey and captures it so both can share. See?"

"I'm not sure . . ."

"I am the badger, who moves along slowly and surely, depending on you to be the coyote and take care of both of us." She tilted her head to gaze at his face. "Now do you see?"

"Yeah," he answered, not at all sure he fully appreciated being compared to a coyote. "You've got very regional metaphors, Jolie."

"Now I don't understand . . ."

"It doesn't matter. I only meant that sometimes I don't understand your comparisons." He pulled her closer and laid his cheek against her damp forehead. "If we don't get some sleep, we won't be able to get up in a few hours."

"A small price for the pleasure you gave me," she said simply.

Jordan lay quietly, startled by the depth of her emotions. So many doubts ran through his mind, doubts about the future—their future together. What would he say to his family in Texas, who had battled Indian raids time and again and lost friends to the Apache? What would he say to the memories of those men he'd lost on the Malpais to the Apache? How could he justify loving a girl whose people had massacred men who had trusted him to lead them to safety? When the time came to make a choice between Jolie and his beliefs, he did not know which he would choose.

Chapter 21

Prickly pear, tall bunches of different grasses, buffalo gourds, mesquite, piñon trees and an occasional, rare cactus grew in the arid region of the San Andres mountain range. The plants attracted insects, which attracted a variety of birds, which in turn attracted small carnivores, whose droppings nourished the plants. It was a never-ending cycle of life.

"I still can't figure out why animals avoid the basin," Amos muttered to no one in particular as their pack animals trod the hard-baked path from the Jornada into the foothills of the San Andres. "Just think—the grass is greener than anywhere else because of that fresh-water spring, and there still ain't no animals around! It's plain damn spooky is what it is."

"You're just a nervous old woman, is all you are, Amos," Griffin observed cheerfully. He tugged at the lead line tied to his allotment of mules, guiding them around a rock jutting up at the edge of the path, and said over his shoulder, "All the animals probably leave for safer ground when they hear us comin'. None of us are exactly as quiet as Indians, you know."

A faint laugh—quickly smothered—drifted to his ears, and Griffin slanted Jolie a grin.

"*Almost* none of us anyway," he amended.

"Anyway," Amos was saying, hardly hearing Griffin's comments, "it sure seems funny, don't it? I mean, last time we were there I could have sworn I saw strange lights in the sky . . ."

"Shooting stars?" Jordan suggested, but Amos shook his head.

"Naw, I know what stars look like. And I heard these strange noises."

"I'll bet I know what *those* were," Griffin put in, giving Jordan and Jolie a significant glance that indicated the direction of his thoughts.

"No, I'll bet you don't," Jordan said flatly. "Your imagination runs full steam ahead with less fuel than it'd take to fire up a canoe, Griffin. Don't talk about things you don't know about."

"Why stop now?" Griffin asked in mock surprise, refusing to take offense. "I've never known what I was talking about before, have I?"

Jordan grinned. "That's true. Sorry—lost my head."

"You're forgiven," Griffin retorted, hauling his mules to a halt at the crest of a steep descent. "How about us stopping for the night? I've about had it with these damned mules pulling at me. My arm and shoulders are so sore I can't even feel 'em."

"Fine with me." Jordan shrugged. "What do you think, Amos? You ready to quit for the day?"

Squinting up at the sky where the sun was a blazing red ball of fire, Amos nodded. "Yeah, might as well. But don't think you're pampering me because of my side, 'cause I don't need to be coddled."

"Maybe you don't," Griffin put in, "but I sure do!" He swung effortlessly from his saddle, grimacing at the strain on his aching arm and shoulder. "Of course, I'm not as *weathered* as you are . . ."

Amos smorted. "You can say that again, you smooth-faced baby! This grizzled old face has character and experience carved all on it, I can tell you."

Smiling to herself, Jolie listened to the careless comments tossed back and forth between the men as she did her share of the work, unloading the pack mules and tending to their sweaty coats so sores would not be rubbed on them. It was hard, time-consuming labor made even more difficult by the fractious natures of the beasts, so that she was almost as sweaty as they were by the time she finished.

Sweeping the hat she had borrowed from Griffin from her head, Jolie wiped her damp forehead on her shirt sleeve. She still had a slight limp that bothered her as she walked toward the campfire where Amos was cooking their evening meal. A soft light lay over the hills and campsite, giving a golden glow to the twisted shapes of the bushes and the humps of rock surrounding them and bathing Amos with muted color. With the imminent setting of the sun the temperature had grown cooler, and a breeze wafted tantalizing odors from the black iron skillets to her nose, luring her to a perch upon a rock not far from the fire.

"It smells good," she said, flinging back her hair and tying it with a thin strip of rawhide to hold it out of her eyes. "What is it?"

Flicking a glance from the sizzling skillet to the girl watching him, Amos said, *"Gúuchi bik'a, bán dijúúlí, bééskants'udze . . ."*

"What in the hell?" Griffin interrupted, coming up behind them in time to hear Amos's menu. "I ain't eating any of that stuff!"

"Any of what stuff?" Amos asked innocently. "What are you talking about?"

"You know," the boy said, slinging his blanket over a rock and sitting down. "All that Apache stuff like prairie dog and cactus!"

Jolie burst into peals of laughter, and Amos joined her.

"What's so funny?" Griffin asked in a suspicious tone. He looked from one to the other. "All right—what's the joke?"

"This 'prairie dog and cactus' you don't want to eat is bacon grease—for gravy, biscuits, and pinto beans," Amos answered with a wide white grin. "That too Apache for you?"

"Well, you know why I thought . . . you two work too hard to be funny," he responded, but couldn't help a matching grin. "How do I know what you're going to cook? For all I know, I could end up eating buffalo chips one morning for breakfast while you both laugh yourselves silly."

"That does give me some ideas," Amos said, expertly flipping the biscuits from their covered pan into a tin plate. He gave the beans a quick stir and threw a handful of flour into the bacon grease bubbling in the skillet. Griffin looked askance when Amos wiped his white-crusted hands on a less than clean rag tucked into his belt, but didn't say anything as Amos cheerfully continued, "Yeah, Rooster, I just might cook you up some *'ich'ii'* one day soon and see how you like it."

"More icky?" the youth questioned with lifted brows. "That seems to be a favorite Apache food."

"No, Griffin, this is different," Jolie corrected him. "*'Ich'ii'* is beef guts. You're thinking of *'iigaa'í*, the yucca blooms we talked about."

-276-

"Enough!" Griffin threw up his hands and laughed. "You win. I'm completely confused and will never learn to speak Apache!"

"You need to learn English first anyway," Jordan said, coming up behind them and bending his long legs to sit beside Jolie. "Schooling is important."

"Not as important as adventure," Griffin said. He leaned back and rested his elbows on the top of a neighboring rock. "We're having great adventures, aren't we? I kinda like it."

"Don't forget your promise," Jordan said.

"What promise is that?" Jolie wanted to know.

"Aw, Jordan made me promise to go home and go back to school after this summer is over." Griffin's face was a youthful caricature of woe. "I only promised so he wouldn't put me on the first mail stage back home."

"But you did promise," Jordan pointed out. "Here, Amos, let me help you with that skillet. Your arm still bothering you pretty bad?"

"Naw, just a little, Cap'n. I can handle the skillet if you'll just get the plates."

While they ate, the skies grew dark, putting on a splendid show for the quartet, who watched with an awe akin to reverence. Brilliant shades of mauve, crimson, and saffron shimmered on the horizon, turning the surrounding peaks to a rainbow of reflected colors. And as the curtain of night fell, one star brighter even than the pale slice of moon twinkled with a shivering crystal light.

"See that, Jolie? Griffin asked, pointing to the star. "That's the first star, and you always make a wish on it. If you do, it will come true."

"Is this so?" she asked, impressed with the knowledge. "Then I shall do so."

"Make your wish silently or it won't come true," he warned hastily when she opened her mouth.

It didn't take a genius to figure out what Jolie was wishing as she tilted her head to look at Jordan and smile, her lips moving in a silent wish.

"Gee, I wonder what she wished for?" Amos said to the world at large, and earned a scowl from both Jordan and Griffin. "You two," he said mildly, "need to step back and take a good look at yourselves. You're both as jumpy as a cat on hot rocks."

"Thanks for your advice," Griffin muttered, but Jordan only raised his brows and said nothing.

Jolie, oblivious to their soft bickering, was gazing up at the star and smiling, absently twisting a long strand of her hair between her fingers. Wishing couldn't hurt, and who knew what might help? After all, Jordan was just too stubborn to admit what all could plainly see. Their coming together had been inevitable, just as their meeting had been. From that first moment in her mother's camp, she had known that Jordan was her future. It seemed sometimes that the *'indaa'* were much slower at seeing things than the Apache. Perhaps it was because they allowed so many small matters to cloud their vision.

"Jolie," Griffin was saying, interrupting her reverie, "want to play poker with us?"

"Ah, Griffin," Jordan objected, "haven't you corrupted her enough? You've already taught her every swearword you know as well as all those bawdy songs that Jassy would take a stick to you for singing. Now you want to teach her to gamble?"

Shrugging, Griffin said, "It's fun. Besides, I'll bet she can beat the pants off you."

"Five dollars says she can't," Amos spoke up immediately.

"Done!" Griffin shot back. "Who's going to stake her?"

"Why don't you?" Jordan asked. "It was your idea."

The mesquite branches fueling the fire popped and crackled merrily as the three men and the girl sat cross-legged on a blanket and played poker. Jolie—true to Griffin's prediction—proved to be a cagey poker player. A lifetime of learning not to show reaction stood her in good stead when she drew a full house to Jordan's three queens.

"I can't believe that!" an astounded Jordan said as he watched her solemnly rake in the pot of coins. "Did you help her, Griffin?"

"You askin' if I dealt off the bottom?" the youth demanded softly. Jordan gave him a sharp glance.

"No. You know better than that. If I was going to accuse you of cheating, I'd say it plain. I'm just asking if you helped her, that's all."

"Did you see me help her?"

"Don't be so touchy. No, I didn't see you help her." Jordan leaned back against a rough-edged rock and pulled out the makings of a cigarette from his shirt pocket. The little cloth bag held papers and tobacco, and he quickly and expertly rolled a cigarette and lit it with a burning branch from the fire before saying, "Amos, you lost your bet. Jolie just won the biggest pot of the night."

"I concede," Amos said gracefully, and tilted up the small brown bottle of whiskey he had fished from his packs. "A toast to the loveliest winner in the entire territory," he said, and swallowed a healthy draught. "Griff?" he offered, holding out the bottle.

"Thanks," Griffin said, slanting his uncle a defiant glance as he took the bottle from Amos. "Here's to you, Jolie—the most beautiful girl I ever kidnapped!"

Laughing, Jolie sat back on her heels and weighed the

coins she'd won in both her cupped palms. They glittered in the soft light of lantern and campfire like small chips of sunshine, and she held them out to Griffin. "I had a good time," she said. "Thank you for letting me play, but I do not want this. It is too heavy, and will only get in my way if I keep it. Beside, you gave me the money to play."

Griffin waved the bottle at her, wiping his mouth on a shirt sleeve. "I can't take that, Jolie. Jordan will really think I cheated then."

"Don't be stupid," Jordan said and reached out to take the bottle. A cold smile curled his lips when Griffin would not release it. "Oh? You don't want to share with me?"

"It's not that—I just don't want you to think I helped her win. She won that money on her own because she's smart, Jordan."

"I know that," he replied softly. "But you and I never seem to be able to talk to each other on a sane level when we're discussing Jolie. Now, let's forget it and let me have a drink."

Griffin relinquished the bottle. Jolie piled the coins back on the blanket in front of him and waited patiently for Jordan to lower the brown bottle from his lips. When he did she held out her hand expectantly.

"You shouldn't drink," Jordan said shortly.

Jolie gazed at him for a moment, then said, "Why not?"

"You're too young."

"I'm older than Griffin," she pointed out.

"Yeah, but you're a female."

"What difference does that make, Jor-dan? Do men not get drunk also? If that is true, then what about the time when you came to that little room and were stumbling about as if you had been drinking mescal . . ."

"That's different," he snapped, eyes narrowing at Griffin's wide grin.

"Why?" she persisted.

"For Chrissake, Jolie!" Jordan exploded. "You're more worrisome than a damn sand flea!" He shoved the bottle into her hand and rose in a fluid movement to stride from the pool of light created by campfire and lantern and into the darkness beyond their camp.

Stricken, she sat staring after him until Griffin reached out to remove the bottle gently from her nonresisting hand.

"He just hates being wrong," Griffin said, but she shook her head.

"No, that's not it. He has doubts about our future, and I don't know how to take them away."

"Well," Amos said, "don't you think that's normal? Hell, everybody's got doubts about the future. Who knows what tomorrow might bring? We might all be dead for all we know, or we might stumble across a rich vein of gold and be richer than old King Midas!"

"Who's that?" Jolie asked distractedly. She was straining to see past the shadows wavering just beyond their camp, trying to see Jordan.

"King Midas?" Amos echoed, snaring her attention by handing her the bottle again. "Drink that, little gal, while I tell you a story about a guy who had *real* problems! Now this king . . ."

In spite of herself, Jolie found the story fascinating. And later, when she lay alone and wide awake on her rough blanket near the fire, she contemplated the white man's absorption with the yellow metal. Surely Jordan would not covet gold more than he did her, she thought vaguely and wondered how he would feel if he should turn her to gold with just his touch. But King Midas's most precious possession had been his daughter, so it had broken his heart to turn her to that cold metal. Perhaps Jordan would not care if his touch had turned her heart to gold. . . .

Turning restlessly, she regarded Jordan's long, blanket-wrapped form lying several feet away. He was asleep already, she assumed, since he did not move and was not smoking a cigarette. Determinedly tamping down the urge to go to him, Jolie turned her back. No. She would not make the first move again. Any overtures would have to come from Jordan. He must show her that he cared for her, truly cared for her, before she could make herself vulnerable again.

"Pssst!"

Startled, Jolie jerked awake, slowly realizing that she must have finally fallen asleep as she saw Amos looming over her in the dark.

"What is it?" she mumbled sleepily, rubbing at her eyes. "Is it time to get up? I do not see the sun. . . ."

"Shhh! No, it ain't time to get up yet. I just thought you might like to join in the fun," Amos whispered, his teeth flashing whitely in the deep shadows.

Interested now, and wide awake, she nodded. " '*Au*, I would like to join in the fun," Jolie whispered back. "What do I do?"

"This," Amos said, and rapidly outlined his plan. Jolie cupped a hand over her mouth to stifle the laughter welling up and gleefully agreed to his suggestions.

By the time the sun had begun to rise, Amos was back in his blankets pretending to sleep. Jolie lay quietly watchful and expectant, with only one eye open. When Jordan nudged them all awake, first Griffin, then Amos and last Jolie, there was the usual stretching and yawning.

Griffin, sleepy-eyed and slow to wake, stumbled up from

his bedroll and into the bushes, while Amos stirred up the slumbering fire for their breakfast. Jolie began folding her blankets, and Jordan took care of the pack mules and horses.

When Griffin returned from his morning stroll, Jolie slid Amos a careful glance, but he was concentrating upon the slab of bacon sizzling in the black iron skillet over licking orange flames. Griffin's hair was slicked back from his forehead, the curling strands dark with water and sticking up like feathers as they slowly began to dry under the morning sun.

"What're you two lookin' at?" he asked, slanting them a curious look as he sat down and picked up his boots.

"Nothing," Jolie said, and Amos answered at the same time, "Jus' waitin' on you to git through foolin' around so we can git goin', Rooster!"

Griffin shrugged and stuck one foot into a boot, muttering, "Don't you ever take time to enjoy life? Hurry here and hurry there . . . what the—!" Leaping up, he shook his foot furiously, dislodging the boot so that it went flying through the air. "Yeow!" he howled, hopping on one leg. "There's something in my boots!"

Jordan's attention was caught by the commotion, and he left the horses and strode toward them. He found Jolie with her head down as she concentrated on folding up her blankets, and Amos was studiously browning an already overdone slab of bacon in the skillet. Griffin was dancing up and down like a demented puppet in a carnival show.

"What's going on?" Jordan demanded, thumbs tucked into his belt and his eyes narrowed. His suspicions were immediately alerted by the averted gazes and quivering lips.

"There was something in my boot!" Griffin gasped. 'I felt it!"

"Like what?"

"I dunno—I think it jumped out when I flung my boot," Griffin said a little breathlessly. His gaze moved to Amos and Jolie, and his eyes narrowed just like Jordan's. "Hey! What's goin' on?"

Unable to contain herself any longer, Jolie burst into peals of laughter, muffling the sound with the palm of her hand. Jordan's lips twitched, and amusement gleamed for an instant in his eyes before fading.

"Boy, you sure did jump high, Rooster!" Amos said then, his face nearly splitting with a wide grin. "I wisht you coulda seen yourself!"

Griffin's eyes were a frosty blue as he glared at first Amos and then Jolie, and his tone was icy when he asked, "Just what did you put into my boot?"

"Lizards," Jolie answered promptly, dissolving into gales of laughter again.

"Lizards?" Griffin's voice rose on the last syllable.

"Lizards," Amos confirmed between chuckles. "You're lucky they were in your boot, Rooster! I was gonna cook a few up for you, but Jolie talked me out of that notion . . ."

"How kind," Griffin said coldly.

" . . . so I ended up settlin' for your boot. I just wisht you coulda seen your face!"

"I believe you've already said that!" Griffin snapped. His hot gaze shifted from Amos to Jolie, lingered accusingly, then came to a rest on his uncle's face. Even Jordan was struggling to hide his amusement, and the absurdity of how he must have looked leaping about like a cat on hot rocks finally appealed to Griffin's humorous side. A reluctant grin pressed at the corners of his mouth for a moment, then won, and he shook his head ruefully. "I must've looked pretty funny," he said at last.

"Oh, you did, Griffin," Jolie assured him with a gurgle of laughter. "What did you do with the poor lizards?"

"I think they must be in the bushes with my boot. Or maybe halfway to Texas by now."

Shaking his head, Jordan interrupted, "Now that we've all had our fun—shall we move on? I'd like to find this gold before I'm too damn old to spend it."

Chapter
22

Winding up trails toward Hembrillo Pass, the caravan was fast approaching the peak they had previously explored, with its sister peak looming just beyond. It was an area familiar to Amos, as he and the Ninth Cavalry had fought there three years before, but he still had trouble following Jolie's directions.

"Are you sure?" he asked, removing his cavalry cap with its attached scarf and scratching his woolly head. His hair had grown long and thick, so that his fingers tangled in the crisp, kinky curls as he raked them through, leaving them standing on end to give him a wild appearance. "I sort of remember comin' up on that mural—you recollect the one? —and then runnin' up on this particular peak."

"But that was if you came into the basin from the east instead of this way," Jolie explained. "We are going the opposite way now."

"Yeah, I reckon you're right," Amos admitted, replacing his cap to shade his eyes and shifting in the saddle. "So—lead on!"

Jolie, who was helping lead some of the pack mules, guided her mount down the rocky path and around bunches of stunted grass before beginning the slow ascent up the path leading to Hembrillo Pass. Well ahead of them was Hembrillo Peak, a huge shadow looming on the horizon like a brooding giant watching them. Behind them was the cheerless tableland of the La Jornada del Muerto, of which they had traversed only the southernmost tip in their travels, and which stretched between the San Andres and the Río Grande some forty-five miles wide by ninety miles long. Lava beds bordered the north, the same Malpais where Jordan had lost his men to the Apache, and the Río Grande edged the south. The hard-baked red sand appeared even more desolate from the vantage point of a high peak.

Griffin gave a last look over his shoulder as the more familiar flat land of the Jornada gave way to the bleak San Andres. Once through the narrow confines of Hembrillo Pass, he surveyed the crater of the Hembrillo Basin with a jaundiced eye. "Reminds me of a volcano," he muttered, catching Jordan's attention.

"Where'd you ever see a volcano?" he asked his nephew, and Griffin shrugged.

"We had drawings of volcanoes in our schoolbooks. I remember a famous one—I think it was Ves . . . Ves . . ."

"Vesuvius?" Jordan answered for him, and Griffin nodded.

"Yeah, that was it. The pictures were awesome, and this place reminds me of those drawings." He glanced around the area, which did indeed resemble a dormant volcano. The craggy rim of the basin surrounded a desert floor, and the twin peaks thrust skyward like solitary whales in a sandy sea. From their viewpoint on the crest, the entire area appeared to be desolate and barren of life.

It was Jolie who pointed out the disconcerting fact that they were not alone.

"Over there," she murmured, edging her mount closer and nudging Amos's leg with her bare toes. "Do you see them?"

Standing up in his stirrups, Amos pushed back the bill of his cavalry cap and squinted into the distance. "Nope," he said after a moment. "I don't see anything."

"See what?" Griffin asked, his attention diverted by their tone and stance. "What do you see?"

Flinging back her heavy ribbon of dark hair, Jolie pointed to a spot where the land dipped into a stand of mesquite.

"*Shái' ánde,*" she said softly.

Griffin stared at her blankly. "Shy who?"

"*Shái' ánde,*" she repeated. "Geronimo's band."

As if with a concerted movement, Jordan, Amos, and Griffin all gripped their rifles more tightly and hefted them to a level easy for aiming.

"Where?" Jordan asked tersely, narrowing his eyes in the direction she was pointing. "I don't see anything."

"Do you not see the bushes move? And the darker shadow behind them?" Jolie asked. "Look closely."

The three men finally saw what she had seen, their eyes slowly adjusting to the subtle differences among shadows. A slight movement captured their attention, and they could discern the blurred outline of a man crouching behind the leafy branches of a bearberry. Skillfully disguised to blend in with the landscape, the figure shifted position the slightest bit, and a branch quivered.

"How many do you see?" Jordan asked her after a few moments of squinting at the clump of bushes, grasses, and stunted trees.

"Only a few. Let's move on so we don't appear to notice

them. I think they must be just scouts for a larger band,'' she said, nudging her piebald forward and tugging at the lead lines of her mules.

"Damn, *that* makes me feel better,'' Griffin muttered, following her example and moving on. "More Apaches—I ain't at all sure I like the idea of fighting Apachs on their home ground.''

Amos snorted. "And where *ain't* their home ground, Rooster? Apache—no offense, Jolie—make their home ground wherever they want it without much trouble. Just ask Jordan.''

Jordan's expression was dark, and he remained silently contemplating the rocks and brush in front of them. He didn't mind a confrontation with the Apache; in fact, he even welcomed it, but he wasn't at all certain he wanted it now. Not with Jolie around. Whose side would she take?

Sliding a wary glance toward him, Jolie immediately guessed the direction of his thoughts, and sighed. Both of them had suffered losses. Couldn't he accept the fact that *she* was not his enemy?

"Remember, Jor-dan,'' she said, her voice floating softly across the space between them, "that it was I who saw them hiding in the brush and warned you.''

His eyes met hers, thick with suspicion and distrust, and she flinched. "That doesn't mean a whole lot, green eyes, but I'm willing to believe that you're on our side. I just hope you remember that if it comes down to shooting.''

"I hope *you* remember it,'' she returned, and looked back toward the bushes. The shadows were gone now, fading into the surrounding terrain as if they had never been and leaving her uneasy. She knew most of Geronimo's band but could not guess their mood or purpose for being in the basin.

Were they just hunting, and if so, what—or whom—were they hunting? Jolie wasn't sure how much she'd like to know the answer to those questions.

They moved along the rocky, narrow ledge into the basin floor and camped where they had camped once before, close to the freshwater spring at the base of Hembrillo Peak. It was familiar territory to all of them by now.

"Do you remember the last time we camped here, Jordan?" Jolie asked that evening after they had unloaded the mules and taken care of the horses.

Startled because he had not heard her come up behind him—it was the way she walked, just like an Apache, and the fact that she never wore shoes—Jordan swung around with a scowl. He was sitting on a rock replacing a worn D-ring on his bridle, and he remained seated, returning his attention to what he was doing. After a moment he answered, his voice a low mutter.

"Yeah, I remember. Why?"

She refrained from touching the dark, damply curling strands of hair that waved across the back of his neck in the same rebellious manner as a small boy's, and instead she shoved her hands deep into the pockets of her Levis. It was an effort not to reach out and touch him.

"Much has happened since then," she ventured. Late afternoon light played across Jordan, tangling in his hair and making it gleam with a deep, rich luster. Even with his face averted so that he presented only a carefully blank profile, she could sense his tension.

"Yeah, it has," he finally answered, his voice again a monotone, noncommittal and careful. His mouth was compressed in a straight line, deep grooves bracketing his nose and lips, and the dark sweep of his lashes veiled his eyes. He flicked her a glance when the silence stretched too long and was startled to see the bright sheen of tears in her eyes. "You okay?" he asked carefully.

She flung her head, whipping back her thick mane of hair like a whip. The thin strip of rawhide circling her forehead just above delicately arched brows was cutting into her skin slightly, and she reached up to pull it off, keeping her gaze locked on Jordan. He was gazing at her so intently, as if trying to read her thoughts, that she almost reached out to him before she caught herself. No. Now was not the time.

So she returned his look levelly, forcing her lips into a smile as careless as his, and said, " '*Au*. I am 'okay.' I just thought you might want to talk with me."

"Is that like 'sitting' with you?" Jordan couldn't help teasing, his eyes crinkling at the corners and one side of his mouth quirking in a genuine smile. "Sitting with you had some serious repercussions, and I just wondered if talking with you could do the same damage to all my good intentions."

"I'm not sure what . . . repercussions . . . means, but I never meant to damage you . . ."

"Liar," he said softly and put down the bridle. "You meant to damage me from the first moment you set eyes on me, Jolie La Fleur, and I've got to admit that you've succeeded. I don't know quite what I want any more, or even what I don't want. It seems like every time I turn around, I see your face and hear your voice and feel you close to me. Now, that's serious damage."

Her breath caught at the soft gleam in his eyes and the impassioned tone of his voice, and she realized at last that she was tormenting Jordan Sinclar as badly as he was tormenting her. It made her feel much better.

"Then we are both damaged," she replied. "May I sit down with you?"

Jordan moved over on the rock to make space, slanting her a quizzical glance as he picked up the bridle again. "Bored already?"

"Why do you ask that?" she wanted to know, scooting across the gritty surface closer to him.

"Well, out of all the things you could be doing, like gathering firewood with Amos or standing watch with Griffin, you chose to come and watch me repair my bridle." His gaze drifted over her more closely, noting the way her breasts pressed against the thin cotton material of the shirt she wore, and how she had tied it in a knot just beneath them so that her midriff was bare above the loose waistband of Griffin's Levis. If anything, she had tanned even darker than when he'd first seen her, a dusky maiden as ripe and luscious as a Georgia peach, with skin as soft and velvety and golden as that celebrated fruit. How could she be so lovely after all this time on the trail, when any other woman would be drawn and haggard from the hours of riding and miles of choking on dust and pulling at a string of cantankerous mules? But she was. The tawny flush on her high cheekbones accentuated the brilliance of the glowing green eyes that were almost almond-shaped, slanting slightly upward at the corners to give her a unique, exotic appearance.

Jolie La Fleur was a woman who could hold her own in any gathering, Jordan realized at last. Though inexperienced, she was quick enough to adapt to any given situation so well as to be considered charming and perhaps slightly naive. He began to recall the thousand tiny details that he'd overlooked— the times when Jolie had been the one to remain calm under pressure; the times when she had reacted to danger with intuitive competence; and the times when she had made a concerted effort to please him by adapting dress and manners to which he was more accustomed. That was a Jolie he had overlooked.

When he turned and looked at her again, his gaze moving from head to heels, it was with a new understanding of who she was, and that she had accepted him without demanding or expecting him to change. All she asked from him was a return of the same love she was so freely offering, and he had been too thick to comprehend.

Jordan struggled silently with his doubts about the future. It was still something he had not fully resolved within himself. How could he explain to her how he felt?

So he said nothing, but his smile and the softening in his eyes said more than he could have said in words. Encouraged, Jolie smiled back, her lips curving in a winsome line that made him sigh and say, "You're pretty disarming, you know."

"Disarming?" she echoed, searching her memory for the correct definition of the word. "I have not removed your weapons," she guessed wrongly, and Jordan laughed and shook his head.

"Wrong definition," he said. "Though on second thought, maybe it's right after all. You've pretty effectively taken away the weapons of detachment and misunderstanding, leaving me with only deliberate malice as a possible defense against you, Jolie."

Confused, she could only look at him and shake her head, wondering what he was talking about.

"Why do you need a weapon against me?" she asked. "I am not your enemy."

"Oh, you're much worse than my enemy, green eyes." He snaked the D-ring through the leather loop of his bridle and fastened it tightly, then buckled the straps he'd loosened on the bit. "There, all fixed. No," he continued, glancing up at her, "an enemy is much easier to understand and to dispose of. You, my lovely antagonist, are much more complicated than that. You torment me without speaking to me. You are capable of enraging me with a look, or a smile in another man's direction. I cannot sleep if we are angry with one another, and if we are together—I still cannot sleep.''

Jordan rose from the rock and held out a hand, which Jolie took with cold, nerveless fingers. "Are you trying to tell me that I should go away, Jor-dan?" she asked, flinging back her head to face him with a defiant thrust of her chin.

"Don't be ridiculous, Gáadu—isn't that what they call you in your village? If you left, I would follow you. It's that simple.''

Jolie's heart was pounding so loudly that it sounded to her like thunder rolling across the basin floor from the towering mountain peaks, and she hardly dared look at him too closely. Instead, she stared down at her bare toes curling against red rock. Dark wings of hair fell on each side of her face, and she remembered that she had removed the strip of rawhide. It must have fallen to the ground, but she could not summon the strength to look for it. She was too aware of Jordan's hand holding hers, of his proximity and his amused stare as she rose to stand with her chin lifted, gazing deep into his eyes.

"Does this mean . . . ?" she began, but he stopped her with two fingers across her lips.

"Don't rush me. I don't know yet what I mean. Give me time, okay?''

She smiled, and it was as if the sun had broken through the clouds, iluminating her face with a bright glow. " '*Áxah*— hokay," she said softly. "I will give you time to find your answers, Jor-dan. Just remember that I am waiting.''

"How could I forget that?" he murmured softly, his smile mirroring hers. Warm fingertips brushed lightly from her mouth up the slope of her cheek and to her ear, making her shiver. "Every time I turn around, I see you, whether you're actually there or not. It's like magic, tricks with mirrors, aces up the sleeves, rabbits out of silk top hats, and sleight of hand . . . why are you pulling away? I'm just teasing you, love.'' His hands shifted to the small of her back, pulling her close, and he ignored her faint protests that Amos and Griffin were watching.

"Do you care? I don't. What do you think they think we're doing when we're alone in our blankets on a dark night? Or in a hotel room? Neither one of them are naive enough to believe we're knitting scarves or swapping war stories."

This was a Jordan she wasn't accustomed to seeing, a Jordan who was pursing instead of being pursued, and Jolie wasn't certain what she should do.

"Do you want to knit a scarf or swap a war story?" she asked against the shoulder of his damp cotton shirt. He smelled of wind and sun, and tobacco and leather, that familiar, male fragrance that she would always associate with Jordan. "I can't knit, but I do have stories I can tell."

"I bet you do," he said, tucking her hand under his arm and guiding her toward a stand of mesquite. "Tell me, Jolie, who were those Apache we saw earlier?"

"I already told you," she began, "*Shá'i'ánde . . .*"

"No, I know that. Did you know any of them? Do you think they're following us?" Jordan led her to a gnarled root thrusting up from the ground and forming a perfect bench.

Jolie shrugged helplessly. "I recognized Geronimo. I hope they are not following us. He is the most ruthless leader, besides Nana."

"Yeah, I got that impression back in your village that time." A smile crooked his mouth. "I thought I was a goner then for sure. What saved me?"

Another shrug and a half-smile. "I do not know. A whim,

perhaps. Geronimo has no love for the '*indaa*', so it was a surprise that he let you go without harm. Nana is even more fierce than Geronimo, because he has the fires of hatred burning inside him.'' She paused for a moment, obviously struggling with herself, then took one of Jordan's hands between her own. ''This gold you seek, Jor-dan, please—do not pursue it any further. I am afraid.''

Amusement curled his mouth as he echoed, ''Afraid? Now? After all this time? Why now, green eyes? Because of those warriors?''

She nodded. '' '*Au*! They have seen us, and they must know why we have come here.'' She gripped his fingers even more tightly, as if trying to transfer her own anxiety to Jordan. ''Let me tell you about something that happened long ago, when I had seen no more than fourteen summers. My papa was gone deep into the mountains hunting, and I traveled with my mother and our people to Mexico. There, Nana joined up with Victorio, Geronimo, Juh, and others. They raided to obtain ammunition and supplies, but soon the ammunition ran out.'' Jolie paused for a moment, then continued, ''In the summer, Nana ambushed a mule train that was traveling a smuggler's path across the border. We all thought the mules must carry ammunition and supplies, and we took them with us back into Mexico. Nana did not open the packs until that night.'' Now Jolie paused for effect, her voice lowering as she said, ''I can never forget the expression of disgust on Nana's face when he pulled out a heavy, dull-looking bar and threw it to the ground. His voice was contemptuous when he said, 'Silver!' Then one of the others suggested we take the silver to Casa Grandes to exchange it for ammunition with the Mexicans, but there was no time. We buried the silver right there.''

''But what is the point of this story?'' Jordan asked

impatiently. A gust of wind pushed his hair back from his forehead as he fumbled in his shirt pocket for his tobacco pouch. "What does this have to do with the Apache we saw today?"

"Wait and you will see," Jolie returned. Jordan recalled how she liked making a long story out of a short one, so he settled himself on the tree root beside her to hear her out.

"Okay, green eyes. Tell your story," he muttered around the cigarette paper dangling from between his lips. He curled the paper around—no mean feat in the freshening breeze—and filled it with tobacco, not spilling a drop.

Jolie laced her fingers around a bent knee and leaned back against the rough bark of a shading mesquite as she continued, "Later that night around the campfire, I heard Nana tell Kaytennae—one of the subchiefs—that he knew of several places where gold or silver could be found in great quantities. I heard him say. . ." She pursed her mouth as she tried to recall his exact words, then recited, " 'There is a canyon in the mountains west of Ojo Caliente—a long way West—where chunks of the yellow stuff as large as grains of corn can be picked up if I did not fear the wrath of Ussen. I know of cliffs with layers of silver so soft that it can be cut with a knife. I know a cave where bars of gold are stacked as if firewood by the soldiers.'

"We all moved closer to hear what else he would say, as we had never heard Nana talk about gold before," Jolie said softly, her eyes bright with the memory. "I heard him say to the others that he had seen another cave of gold a three-day walk from Casa Grandes. And then he said, 'Just beneath the rim of a cliff I found a cave almost filled with it. It could not be reached from above, so the Mexicans must have carried those bars up ladders from one ledge to another to hide it.'

"Not long after that night, Victorio was ambushed and

killed. Nana and the rest of us who survived fled back to the San Andres, but the area was filled with Mexican and American soldiers. We were almost out of ammunition, so Nana listened to the pleas of the others and agreed to go back for the silver we had left a few short months before. We intended to trade the silver for bullets.

"Nana did not want to, but he let the others—who were our best trackers—lead the way to the cache." Here Jolie drew a deep breath and lowered her voice as if whispering a secret. "We never found the silver. We searched for a week, but none of us could find it again. He did not say so, but Nana was pleased that we did not."

Jordan's cigarette had gone out, and he'd been so engrossed in Jolie's story that he hadn't relit it. He did so now, squinting at her over the glowering tip.

"So, what you're telling me is that we may never find the gold or silver, and even if we do—we're liable to die for it. Is that right?"

She nodded. "'*Au*. Gold is dangerous, Jordan. Men are willing to lie for it, to die for it, and even to kill for it. It should be left alone."

"Then why are you with us now, if you believe this?"

"You know why. I did not come for the gold. I came for you."

He grinned. "I knew that."

"Then you will go back?" she asked hopefully, leaning forward to curl her fingers around his forearm. Disappointment shadowed her eyes when he shook his head.

"No, Jolie. I came with Amos to find gold, and that's what I intend to do. If you are afraid, I will send you back with Griffin."

"*Dah*! I am your woman. I go where you go, even if it is into death."

Jordan's brows lowered. "Damn! You sure sound pessimistic about this thing, Jolie."

She shrugged. "I do not understand pess . . . pess . . . what you said, but I do understand death. I am not afraid if that is what you are willing to risk."

"That's comforting," he muttered, taking a last drag from his cigarette and throwing it to the ground. "Why is it I suddenly feel like somebody's got my name on one of his bullets?"

"You know there has been much trouble between the '*indaa*' and the *shá'i'ánde*. Why do you act so surprised?"

Now it was Jordan's turn to shrug. "I don't know. I guess maybe I thought you were my magic charm, my protection against harm from the Apache." His half-smile was wry. "After all, that's why you were brought along in the first place."

"Are you sorry you captured the wrong one?" Jolie asked softly. "Victorio's granddaughter would be much more protection, but she would also be much sought after. While I—I am not missed yet. Only my papa will search for me when he returns from his hunt."

"And when will that be?"

"When the snow falls in the mountains." Her throat tightened. He had not answered her question. Was he sorry he had kidnapped the wrong girl?

But then he was pulling her into the angle of his arm and shoulder, smoothing back her long, gleaming hair and saying tenderly, "In spite of everything, I would not trade you for Victorio himself, green eyes!"

Chapter 23

Jordan was no fool, and he had not resigned from the army in order to risk his neck foolishly now. While Jolie was splashing about in the cool, refreshing waters of the small spring, he drew Amos and Griffin aside and briefly recounted a much shorter version of her story.

Amos listened silently, squatting by the fire and occasionally poking at the smoldering embers under the blackened coffeepot.

"Well," he said when Jordan had finished, "the way I see it is this: We knew the odds when we started this, and they haven't changed much since. Course, I had no idea we'd be trespassing on some Apache notion of forbidden fruit, but that's the way it is. This time last year, I was fightin' with the Ninth against the Apache while they played hit and run. It's a game they're damn good at playin'."

"Yeah. I remember how good they are at it," Jordan said.

Amos poured scalding coffee into his tin cup and stared into the flames, his voice softly recalling, "It was July twenty-ninth. Lieutenant Guilfoyle and a small detachment of the Ninth almost caught up with a band of renegades led by Nana or Naiche near the White Sands.'' He grimaced. "*Almost* caught up with 'em, but not quite. They'd just killed three Mexicans. We figured there were only about a dozen Apache, so Nana's main force had to be somewhere else.'' He took another sip of coffee, dark eyes as hot and smoldering as the black liquid he drank, staring into the fire as if still seeing the elusive Apache warriors.

"We followed 'em, trekking across the desert until we got here, in the San Andres. God, we were saddle-sore and tired, but we gave 'em a hell of a fight! We ended up taking two of their horses, a dozen mules, blankets and all of their supplies. Shot two of 'em pretty bad, but the rest crossed the Río Grande about six miles below San José, killing two miners and another Mexican who got in their way.''

"Did they come back?'' Griffin asked, fascinated by the tales he'd never been able to coax from either Amos or his uncle. "God, I wish I'd been there!''

Amos sliced him a weary glance. "Yeah, Rooster, they came back—with a vengeance. All through July and August they kept it up, sometimes riding seventy miles in a day, jumpin' back and forth, fightin' rear-guard actions and comin' out on top . . . yeah, they came back, all right. Four Mexicans killed in the foothills of the San Mateos; thirty-six ranchers who were out hunting *them* were eating their dinner in Red Canyon in the San Mateos when they got surprised and shot up. Killed one man, wounded seven, and they lost all their horses to the Apache.''

Disgruntled, Griffin sat back and asked, "Didn't we win any of the battles?''

"Every once in a while. Captured eleven horses and wounded a couple of Apache at Monica Springs in early August; caught up with 'em about ten days later twenty-five miles west of Sabinal. Then we lost one of our men, had three wounded, and another one missing. Still don't know how many the Apache lost, 'cause we couldn't follow them. Captain Parker wouldn't risk any more of our detachment in pursuit because of the wounded.

"A week later, fifteen miles from the McEvers ranch in Hillsboro country, Lieutenant Smith and a detachment of twenty men from the Ninth attacked the hostiles again. This time they were defeated, but it cost us Lieutenant Smith and four of his men as well as a party of citizens under the command of some guy named George Daly."

"Je-e-zus!" Griffin drew out the word. "How'd that happen?"

"Hell, it was Daly's own fault he got killed. The Ninth and the civilians were closin' in on Nana, when that wily old Apache chief led his men into Gavilan Canyon. Lieutenant Smith commanded a halt, but Daly's miners wouldn't stay back and Smith couldn't let 'em go in by themselves and get shot. So he went in with 'em. One volley did for Daly and Smith. The rest of those ignorant bastards got out of there as fast as they could, tails between their legs and bayin' like hounds!"

Griffin was silent for a moment, digesting this bit of information, then he asked, "Did you ever get Nana?"

Amos flicked his wrist to send the dregs of his coffee hissing across the hot stones in the fire.

"Naw. That old chief hightailed it across the Mexican border around the end of August, and as far as I know, he's still there. Maybe he's done with war for a while."

"He must've had quite a big army of braves," Griffin observed after a few moments of silence.

Jordan laughed cynically. "Yeah. Old Nana started out with fifteen warriors, and by the time he got to Mexico, he had maybe forty. Hard to believe, isn't it? That wily old Apache, crippled with age and rheumatism, led a handful of men over a thousand miles of enemy territory. He fought somewhere around seven or eight battles—winning all of them—and killed maybe fifty Americans, wounded God only knows how many more, as well as capturing two women and not less than two hundred horses and mules along his way. Somehow, he managed to elude more than a thousand soldiers, not to mention three or four hundred civilians, and all with less than forty warriors." Jordan shook his head. "Any wonder why I got disgusted and quit?"

"And you're saying that's what we're up against now?" Griffin said softly.

"Yeah. That's why I decided to let you make your own choice, Griffin. We know they're here, and worse than that—they know we're here."

"But even if we backtrack, go back to Franklin or wherever, we've got no guarantees they won't follow us and ambush us somewhere along the trail."

"That's right," Jordan agreed. He propped his foot on the rock where Griffin was sitting. "It may be Nana, it may be Geronimo, or Naiche, but there's a band of renegade Apache waiting for us to do something they don't like."

"Jolie said it was Geronimo's band," Griffin muttered.

"She said it was Geronimo," Amos pointed out, "but yeah, it's about the same thing."

"What do you want to do, Amos?" Griffin asked, turning to look at him. "Go on, or turn back?"

"Like I already said, we knew what we might run into when we started out. I'm for going on."

"Me, too," Griffin said after a moment. "What about you, Jordan?"

Shrugging, his thumbs hooked in his belt, Jordan slid a

glance in the direction of the spring where Jolie was bathing before he answered. The Apache were her people, her family, and while she swore loyalty to him because of her love, what would it do to her to be forced to make a decision?

"Jordan?" Griffin prompted, staring at his uncle with a quizzical expression. "What about you?"

"I'm still in." He jerked his thumb in the direction of the spring. "Maybe we should ask her how she feels."

Now Griffin was amazed. He rocked back on his heels and stared at his uncle for several moments before saying, "Do you mean you're actually thinking about how she might feel for a change? I'm shocked!"

Jordan's narrowed glance hushed Griffin effectively, and the youth watched with open mouth as his uncle pivoted and strode away.

"Well, will you lookit that," he said to the world at large. "Jordan Sinclair finally places some importance on what really matters."

Amos laughed. "You're a little behind, Rooster. He's been doin' that since that first night in Franklin."

"How do you figure?" Griffin asked, swerving to gaze at Amos's bland face. "Hell, he's done his best to make Jolie completely miserable since the first night we got her, and I ain't seen a whole lot of changes since."

"Then you ain't been lookin' in the right direction, boy. Or, you ain't been seein' what you been lookin' at." Amos winked. "He's been payin' attention, all right, only he wasn't in no hurry to do anything about it. And that's the way it should be. It's only the very young who rush in without considerin' all the consequences."

"And you're saying that's what I would have done?" Griffin demanded irritably.

"Now, don't get your back up, Rooster. That *is* what you did, ain't it?"

Griffin thought about it for a moment, then said, "Yeah, I reckon you're right, Amos. How'd you get so smart?"

Chuckling, Amos held out a tin mug of steaming coffee. "I was born that way, boy. When you're born black in the South, you gotta be smart to stay alive sometimes."

Slanting Amos a curious glance, Griffin took the proffered mug and asked, "Were you a slave or something before the War Between the States?"

"I take it you're wantin' to know all my business now," Amos replied, and Griffin hurried to assure him that wasn't true.

"No, I'm just curious. I never knew too many black men before, though every now and then we'd get one who hired on as a cowhand. They never seemed to stay long."

Stretching out with his legs parallel to the fire, Amos leaned back with his saddle as a backrest and said, "No, I was born a free man not far from Natchez, Mississippi. Grew up on the river in a little shanty that had wild roses growing all around it, with honeysuckle bordering the cotton fields. Funny, but as a kid I didn't know that much about prejudice. Maybe that's why I feel some kind of a kinship with the Apache. They're gettin' a raw deal just like some of my people are gettin'."

"Aw, come on! No prejudice in the South?" Griffin scoffed. "I know enough about history and life to know that can't be true."

"I didn't say it wasn't there. I just said I never had much experience with it until I grew up and left home. See, the man who my daddy worked for didn't care what color a man was as long as he did honest work for honest pay. He was fair, and he expected us to be fair with him."

"What'd your daddy do?"

"He was a fisherman. Fished in the back bayous and along the river and sold what he got. We ate good. You ever eaten a Mississippi River catfish, Griffin? No? Boy, you ain't lived 'til you've had cornmeal-breaded catfish fried up in hot grease with a handful of hushpuppies alongside. Add some collard greens or poke salad, and you're in hog heaven!"

"Poke salad?"

"Yeah, it grows wild, and you pick it and stuff it into a bag—or poke—carried over one shoulder. When you're done pickin', you carry it home and cook it up with fatback and maybe some onion . . ."

While Amos was reciting culinary masterpieces from his childhood, Jordan was approaching Jolie. She was still splashing about in the spring, enjoying the cool water and the refreshing feeling of being clean for the first time in several days.

"Need any soap?" Jordan teased from the vantage point of a flat rock jutting out over the tumbling stream.

Slicking back the wet ropes of her dark hair, Jolie rose dripping from the stream to stand in the shallows. Curls of water barely covered her breasts, skimming past in a chilling froth. Trickles slid over her face and neck, wet drops clinging to the tip of her nose and chin, and she laughed as she wiped her face.

"*Dah*. But I do need '*izhee*' for my hair."

"Shampoo?" Jordan guessed, and she nodded.

"You learn quickly, *shitsíné*."

"Now what does that word mean?" he asked, tossing her the long strip of cloth used for a towel.

Jolie's expression was mischievous as she caught the towel and rose from the water, standing knee-deep in the shallows as she wrapped it around her. Her dusky skin shimmered wetly above the edges of the towel, long hair dripping over one shoulder and clinging to the rounded thrust of a breast.

"Which word do you mean?" she asked innocently when Jordan repeated himself. " *'Izhee'*?"

"No, the other one."

"Oh." She wrinkled her nose at him as she walked up the shallow slope of the bank. "That one. I shall tell you the meaning another time, perhaps."

Jordan's brows lifted. "Why not now?" When she shrugged and reached for the clean clothes she had draped over the bushes, he grabbed her around the waist and lifted her high over his head, ignoring her laughing squeals. "Tell me," he threatened, "or I'll dump you back in the water, towel and all!"

" *'Aál*, Jor-dan," she cried between breaths of laughter, "enough!"

"Give up?" he growled with mock severity, still holding her in his arms, and she nodded and put her arms around his neck.

" *'Au*. I give up, Jor-dan."

He swung her down then, setting her on her feet. "Okay, green eyes. What does it mean?"

" *Shitsíné* means my dear, or honey. It is a term used by family, or perhaps lovers."

He pulled her close, ignoring the fact that the towel was falling away in spite of her efforts to grab it, and wrapped his arms around her squirming, wet body.

"So what is the Apache word for this?" he murmured, his head lowering and his lips capturing hers in a long, lingering kiss.

" *Yiits'us*," she answered when she could speak, her voice a little breathless. She clung to him tightly to keep from falling.

"*Yiits'i*?" he said, curling his tongue around the unfamiliar Apache word, and she shook her head and laughed.

"*Dah*, this is *yiitśi*," she replied, grabbing the skin of his forearm in a swift, hard pinch. Before he could do more than say "hey!", she was standing on her tiptoes and murmuring against his mouth, "This is *yiits' ús* . . ." Jolie kissed him deeply, pressing her tongue between his lips in hot, fiery darts that made him breathe more deeply.

"Yeah," he husked several minutes later, "I can definitely tell the difference between the two. Any other words you feel like teaching me, *shitsiné*?"

"Umm-hmm. Come with me and I will show you," Jolie said with a sly glance up at him, leading him toward the shallows where the bushes and reeds grew thickly.

" 'Bout time you two showed up," Amos observed, lifting his charred stick with the meat on the tip and gazing at it critically. Showers of sparks flew upward from the fire as the grease dripped onto the coals. "We thought maybe you'd drowned down there. Heard a few strange sounds like cats drownin' or somethin' . . ." His voice trailed into silence as Griffin smothered a laugh behind his cupped palm, and Amos finally glanced up at the pair who stood just beyond the ragged pool of firelight.

Fortunately, the dark shadows of night hid the flush on Jolie's high cheekbones, but it did nothing to disguise the rumpled state of her clothing, nor the fact that she and Jordan were both wet and grass-stained. She dug her bare toes into the hard dirt of the ground as Jordan said, "You must be getting old, Amos. I didn't hear anything unusual out there."

"Yeah, mebbe that's it. I'm hearin' things in my old age.

I shoulda thought of that. Want some roast rabbit? Griffin managed to find us one out there in the brush.''

Taking Jolie's hand, Jordan led her around the ring of rocks and into the light, where she stood self-consciously trying to smooth the wrinkles from her shirt.

''Did you shoot it?'' he asked the youth, who shook his head.

''Nope. Amos showed me how to rig up a snare. Said we didn't want to let anybody know anymore than we had to about where I was.''

''Yeah, no sense in alerting the Apache to our exact location—as if they didn't already know it anyway,'' Jordan muttered sarcastically.

Jolie couldn't help a laugh. ''Our fire would tell them all they needed to know,'' she said, gesturing to the smoke and sparks. ''Didn't you think of that?''

Amos shared her amusement. ''They've been following us for two days, little one! Of course we thought of that! But why bother eating cold food unless we have to? Let the Apache be the ones who sit all hunkered down in the tall grass and smellin' our food while their bellies growl. This fire ain't goin' to invite 'em in before they feel like it, and it ain't goin' to discourage 'em none, either. I just didn't want our little quick-draw kid here to find hisself with an arrow in his back 'cause he didn't watch over his shoulder. That's the reason for the snare instead of the rifle.'' He took a big bite from his chunk of meat. ''Nope,'' Amos continued, licking his fingers, ''no point in doin' without the creature comforts 'til we have to.''

''And when will that be?'' Griffin asked sourly.

Amos shrugged. ''Soon enough, Rooster, soon enough.''

Soon enough didn't come for a while. There was no sign of the Apache who had followed them while they made their way to the peak north of Hembrillo Peak. It was deathly quiet when they finally stood upon the rocky, brush-studded slopes of the north cone jutting from the basin floor.

"So," Griffin said jauntily, looking around the area as he dismounted from his bay, "what do we do now?"

"Hunt and dig," Jordan answered, tossing the boy a pick and shovel.

Griffin gave him a disgusted glance. "Hey, we coulda done this on Hembrillo Peak. What's the point in coming over here and doing the same thing, when we aren't even sure there's any gold here?"

"There's gold," Jolie broke in, glancing around her. "I remember this place."

"What do you mean, you remember it?" Jordan asked.

She shook her head, long sable braids whipping about her face. "I told you, a long time ago I traveled with Victorio. The gold is here."

"Instead of the other cave?"

She nodded. " '*Au*. Let me think a few moments, and perhaps I will remember where the entrance lies."

"Sounds good to me," Griffin spoke up, and Amos snorted.

"Anything that don't involve hard labor sounds good to you, Rooster!"

"Hey! I've done my share without complaining—too bad," he protested.

Jordan frowned. "Why don't you two give her some peace and quiet so she can think? Maybe she *will* remember where the entrance is."

It took the rest of the afternoon, but Jolie did recall the location of the entrance. She circled the peak in ever widening loops until she stumbled across a vaguely familiar area with an odd jumble of boulders that suggested the outline of a misshapen owl.

"It is here," she said confidently, turning to Jordan. "I remember those rocks."

"Well, we can give it a try," he said, wiping beads of sweat from his brow with the back of one hand. He pushed back his hat and squinted at the cleft she'd identified, shaking his head. "It'll take hours to dig into that. Why don't we wait until morning, Amos?"

Nodding, Amos said, "Suits me. We've waited this long, a few more hours ain't gonna help or hurt."

"Oh yeah?" Griffin put in impatiently. "Remember last time? If we'd gotten in that cave sooner, we might have more gold bars to play with than just one small one!"

"You're welcome to go ahead and start, Rooster," Amos said. "I'm gonna rest."

While the others unsaddled the horses and unpacked the mules, Griffin hacked with his shovel and pick at the rocks, brush, and logs that covered the entrance.

Late afternoon shadows crept along the slopes, signalling dusk, and still Griffin pecked at the debris-littered spot Jolie had chosen. He didn't give up until it was dark and he could no longer see where he was working.

"Tired?" Jolie asked when he slumped wearily against the scant comfort of a rock and poured the contents of a water pouch down his throat.

"Yeah, but at least I'm doin' something," Griffin said in the direction of his uncle and Amos.

"And we appreciate it," Amos said, taking another swig from his whiskey bottle. "Don't we, Jordan?"

"Yeah," Jordan answered. He rubbed the stiff bristles of his beard thoughtfully. "Fact is, we appreciate it so much, we're thinking about letting you get up early and do it again in the morning, Griffin.''

"Go to hell," the boy said tonelessly, not even opening his eyes to glance in Jordan's direction. He groaned softly and ignored their laughter.

Jolie defended him. "Leave him alone," she said. "He is tired, and he has worked hard."

"Maybe so, but if he can't stand the heat in the kitchen . . ." Jordan began, letting his voice trail off into another chuckle.

But in spite of their teasing, Griffin's hard work proved to save them time. The morning sun was barely over the tops of the peaks before they had broken through the barrier of dirt and logs and were standing inside a musty tunnel.

"Light the torches," Jordan ordered, and Griffin fumbled to obey. Faint, flickering light lit the interior with rosy light and erratic shadows.

"Well," Amos said, "this is it. Let's get some packs to carry our future back in."

Griffin fetched the packs for them, his excitement spilling over in half-finished sentences and jerky movements that made them all laugh, easing some of the tension.

"Look," Jolie managed to say calmly over the unsteady thumping of her heart. "Steps." She held her torch high.

"Damn!" Amos breathed. "There sure are! Well, here we are, folks, so let's get on with it!"

He led the way down twisting corridors damp with time. The tunnel descended in a series of steps that Griffin dutifully counted as they went, and reported when they finally reached the bottom that he'd stopped at thirteen hundred and fifty-four.

"And that was a ways back," he added, breathing a sigh of relief as he trod upon the last sloping step. To his surprise it rolled slightly, and he gave a startled yelp, leaping aside and bumping into Amos. "What the hell . . . ?"

"Rigged for ambush," Amos observed, gesturing to a bow and arrow fastened to the cave wall. "Good thing the rawhide strip tied to it rotted a long time ago, huh?" Torchlight flickered over a long bow with a lethal arrow notched and ready to skewer the unfortunate party who disturbed it.

"Yeah, good thing," Griffin muttered uneasily. "What made the step roll?"

"The bottom's been cut so it's round. When you step on it, it rolls."

"Any more surprises like this one?" Griffin wondered aloud, and Amos shrugged.

"Probably."

"Great! Hey—what's that sound?"

Jordan, who had already gone slightly ahead, held his torch high. They were in a huge room bisected by a fast-running stream. Bending forward to scoop up some of the water, Jordan said with surprise, "This water is hot! And it smells like sulphur." They stood at the edge, listening to the rush and roar of the stream as it cut through the cavern.

"Let's follow it," Jolie suggested after a few moments. "I think I remember doing that before."

They followed the underground stream from room to room of the cavern. In some places they had to crawl on hands and knees to continue, and in others they had to wriggle forward on their bellies, torches thrust in front of them and endangering anyone ahead who did not manage to stay out of reach.

"So where's the gold?" Griffin was heard to mutter. His

question was almost instantly followed by an excited whoop from Amos.

"Looky here, looky here!" Rising to his knees, Amos held his torch high, illuminating several dully gleaming stacks. "Gold...silver...and something that looks like copper with it!"

"Al-l-l right!" Griffin exulted, leaping to his feet and flinging himself toward the stacks.

"Careful!" Jordan snapped, snatching Griffin back by one arm. "Remember that rolling step?"

"Oh yeah." Griffin skidded to a halt, slicing a more wary glance toward the waiting fortune.

Cautious explorations revealed no unsprung traps, but they decided not to carry any gold with them at this point. They would wait until their return and not be bogged down with the heavy metal bars in their packs.

"Besides," Jordan said, "there's no telling how far back this cave goes."

"All the way to Hembrillo Peak, do you think?" Griffin wondered aloud.

"Could be. Come on. We're wasting time talking about it," Amos said, earning the caustic query from Griffin, "*Now* who's in a big hurry?"

They continued, and in spite of the cool underground air that brought goose pimples to their flesh, they were all beaded with perspiration. Two of the torches were extinguished to be saved for later, and they stumbled along with the pale light offered by the remaining brands.

One huge cavern revealed ancient drawings painted and carved on the stone walls. Sitting down to rest, Griffin leaned back against a rock the size of a blacksmith's anvil and immediately gave a startled cry.

"What's the matter?" Jordan demanded, swinging his torch around to illuminate Griffin's pale face.

Silvery strands of hair clung damply to the youth's scalp even though it felt to him like it was standing on end.

"The rock moved," he offered weakly, indicating with a wave of his hand the offending stone.

Amos peered closely at him, then snapped irritably, "So? Rocks are always shifting!"

"So, it shouldn't have moved," Griffin insisted stubbornly. "It's too big, and I ain't *that* heavy."

Griffin's rock turned out to be a cover for another shaft, one that descended at a sharp angle. It sloped down for approximately 125 feet before levelling out and then ascending. At the end of this shaft was another large room big enough for a freight train to travel through. This cave also had a stream, and like the other one, it was hot, boiling and hissing a path through the rock.

Once more they followed the stream, moving from room to room, sometimes the only sounds the scuffle of their feet on rock, the eerie whisper of the stream, and their ragged breathing. It was Amos's torch that picked out a horrifying sight that prompted a scream from Jolie.

Amos steadied himself against the clammy wall of the cave and swallowed hard, finally murmuring, "It's okay, little one. He ain't gonna hurt nobody..."

Griffin gulped loudly, and even Jordan seemed shaken by the sight of the grinning skeleton. A sketchy tuft of red hair still adorned the bleached skull, and blank eye sockets gazed into eternity beside the rushing stream.

"I...I...don't remember that," Jolie whispered sickly, averting her eyes from the sight.

"Well, if you'd seen it, you'd remember it," was Jordan's grim comment. He walked forward and stood beside the skeleton, which had collapsed from what appeared to be a kneeling position. The bony wrists were still bound with the remains of a half-rotted rope, fastened to what was left of a wooden post. Jordan lifted his torch, and the fitful light sprayed across a row of more skeletons, all bound to posts like the first, stretching in a neat line.

"Quite an impressive army of ghosts to guard nothing," Jordan muttered. "There's got to be more gold close by."

In a smaller cave just beyond the grisly guards, they found what they were searching for. It leaped out at them when the torch light swept over it: Wells Fargo chests—half-open and crammed with damp, rotting paper money; old Spanish swords, guns, saddles, jewels, boxes filled with letters that would never be received, and enormous piles of gold and silver coins that would burden many more than the seven mules they had brought—littered the rocky room.

Laughter and excited shouts bounced eerily from the walls, ricocheting from the stone ceiling as they sprang forward and seized handfuls of the treasure.

"We found it!" Amos exulted, throwing up a shower of gold and silver. "Just look-a-here!"

Griffin was equally as excited, scrambling from chest to guns, to jewel boxes, to the piles of coins.

"I can't believe it!" he cried. "We found it! We'll be rich the rest of our lives! Look, Jolie...."

Jolie hung back near the entrance, reluctant to enter the room, reluctant to rejoice in the treasure. They had found it, and though she should feel happy for them and relieved that they had realized their quest, she could not summon any emotion other than apprehension.

"What's the matter?" Jordan asked her in a low voice, and she glanced up to see concern in his eyes. "Do you feel the same way I do?"

"I don't know. How do you feel, Jor-dan?"

He shrugged. "I'm not sure. Glad, I guess. Not as glad as I thought I'd be, though."

Their gazes traveled to where Griffin and Amos were delving into the treasure with both hands, looking for all the world to Jordan like children on Christmas morning. But Jolie wouldn't understand that comparison, he thought with a rueful smile.

"Jor-dan?"

He turned his gaze back to Jolie, his expression softening at the sight of her huge green eyes and lovely face. "Yeah?"

"Something's not right. I feel it."

The hairs on the back of his neck prickled, and he felt his throat tighten at the intensity of her tone and eyes.

"Like what?" he asked, striving for composure. Her answer gave him a brief moment of relief.

"We have angered the gods . . ."

"Ah, sweetheart, you know that's just a lot of nonsense cooked up by the local medicine man to scare people into doing what he and the chief want done." Still holding the torch in one hand, he leaned back against the curved side of the arch leading into the treasure room and smiled. "Common sense tells you that. . . ."

Jordan broke off as the walls began to tremble, and a long, low growl rumbled around them. The ground shook, and showers of rock and dust began to pelt them. Alarmed, he leaped away from the opening.

Flinging herself forward, Jolie just managed to avoid the huge, crushing weight of a rock as it rolled forward and blocked the doorway. Jordan caught her, his torch pitching forward and plunging the room into dark shadows.

Chapter
24

For a frozen moment in time, no one spoke. The only sounds were of the underground stream trickling in its ancient bed through the cave and the hollow echo of the giant stone's shift across the doorway. Jordan could have sworn he heard the faint, hollow echo of ancient laughter as well, but put it down to nerves.

He was the first to recover from the shock, making his tone as light and casual as possible as he reached for his doused torch and fumbled to relight it. There was a brief splutter and hiss as the torch finally caught, shedding a welcome pool of light across the cavern.

"Well," he managed to say in a low voice that still ricocheted from wall to cavernous ceiling and back, "the doorway must have been rigged, too. We better figure out what to do next."

There was the dull clink of coins spilling from Griffin's hands back into the pile at his feet, and his youthful voice quavered, "What *can* we do, Jordan? I don't see any other way outa here."

Amos cleared his throat loudly. "There's gotta be a way, Rooster. This cave is like a honeycomb."

"Amos is right," Jolie said, but Jordan's words rolled over hers as he came up with another idea.

"Look, this stone is big, but it's not that big. We can roll it away just enough to squeeze through, and go back the way we came. Come on Amos, Griffin."

So, ignoring Jolie's faint suggestions that they look for another exit instead, Jordan, Griffin, and Amos bent to the task of dislodging the boulder blocking the opening. The stone, though not that large, was dense. Its weight, even with the help of makeshift levers made from scavenged poles and smaller rocks and pebbles, would not budge. The three men were soon in a sweat.

Jolie perched upon an old leather chest to watch, biting nervously at the ends of her fingers. She listened to them grunt and swear, pause in their labors, then grunt and swear again as they threw their weight against the rock and attempted to shift it with muscle and ingenuity.

Pulling her knees up, she clasped her arms around them and narrowed her eyes. Her gaze scanned the room they were in, seeking the deeper shadows, until finally one caught her attention. It was across the thin ribbon of the stream, barely discernible because of the poor light, a narrow outthrust of rock that angled back sharply.

Rising from her perch, she crossed the treasure-littered floor of the cave slowly, picking her way along carefully in the musty gloom, hoping not to set off another trap. This cavern must be riddled with them, she thought, snares craftily placed for the unwary to step into and be crushed to death or pierced with an arrow or spear.

The torches had been wedged between rocks used as holders for them and were giving off sporadic light the farther she moved away from them, so that Jolie stepped more slowly. Once, her bare foot encountered a thin rope strung across the rough stone floor, obviously attached to another device meant to kill, and she froze.

When nothing happened, she proceeded warily, her heart in her throat and her hands as cold and clammy as the stones she walked upon. Pausing at the edge of the stream hissing and steaming in the deep, narrow cut, she took a deep breath. One false step, and she would be plunged into it and risk being burned badly, if not boiled alive. A flat rock jutted up from the middle, steam vapors wreathing it in tiny clouds, and she decided to ford at this point and not take a chance on leaping across.

One step, then two, and she was across, the scalding water and steam barely licking at her feet as she stepped nimbly over them. It seemed to take an eternity, but she finally reached the cleft in the far wall, and her quickly murmured prayers were answered. Pale, dusty light shimmered just around the edge of the cleft. It was another corridor, and it led from this cavern into another, larger one, with more tunnels fanning out. One of them should lead out of the catacombs and up to the surface.

Ducking back into the treasure room, she waited for several moments until Jordan, Amos, and Griffin paused to rest.

"Look!" she called out, waving her arms over her head. "I have found a way out."

Jordan, stretched out upon the damp floor of the cave, slowly turned his head in her direction. Sweat rolled down the sides of his face and into the stubble of beard on his jaw, glistening like diamond chips in the fitful light of the torches. Amos was beside him, half-sitting, one leg drawn up and his arm draped over his knee, sweat glittering on his face also. Only Griffin was still standing, propped against the stone, weariness written in every line of his youthful countenance.

"How?" Griffin called doubtfully. "Maybe it's just another room like this one."

"Then it's a room with a window," Jolie shot back, smiling as this information galvanized the men into reaction. "There is *sha*—sunlight shining into it."

Leaping to their feet with much more energy than they had just exhibited, Jordan and Amos grabbed their packs and began stuffing them with jewels and coins. Griffin, whose pack had been left on the other side of the blocked opening, shrugged quickly out of his shirt and filled it with as much as he could carry.

"Let's go," Jordan said a few moments later, grabbing his torch. "Let's leave marks on the walls so we can find this place again later. You got a knife, Amos?"

"You know I do," was the quick response. "I'll take care of leaving signs. You lead the way now."

Jordan paused at the edge of the stream as Jolie had done, fully aware of the danger even without her urgent, anxious warnings.

"Be careful, Jor-dan! *Yaagudziłtéélé*—the rocks are slippery, and the water is hot . . ."

"Don't worry about me, green eyes," he said, gauging the distance across the stream as he spoke. "I've been around a lot longer than you, and I can take care of myself pretty good."

Instead of fording the water as she had done, he decided to leap across. The thin edges of the rocky banks on each side, however, were too brittle to support the sudden impact of his weight, and crumbled beneath his boots. Jordan slid abruptly toward the boiling water of the stream.

Only Jolie's swift reaction saved him from slipping beneath the water and being cooked. Leaping forward, she grabbed the straps of his pack and threw herself backward, hoping the force of her weight would keep him from going under. It worked, though Jordan still plunged in up to the tops of his boots.

The water was hot enough to burn him through the cowhide, and he rolled from atop Jolie and yanked off his boots as quickly as possible.

"Dammit!" he muttered, stripping away his thick socks. His bare feet were bright pink, and tiny blisters were already forming.

"*Ndiih né?*" Jolie asked, bending to examine his feet.

"What?"

"Does it hurt?" She poked gently at a small, watery pocket with the tip of a finger.

"A little." Jordan winced and slanted her a rueful glance. "I should have used the stepping stone like you said."

"'*Au*, but that does not matter now. Can you walk?" She helped him to his feet, and Jordan gingerly tried first one foot then the other.

"Yeah, it's not too bad. Most of the blisters are on the top of my feet instead of the soles."

Griffin and Amos—who profited by Jordan's mistake and used the rock in the middle of the stream—halted beside him.

"It looks worse than it is," Jordan told them, "and I won't slow us down any. Let's go."

Suiting action to suggestion, they forged ahead, following Jolie around the sharp edge of the cleft and descending into the next cavern. There was no stream here, nothing but a huge, empty cavern with a hole at the top of the vaulted rock ceiling. This natural skylight was over two hundred feet above the rocky floor, flooding the area with warm, dusty light.

"I was beginning to wonder if I'd ever see the sun

again,'' Griffin muttered, squinting up at the golden streamers filtering into the cave. "Let's get outa here."

Amos's voice was ripe with amusement. "You rich enough already, Rooster?"

"No, but I'm gettin' a little nervous about stayin' down here too long," the boy replied. He gave a quick glance around the cavern. "And I still don't see any escape hatch."

"There are more tunnels leading out," Jolie said quickly. "But I'm not sure which one leads to the top, and which leads to the other peak."

"Great!" Jordan snapped. "I hope we aren't going to depend on your guesses to get out of here."

Hands on her slim hips, Jolie glared at him. "*Dah*! You can do what you like if you don't trust me!"

"I didn't say that, *shitsiné*. I only said . . ."

Jolie shook her head. "It doesn't matter, Jor-dan," she said. "*Hiyaa*—I'm tired, and I want out of here, also. If you prefer exploring the tunnels yourself, I do not care. I only want to breathe sweet air again, instead of air that has not seen *sha*."

"Yeah," Amos agreed, "I'd like to feel the sunshine on my face again, too."

"Well, I think Jolie should lead us out," Griffin said. "She ain't done too bad so far."

So Jolie led them out, feeling much like the man in one of the stories related by the little priest at the mission when she was a child. The story had been about a man with a long white beard who had led his people from the wilderness into safety. For the first time, she understood the weight of the responsibility in leading others, a fact the little priest had often tried to get across to the children. Of course, he had been more concerned with convincing Apache children that they should follow the right leaders—who were the bluecoat soldiers—instead of the wrong ones, to emphasize the points he should have. It was a fact that had not escaped Jolie's notice even then.

So now, as she led them down twisting corridors and time-warped tunnels, she debated on the wisdom of this search for gold. Ussen, the Apache god, was represented by the sun, the color of gold. The Sacred Mountain—*dzil dighine*—was in the San Andres. Could not this gold belong to Ussen? she rationalized. And who was to say that Ussen and the *'indaa'* god were not one and the same?

The son of Chief Juh, Daklugie, had once observed that the mountain gods were angered by the gold mining and they danced and shook the mighty shoulders and opened up and swallowed towns. The rivers changed their courses.

He had been referring to *niigudiyeena*—an earthquake—that had occurred in 1880, only three years before. Even Nana, Victorio's successor, had considered the white man's lust for gold sacrilegious.

As she felt her way along the dark tunnel, Jolie nervously recalled Nana's comments of not long before. He had been speaking to a man from the agency that regulated Indian affairs, and he had said, "The white-eyes are superstitious about gold. Their lust for it is insatiable. They lie, steal, kill, die for it. If forced to choose between it and things many times exceeding it in value, they unhesitatingly choose gold. Little do they care that they incur the wrath of the mountain gods . . ."

Jolie shivered. Daklugie and Nana's words seemed a prophecy.

"Cold, *shitsíné*?" Jordan murmured close behind her, once more using the Apache endearment, and she smiled.

"*Dah*. I am not cold, Jor-dan, only worried. I do not

wish for anything bad to happen because we have disturbed the gold.''

"Well, I'm certainly not going to say anything else about silly superstitions," Jordan muttered. "Another rock might roll over us, or the roof might fall in."

In spite of her apprehension Jolie laughed. "I shall pray that it does not. Look, Jor-dan—there, far away, do you see light?"

A tiny speck flickered briefly at the end of the tunnel, then seemed to disappear. Behind them Jordan could hear Griffin complaining softly about the knee-deep dust on the cave floor.

"What is this stinky stuff?" Griffin asked Jolie, in a tone of disgust. "It clings to everything!"

"*Guano*," she answered briefly, more concerned about the speck of light than the dust.

Griffin sneezed, then coughed. "Well, it's makin' me sick. It's making my eyes and nose run, too, and I think my legs are breaking out into a rash. How about you, Amos?"

"Yeah, it's makin' me a little queasy, too, but if we can just get outa here, I'll be happy."

"What's *guano*, anyway, Jolie?" Griffin continued, brushing at his clothes and arms.

"Bat dung," was the short answer, and Griffin choked.

"*Bat dung*!" he exploded. "Dammit! Why didn't you tell me before?"

Jolie halted and swung around, gazing at him in the dim light afforded by the torches, and for the first time since he had brought her from the Apache village, her voice was sharp to Griffin.

"What difference would it make? Do you wish to leave this place or not? If we had to wade through buffalo dung neck-high, would you not do it to get out?"

Griffin just stared at her for several seconds, then muttered, "Yeah, I guess so. Sorry, Jolie."

Her expression softened, and she put out her hand to touch him on one arm. "It is well, Griffin. I did not mean to be ugly to you. I am worried, that is all."

"I understand, and I guess I'm worried, too. Maybe that's why I'd rather talk about *guano* than whether or not we're ever gonna get outa here," he replied, a half-smile slanting his mouth. Blue eyes met hers for a moment, then he shrugged. "Let's move on"

"Don't get too happy about it now," Jordan said, jerking his thumb toward the tunnel ahead of them, "but I think there's a light at the end of the tunnel."

"So *that's* where that saying came from," Griffin muttered as he shifted his backpack and waded through the *guano* behind Jordan. "It makes more sense now than it ever did before."

They pushed on, sometimes having to get down and crawl on hands and knees again, in some places having to walk stooped over, while the tunnel zigzagged through the center of the mountain. Finally, reaching that area where the light proved to be another high window, they sank down on the rock to rest.

"Well, what now?" Griffin asked after a few moments, resting his head against the wall. He had selected a spot thankfully free of *guano*. "None of us can make that climb up to the window, and I don't see any other way out."

"You've said that before," Jordan pointed out. "There're more tunnels leading out of here."

Amos heaved his pack down and sat on it. "Sooner or later one of the windows is bound to be closer to the cave floor, Rooster. Don't go gettin' all down in the mouth again."

"Yeah, but it might take weeks; or it might be rigged with another trap; or it might . . ."

"Might!" Amos exploded irritably. "Mites is on a chicken's ass, boy! Don't be talkin' none of this 'might' stuff around me! I intend to get out of here, and I intend to be rich when I do!"

In spite of his tension, Griffin grinned, and the torchlight shimmered on his pale golden hair. "Me, too," he said softly. "I'm gonna buy my mama the prettiest dress you ever saw, and then I'm gonna buy me that bay stallion Charlie Bradshaw has over on the Circle X Ranch. And then . . ."

"And then you're going back to school," Jordan finished for him. "Remember?"

"School? If I've already got money, what's the point in going to school?" Griffin wanted to know. He took a swallow of water from his leather water pouch and wiped his mouth on his sleeve. "School would just be a waste of time then."

"You need to learn how to keep your money, or at least how not to waste it," Jordan answered. "Besides, you promised me you would."

"Yeah, but I didn't figure you'd make me keep that promise if we got rich, Jordan."

"Well, you figured wrong."

Jolie listened silently, thinking of all she'd ever heard about men and their search for gold, and wondering if it would taint Jordan and Griffin and Amos as it had others. She wrapped her arms around her knees and pulled them up to her chest.

Jordan leaned close, his mouth stirring damp strands of hair over her ear. "I know what you're thinking, green eyes."

She turned, laying her cheek against her knee and looking at him. "Do you?" she asked softly.

"Yes. But I'm not Apache, Jolie, and I do not feel the same way you do about gold. I sometimes think of all the things I can do with it that I've never done before, things that will make a difference in my life."

"What kind of things, Jordan? Will you buy a new horse, perhaps, or new clothes? Will those make a difference in your life?"

"No, but I can buy a ranch and start my life over." He put his arm around her shoulders and drew her into the angle of his arm and chest. "I've been thinking—I don't have to go to Mexico and lie on a beach and do nothing. I can buy cattle and horses, and have a piece of ground that belongs to me . . . to *us*. We can have those children you once spoke of, and live together a long time, man and wife."

Jolie was silent, and Jordan stiffened thinking that she did not want to live on a ranch, or had changed her mind about marrying him.

"Guess I spoke too late, huh? Maybe you don't want to get married to me anymore, or . . ."

Turning into him, Jolie half-rose on her knees and put two fingers over his mouth.

"You are wrong, Jor-dan. I want to be *nighaasd zq'*. I want that more than anything." Her voice faltered. "But I want it to be right. . . ."

He crushed her close, his mouth grazing her cheek and ear, his breath warm against her. "It will be, love," he promised, "it will be."

"I hate to interrupt this tender little scene," Amos drawled, "but I'd kinda like to get out of this cave. From what I can tell, the light seems to be fadin' in our little

natural window up there, which means it must be gettin'
dark outside. Dark seems like a good time to try and find
our way back to where we started, especially as these
torches we're carrying won't last forever.''

Griffin groaned. "That's all I needed to hear..."

"Come on, Rooster! Do something besides gripe about
where you are," Amos retorted. "Carry this torch awhile."

Heaving himself up from the rock floor, Griffin took the
torch and followed the others.

They wandered in the caverns beneath the ground for a
day and a half, coming close but never quite finding the way
out. Each tunnel seemed to meet with a dead end or another
huge room, and it was in one of these rooms that they made
their greatest find.

It was Griffin, actually, who found the gold. He'd paused
just ahead of the others and leaned against a wall for
support. He was weak from hunger and worry, and his legs
were too shaky to support him much longer.

What good was his gold if he died underground, buried
alive in the vast caverns that seemed to run beneath all of
New Mexico territory? he wondered bitterly. He pushed
away from the wall, his palms against it, and froze.

Instead of the cold stone he'd expected to feel, it was
rough and hairy, like an animal skin. Swallowing hard,
Griffin reached for the torch he had propped against a stone
and held it up, half-turning to look closely at the wall.

It was no wall. Stacked as high as a man and covered
with old buffalo robes were dull bars, looking for all the
world like pig iron. Hardly daring to hope, Griffin reached
for one of them with trembling fingers. It clung stubbornly
to its position, and he jerked hard. The bar was heavy, and
certainly didn't look like gold, but he rubbed it against his

shirt to remove the film of dust and age and was rewarded with a dully gleaming shine that he couldn't mistake.

Turning to the others, he said in a voice that was quite calm, "Gentlemen—and lovely lady—we have found gold again."

Silence greeted this statement, as the others were as tired and despairing as he was, so he cleared his throat and repeated himself, and was met with a chorus of weary astonishment. He held up the bar and let the light from the dying torch flicker over it.

"Looks like you knew what you were talking about when you told us about Padre La Rue's mine," Jordan said to Jolie after he'd examined the finding. "There's thousands of bars here, *thousands*!"

"Yes," she said simply, too distraught to care. Her tired mind struggled with this information, and some tiny fact that should have been important now eluded her. She closed her eyes. Her feet were sore from walking, and her legs were aching, and her eyes hurt from straining them in the dark. Jordan's feet were bleeding and raw from his burns, but he never complained. Amos had fallen once and broken open his recent wound, necessitating the destruction of a shirt to bind it more tightly. Jordan had donated the shirt.

All these facts and the vague impressions of the past day and a half circled endlessly in her mind, whirling past at a dizzying rate while she struggled for composure. There was something she should remember, some small detail that she had overlooked.

Rubbing her eyes, she glanced up and watched as the men began counting the gold bars stacked like cordwood. Would they never tire of gold? she wondered wretchedly. Gold. That was the fact that kept haunting her—it was the vague memory of gold covered with old buffalo robes and resting only a few hundred feet from a tunnel leading out onto the Hembrillo Peak.

Her head jerked up, and she surged to her feet. "Jordan!" she cried out, stumbling forward to catch him by one arm. "I remember, I remember! The tunnel to go out is not far away... it is in that direction. I remember now."

Pausing, hardly daring to believe that this time she might remember, Jordan asked carefully, "Are you sure?"

"'*Au*! I am sure this time! I came here several times, you see, and I remember this. I can remember an old sword lying behind the stacks, because I was playing with it and was made to stop... it is broken in two... here it is!" she cried triumphantly, dropping on her hands and knees to search at the bottom of the gold stacks. She held up a sword with a rusted hilt, its blade broken in half. "See?"

"Yes, we see," Jordan said. "Mark the way, Amos, and let's get out of here. I'm ready to see some sunlight."

Griffin lifted several of the gold bars and tied his leather belt around them. "I'm taking these with us, just in case we don't find it again. Gold seems to have a way of getting lost too often," he said gleefully.

"Leave it!" Jolie said sharply. "It is forbidden."

"Aw, Jolie, you're not going to try that superstitious stuff on me again, are you?" Griffin moaned.

"You are young and greedy," she snapped. "Leave it."

Hesitating, glancing from his uncle to Jolie, Griffin opened his mouth to present another argument in favor of taking the gold bars. An unfamiliar rumble pre-empted anything he might have said.

Amos's eyes rolled wildly. "What's that?"

The rumble was something that Jolie remembered. There had been another rumble a few years before, and then the ground had shaken and the earth had moved also.

"Run!" she said, and as the walls began to dance in a peculiar shimmy, no one doubted what it was.

Earthquakes above ground were bad enough, but experiencing an earthquake when one was deep within the bowels of the earth was something else. It was all too possible for the fissures to open and cavern walls to collapse in a shower of twenty-ton boulders and sheets of rock.

There was no time for conversation, no time to pick up extra packs or the torches. They ran. They ran like terrified sheep from the wolf, bent over with arms above their heads to shield them from falling rocks and pebbles, leaping chasms that opened beneath their feet, running blindly. Griffin's torch was knocked from his hand by a falling rock and he didn't pause to pick it up. Jordan and Jolie shredded their bare feet on the rocks and lethal edges of the stone and didn't pause. Amos staggered from a wicked blow to the head, recovered his balance, and pushed on. It was a nightmare from which there was no hope of waking, reality that had intruded into the dream for gold.

"Come on!" Jordan rasped when Jolie fell, gasping for breath, her tortured lungs and leaden legs refusing to respond to her signals to go on. "Get up, damn you!" He grabbed her arm and dragged her until she could regain her feet, relentlessly forging ahead.

An eternity passed, and then another one, and in the kind of miracle that all pray for but few see, a large square of light appeared just ahead of them. When they staggered through it, sunlight struck them with blinding force, and they collapsed on the trembling ground covered with dust. The earth was still shaking, still dancing in the final throes of the quake, and they could do nothing but hold to blades of grass as if that would keep them from tumbling down the slopes of the peak.

When the final tremor had faded, they opened their eyes and looked at each other in silent awe. Eyes unaccustomed to light ached, and they were covered with bruises and bleeding cuts from head to toe, but they were alive.

Laughter borne of relief and strain welled up in four throats at the same time, bursting forth, an alien sound in a silent world. Shudders of laughter rocked them, and each time one of them met the others' eyes, they dissolved into more spasms.

"We did it!" Amos said when he could speak again, wiping tears from his eyes. "We went to hell and came back to tell about it!" He rolled onto his back and lay looking up at the blue sky he'd thought he'd never see again. It was beautiful. The grass was beautiful, and the mountains, and even the burning sands of the Jornada stretching beyond the mountains was beautiful. It was a beautiful day, and Amos said so. He closed his eyes, a big smile still pasted on his bearded face.

"Amos," Jordan said quietly a few moments later, "open your eyes."

Amos's head rolled back and forth on his pack. "Nope. I'm goin' to lie right here and sleep with the sun beatin' down on me! Never thought I'd be glad to feel that hot ole sun again, but damn if it don't feel good!"

"Amos," Jolie added, "it would be good if you were to open your eyes . . . *déduudí.*"

"What is so important?" Amos began, turning over and opening his eyes. His mouth sagged, and his eyes opened even wider. Ranging just beyond where they all lay in front of the tunnel entrance, was a half-circle of armed Apache warriors.

Jordan, Griffin, and Jolie were still in the same postures

of relaxation, but there was nothing relaxed about the expressions on their faces. They had been delivered from the earthquake into the hands of Nana, one of the fiercest Apache leaders ever to roam New Mexico territory.

Chapter
25

Griffin strained against the ropes binding him to the wooden stake driven into the ground. It was no use. The thin strips of rawhide would not give at all. The Apache had wet them before looping them around the wrists tied behind him, and as the searing New Mexico sun dried them, the rawhide shrank, digging painfully into his skin.

"Tied up tighter than a pig trussed for market," Griffin muttered morosely. He squinted toward where Jordan and Amos were tied, only a few feet away, awaiting the same fate, whatever that would be.

"And we're likely to be butchered just like a pig," Amos added gloomily. His gaze moved to Jordan, who sat with his head back against the pole, staring straight ahead. "Anybody seen Jolie yet?" Amos asked hopefully.

Jordan shook his head. "No. I haven't seen a sign of her since one of the warriors put her on back of his horse and rode away from Hembrillo Peak." He shut his eyes, still haunted by the memory of her bleak face when Nana had ignored her pleas and taken them all prisoner.

"You know," Griffin mused aloud, "maybe there's something to that superstitition stuff after all. Seems like every time we found some gold, something bad happened. Maybe since it's Apache gold, their god really is protecting it."

"Oh, for Chrissake!" Amos muttered wearily, closing his eyes again and resting his head against his pole. "It's bad enough I gotta be tied up waiting to be skinned or something, but now I gotta listen to this fairy tale!"

"No," Griffin insisted, "just think about it, Amos! What happened when we found all that gold and silver and jewels in that room? A big stone trapped us inside!" he answered for him. "And then, when we found all those gold bars, what happened?" When Amos refused to answer, Griffin answered for him again. "An earthquake! Now don't that tell you something?"

"Yeah," Amos finally said, "it tells me that I was in the wrong place at the wrong time again, that's what it tells me! Will you stop this useless junk, boy? It's bad enough that every gnat and flyin' or crawlin' insect in all of New Mex territory has found us, but I don't want my last hours to be spent listening to a bunch of wild maybes!"

After a few minutes of silence spent contemplating the burning blue bowl of the sky and the teeming Apache village below them, Jordan commented, "Wish I knew where Jolie was and what she's doing."

"While you're wishin'," Amos said, "wish we was all where we ain't!"

Jordan closed his eyes against the searing prick of the sun and sighed. Amos was right about the insects. As if lured by the prospect of a delicious meal, flies and ants had arrived in droves to bite any area of skin unprotected by clothing. His feet hurt, and his wrists were aching. The circulation in his hands had been cut off and his fingers were numb, but at least he was alive. As long as there was still breath in his body, there was hope, and he didn't intend to give up anytime soon.

If only his brain weren't so tired. He'd had nothing to eat in two days, and in the last eight hours, no one had thought about giving the prisoners water. His mouth was dry, and his throat almost closed. Where the hell was Jolie?

Jolie was also fighting for survival, and not just her own. Stubbornly, she faced the Apache subchief who was interrogating her, demanding that the prisoners be freed.

"They have not harmed anyone," she argued, careful to keep her tone courteous so as not to offend. "And they are not our enemies."

"Maybe not *yours*, Gáadu," the chief returned, gazing at her with hostile eyes, "but they are most certainly enemies of the *nde*."

"Do you doubt my loyalty to my mother's people?" she shot back. "I was born into The People, and I have lived most of my life with you. Who dares say I am not *nde*?"

The other three men in the brush and mud wickiup did not speak, just exchanged glances. Outside the hut formed by fastening leafy branches over an oven-shaped framework of slender saplings, the familiar chatter of the women and the laughter of the playing children provided a busy backdrop to the scene unfolding inside.

Jolie could hear snatches of song and the clatter of hooves across the ground. Gone were her faded Levis and the thin cotton shirt she'd worn for the past months, and in their place was a costume that accentuated her heritage. She stood before the council arrayed in her best *'eutsa* trimmed with a fringe of beads and shells received in a long-ago trade. The shells made a faint tinkling sound with each movement, and her long, dark hair, bound in neat braids, swung against the musical collar of the buckskin dress.

She stood stiffly, head bowed slightly in deference. "I know these *'indaa'*," she said. "They are good men and have been kind to me. They are not like the others but are smart and willing to . . ."

"*Dah!*" The chief made a gesture of contempt. "'*Indaa dogoyạạda! 'Indaa' nant' án 'agodil' ịị.*" He folded his arms across his chest, signalling the interview was at an end for the moment, and Jolie stepped aside to let him pass. Only after the other men had filed out behind him did she leave, bending slightly under the curved arch of the doorway.

The first sight that met her eyes was the three captives on the mound above the village, and her throat tightened. She had to do something.

Jolie cast furtive glances around the open area circled by brush wickiups. Cooking fires dotted the ground here and there, with pots suspended over some of them, and the camp dogs sniffed among piles of garbage looking for discarded bones or meat. She'd forgotten the distinct odor that permeated the village in the summertime, the rich mixture of smells that combined thick smoke from the fires, rotting piles of garbage, boiling cooking pots, and meat dripping over glowing coals.

A few feet away, three dogs circled one another with bared teeth, stiff-legged and snarling, until a rotund woman snatched up a length of wood and began to thrash them soundly. Loud yelps rent the air, and the dogs fled in three separate directions. Two young boys ran past with sticks intended to be spears and tiny bows and arrows clutched in their fists. Cottonwood and green willow branches burned in the fires, the smoke discouraging gnats, green flies, and mosquitos, and penetrating clothing and hair.

Not far away, some men were playing a wheel game, in

which the contestants threw arrows or sticks at a rolling hoop laced with rawhide. Shouting and laughing, they bragged good-humoredly and gambled on the outcome with whatever valuables they possessed. It was a noisy, active scene, and one familiar to Jolie.

To the three men on the slope, the scene was chaos. They didn't understand what was going on and didn't like the festive air that seemed to indicate a ritual killing of the prisoners.

"I'd like to know what we're in for," Amos said in a voice that was thick from lack of water. He attempted to lick his lips, but his tongue was too swollen. "Then again, maybe I wouldn't," he added a moment later.

Night shadows finally began to fall, creeping down the mountain face slowly. Scattered fires glowed like huge, sullen eyes, appearing to the men on the hill as evil. It seemed to be a time for social gathering, with dances in a dozen different places.

The captives' relief afforded by the burning sun's descent was dulled by apprehension. Drummers set up brightly painted drums, with several men grouped around one to pound on the tightly stretched skin with the heels of their palms and their fingers. The thumping beat crescendoed as men and women danced side by side, forming a circle that contracted and expanded. The line of dancers resembled a snake writhing across the ground, ominous and deadly. Deep baritone voices rang in song, accompanied by the shriller voices of the women and occasionally broken by the high, plaintive chanting of an old man. Hand rattles made of hollow gourds, dried, stiffened hides or dried buffalo scrotums knocked and clattered, keeping rhythm with the beat of the drums.

"This is one party I hope we don't get invited to," Jordan said in a croaking voice as the sun disappeared behind a peak, leaving the men in total shadow. "I've got a feeling we wouldn't like it."

Griffin, who was keeping his youthful composure extremely well, considering the fact that he was terrified beyond belief, managed a weak, rasping laugh.

"Humorous to the end, huh?"

"It ain't the end yet, boy," Amos put in. "It ain't over 'til . . ." He halted abruptly.

" 'Til what?" Griffin demanded, " 'til we're dead? That's what you mean, so why don't you say it? I'm not a baby you have to coddle." He flexed his arms against the painful leather strips. "I'm in the same shape you guys are in, so don't try to sugarcoat it for me."

"I didn't mean that," Amos said softly. "It's just that I find it a tad hard to discuss my death. Especially as how I happen to think I'd make a mighty ugly corpse."

Leaning his head back against the post, Jordan laughed weakly. "Not me," he said. "I think I'd make a damn goodlooking corpse."

"Dah," a soft feminine voice disagreed, "you would make a most disagreeable corpse, Jor-dan Sinclair!"

"Jolie!" three voices chorused in perfect unison.

"Shhh!" She put her fingers over Jordan's lips from behind and was appalled at how dry and swollen they were. Muttering imprecations about their lack of humane treatment in first French, then Spanish, then Apache, Jolie continued in a low voice, "You must be quiet. I will loosen your ties and give you water, but that is all I can do right now. I will think of something else later."

"Like what?" Jordan peered at her in the dark shadows of night, trying to fill his eyes with the sight of her. "Don't do anything that will endanger you, green eyes."

She shook her head. "No, I must be careful in order to be

able to help you. If . . . if only *shitáa* would return from the mountains, then perhaps . . ." Breaking off, she gave her head another shake. "It is not to be."

"How could your father help us?" Amos asked, wincing as she loosened his bindings. The rush of blood back into starved flesh was painful, and he could barely wiggle his fingers. "Does he have some kind of influence over the chief?"

"Papa? No, he has no influence, but they respect him. He is one of the few *'indaa'* who has married into the tribe and been accepted. Even Nana listens when my father speaks."

"Maybe you could ride to Fort Sheldon or something and bring us back some help," Griffin suggested hopefully, but that idea was met with immediate refusal.

"*Dah*. They would kill you as soon as they saw soldiers coming," she said. "But I do know they do not mean to kill you right away."

Jordan frowned. "I'm not sure if that's good or bad. I'd rather die quickly than slowly, and I've seen what they can do to a man, Jolie."

She held a gourd of water up to his lips and let him drink, tenderly wiping his face and the stubble of beard on his jaw when he was through.

"I would not let you be tortured," she said. "I would kill you myself first."

In spite of the hours spent in the broiling sun, Jordan could not halt the sudden chill that shivered through him. There was no smile on her lips, nor note of jest in her tone, and he knew she would do just that.

Jolie gave Griffin and Amos water, then poured the remainder over their heads to cool them. Pausing next to Jordan she said, "I must go back before I am missed. I will do what I can, *shitsíné*."

Her fingers skimmed over the rugged planes of his face as

if committing it to memory, and, kneeling beside him, she leaned forward and kissed him gently on the lips, her mouth moving sweetly on his.

"Mmm, again," he husked when she drew back, his mouth crooking in a smile. "Your lips are as sweet as sugar—what is the Apache word for sugar, green eyes? I want to learn all I can from you in case your people are right."

Puzzled, she stared at him in the dim light and asked, "What do you mean?"

"In case the Apache are right about their god. Maybe I should know how to speak your language just in case you forget mine in the next life."

She laughed softly. "Now I know the sun has baked your brain, foolish one! You are funning me again." Jolie gave him a quick, hard kiss and gathered up her gourd. "I have to go now, but I will be back," she whispered and disappeared into the deep shadows behind them. Her voice floated back a moment later, *"Gulkǫǫde,* Jor-dan . . ."

Beside him, Amos laughed, and Jordan asked what she'd said. "That's the Apache word for sugar, Cap'n," Amos replied with a grin that shone brightly in the dark.

Dawn stole softly over the sleeping Apache camp, bright fingers of light peeking over the rims of verdant peaks in shimmering rays. Blinking against the light, Jordan tried to ease the muscles cramped from long hours spent stretched out with his hands tied behind him, and found it impossible. He attempted wetting his lips with his tongue, but it was too dry.

Beside him, Griffin moaned softly and Jordan winced. He was responsible for the boy, and now look what had happened.

He was only sixteen and should have stayed at home with his mother. Would Jassy understand what drove a boy to try his wings and seek adventure? Or would she blame her brother for letting him come along and be killed by the Apache? The latter was more likely.

Amos echoed his thoughts as he said, "Hell, I don't mind it so much for me, but I sure hate this for the boy. He's too damn young, and I feel responsible."

"How do you think I feel?" Jordan asked in a tortured voice. "He's my nephew, and Jassy trusted me to take care of him."

"Will you two quit talkin' about me like I'm already dead?" Griffin cut in irritably. "And I ain' no *boy*! I'd like to think that I'm grown up enough to at least be considered a young *man*."

"With a limited future," Jordan returned. "Hell, I'm sorry, Griffin. I should have put you on that mail stage back to Jassy."

"I wouldn't have gone," the youth replied shortly, shutting his eyes against the glare of the early morning sun. "I'd have probably gotten myself shot before I ever got back 'cause I was determined to have an adventure. At least, now I'm with you."

"I'm sure that's a great comfort." Jordan leaned his head back against the post again, wishing his hands were tied in front of him so he could scratch the insect bites on his arms and neck. Then he straightened, staring ahead of him at the wickiups below. "There's Jolie," he observed, narrowing his eyes.

Jolie was walking across the open space in the middle of the camp, accompanied by an older woman who seemed to be berating her for something, her age-puckered mouth moving at a rapid pace in time with the flailing of her withered arms. They walked to a small structure built a short distance away from the other dwellings, behind a row of bushes and small grove of cottonwoods.

Watching, Jordan observed with a pang the bluish glint of the sun on Jolie's hair, and how gracefully she moved, like a willow bending in the wind. It seemed to him that she glanced in his direction before she bent to enter the hut, and he knew she was thinking about him. God, this was as hard on her in a way as it was on him. She must be suffering with just as helpless a feeling as he was.

Jordan was right to a certain extent. Jolie was worried, but she had a plan. She'd spent a sleepless night on a pallet in the wickiup she was sharing with the old crone who had been set to guard her. Finally, just before the first light, she had thought of the perfect solution. It had come to her with the memory of the first time she had seen Jordan and the circumstances surrounding her capture.

Even now, a slight smile curved the soft lines of her mouth as Jolie considered how woman's infirmity could often work for her as well as against her.

Entering the wickiup set aside from the others, she promptly went to a mat and lay down, turning her face to the wall. The old woman busied herself with the making of a pair of moccasins, sitting cross-legged on a *teestl'u*, or weed bed just like the one Jolie was lying upon. Special bowls were piled neatly against one wall, and the large pit used for cooking smoldered in the center of the shelter.

An hour passed, and then another, and finally the old woman dozed off, nodding over the unfinished moccasins. It was the chance Jolie had been waiting for.

Rising from her pallet, she crept past the old woman and out the door of the wickiup, pausing in the entrance to cast furtive glances around the area outside the brush hut. No one even glanced in her direction. All were busy with preparations for the upcoming celebration.

Nana and his warriors had come back from several raids, victorious and filled with satisfaction. They had plundered and looted wagon trains and ranches, dipping down into Mexico before returning. It had been on their return from Mexico that they had happened upon Jolie and the others. Nana was in the habit of storing useless plunder such as gold and silver in that particular cavern, and had been enraged to find his enemies trespassing.

Now there would be a celebration in the camp, with the prisoners as the focus of the activities. Jolie had not seen such a rite, since her father would not allow it, but she had heard often enough how it was done and did not intend for Jordan, Griffin, and Amos to suffer.

Stealing across the camp ground, she made her way undetected to the mound above the village. Tucked within the folds of her *'eutsa* was a sharp knife, which she used with rapid efficiency on the rawhide binding Jordan.

"I cannot risk being seen," she whispered in short, quick tones, "so you must free the others. I leave you the knife. Use your judgment on the proper time for escape, *shitsíné*."

"What about our guns?" Amos asked swiftly. "Where are they?"

"In the wickiup of the council. Forget them. You must use what other weapons you can find. Look in the last hut beyond the stream. It is not guarded well."

Slicing through the thin strips of leather, Jolie pressed the knife into Jordan's palm and brushed her lips across his ear. "*Vaya con Dios*," she murmured.

He grabbed her hand. "My God or yours?"

"Does it matter?"

Jordan smiled. "No, my love. I think either god will be on our side. Where can I find you later?"

"Forget me now. Think only of yourselves. I will not be harmed, but you are part of the celebrations. You must get away..."

"No," Jordan broke in, "I won't go without you!"

Jolie snatched her hand away. "You have no choice! If you are foolish enough to linger, you will be tortured and killed. Don't think just of yourself, *shitsíné*, but of the two you have with you, also," she said when he tried to speak. "Would you have them suffer for your stubbornness?"

With a fleeting smile and another brush of her lips across his cheek, she was gone, gliding gracefully down the slope back to the wickiup while Jordan watched with his heart in his mouth.

"She's right," Amos said after a long moment.

"Yeah," Griffin added, "but I'm not thinkin' of just myself, Jordan. If we try to stick around here, we'll all be dead. You heard her—we're part of the party whether we want to be or not; in fact, we're the entertainment." He closed his eyes and shuddered, recalling all the news stories he'd read about Indians and the atrocities they could commit. Of course, after knowing Jolie, he also knew that the white man was equally as adept at committing atrocities. That left him with the conclusion that both sides were quite capable of savagery.

"We'll have to wait until the right time," Jordan said after a few moments. He flexed his fingers, feeling more comfortable already. "Here, Amos. I'm going to cut your bonds, then Griffin's. This is our only weapon at the moment, so we'll have to do the best we can with it."

"I've been known to be pretty damn good with a knife, Cap'n," Amos said, twisting so that Jordan could get at his bonds without being too conspicuous. "Make this quick—I'll keep a lookout for anybody watchin'."

"Don't move!" Griffin snapped then, tensing. "I see a man looking up here toward us, and I think it's one of the Apache who brought us back."

Several tension-filled minutes passed while the sun beat down, sweat streamed down their faces, and the intolerable flies swarmed around them, but no one came to check on them.

"Okay, *now*," Griffin said, and Jordan edged close to Amos again and swiftly sliced his rawhide cords. The procedure was repeated with Griffin before he settled himself back against the rough wooden post again, hands behind his back as if they were still tied.

"Wait until I give the signal," Jordan said, "and then we'll make a break for it. Amos—you look out for Griffin, okay? Just in case anything happens to me."

Amos gave him a long, considering look that plainly stated he knew Jordan's intentions, and nodded his head. "I'll take care of him, Cap'n. You know that."

"Maybe we should go one at a time," Griffin suggested, but Jordan shook his head.

"No. We go together. Someone would be bound to notice if only one was gone, and I can't risk it. Amos, you take the knife. I'm not that good with one. We'll head for the weapons first."

The right time didn't come until almost dusk. The Apache were gearing up for the coming festivities, and some were already drunk on *tulpái*. It was apparent that they intended to have their captives as the guests of honor before the night was over.

While Jordan was hesitating, agonizing over the right moment to escape, the heavens decided to cooperate. As if a sign from God, showers of meteorites spilled over the ground like snow from the sky, thumping onto the roofs of the wickiups and even into the cooking pots with alarming results.

Women screamed and grabbed their children, while the men snatched up weapons as if to arm themselves against these invaders from the sky. Dogs yelped and horses neighed shrilly, rearing and plunging in frantic efforts to escape the hot shower that pelted them.

"What the hell . . . ?" Amos began, but Jordan was already urging them up.

"Now! Let's run for it!"

"What is that stuff?" Griffin asked, running with his arms over his head, stumbling as his legs buckled under him. He was weak from hunger, thirst, and inactivity.

"I'm not sure, but whatever it is, it may get us out of here," was Jordan's answer as he urged Amos and Griffin ahead of him down the slope away from the camp.

They managed to grab three horses that were running wild. Ropes trailed from crude hackamores left on the animals, to enable the Apaches to capture them more easily.

"Let's go," Amos said, wheeling his mount in a circle. Griffin vaulted to the back of a bay mare and looped the ends of the rope hackamore around her neck, looking to Jordan for direction.

"This way," Jordan said, pointing to a cut that ran between the mountains. "And hurry."

"Where are you going?" Griffin asked when Jordan pivoted his mount in the opposite direction.

"After Jolie . . ."

"Wait! What if they catch you . . ." he said to Jordan's back, but his uncle was gone, racing his mount down the slope at breakneck speed, the animal's legs stretching as far as they would go from fear and urging, neck out and eyes wild as Jordan bent over his head.

"Damn fool," Amos muttered, and reached out to grab Griffin's rope reins when the youth would have followed him. "Let him go, boy! I promised to see to you, and that I will whether you like it or not. Now come on!"

In spite of Griffin's efforts, Amos pulled him along. Frustrated but terrified, Griffin had little choice but to follow. The pair wound around mountain paths and down arroyos that looked as if they would crumble at any moment. The meteor shower had lasted only a few minutes, and Amos knew that the Apache would be looking for them shortly. He ran for all he was worth, until the horses were lathered white and heaving.

"Let's rest here a minute," he said, pulling up beneath a rocky overhang tucked into the granite face of a mountain. "No one can see us here."

"He'll be killed," Griffin said dully, and Amos knew who he was talking about.

"Maybe, Rooster. But look at it this way—it was his choice."

Griffin turned a ravaged face to him, and Amos recoiled from the pain and suffering etched into features that no longer appeared youthful.

"I love her, too, but not enough to die for her." He leaned close, rasping, "I was wrong, Amos! All this time I thought he didn't care, that he was treating her wrong and would leave her, but he loves her more than I do."

"And that's bad?" Amos reached out to snare his arm when Griffin would have turned away. "Listen—just because a man don't go around shoutin' to the rooftops that he loves somebody don't mean he don't! It's time you grew up and learned that not everybody's alike, Griffin Armstrong! So you love her. So does he. And he loves her enough to risk all for her.'' His voice softened. ''He may make it yet, Rooster. Don't give up on an old Army man...''

''That's easy for you to say! He isn't your uncle!''

''No, he isn't, but that don't mean that I don't like and respect him. Are you gonna try and tell me my feelings don't count?''

Griffin looked Amos fully in the face, noticing for the first time the pale lines on each side of his wide mouth, and the suspicious brightness in his eyes.

''No,'' he said in a husky voice, ''I don't think I will try that, Amos. I just hope he comes back.''

Amos shifted atop the wet, sweaty back of his mount and gazed over the peaks they had just fled, his eyes misted. They'd been through a lot together, he and Jordan, and any regrets he might have about the gold were minor compared to the regret concerning a *compadre*. Jordan had been more than a partner. He had been a friend, a man he respected and cared about, and he would feel his loss as deeply as Griffin.

Few illusions about Jordan's fate tempered Amos's hope for him, but he mentioned none of that to Griffin. The boy— no, man—had been entrusted to him, and he would do all he could to keep him going.

''Yeah, Rooster, I hope he comes back, too.''

Chapter
26

Smoke rose in gray wisps above the adobe roofs of Fort Seldon. It was a weary and dispirited pair who rode tired Indian ponies to the Army post on the banks of the Río Grande. A sentry spotted them first and gave the alarm:

"Company comin'!" the cry echoed down the rooftop to the men below.

They weren't sure at first if these men were friends or enemies, and it wasn't until they had ridden close enough for the sentry to discern that one was a Negro and the other a young white man that the double wooden doors swung open to admit them.

Exhausted and stumbling, Amos and Griffin were given shelter, food, and rest. Coherence did not come until later, but Amos's first words were directions to Nana's camp. There was still hope that Jordan and Jolie would be found alive.

The meteorite shower had been a welcome gift from God as far as Jordan was concerned, and he'd seized upon the opportunity to save Amos and Griffin and rescue Jolie all at the same time. Griffin, in much more danger than Jolie, had been his first priority. Reunion with Jolie was the second.

The pony he'd managed to capture had been fractious, bucking and lunging, sidestepping hot stones from the sky with as equal ferocity as it desired to rid itself of the man on its back. Jordan had grimly hung on, determined to scoop Jolie from beneath the very noses of the Apache. It had not been as easy as he'd hoped. He'd searched the crowd and even several of the wickiups for a glimpse of her. In one of the huts, he found his weapons stacked against a wall and had not hesitated in collecting his possessions. The future might see a need for them.

Though most of the Apache had scattered, diving for cover from the sometimes lethal shower that started fires and burned upon contact, there were some of the warriors who had not. Among these was Nana.

When the shower began pelting the brush roof of her wickiup, Jolie had been only faintly alarmed, thinking it was one of the hailstorms that sometimes struck in the summer without warning. Then she had smelled smoke and realized that the roof was burning. Looking out, she had seen the pandemonium and become confused. A quick glance at the mound above the village showed her that Jordan and the others had escaped, leaving her behind.

The old woman, awakened from her nap by the shouts and screaming outside, panicked. She ran from the hut without thinking once about her charge, wailing loudly as she crossed the ground toward her own dwelling and possessions. Alone, Jolie briefly considered her options.

She could attempt to follow Jordan and the others, but she had not been able to see the direction of their flight. If she stayed with the Apache, she would be closely watched until her father's return, an event that would not take place until the fall. It was now *daaneest'águ*—August—and Henri La Fleur wasn't due for two months.

Biting her lower lip, Jolie hesitated in the entrance of the smoldering wickiup. A wave of dizziness seized her, and she swayed, gripping the edges of the doorway tightly. If only she had had time to talk to Jordan, but the time had not been right. She closed her eyes for a brief moment, praying that he would be safe.

Then, gathering her determination, Jolie had swung from the doorway into the chaos outside. Instantly surrounded by scurrying men, women, and children, she tried to force her way through the crowd. All she could think of was escape. Escape from the Apache and into the mountains, where, perhaps, she could find someone who would take her to a town. Once in a town she could search for Jordan. Instinct told her that he would be searching for her, also.

But that instinct had not hinted that he would ride into the face of death and danger to search for her. Jolie gasped in shock when a horse cut in front of her path, cutting her off from the mountain shelters she sought.

"Duu gḣat' įįda!" she cried, shoving futilely at the lathered sides of the horse. Her hands were soaked with the animal's sweat, and she swung out wildly at the man who tried to scoop her from the ground onto his mount.

"Jolie!" a voice shouted three times in her ear before she heard and recognized Jordan. Almost weeping with relief, she put her arms around his neck and allowed herself to be pulled atop the horse and into his arms.

"We need to get the hell out of here before this shower is over with," he said against her ear, and she nodded.

"'Au," was all she could manage for a moment. Her throat was too tight with emotion. He had come back for

her, knowing he could very well die for his recklessness. For all the trouble he had putting his feelings into words, Jordan Sinclair had no such trouble with action.

Nudging the terrified horse forward, Jordan weaved a path through the Apaches with no effort. No one tried to stop them—indeed, no one even seemed to notice them. It wasn't until he had ascended the ridge where he and Amos and Griffin had been tied that he ran into trouble.

Four men in full battle regalia blocked the way, bows drawn and arrows notched.

"Alto!" one of the men said in Spanish, raising his weapon in a threatening manner.

Jordan reined his mount in so sharply it half-reared, snorting in alarm. "Be careful," Jolie warned behind him. "The man on the left is Nana." Her arms tightened briefly around his waist, then she slid from the horse before he could stop her.

Stepping boldly forward, she faced Nana with her head back and eyes level with his. For several moments they conversed rapidly in Apache, their words incomprehensible to Jordan and sounding like gibberish. Jolie spoke quickly and impassionately, while Nana occasionally uttered a sharp, firm remark that sounded like a death knell to Jordan.

When he would have spurred his animal forward in an attempt to snatch Jolie and escape, he found the impulse dying in the face of the ferocious glitter in the Apache eyes regarding him with hatred and contempt. All he could do was wait and hope Jolie was as eloquent as she seemed to be. The air was charged with suspense, an element that transferred to Jordan's stolen pony, and the animal began to prance nervously.

Grinding his teeth, Jordan barely managed to keep the horse under control with his knees and the rough rope reins he held. The meteor shower had passed now, leaving burning bushes and huts behind, and he could hear the Apache beginning to regroup behind him. A stiff breeze blew down the mountain, stirring dark waves of his hair and blowing dust into his eyes, and Jordan's mouth tightened.

"Jolie," he said then, his tone commanding their attention, "tell Nana that I will meet him in hand-to-hand combat if he chooses. I would prefer that to dying like a camp dog at his hands."

Half-turning, Jolie gazed up at Jordan's determined face with frightened eyes. "But—what if he accepts?" she blurted.

"That is what I wish. Tell him," Jordan demanded. "I am not afraid to die like a man, but I will not hide behind the skirts of a woman." He swung down from the Indian pony and moved to stand beside her. Sensing her distress, he said, "Would you wish to remember me as a man who would allow a woman to fight for him? No, *shitsíné*, you would not. Now tell Nana what I asked you to tell him . . ."

"There is no need, *bélu*," Nana interrupted in a contemptuous tone. "I understand your tongue better than you understand mine, and I can speak your language." He made a sharp gesture, and the warriors beside him lowered their weapons.

"So you wish to fight me for your life?" Nana continued. "That is entertaining—and amusing. Do you have any notion of what would happen if I were killed? No, it is obvious you do not. My people would kill you very slowly, *bélu*. You would pray for death for days before it came to you. Do you still wish to risk that?"

"If I were to win, would Jolie be allowed to go free?" Jordan asked instead of answering him. "Would she be given the freedom to make her own choice about where she wished to be?"

"If I commanded it."

"Then, I would ask that of you, as one warrior to another," Jordan said. "If I win, she is to do as she pleases."

There was a long moment of silence while Nana digested this suggestion. His weathered face, like the crags and peaks of the mountains he loved, was set in a thoughtful pose, and the black eyes that had witnessed the deaths of hundreds of white men regarded Jordan with a glimmer of respect. Courage he could understand, and he considered it rare among the white men he had encountered. Love for another human being beyond regard for one's own life was also respected. Unselfish love for a woman of The People was unheard of.

Holding her breath, Jolie was the first to recognize the subtle softening of Nana's expression that indicated he might relent, and she struck before the great chief could reconsider, pleading with him to let them both go.

"Do you recall Lozen, Victorio's sister?" she asked, knowing he knew her well. "I feel as she did. Lozen had her Gray Ghost, and this man is my chosen mate. If I do not have him, I will take no man. I will be as Lozen and spend my life without a man, embracing war as a mate. Is that what you wish, Great Chief—that your women lose their husbands, lovers, and children to this strife between the white man and the Apache? Have not enough men died, leaving wailing widows and hungry children behind?" Her voice quavered, and she saw in the opaque eyes watching her that Nana was recalling the hundreds of deaths he had seen, deaths that had affected him greatly.

Then, with a sharp gesture of one hand, he brusquely dismissed them both, telling Jolie to take her man and leave at once before he changed his mind.

"I am not a soft man, but I yield to you, Gáadu, in this. I knew your mother, Nañdile, and I liked her well. She would not want her daughter to sorrow. Go now, and do not return to the camp of The People. You have chosen your path and shall not be allowed to come back.''

Pivoting on one heel, Nana strode swiftly away, a straight-backed warrior with the weight of hundreds of lives upon his shoulders.

''Swiftly,'' Jolie hissed, ''before he regrets his lenience or others resent our escape!''

Jordan needed no urging. Boosting Jolie atop the skittish Apache pony, he vaulted behind her and reined the animal in the direction of the valley beyond the Organ Mountains.

The San Augustin Plains bordered the Jornada on the west and the Organ Mountains on the east. Tall grasses thickly covered the ground, ranging to the foot of red cliffs jutting like ragged teeth from the ground, and mesquite, piñon, and pine trees provided shade and shelter from the elements.

Nestled under a grove of sharply scented pine trees, Jordan and Jolie were wrapped in one another's arms, rejoicing in their escape. The weary pony was tethered close by, and the weapons and possessions Jordan had managed to retrieve lay in a pile at their feet.

''Do you suppose Amos and Griffin are safe?'' Jolie wondered aloud, nuzzling Jordan's neck with her nose. ''I do not think Nana sent warriors after them.''

''I imagine the camp is in ruins, and they have moved on by now,'' Jordan said. ''The lives of such miserable human beings as we are not regarded as highly as shelter from rain and sun.'' He stretched lazily, cuddling her closer. It felt good to be free from danger, and he'd been too near death not to appreciate life and all its pleasures.

One of the greatest pleasures, Jordan reflected, was Jolie.

He still smiled at the memory of her courage in standing up to Nana and pleading for his life, and he would always carry that picture in his mind.

Turning slightly, Jordan found Jolie's eyes fixed upon him in an unwavering stare that reminded him of the first days after she'd been captured by Griffin.

"See something you like?" he teased.

"'*Au, Ninii'. Nitele. Nibide. Nichuu'* ..."

"What? Translate," he ordered with mock severity, rolling over with her beneath him, and she laughed.

"Your face. Your chest, Your stomach. Your..."

"Never mind!" he broke in, "I know what part of my anatomy lies below my stomach, you brazen wench."

It was Jolie's turn to ask for a translation, which she did without hesitation.

"Brazen... did anyone ever tell you that your eyes glow like summer grass on the mountains? Bold, daring, shameless wench—ah, Jolie, your skin is so soft, like the down of a thistle, and your hair gleams with the shadows of night— where was I? Oh yes, wench. A woman. A girl, a lover, *my* lover... Jolie."

The last word was a hot whisper against her ear, making her shiver with delight, and she turned into him with a sigh. "I am... *shika,* Jor-dan?"

"*Shika?*"

"Your lover..."

"Yes, for now. But that will soon change." He was silent for a moment, then asked, his lips moving against the gentle sweep of her jaw, "What is the Apache word for wife?"

Jolie drew her breath in sharply, then said, "It depends on how you use it. If you are saying one's wife, then it would be *kághaasdzą',* of if you were to say, my spouse, you would say *biłnaash'aashń.* Why do you ask such a thing?"

Jordan's lips had moved from her jaw down her throat, and were lingering on that faint, fluttering pulse in the dusky hollow. Jolie closed her eyes, and he was pulling down the neck of her dress, baring the gentle swells of her breasts. Lightly, teasingly, he nipped at the dark rosebuds jutting up proudly, making Jolie moan softly.

Opening her eyes, she forgot about the question, the time and the place, and everything but Jordan. Her fingers were swift and efficient on his shirt and belt, and in just moments they were both bare of clothing. Overhead in the thick branches of the pine a bird was singing, a lighthearted melody that serenaded the entwined pair lying on thick grasses below.

Words and thoughts drifted away on the crisp wind that blew down the valley and across the plains, and the bright burning bowl of the blue sky overhead faded away as she saw only Jordan. He filled Jolie's world with his searing blue eyes and thick waves of chestnut hair that fell over his forehead and into his eyes. She rested her palms against Jordan's flat, muscular abdomen and began teasing explorations with the pads of her fingers. She caressed his sides, the ridged swell of his ribs and the lean, tight muscles in his belly, then skimmed over his smooth, sun-bronzed flesh to the sharp angle of his hips. A smile curved her mouth as Jolie's hands circled around and traced a path from his buttocks to his thighs, stroking his inner thighs with an erotic motion that made him groan aloud. Just when her fingers found and held him, he caught her hand, holding it as he buried his face in the golden hollow of her neck and shoulder.

"What's the word for witch, Jolie, for the magic you create?"

"*'Ént' Hn . . .*"

"I can't say that . . . I can't even speak English right now . . . yes, do that . . . kiss me again, my sweet, here—on my mouth like that . . ."

Her lips obediently found his, touching lightly and lingering, holding him in her spell. Nothing else mattered at this moment. There were only the two of them and this powerful magic between them, this inexorable pull that had grown stronger and stronger in the past two months, keeping them together even when Jordan had resisted. Now his resistance was gone as if it had never existed.

Unable to wait any longer, wanting her, Jordan suddenly rolled over and nudged her thighs apart, filling her with his body and making her cry out. She was his, and he would never let her go. . . .

When the shattering release came only a few moments later, both of them were unprepared for its intensity. It rolled over them and left them weak and exhausted, lying in one another's arms damp and trembling.

Muffled hoofbeats woke them from a sound, satisfied sleep, jerking Jordan awake instantly. It was dark, and the night sky was peppered with bright, flickering stars and a ragged half-moon. There was the faint, metallic clang of an iron-shod hoof against rock, and he frowned. Apache ponies were barefoot. Who would be riding this late at night in such great number? It sounded like an entire troop.

It *was* an entire troop. The soldiers from Fort Seldon had stumbled across the small camp in the dark.

"Captain Jordan Sinclair?" the leading officer asked, his mouth set in a straight, harsh line as his glance moved from the man before him to the slender, wild-haired Apache maiden obviously warming his blankets. "We had word that you were in possible trouble . . ."

"As you can see, Lieutenant," Jordan answered smoothly with a wave of one arm, not liking the expression on the man's face as he stared at Jolie with bold eyes, "we are safe now."

"More than safe, I'd say," was the short, sneering reply, and Jordan stiffened.

"How did you know about us?" he asked instead of allowing the man to provoke him.

"Two men, one an ex-Army man like yourself, staggered into Fort Seldon. They seemed pretty worried about you. Is this woman your prisoner?" He indicated Jolie with a jab of his drawn saber in her direction, licking his lips as if in anticipation. Even disheveled and wrapped in a shapeless blanket, the girl was quite beautiful. "It's been a while since I've been with a woman, even a squaw." He paused at the dangerous glitter in Jordan's eyes, half-expecting his answer.

"No. She is not my prisoner. She is *biłnaash'aashń*."

"What?"

"My wife," Jordan explained softly, his eyes narrowing up at the uniformed cavalry officer. "And she deserves and will get respect."

Shrugging at the menacing gleam in Jordan's eyes, the lieutenant asked if they could dismount and spend the rest of the night there before going on in the morning. "Guess there's no point in going any further tonight," he added, swinging down from his saddle when Jordan gave a curt nod.

While the other men dismounted, the lieutenant stretched his cramped muscles and sheathed his saber, moving to crouch by the fire and stir it with a stick. His obvious disgust at finding Sinclair bedding down with an Apache wife was evident in the creases on each side of a wide mouth, and his small brown eyes were narrowed and cold.

"Your nephew claims that you were being held by Nana," the lieutenant said when Jordan moved to stand near him. "Is that so?"

"Yeah." Jordan's dislike of the lieutenant thickly coated his tone, and he stood with his arms crossed over his bare chest, staring down at him. "Why?"

The lieutenant grinned humorlessly. "I'd be a pretty popular officer if I was to bring the old man in, now wouldn't I?"

"If you lived to bring 'the old man' in," Jordan replied tersely.

"Yeah, well, I ain't got no squaw-wife to hide behind, but I might could . . ."

That was as far as he got before Jordan was hauling him up by his shirt collar and shaking him as if he were a scruffy mutt. "You've overstayed your welcome, Lieutenant," he snarled. "Now mount up and get out of here!"

Jerking away, the lieutenant was breathing hard, and his voice was shaking as he said, "Pretty cocky, aren't you? I've got all these men with me, and we could take you and your Apache squaw in with no trouble." He stepped closer and lowered his voice. "Or we could just claim that Nana got to you first."

"You could, but you won't," Jordan said, and the lieutenant felt the hard press of naked steel against his belly. The knife sliced off one of the gold buttons on his coat, and he could have sworn Sinclair had never moved a muscle. "My advice is that you don't say another word, Lieutenant, and I just might be nice enough to tell you where you can find Nana. It'd be a big feather in your cap to take him in, remember?''

Licking suddenly dry lips, the lieutenant nodded.

''Jor-dan?'' Jolie asked, staring into the blue flames of their campfire and hugging her knees to her chest. ''Why did the soldiers ride away so quickly? I thought they wanted to stay the night here in our camp.''

Jordan shrugged. ''Changed their mind and decided to go after Nana, I guess. With any luck, that cocky lieutenant just might find him.''

Jolie gave him a quick glance, then smiled. For a moment she remained silent and thoughtful, hugging to herself the words she'd heard him say earlier, claiming her as his wife. The fire crackled and popped, golden, licking flames straining higher, and she sighed reflectively.

''Jor-dan? Will you not miss the gold you wanted? Will you regret that you have me instead of the yellow metal that would make you rich and happy?''

Glancing up from the stick he was sharpening to use as a spit over the fire, Jordan was silent for so long that she bowed her head, fearing his answer. Then he was saying, ''All the gold in the world would not replace one moment's happiness with you, Jolie. I do not need gold when I have life's greatest treasure in you.''

Tears pricked at her eyelids, and when she lifted her gaze to his, she knew from the expression of love and tenderness on his face that he meant every word. For a moment Jolie spared a regret for Lozen, who had not found such happiness with her Gray Ghost, then thanked her god and his that she had found Jordan.

Rising, Jordan crossed the short distance between them in two steps and took her into his arms. She could feel the steady beat of his heart beneath her palms, and his beard-stubbled jaw rubbed roughly against her forehead.

"Would you hate it if I were to have gold, Jolie?" he asked, still holding her, and she shook her head.

"*Dah.* It no longer means anythng to me. But you do not have the gold, Jordan." She drew back fearfully. "You do not plan to go back?"

"No, no, green eyes," he assured her, drawing her back into his arms, "I just wondered if you would object if I managed to . . . acquire . . . gold."

"But—how?"

Grinning, Jordan pushed her away to arm's length for a moment and held her there. "Well, when I was looking for you in all the confusion in the camp, I went into this hut and found our weapons. I grabbed my gun and one of Griffin's I think, and a pack." His grin broadened. "It was Amos's pack that I grabbed, and that man had somehow managed to stuff it with gold bars, silver, and jewels! Not enough to make us as rich as we'd hoped, but enough to divide and still be able to buy a ranch apiece, or whatever. I don't know what Amos and Griffin plan on doing with theirs, but I know of a little spot close enough to the Organs that I think we'd be pretty happy on . . ."

"What about your plans for Mexico, or . . . or . . ." She frowned, trying to recall the other place he had mentioned, and Jordan finished for her, "Europe?"

She nodded. "'*Au.*"

"Wherever I go, you go. We are two, Jolie." He pulled her into his arms again and held her close.

Smiling, she thought of the secret knowledge she carried in her heart, and the new life growing within her. This tall, handsome man would be a father in the spring; when the snows had melted and the land was bursting with the promise of new life, a child would be born to them. It would be a son, tall and strong like his father, with the dark hair of his heritage and eyes as blue as the blazing sky over New Mexico territory.

Life's cycle repeated itself over and over; it was the way of the Apache and the white man, and perhaps one day they would all live in peace. Sighing with contentment, Jolie thought of the new life ahead of her. She laid her hand in Jordan's and felt his fingers close around hers, holding her in a loving clasp for all of time.

Epilogue

September 27, 1886

A soft wind blew across the neat frame house situated beneath tall, shading trees. Beyond the house a spring-fed creek twisted and turned in a meandering path through high, grassy fields thick with cattle.

To the casual observer, the ranch house was as ordinary as the next one. Only a few might notice the odd dwelling several yards behind the house, the conical shape and hide-covered structure that was almost identical to a tipi. It was, in fact, a tipi, and it belonged to the lady of the house.

"Does she stay in that thing often?" Griffin asked his uncle in a doubtful tone, gazing skeptically at the tipi from his chair on the porch.

"Only when the four walls of the house quit breathing," Jordan replied with a grin. "When she gets stifled inside, she retreats to a house that breathes." He shrugged at Griffin's questioning glance. "It doesn't usually last long, so I don't mind."

"How does little Johnny feel about that?" Amos leaned forward to ask, a wide white grin on his dark face.

A booming voice answered before Jordan could speak, "Leetle Zjohn Henri does not mind eet at all, *monsieur*! He has his *grandpère* to play weeth when hees *maman* hides in her tipi!" Beaming, the huge rugged bear of a man known as Henri La Fleur bounced the afore-mentioned toddler on his lap while the child squealed with delight. "He ees the speeting image of his *grandpère*, no?" Henri boomed.

"No," Griffin answered, laughing. "He looks just like the Sinclairs, and of course, his handsome Uncle Griffin!"

"He has his mother's hair and complexion," Amos put in, "and his father's eyes . . ."

"And he is as smart as his father," Jolie said from the doorway, and Jordan immediately stood up and went to her.

He put a solicitous arm around her slender shoulders and helped her to the white wicker rocking chair on the porch. Easing her swollen body into the chair, Jolie smiled at the group, who were staring at her with wide, interested eyes.

"What's the matter?" she teased. "Have you never seen a woman big with child before?"

"Yeah," Amos said slowly, "but not that big!"

"It must be another boy," Jordan said proudly, and Henri shook his head.

"Non!" he roared. "Thees one ees a *petite fille*—a girl as lovely as her *maman*!"

"I want a pony," Johnny Sinclair piped, and they all laughed at the boy's obvious distaste for a sibling.

Griffin, glancing again at Jolie, muttered, "He may be getting his wish."

After the shared laughter died, Jordan asked his nephew, "How's school?"

Griffin smiled, his handsome face creasing into an expression of pride. "Fine. I started my second year of law school a few weeks ago."

"Always figured a boy as silver-tongued as you are would make a good lawyer," Amos commented slyly. "I s'pose I'll have to be votin' for you as Governor one day."

"Maybe," Griffin retorted, "and maybe for President!"

"Don't get ahead of yourself, boy! You ain' even a lawyer yet!" Amos grinned hugely, and Griffin grinned back.

"So how's Dahlia, Amos?" Jolie asked. "I was hoping she could come over some time soon."

"Well, her time is almost on her, so she ain't doin' no travelin' right now,' Amos answered, beaming with pride at the mention of his beautiful wife. "And as big as she is, she'd break the back of any horse she rode and ruin the axles on my buckboard."

"A boy," Jordan guessed, "must be a boy!"

"Maybe two," Griffin added, and Amos groaned with mock dismay.

"Have you had any more trouble, Amos?" Jordan asked after a moment, referring to a recent spate of cattle-stealing from Amos's ranch.

Shaking his dark head, Amos said, "Naw, not since they cornered Nana in Mexico, and sent him and Geronimo off to Florida. A shame, really, that it had to end that way. I kinda respected those fightin' men."

"I thought Geronimo escaped again, ran off after a big drunk and decided not to surrender," Griffin said.

"He did, but they talked him into coming in, promised him God only knows what, and ended up breaking faith with all of them." Jordan's tone was slightly bitter. "You know, I may not have thought so for a long time, but I think that we have almost destroyed an entire race of people. It's not anything that I'm proud of. . . ."

"*Dah*, Jor-dan," Jolie said, "you have not destroyed them. The Apache may be small in numbers now, and perhaps they have been rounded up like cattle and placed in little pens to live, but they are not destroyed. They will survive just as we survived."

She flung back her head, her eyes meeting his with common understanding, and Jordan nodded slowly.

"Yeah, I guess you're right," he murmured. He glanced at his son, at that sturdy boy with dusky skin, hair the color of a crow's wing, and sky-blue eyes, and knew that she was right. The Apache had survived the Spanish, the French, other Indian trides, and the white man, and they would always survive. It was a good thing to know. And it was a good thing to know that the hate he had once felt toward those warriors of the desert had faded away and had been replaced by respect and tolerance. Jolie had done that for him. She had taken his prejudice and replaced it with love. He was the most fortunate man alive.

Twilight descended upon the Bar *S* ranch in purple shadows and as the sky darkened, Griffin said, "Hey, Jolie, there's the first star! Do you remember that verse I taught you and how we wished on it?"

Smiling, she said, "'*Au*. And my wish came true, Griffin." Glancing around at her family, at Jordan, so handsome and content, and her son, her father, Amos, and Griffin, she repeated, "My wish came true."

DEAR READERS:

If you liked this book, please let me know. I welcome your comments—good and bad—because that way I know what pleases you and what doesn't.

You may write to me in care of Warner Books, 666 Fifth Avenue, New York, N.Y. 10103

Virginia Brown

Bibliography

The Mescalero Apaches, by C.L. Sonnichen, Oklahoma Press, copyright 1958, 1973

100 Tons of Gold, by David Leon Chandler, Doubleday, copyright 1975, 1978

Mescalero Apache Dictionary, by the Mescalero Apache Tribe, Mescalero, N.M., copyright 1982

Portraits of "The Whiteman," by Keith H. Basso, Cambridge University Press, copyright 1979

Excerpts from *The Mescalero Apaches* were used in quoting Apache Chief Nana's words concerning his feelings about gold.

The entire concept of the gold hidden in Victorio, or Hembrillo Peak was researched in *100 Tons of Gold*. It has, of course, been greatly fictionalized in this story.